Welcome to a World of Wonders

Explore—
- The nature of reality
- The effects of time travel on time itself

Investigate—
- Killer chipmunks
- A religious document scripted in blood

Discover—
- A killer sport played by genetically engineered humanimals
- The resurrection of the human race

The Future is back as never before
in the

YEAR'S BEST SF 5

Edited by David G. Hartwell

Year's Best SF
Year's Best SF 2
Year's Best SF 3
Year's Best SF 4

YEAR'S BEST SF 5

EDITED BY
DAVID G. HARTWELL

An Imprint of HarperCollins*Publishers*

These are works of fiction. Names, characters, places, and incidents are the products of the authors' imaginations or are used fictitiously and are not to be construed as real. Any resemblance to actual events, locales, organizations, or persons, living or dead, is entirely coincidental.

Individual story copyrights appear on pages 493-94.

EOS
An Imprint of HarperCollins*Publishers*
10 East 53rd Street
New York, New York 10022-5299

First Eos mass market paperback printing: June 2000

Printed in the U.S.A.

This year's volume is dedicated to my attorney, Vivienne Garfinkle, Esq., because it pleases me to do so, and to Geoffrey S. Hartwell, B.A., for jobs well done, and with particular gratitude to John Silbersack, who understood the idea, without whom this book would not exist.

Acknowledgments

I would like to acknowledge the valuable assistance of Caitlin Blasdell, Jennifer Brehl, and Diana Gill in the creation of this year's volume, all of whom performed with faultless grace under difficult circumstances.

Contents

xiii   Introduction

1   Geoff Ryman
Everywhere

14   Elisabeth Malartre
Evolution Never Sleeps

36   Kim Stanley Robinson
Sexual Dimorphism

57   Robert Reed
Game of the Century

94   Michael Bishop
Secrets of the Alien Reliquary

97   Sarah Zettel
Kinds of Strangers

124   Cory Doctorow
Visit the Sins

145   Greg Egan
Border Guards

174   Terry Bisson
Macs

186   Chris Lawson
Written in Blood

204   Gene Wolfe
Has Anybody Seen Junie Moon?

222   Robert J. Sawyer
The Blue Planet

229   Mary Soon Lee
Lifework

238   Fred Lerner
Rosetta Stone

255   Brian Aldiss
An Apollo Asteroid

271   Curt Wohleber
100 Candles

288   G. David Nordley
Democritus' Violin

311   Tom Purdom
Fossil Games

362   Chris Beckett
Valour

379   Stephen Baxter
Huddle

404   Brian M. Stableford
       Ashes and Tombstones

422   Michael Swanwick
       Ancient Engines

433   Hiroe Suga
       Freckled Figure

457   Barry N. Malzberg
       Shiva

466   Lucy Sussex
       The Queen of Erewhon

Introduction

Nineteen hundred and ninety-nine is one of the legendary years of the science fiction future, and we have lived through it. When I was a boy reading SF, 1999 was the setting of stories such as C. M. Kornbluth's "The Rocket of 99"; when I was older, it was the setting of a TV show, *Space 1999*. And now it is gone, and all the SF written about the 80s and 90s is just fiction—now robbed of most of its significant prophetic power—and must stand or fall as fiction, on the merits of its execution and/or on its historical importance. It is a sobering thought to consider that fifty years ago 1999 looked like the relatively distant future, a time of wonders and radical difference. Fifty years is not so long, less than the career of Jack Williamson for instance, who published in 1929 and this year too, in the course of seven decades of writing SF. I leave you with the thought that we should set our SF stories further ahead in time, lest we become outdated fantasy too soon.

This was the year that people started talking seriously about instant books, printed on demand in bookstores or in publishers' warehouses and delivered in hours or days to readers, and of electronic books to be read on hand-held readers or on computers. Both of these media became everyday reality, though not yet widespread and popular, in 1999. And the business sections of major newspapers predicted a coming revolution in wireless telecommunications, with the advent of hand-held devices capable of making phone calls, connecting to the internet, sending and receiving e-mail, and indeed reading electronic books. It gives me pause to think that some of you may well be reading these words on such a device . . . because I have devoted my life to books on paper—comfortable, beautiful objects, sometimes usable and disposable, sometimes treasures to keep. Remember that something published electronically can vanish much more quickly and thoroughly than when printed on paper. If it's a keeper, you want a book . . . at least until the revolution after this one.

Science fiction in 1999 had a particularly good year, the best year for commercial success in more than a decade in book form. There were SF books on the bestseller lists in the U.S. often in 1999. Short fiction continued strong, but without one focal original anthology. The best original SF anthology of the year was probably editor Robert Silverberg's *New Horizons* (but the contracts prevent the authors from reselling stories in that book to this one, so no stories are represented here). However, *Moon Shots,* a paperback original edited by Peter Crowther, was very strong, the best paperback original anthology of the year. There were several other respectable original anthologies in '99 (*No Woman Born*, edited by Constance Ash, was nominated for the Philip K. Dick Award as best paperback original of the year) and the usual bunch of weak ones—a sad state of affairs below the top ranks.

Asimov's SF had a particularly good year, as did *Fantasy & Science Fiction*, in its 50th Anniversary year. *Interzone* had an exceptional year, nearly as strong as *Asimov's* or *F&SF's*, perhaps because of the growth of so much strong U.K. talent in SF over the last decade. Amazing returned impressively in 1999, *SF Age* continued, as did *Analog*, and each of them published a number of distinguished stories. *Century* returned to produce one issue late in the year. Australia produced another issue of *Eidolon,* as well as new issues of several other magazines in time for the World SF convention in Melbourne in September, and Canada produced more issues of *On Spec* and a transformed *Transversions.*

I repeat, for readers new to this series, my usual disclaimer: this selection of science fiction stories represents the best that was published during the year 1999. I could perhaps have filled two or three more volumes this size and then claimed to have nearly all of the best—though not all the best novellas. I believe that representing the best, while it is not physically possible to encompass it all in one even very large book, also implies presenting some substantial variety of excellences, and I left some writers out in order to include others in this limited space.

My general principle for selection: this book is full of science fiction—every story in the book is clearly that and not something else. I personally have a high regard for horror, fantasy, speculative fiction, slipstream, and postmodern literature. But here, I chose science fiction. It is the intention of this year's best series to focus on science fiction, and to provide readers who are looking especially for science fiction an annual home base.

Which is not to say that I choose one kind of science fiction—I try to represent the varieties of tones and voices and attitudes that keep the genre vigorous and responsive to the changing realities out of which it emerges, in science and daily life. This is a book about what's going on now in SF.

And now let us move on to the stories.

—David G. Hartwell
Pleasantville, NY

Everywhere

GEOFF RYMAN

Geoff Ryman is a Canadian-born writer who moved to the USA at age 11, and has been living in England since 1973. He began publishing occasional SF stories in the mid-1970s, and has also written some SF plays, including a powerful adaptation of Philip K. Dick's The Transmigration of Timothy Archer *(1982). The first work to establish his international reputation as one of the leading writers of SF was "The Unconquered Country: A Life History" (1984, rev 1986), which won the World Fantasy Award. It is reprinted in his only collection to date,* Unconquered Countries: Four Novellas *(1994). Ryman's first novel was* The Warrior who Carried Life *(1985), a fantasy. His second,* The Child Garden *(1988), won the Arthur C. Clarke Award and the John W. Campbell Memorial Award, and confirmed him as a major figure in contemporary SF. His most recent books are not SF.* Was *(1992) is the supposed true story of the real-life Dorothy who was the inspiration for L. Frank Baum's first Oz book, and of a contemporary man dying of AIDS.* 253 *(1998) is a work of hypertext fiction linking the lives of characters in a subway car. It won the Philip K. Dick Award in 1999.*

This story, from Interzone, *is uncharacteristically short for Ryman (most of his stories are novellas) and utopian (most of his works are dystopian, or at least seriously grim). As we enter a new century and a new millennium, leading the Year's Best with a utopian vision seems appropriate. Here's to a brighter future!*

When we knew Granddad was going to die, we took him to see the Angel of the North.

When he got there, he said: It's all different. There were none of these oaks all around it then, he said. Look at the size of them! The last time I saw this, he says to me, I was no older than you are now, and it was brand new, and we couldn't make out if we liked it or not.

We took him, the whole lot of us, on the tram from Blaydon. We made a day of it. All of Dad's exes and their exes and some of their kids and me Aunties and their exes and their kids. It wasn't that happy a group to tell you the truth. But Granddad loved seeing us all in one place.

He was going a bit soft by then. He couldn't tell what the time was any more and his words came out wrong. The Mums made us sit on his lap. He kept calling me by my Dad's name. His breath smelt funny but I didn't mind, not too much. He told me about how things used to be in Blaydon.

They used to have a gang in the Dene called Pedro's Gang. They drank something called Woodpecker and broke people's windows and they left empty tins of pop in the woods. If you were little you weren't allowed out cos everyone's Mum was so fearful and all. Granddad once saw twelve young lads go over and hit an old woman and take her things. One night his brother got drunk and put his fist through a window, and he went to the hospital, and he had to wait hours before they saw him and that was terrible.

I thought it sounded exciting meself. But I didn't say so because Granddad wanted me to know how much better things are now.

He says to me, like: the trouble was, Landlubber, we were just kids, but we all thought the future would be terrible. We all thought the world was going to burn up, and that everyone would get poorer and poorer, and the crime worse.

He told me that lots of people had no work. I don't really understand how anyone could have nothing to do. But then I've never got me head around what money used to be either.

Or why they built that Angel. It's not even that big, and it was old and covered in rust. It didn't look like an Angel to me at all, the wings were so big and square. Granddad said, no, it looks like an airplane, that's what airplanes looked like back then. It's meant to go rusty, it's the Industrial Spirit of the North.

I didn't know what he was on about. I asked Dad why the Angel was so important and he kept explaining it had a soul, but couldn't say how. The church choir showed up and started singing hymns. Then it started to rain. It was a wonderful day out.

I went back into the tram and asked me watch about the Angel.

This is my watch, here, see? It's dead good isn't it, it's got all sorts on it. It takes photographs and all. Here, look, this is the picture it took of Granddad by the Angel. It's the last picture I got of him. You can talk to people on it. And it keeps thinking of fun things for you to do.

Why not explain to the interviewer why the Angel of the North is important?

Duh. Usually they're fun.

Take the train to Newcastle and walk along the river until you see on the hill where people keep their homing pigeons. Muck out the cages for readies.

It's useful when you're a bit short, it comes up with ideas to make some dosh.

It's really clever. It takes all the stuff that goes on around here and stirs it around and comes up with something new. Here, listen:

The laws of evolution have been applied to fun. New generations of ideas are generated and eliminated at such a speed that evolution works in real time. It's survival of the funnest and you decide

They evolve machines too. Have you seen our new little airplanes? They've run the designs through thousands of generations, and they got better and faster and smarter.

The vicar bought the whole church choir airplanes they can wear. The wings are really good, they look just like bird's wings with pinions sticking out like this. Oh! I really want one of them. You can turn somersaults in them. People build them in their sheds for spare readies, I could get one now if I had the dosh.

Every Sunday as long as it isn't raining, you can see the church choir take off in formation. Little old ladies in leotards and blue jeans and these big embroidered Mexican hats. They rev up and take off and start to sing the Muslim call to prayer. They echo all over the show. Then they cut their engines and spiral up on the updraft. That's when they start up on Nearer My God to Thee.

Every Sunday, Granddad and I used to walk up Shibbon Road to the Dene. It's so high up there that we could look down on top of them. He never got over it. Once he laughed so hard he fell down, and just lay there on the grass. We just lay on our backs and looked up at the choir, they just kept going up like they were kites.

When the Travellers come to Blaydon, they join in. Their wagons are pulled by horses and have calliopes built into the front, so on Sundays, when the choir goes up, the calliopes start up, so you got organ music all over the show as well. Me Dad calls Blaydon a sound sandwich. He says it's all the hills.

The Travellers like our acoustics, so they come here a

lot. They got all sorts to trade. They got these bacteria that
eat rubbish, and they hatch new machines, like smart door
keys that only work for the right people. They make their
own beer, but you got to be a bit careful how much you
drink.

Granddad and I used to take some sarnies and our sleeping bags and kip with them. The Travellers go everywhere,
so they sit around the fire and tell about all sorts going on,
not just in England but France and Italia. One girl, her Mum
let her go with them for a whole summer. She went to
Prague and saw all these Buddhist monks from Thailand.
They were Travellers and all.

Granddad used to tell the Travellers his stories too. When
he was young he went to Mexico. India. The lot. You could
in them days. He even went to Egypt, my Granddad. He
used to tell the Travellers the same stories, over and over,
but they never seemed to noticed. Like, when he was in
Egypt he tried to rent this boat to take him onto the Delta,
and he couldn't figure why it was so expensive, and when
he got on it, he found he'd rented a car ferry all to himself
by mistake. He had the whole thing to himself. The noise
of the engines scared off the birds which was the only reason he'd wanted the boat.

So, Granddad was something of a Traveller himself. He
went everywhere.

There's all sorts to do around Blaydon. We got dolphins
in the municipal swimming pool.

We dug it ourselves, in the Haughs just down there by
the river. It's tidal, our river. Did you know? It had dolphins anyway, but our pool lured them in. They like the
people and the facilities, like the video conferencing. They
like video conferencing, do dolphins. They like being fed
and all.

My Dad and I help make the food. We grind up fish
heads on a Saturday at Safeways. It smells rotten to me,
but then I'm not an aquatic mammal, am I? That's how we
earned the readies to buy me my watch. You get everyone
along grinding fish heads, everybody takes turns. Then you
get to go to the swimming.

Sick people get first crack at swimming with the dolphins. When Granddad was sick, he'd take me with him. There'd be all this steam coming off the water like in a vampire movie. The dolphins always knew who wasn't right, what was wrong with them. Mrs Grathby had trouble with her joints, they always used to be gentle with her, just nudge her along with their noses like. But Granddad, there was one he called Liam. Liam always used to jump up and land real hard right next to him, splash him all over and Granddad would push him away, laughing like, you know? He loved Liam. They were pals.

Have a major water-fight on all floors of the Grand Hotel in Newcastle.

Hear that? It just keeps doing that until something takes your fancy.

Hire Dad the giant bunny rabbit costume again and make him wear it.

We did that once before. It was dead fun. I think it knows Dad's a bit down since Granddad.

Call your friend Heidi and ask her to swap clothes with you and pretend to be each other for a day.

Aw Jeez! Me sister's been wearing me watch again! It's not fair! It mucks it up, it's supposed to know what I like, not her and that flipping Heidi. And she's got her own computer, it's loads better than mine, it looks like a shirt and has earphones, so no one else can hear it. It's not fair! People just come clod-hopping through. You don't get to keep nothing.
Look this is all I had to do to get this watch!

Grind fishfood on 3.11, 16.11, 20.12 and every Sunday until 3.3
Clean pavements three Sundays
Deliver four sweaters for Step Mum

Help Dad with joinery for telecoms outstation
Wire up Mrs Grathby for video immersion
Attend school from April 10th to 31 July inclusive

I did even more than that. At least I got some over. I'm
saving up for a pair of cars.

Me and me mates love using the cars. I borrow me Dad's
pair. You wear them like shoes and they're smart. It's great
fun on a Sunday. We all go whizzin down Lucy Street
together, which is this great big hill, but the shoes won't
let you go too fast or crash into anything. We all meet up,
whizz around in the mall in great big serpent. You can pre-
program all the cars together, so you all break up and then
all at once come back together, to make shapes and all.

Granddad loved those cars. He hated his stick, so he'd
go shooting off in my Dad's pair, ducking and weaving,
and shouting back to me, Come on, Landlubber, keep up!
I was a bit scared in them days, but he kept up at me til I
joined in. He'd get into those long lines, and we shoot off
the end of them, both of us. He'd hold me up.

He helped me make me lantern and all. Have you seen
our lanterns, all along the mall? They look good when the
phosphors go on at night. All the faces on them are real
people, you know. You know the ink on them's made of
these tiny chips with legs? Dad's seen them through a microscope, he says they look like synchronized swimmers.

I got one with my face on it. I was bit younger then so
I have this really naff crew cut. Granddad helped me make
it. It tells jokes. I'm not very good at making jokes up, but
Granddad had this old joke book. At least I made the effort.

Let's see, what else. There's loads around here. We got
the sandbox in front of the old mall. Everybody has a go
at that, making things. When King William died all his fans
in wheelchairs patted together a picture of him in sand.
Then it rained. But it was a good picture.

Our sandbox is a bit different. It's got mostly real sand.
There's only one corner of it computer dust. It's all right
for kids and that or people who don't want to do things

themselves. I mean when we were little we had the dust make this great big 3D sign Happy Birthday Granddad Piper. He thought it was wonderful because if you were his age and grew up with PCs and that, it must be wonderful, just to think of something and have it made.

I don't like pictures, they're too easy. Me, I like to get stuck in. If I go to the sandbox to make something, I want to come back with sand under me fingernails. Me Dad's the same. When Newcastle won the cup, me and me mates made this big Newcastle crest out of real sand. Then we had a sandfight. It took me a week to get the sand out of me hair. I got loads of mates now, but I didn't used to.

Granddad was me mate for a while. I guess I was his pet project. I always was a bit quiet, and a little bit left out, and also I got into a bit of trouble from time to time. He got me out of myself.

You know I was telling you about the Angel? When I went back into that tram I sat and listened to the rain on the roof. It was dead quiet and there was nobody around, so I could be meself. So I asked me watch. OK then. What is this Angel? And it told me the story of how the Angel of the North got a soul.

There was this prisoner in Hull jail for thieving cos he run out of readies cos he never did nothing. It was all his fault really, he says so himself. He drank and cheated his friends and all that and did nothing with all his education.

He just sat alone in his cell. First off, he was angry at the police for catching him, and then he was angry with himself for getting caught and doing it and all of that. Sounds lovely, doesn't he? Depressing isn't the word.

Then he got this idea, to give the Angel a soul.

It goes like this. There are 11 dimensions, but we only see three of them and time, and the others are what was left over after the Big Bang. They're too small to see but they're everywhere at the same time, and we live in them too, but we don't know it. There's no time there, so once something happens, it's like a photograph, you can't change it.

So what the prisoner of Hull said that means is that everything we do gets laid down in the other dimensions like train tracks. It's like a story, and it doesn't end until we die, and that does the job for us. That's our soul, that story.

So what the Prisoner in Hull does, is work in the prison, get some readies and pay to have a client put inside the Angel's head.

And all the other computers that keep track of everyone's jobs or the questions they asked, or just what they're doing, that all gets uploaded to the Angel.

Blaydon's there. It's got all of us, grinding fish heads. Every time someone makes tea or gets married from Carlisle to Ulverton from Newcastle to Derby, that gets run through the Angel. And that Angel is laying down the story of the North.

My watch told me that, sitting in that tram.

Then everyone else starts coming back in, but not Dad and Granddad, so I go out to fetch them.

The clouds were all pulled down in shreds. It looked like the cotton candy Dad makes at fêtes. The sky was full of the church choir in their little airplanes. For just a second, it looked like a Mother Angel, with all her little ones.

I found Dad standing alone with Granddad. I thought it was rain on my Dad's face, but it wasn't. He was looking at Granddad, all bent and twisted, facing into the wind.

We got to go Dad, I said.

And he said, In a minute son. Granddad was looking up at the planes and smiling.

And I said it's raining Dad. But they weren't going to come in. So I looked at the Angel and all this rust running off it in red streaks onto the concrete. So I asked, if it's an Angel of the North, then why is it facing south?

And Granddad says, Because it's holding out its arms in welcome.

He didn't want to go.

We got him back into the tram, and back home, and he started to wheeze a bit, so me Step Mum put him to bed and about eight o clock she goes in to swab his teeth with vanilla, and she comes out and says to Dad, I think he's stopped breathing.

So I go in, and I can see, no he's still breathing. I can hear it. And his tongue flicks, like he's trying to say something. But Dad comes in, and they all start to cry and carry on. And the neighbours all come in, yah, yah, yah, and I keep saying, it's not true, look, he's still breathing. What do they have to come into it for, it's not their Granddad, is it?

No one was paying any attention to the likes of me, were they? So I just take off. There's this old bridge you're not allowed on. It's got trees growing out of it. The floor's gone, and you have to walk along the top of the barricades. You fall off, you go straight into the river, but it's a good dodge into Newcastle.

So I just went and stood there for a bit, looking down on the river. Me Granddad used to take me sailing. We'd push off from the Haughs, and shoot out under this bridge, I could see where we were practically. And we'd go all the way down the Tyne and out to sea. He used to take me out to where the dolphins were. You'd see Liam come up. He was still wearing his computer, Liam, like a crown.

So I'm standing on the bridge, and me watch says: go down to the swimming pool, and go and tell Liam that Granddad's dead.

It's a bit like a dog I guess. You got to show one dog the dead body of the other or it will pine.

So I went down to the pool, but it's late and raining and there's nobody there, and I start to call him, like: Liam! Li-am! But he wasn't there.

So me watch says: he's wearing his computer: give him a call on his mobile.

So me watch goes bleep bleep bleep, and there's a crackle and suddenly I hear a whoosh and crickle, and there's all these cold green waves on the face of my watch, and I say Liam? Liam, this is me, remember me, Liam? My Granddad's dead Liam. I thought you might need to know.

But what is he, just a dolphin right, I don't know what it meant. How's he supposed to know who I am. You all right then, Liam? Catching lots of fish are you? So I hung up.

And I stand there, and the rain's really bucketing down,

and I don't want to go home. Talking to yourself. It's the first sign, you know.

And suddenly me watch starts up again, and it's talking to me with Granddad's voice. You wanna hear what it said? Here. Hear.

Hello there, Landlubber. How are ya? This is your old Granddad. It's a dead clever world we live in, isn't it? They've rigged this thing up here, so that I can put this in your watch for when you need it.

Listen, me old son. You mustn't grieve, you know. Things are different now. They know how it works. We used to think we had a little man in our heads who watched everything on a screen and when you died he went to heaven not you. Now, they know, there's no little man, there's no screen. There's just a brain putting everything together. And what we do is ask ourselves: what do we think about next? What do we do next?

You know all about those dimension things, don't you? Well I got a name for them. I call them Everywhere. Cos they are. And I want you to know, that I'm Everywhere now.

That's how we live forever in heaven these days And it's true, me old son. You think of me still travelling around Mexico before I met your Mamby. Think of me in India. Think of me learning all about readies to keep up with you lot. Think of me on me boat, sailing out to sea. Remember that day I took you sailing out beyond the Tyne mouth? It's still there, Landlubber.

You know, all the evil in the world, all the sadness comes from not having a good answer to that question: what do I do next? You just keep thinking of good things to do, lad. You'll be all right. We'll all be all right. I wanted you to know that.

I got me footie on Saturdays, Granddad. Then I'm thinking I'll start up school again. They got a sailing club now. I thought I'd join it, Granddad, thought I'd take them out to where you showed me the dolphins. I'll tell them about Everywhere.

Did you know, Granddad?

They're making a new kind of watch. It's going to show us Everywhere, too.

Evolution Never Sleeps

ELISABETH MALARTRE

Elisabeth Malartre is a new writer, a biologist, with a Ph.D from the University of California at Irvine, who works as an environmental consultant and science writer. Her first sale was a 1997 novella about the first Mars expedition, co-authored with Gregory Benford, "A Cold, Dry, Cradle," that Benford expanded it into his novel, The Martian Race.

"I consider myself first and foremost a science educator, and everything I do is related to that. I've spent 20 years successfully preserving land in Orange County, CA, a bastion of reactionary conservatism, but then I'm pretty stubborn. Sometimes I teach at local colleges—human evolution, human ecology or environmental science. I also train people to be volunteer naturalists. I write a regular science column for a weekly paper, bringing biological theory down to the level of everyday experience. Although I have a loyal readership, there are many people who will never look at a science article. Those are the people I'm trying to reach through my fiction.

"Although I started writing science fiction only about 4 years ago, I've been reading it for well over 40 years. My speciality is hard sf with biological themes"

"Evolution Never Sleeps" is her second published story. It appeared in Asimov's, *which had a great year in 1999. The hard science is evolutionary biology and the idea, while reminiscent of the riotously rubber-science B-movies of the 1950s, is rigorously executed and made serious. It teaches us something about the bedrock scientific theory of Evolution, upon which so much SF has been based since 1895.*

Death came instantaneously to the deer. The dark blue semi had been laboring up the final quarter mile of the Sherwin grade, fighting the rapidly thinning air. Its headlights picked out roadside pine trees, their nearest branches blown away by the snowblowers of winters past. As it crested the summit the truck began to pick up speed, hitting its stride on the gradual downhill. It was a crisp summer night, sky sprinkled with stars, light traffic on route 395.

A few miles later, just beyond the offramp to Mammoth Lakes, a six point buck leaped off the shoulder of the road into the truck's grille. The lifeless body arced back to the right shoulder of the road, landing in a crumpled heap amidst the low shrubs. The truck swerved slightly, shifted gears and roared off toward Bridgeport. The stars glittered coldly over the slightly twitching body. Blood no longer pumped by the stilled heart trickled out of its open mouth. After a few minutes there was a soft stirring sound in the shrubs near the deer.

Fred Morales aimed his orange stakebed truck at the shoulder where the deer lay, happy to have finally found the carcass. He'd driven by the site twice without noticing it hidden there in the bushes. But the motorist who'd called it in to Caltrans had been right about the location after all. This was the last one before lunch. The sun reflected off the hood of the truck into his eyes and he was thirsty. What a job—collecting road kills. This one was pretty fresh, belly not too full of gas. It wouldn't be half bad, and there was a breeze to boot. Nevertheless, he stood carefully upwind as he tied the rope around the legs.

There was a sudden rustle and a flash of movement in the small grey-green shrubs next to the carcass as the winch started to move it toward the truck. Fred Morales leaped back onto the asphalt reflexively, before the front of his brain realized what he had seen.

"Squirrels," he said out loud. "Just squirrels." His heart pounded. Sometimes there were snakes under the bodies. Fred Morales didn't like snakes, didn't like to be surprised by them. He blew out a long breath to steady himself. "Just fuckin' squirrels." Nevertheless, he hurriedly finished winching the carcass onto the Caltrans truck with the other road kills and drove away without looking back.

"What do you do—sample 'em before you bring 'em in?" Ron Feister squatted down and poked at the carcass Fred had unloaded at his feet at the dump site.

"Huh?" Fred looked where the Fish & Game biologist pointed. Several places on the carcass had been nibbled, small red patches against the dusty brown of the pelt.

"See what was eating this deer?"

"Wasn't nothing on it—no birds . . ."

"Nope, no smell, too soon for buzzards. Not right for coyote either. They tear off pieces, drag 'em away to eat."

"Only thing I saw was squirrels."

"Squirrels? What did they look like?"

"Dunno . . . little, fast, you know . . . with stripes."

"Chipmunks, you mean? Stripes on the head?"

"Guess so."

Feister stood up. "Huh. Where did you get this one?"

"On 395, near 203. Why, something funny?"

"Just a little unusual. Let me know if you get another one like this, okay?"

"Sure. You done? I want to dump the rest of these stinkers."

"Go for it. See you, Fred." Feister strode off toward his truck. *Chipmunks? I'll be damned.*

*   *   *

Janice Reidel stopped her jeep as she came to the dead snake lying on the grey asphalt. In her mind she spun a prayer wheel for the soul of the dead animal before alighting from the vehicle. She admired the smooth scaly carcass. The graceful sweep of its body was interrupted where the car tire had squashed it. A small pocket of pink guts squeezed out through the dark stripes on the scales. *Striped racer*, she decided, picking it up by its tail and gently tossing it into the roadside bushes. She always did this to road kills. Left on the asphalt, the kill would tempt scavengers like buzzards, ravens or coyotes onto the roadway, where they were apt to be hit themselves. How often had she seen ground squirrels scatter from a fallen colleague's body as the jeep approached? The tar pit syndrome. *I'll tell Jeff about this one when he calls tonight*. She headed back to her research quarters at the Sierra Nevada Aquatic Research Lab, SNARL emblazoned on her cap. She particularly enjoyed the scenery, rugged colorful mountains meeting the flat sage-covered plains of the Great Basin, here on the dry east side of the Sierra Nevada mountains in California.

Janice was one of a dozen first year graduate students doing summer internships at SNARL, hoping to find an interesting problem for a thesis. Despite the lab's name, most of them were working that summer on terrestrial problems, especially ground squirrel behavior.

She and some of the other interns spent four-hour shifts observing the animals in a large enclosure. It was organized tedium, like much of scientific research. She was learning, however, that it was the only way to attack the complexity of nature.

"A striped racer? No way." Jeff's voice came through faint crackles on the phone. "You're at 8000 feet—they don't get up that high."

"The snake didn't know that. I'm sure it was a racer—black with long pale yellow stripes on the sides—what else could it have been?"

"A flattened chipmunk?"

"No, really. It was a snake. You're the herp expert. I expect you to know everything about them."

Despite being a graduate student in math, Jeff was an avid snake hobbyist. It was one of the unexpected twists in his personality that set him apart from other men Janice had dated.

"Hm. How far from Highway 395 was it?"

"A few hundred yards, why?"

"You sometimes get unusual sightings near the interstate. People lose animals from their cars, or they dump 'em."

"Sounds far-fetched to me."

"So's that snake at that altitude."

"Look, I'll go get it tomorrow and preserve it for you."

"Yum. Snake preserves. My favorite."

"Ha ha. Listen, when are you coming up? It feels like forever since I've seen you."

"Miss me, eh?"

"Mmm, you bet."

"Woman, you're the one who left, not me."

"It's just a summer fellowship. I didn't emigrate. Look, you could write those old equations just as easily up here in the gorgeous mountains as in sweaty old Berkeley. There's even a spare cubicle in the lab building until the end of July. And you could explore for snakes while you're up here."

"Hm. Tempt me some more. What are the sleeping arrangements?"

She laughed. "The natives are still *very* friendly."

The next morning, before her four-hour shift watching the squirrel enclosure, Janice went back to look for the snake. She leaped from the jeep, strode over to the bushes with her usual no-nonsense gait and was surprised to find only a few scraps of bone. Surprised, she pulled back. *Wow, that was fast. Someone was hungry.* She started searching carefully, hoping there was still a piece with some skin on it, enough for Jeff to look at. *There.* About three inches of snake tail lay just beyond her reach.

As she stepped around the low bushes, there was a flurry of activity as a chipmunk darted away from her, scattering the pumice gravel. *So that's who's been eating my snake. Hungry little bugger.* There was a flash of movement to her right, and she became aware of several more chipmunks among the shrubs. They were all watching her. *Sorry, guys, but I need this bit.* She squatted down and reached for the piece of snake.

Before she could touch it, a chipmunk dashed forward, causing her to jerk her hand back. She expected that the movement would send it running in the opposite direction, but instead, the small animal crouched down and started making its alarm cry: shrill repetitive bursts of sound, tail jerking furiously. *It's almost as if he's defending it.*

She felt suddenly vulnerable, in shorts and sleeveless top, without even her trusty leather gloves. Rodent bites were painful and took a long time to heal. An encounter with a lab rat had left a permanent scar on her third finger. This was certainly atypical behavior. Maybe the animal was rabid.

Off to her right another chipmunk started to chirp, then another. The stereo effect was unnerving. There seemed to be about a dozen chipmunks scattered throughout the shrubs in front of her.

She looked again at the closest animal. It showed no sign of wanting to leave, back arched slightly, head high, tail jerking spasmodically with each shrill bark. She felt the sun hot on her scalp. Up this high, with little protective atmosphere above, she burned easily. Her hat was in the jeep, of course. Another minute passed. Stalemate. If she went for her hat she'd lose the snake. Her knees began to ache and she knew she'd be lightheaded when she did finally stand. The piece was probably too short to be diagnostic anyway. "Oh, all right, keep your damn snake if it's that important."

She stood up, stars swimming in her vision. *Damn low blood pressure.* The closest chipmunk lunged forward, grabbed the piece of snake with its teeth and ran off. As it reached the others they spun around, and followed it into the shrubs.

Bizarre. They seemed to be working together, like a pack.

Professor Daniel Branton scowled at her as he meticulously picked a tiny crumb of sandwich from his forearm. "Chipmunks don't exhibit coordinated behavior. They're basically loners, scavengers."

"But it was so definite, I know they were working together."

"There's never been anything in the literature to indicate that chipmunks behave in groups."

"Well, maybe this is something new."

"What you saw was just normal duetting behavior. One animal barks, then the others join in. That's all."

"What about the animal that wouldn't let me have the piece of snake? That's not normal behavior."

He snorted. "You students need to be more observant and less imaginative. An animal of that size is not going to stand up to a human."

"But that's the point, it did. And furthermore, it wasn't alone . . ."

"I doubt that." Branton crunched the empty sandwich wrapping into a ball and picked up his empty drink can.

Janice swallowed her annoyance, felt her face flush. Branton was known as a prissy nitpicker. She should've known he wouldn't believe something out of the ordinary from a mere graduate student. Unfortunately, he was the ranking professor at the lab, and would be on her advisory committee if she picked a thesis problem in animal behavior. She could not afford to alienate him, but this was too intriguing to just let go.

"But if they are cooperating it would certainly be an interesting problem."

He looked at her sharply. "Open-ended research like that is not for graduate school. You need to pick a problem with a definite answer, or you'll never finish. The university can't afford to keep on supporting doctoral candidates indefinitely, you know."

"But if I wanted to test the hypothesis that they were cooperating, what would you suggest . . . ?" *Can't hurt to ask his advice.*

He stood up to return to the research center. "That's pretty obvious. Duplicate the conditions, observe carefully, and record the data meticulously, the way I've taught you for enclosure research. But it's a waste of time. Stick to your enclosure observations. Ground squirrels are inherently more interesting."

"I'll do it on my own time. And thanks for the advice." *A good graduate student must always be submissive.*

Branton strode off, waving his hand vaguely behind him in response.

Amy Chang, another first-year graduate student, grimaced at his retreating back. "Ground squirrels are inherently more interesting," she muttered in a low voice that aped his didactic tone. "What an asshole."

Janice suppressed a smile. She also didn't share Branton's enthusiasm for the endless mate-substitution experiments he was conducting in the enclosure. Few of the graduate students did. Still, that was her summer grant money.

Amy brushed black bangs out of her eyes. "For what it's worth, I believe you. The chipmunks have always seemed to be brighter than the ground squirrels anyway."

As if on cue, a chipmunk began its alarm cry from the tree a few yards away. They were sitting outside, in a small clump of pines close to the lab buildings that functioned as a rustic picnic area. Janice studied the ground next to the log she was sitting on: large black ants were busily combing the fallen pine needles. "Nature's garbage collectors," she said. "Without ants, we'd be knee deep in dead moths."

"They're great scavengers, all right," agreed Amy, "and what a system they have: a lot of unremarkable individual units that together make an unstoppable army. And they find everything that's edible. There's no hiding from them."

"You know, in a way, those ants make me think of the chipmunks. If they were organized like ants, how would we live with them?"

"What do you mean?"

"Think about it—you know what a nuisance ants are at a picnic. What if an organized group of chipmunks descended on a table full of food?"

Amy paused. "Hm. I'll bet they could carry off most of the stuff without much trouble."

"Right. And do you know what would happen if someone tried to stop 'em?"

"Dunno, what?"

"They'd be picking teeth out of their hand. Rodents are pretty aggressive. Despite what Branton said, they don't hesitate to attack an animal much larger than themselves. Look at this." She showed Amy the scar on her finger—two white semicircles left by the sharp incisors of a harmless-looking white lab rat. She remembered her surprise at the rat's unprovoked attack.

"I remember reading that rats in slums bite sleeping babies. Even kill some of them," said Amy.

"Yeah, and during plague years in Europe the rats crunched the bones of the dead bodies."

"Ugggh. But those were rats."

"Chipmunks are just rats with stripes, bona fide rodents with all that implies."

"Yes, not like my birds. Even sea gulls are better mannered than rats."

"Oh yeah? Remember that Hitchcock movie about a lot of birds attacking the people in a little town?"

"Oh, that one. I read somewhere how they trained all those birds to peck people. But it wasn't real. There wasn't any reason for them to act like that all of a sudden."

Janice let out a deep breath she didn't know she'd been holding. "I always thought it was a frightening movie, to have benign creatures suddenly become threatening. And what I saw today was real. Those chippies really weren't very friendly. I'd hate to go into the woods alone if large groups of any kind of rodent were out looking for trouble."

" 'The Attack of the Killer Chipmunks' eh?"

"It sounds silly, but that's because we've been conditioned by Disney cartoons to think of them as lovable, harmless little creatures."

"Well, you have to admit they're pretty cute."

"Only if you romanticize them. Take those damned ground squirrels, for example. If the females get too upset at living conditions, or if they're caged with a strange male, they kill their young. Bite off their heads."

Amy shuddered. "You're really serious about this rodent menace, aren't you?"

The chipmunk continued to call from the tree. Janice lobbed a pine cone at it halfheartedly.

"Well, before I get too carried away I need to prove what I saw. Branton said to duplicate the conditions."

"So throw them some more snakes."

"Huh? Oh, you mean road kills. Yeah, there must be plenty. Maybe when Jeff comes up he can find some."

Late that afternoon, Janice was working in her cubicle in the lab when she heard a familiar male voice outside her open door. "Janny babe? You in there?"

She leaped up from her chair and flung herself at the tall, lean, and slightly disheveled figure in the doorway. "Jeff! Wow, you got here fast! And it's so good to see you." They were instantly in a mad whirling embrace around her cubicle.

Amy chose that moment to knock on the doorframe. "Hey, cool down, you two. I can hear you giggling all the way down the hall."

Jeff slowly put Janice down, sliding her body down his while staring intently at her. Finally her feet were on the floor, and she disengaged from him slightly. Still hugging him, she turned to Amy and introduced them. "Jeff, meet Amy, the Pellet Researcher for this year."

Jeff looked blank. "Pleased, I'm sure. What are pellets?"

Amy sneezed. "Barf balls. Birds that prey on small furry things cough up balls of fur and bones. I separate out the bones and identify them. We even find snake scales in 'em."

"Oh yeah, sure. I just couldn't connect for a moment."
He collected himself. "It's the altitude, you know. My
brains are at eight thousand feet. Besides, I was distracted."

Amy grinned. "Okay, I get the hint. But when you're
ready, I've found something about the chipmunks you
should know."

Despite herself, Janice was intrigued. "Tell me quick,
then we can talk about it later." She hugged Jeff. "Much
later."

"Well, basically, this summer's big owl pellets have quite
a few chipmunks in 'em."

Janice looked puzzled. "What's that mean?"

"There shouldn't be chipmunks in these pellets—they're
diurnal animals. They're not active when the owls are out,
so how can they be getting caught?"

"Something's funny."

"Not only that, but I checked the pellet results from past
years—up until two years ago, only voles and mice, nice
nocturnal animals, what you'd expect. No chipmunks."

"Well, either these are early owls, or the chipmunks stay
up late."

"Exactly. And there are no reports of funny owls. So the
chipmunks are changing their behavior."

Over the next week Janice and Jeff retrieved a variety of
squashed and bloody carcasses from the paved roads between Mammoth Lakes and SNARL and transported them
to the site of her encounter with the chipmunks, just north
of the intersection of Highway 203 and Highway 395, on
an old asphalt spur road within sight of the interstate. Her
jeep began to smell like ripe flesh, and her gloves acquired
unpleasant stains.

Thursday morning she dumped yet another squashed rabbit on the edge of the pavement. Then she retired to her
jeep on the side of the road and waited, binoculars and
notebook at the ready, for the chipmunks to respond in the
now-familiar pattern. Jeff pulled out a book and stretched
out in the back seat.

Within minutes there was a stirring in the low shrubs
nearest the carcass. Two chipmunks she called the Look-

outs emerged from the vegetation and approached the rabbit. They circled it cautiously, sniffing the air repeatedly and making low chittering noises. At some unseen signal they flashed quickly back into the shrubs. Next came the noise of high-pitched barking: not the continuous alarm signal common to chipmunks and squirrels, these were short bursts of sound repeated for about ten minutes. This was followed by the appearance of at least a dozen chipmunks around the carcass. Finally came the feeding frenzy, enthusiastic yet curiously disciplined. Some animals tore out chunks and disappeared into the shrubs, to be replaced by others. In about an hour the rabbit was reduced to fascia-covered bones.

"Let's see Disney make a cartoon out of this. They could call it 'Bambi and Thumper Share a Roadkill,' " she remarked.

"Reminds me of stories about piranhas."

"Land piranhas? But they take living prey. These are more like furry vultures. At least so far."

"Oh? Care to explain?" He put his book down.

"Okay. I think they're cooperating because that way they can compete with bigger scavengers like ravens and coyotes. These carcasses disappear so fast the other creatures never have a chance to find them."

"Why do chipmunks eat meat anyway? They're supposed to eat nuts and berries and stuff like that. They're not predators."

Janice sighed. "Deer, squirrels, mice, rabbits and other cute, furry critters are classified as plant eaters, herbivores. We've adopted the view fostered by cartoons and kids' books, that they only eat plant food. But actually, very few animals turn down the chance to eat meat even if they don't hunt."

"Why?"

"Well, for starters, meat is easier to digest than plant food. No tough fibers. Carnivores have much shorter, simpler digestive systems than herbivores. So it's a good source of energy and calories."

"So why haven't chipmunks everywhere realized this before?"

"Good question, especially from a mathematician. It has to do with the evolutionary pressure. It's pretty fierce up here."

Jeff looked blank.

"Look, this is a food-scarce environment. Dry all year and cold in the winter to boot. The pine forest where the chipmunks live is not very diverse—not a lot of different organisms, but many individuals of the few species that do thrive here. It's the classic pattern for a difficult environment."

"But there are twenty square miles of pine forest filled with pine nuts—how tough can that be for a chipmunk?"

Janice considered for a moment, pawed through some papers in the front seat. She tossed Jeff a greyish object.

"Look at this deer leg I found in the forest."

He turned the bone over and noticed that one end was jagged.

"Let's see . . . it has marks on it—looks like tooth marks. Okay, it's been gnawed."

"Yup. Nothing lasts long on the forest floor. When an animal dies its body is quickly scavenged by the living. Even the bones are gnawed for their calcium. So anything the chipmunks can do to improve the food supply is going to be a big advantage for their survival."

"Okay. I'm convinced. But I'm just a humble mathematician. How're you going to prove your idea to the Brantons of the world?"

"Well, I don't know yet, but I think I can predict what the next step is. It's the same kind of thing that happened to our own ancestors on the African savanna. We were originally scavengers, cleaning up after the big predators like lions."

"So much for the Great Hunter idea, eh?"

"It's not a very likely scenario for puny creatures like us without claws or fangs, or at that time, much technology. The point is, a coordinated band can scare or harass a large predator away from its kill."

"But our ancestors did start to hunt."

"They did at some point. Using the same pack behavior they developed for scavenging, they found they could take large living game. And the communication skills they needed for hunting led to human language."

"So the next step for the chipmunks is to talk?"

"No, silly." She bopped him lightly on the head with her clipboard. "Wolves and wild dogs don't talk, but they hunt in packs. So, I predict that the chipmunks are going to hunt living prey."

Janice swam up out of sleep with the comforting sensation of another body next to hers. Jeff was snuggled up against her, breathing deeply and surprisingly quietly, one arm draped over her breasts. She ran her hands lightly over his exposed shoulders and arms. He stirred, grunted contentedly and opened his eyes. Then inhaled deeply and coughed. "Can't get used to the air up here—how can you breathe something you can't even see?"

"Smoghead. Look out there. It's a gorgeous day. Let me show you some scenery."

"What are we doing about breakfast?"

"There's a good place in Mammoth, then we can explore the forest behind the town."

As they drove out of the parking lot they passed Amy carrying a paper sack. She waved them down. "Hey, how'd you like to come out hooting with me tonight? I want to nail down if Owl #6 is a Great Grey. I found some pretty interesting-looking feathers in its territory."

"Is that what you've got in the bag?" asked Janice.

She frowned. "No, unfortunately. These are the remains of Old Reliable, my owl from Doe Ridge. I found it lying under the tree where it leaves its pellets."

"How'd it die?"

"Can't tell, actually. The body was pretty well munched already—not much but feathers and a few bones left. Things sure don't last long on the forest floor around here. I checked the site just two days ago."

Janice turned to Jeff. "You have time to go hooting to-night? I'll bet you've never done it."

He suppressed a smile. "Sure, if it's a hoot, I'm interested."

They all groaned.

"Okay, we're in."

"Great. I'll bring the hot chocolate. Meet here around eight tonight and we'll head off."

Blondie's Kitchen was pleasantly full of T-shirted vacationers, but there was one unoccupied booth left. The smell of coffee permeated the air, sharpening Janice's hunger.

As they perused the menus, she became aware of an animated conversation behind her back in the adjoining booth.

"That's not English—what is it?" asked Jeff.

Janice listened for a few seconds. "French, but with a southern accent, not Parisian."

He stared at her. "Wow, I'm impressed. How did you do that?"

She looked up from the menu and smiled at him. Her frequent trips to Europe as a child had given her fluency in French and Italian and the ability to distinguish regional accents.

"Southern accents are the same all over. People speak more slowly and hang onto the ends of their words. In Australia their south is the north, but the same thing happens."

As she turned in again on the conversation behind her, something about it caught her attention. She motioned Jeff to silence.

"Wait a minute, I want to hear this. . . ." She turned her head to hear better and concentrated.

A man was talking, a long barrage spiked with exasperation and cries of disbelief from others. Janice listened for a few minutes. Finally there was loud laughter from the table behind.

She turned back to Jeff. "He was complaining about squirrels stealing food. A bunch of squirrels, *tout un tas*, he said. They apparently worked over his pack and he couldn't get them to stop. He was pretty upset about it, especially when his friends didn't take him seriously. He kept insisting that they were doing something unusual."

"Where did it happen?"

"Unfortunately, I missed that part, so it could have just been a campground. But there are campgrounds in France, so he should be used to pesky squirrels."

"These were squirrels, or chipmunks?"

"He called them squirrels. But I doubt he'd know the correct name for chipmunks anyway. Most people don't distinguish between the local rodents. They're all just generic squirrels. No, what's funny is that I was discussing this kind of incident with Amy just yesterday, and now it's happened."

"Maybe you have chipmunks on the brain. Here comes the waitress. Ready to order?"

After breakfast they headed out of town on the winding asphalt ribbon of the scenic loop. There were few other cars, in contrast to the busy interstate. The brilliant blue sky illuminated steep-sided hillsides thickly grown with tall stately fir trees.

Janice looked around as she drove. Not a menacing forest at all, in fact a rather straightforward one, she thought. Still, she couldn't help wondering if the placidity hid the secret rustlings of new activity. As if answering her thought, a ground squirrel erupted out of a roadside shrub and dashed across the road in front of them. She slowed the jeep, but it was moving very fast and was in no danger of being hit.

"What was that—a greased chipmunk?" asked Jeff.

"I think it was a golden mantled ground squirrel. The head was orange, and it was a bit bigger."

"How could you tell? All I got was a glimpse."

"It *was* moving pretty fast. Last time I saw a squirrel run like that, there was a weasel behind it."

"Maybe the chipmunk mafia was after it." He grinned.

"Don't you start now."

She turned off onto a gravel forest service road and parked the jeep at the base of a hill. As they walked around the rocky apron of the hill they came to a wooden nest box mounted on a pine tree, one of many scattered throughout the forest. Earlier in the summer she and Amy had amused themselves by guessing what birds were using the boxes, gleaning information from an occasional dropped feather. But as they approached, Janice saw something was wrong. Nest material protruded from the entrance hole, and many feathers were strewn around the forest floor beneath it.

"Something must've raided this box," she said. "Look at the entrance hole—it's chewed all around."

"So what animal could do this? Don't they build these boxes so only birds can get in?"

"I thought so. I've never seen one messed up like this, and it must be a rare event or the Forest Service wouldn't bother putting boxes up."

"Seems to me it'd be easy for squirrels or chipmunks to get into one of these anytime they wanted."

Janice considered for a moment. "I always thought so too, and maybe that's the answer. They don't usually want to."

"But now they do? Your chipmunks again?"

She stared at him. "Well, maybe I'm just jumping to conclusions, but if they were starting to hunt, these would be the easiest prey. Here in the boxes, and in all the dead trees where the other birds nest." She shivered despite the warmth of the late morning sun.

Amy killed the headlights on the pickup truck as they reached the territory of Owl #6. The site was a clump of Jeffrey pines on a low rocky bluff overlooking a pumice flat and the interstate, about a quarter mile north of Highway 203.

"So what's special about this owl?" asked Jeff.

"Well, basically, locating a Great Grey would burnish my credentials as a field biologist. It'd be a real find on this side of the mountains. They're pretty rare even in lusher forests on the west side. I've put in a lot of hours trying to find this puppy. Maybe tonight's the night."

They unloaded the tape recorder, and Jeff slung it around

his neck. It was a big bulky job, an ancient model from the lab.

"So you're not actually going to hoot?" asked Janice.

"Nah, my hoots have a Chinese accent, not 'furry' enough. Owls hate 'em. This way is better."

A flicker of movement caught Janice's eye. A darker shape was gliding noiselessly into the green-black branches of the pines on the edge of the bluff. She touched Amy on the shoulder and pointed.

"There it is. What luck!" Amy whispered.

They walked carefully over the fallen branches and pine cones to a small clearing close to where they had seen the owl.

Jeff set the recorder on the ground and Amy flicked it on. The throaty hoots of a Great Grey floated into the darkness. She repeated the sequence several times, but there was no answering call.

"Well, maybe it's just a Great Horned Owl after all."

She fumbled in the backpack for a small flashlight. "I've got horned owl hoots further along on the tape."

"Here, I've got one," said Janice. As she flicked the light on she heard soft rustling noises among the dry needles of the forest floor. Holding the light at eye level, she scanned around her. A few spider eyes gleamed back at her, and several sets of larger eyes. One set was close enough to discern the striped body behind the eyes. "Look, a chipmunk! Well, that proves they're out at night all right."

"And that's why my owls are catching them."

"Yeah, but what are they doing out?" asked Janice.

"What difference does it make? Snakes come out on summer nights, why not chipmunks?" asked Jeff.

"The snakes only do it because their body temperature is still warm enough to hunt. It's basic physiology for a cold-blooded animal. And it's not something new," she explained.

"Right," put in Amy. "And remember, just a few years ago the owls weren't catching chipmunks."

"So they probably weren't out at night."

"The only other possible explanation was that a new species of owl with slightly different hours had moved in," sighed Amy. "I was counting on a Great Grey, but they almost always answer the tape if they hear it."

The tape recorder was still running and Great Horned owl hoots filled the air. In the recorded silence after the calls they heard again the soft rustling noises. The tape called again, but the owl stayed silent. The rustling sounds increased.

"No wonder those chipmunks get caught—they make a racket."

"I sure wish this one would hoot. Say, you guys, would you mind moving away from the tree? Take a walk or something? Maybe there are too many of us here."

Janice and Jeff moved away from the clearing, walking slowly back toward the truck, then past it down the dirt road and into the forest. A few minutes later, as they rounded the first bend, Janice suddenly stopped and put her hand on Jeff's arm. "Listen. The owl."

The sound of the live owl's answer floated lightly over the forest.

"It's in a higher pitch, but the song's the same," whispered Jeff.

"That's what it usually sounds like. Poor Amy, it's unmistakably a Great Horned Owl."

"Hoping to nail chipmunks, probably," said Jeff.

"Yeah. The Great Horned owls are top predators. Pretty ferocious hunters, the terror of the night to anything smaller. We enjoy the sound of the hooting, because they don't threaten us." She paused. "I wonder if the mice shiver when they hear it."

"Like we do at the scream of a cougar?"

"Or the snarl of a grizzly? Actually, besides the odd tiger attack in India, there are precious few large predators left to threaten humans. We've erased them, starting back about ten thousand years when we—"

They heard Amy curse and stamp her feet.

"What's she doing over there?" wondered Jeff. "I thought the idea was for us to be quiet."

"I don't know. Shhh."

The owl continued to call from the tree every few seconds in response to the tape. As they stood quietly in the darkness Janice slowly became aware of soft rustling sounds around them. She fumbled for her flashlight, but it slipped through her hands onto the duff. She reached down to pick it up, groping around with her hand.

From the darkness something furry leaped at her hand. Warm fur, sharp teeth. "Ow!" she yelled, and shook her attacker free while straightening up.

"What's the matter?"

Janice was nearly speechless with surprise. "It . . . bit me! It leaped on me and bit me!"

"What? Where?" Jeff was instantly all motion and concern.

"On my hand. Goddamn chipmunk bit me. It's absolutely incredible!"

Suddenly from the clearing they heard the sound of running feet, a crash, and Amy yelling.

"What's she saying?" asked Jeff.

"I'm not sure. It sounds like 'stop it.' We'd better get over there."

They retrieved the flashlight and half-ran back to the clearing, stumbling over pine cones and branches. The tape recorder was tipped over on its side.

"Amy? Where are you? What's happening?" yelled Janice.

A rustling commotion in the branches of a tree above them. She looked up. Scrambling noises on the trunk traced the descent of many small bodies.

"Lord, the tree must be full of them!"

From the direction of the owl tree came a strangled screech and sounds of thrashing. Amy was yelling "Stop it, stop it, stop it, you damn things!" In the distance they could see her flashlight playing in the branches of the tree, its stabs raking across shrouded vaults.

"The owl! They're attacking the owl," yelled Janice. They ran to join Amy. Suddenly she was filled with loathing for the swarming rodents.

They found Amy two branches up in the tree, flashlight clenched in her teeth, yelling wordlessly.

There was more commotion in the branches, sharp squeals and thrashings.

Then above her Janice heard something falling, thumping into branches and crashing to the ground on the far side of the tree. She guessed it was the owl, but it sounded too heavy. She had a sudden vision of a cadre of chipmunks attacking the owl as it sat helpless on the branch, the brief death struggle, the failed takeoff becoming a plunge taking both attackers and prey to their doom.

Above them, Amy yelled in pain and stopped climbing. She yelled again and her flashlight fell to the ground.

"Ahhh! I'm being attacked!"

A hastening, liquid sound—made up, Janice realized, of many excited squeals.

"They're swarming all over," Amy shrieked. "I'm coming down."

With a cry she fell from the tree, landing in a crumpled heap. They rushed over to her.

Jeff helped her up.

"Amy . . ." began Janice.

"Oh, my ankle. I must've landed wrong." Her terrified face stared up at them in the flashlight gleam. "D-damn things are all over the tree! One of them b-bit me on the shoulder. They're like in a frenzy or something."

The branches above them were alive with swift scurrying noises.

"Let's get out of here," said Janice. "This is bad news. Maybe these things are sick."

"No," said Jeff. "It's what you said. They've taken the next step. They're hunting."

"But why the owl?"

"It's payback time. Remember the mice shivering at the sound of the hooting?"

She stared at him. "I was only half serious about the hunting. But they're so intense."

"Wait, the owl . . . where is it?" gasped Amy. "Maybe it's still alive."

"Not a chance. Let's just get out of here," urged Janice.

"You two go for the truck, I'll look for the owl," said Jeff.

The two women struggled toward the truck, Amy leaning heavily on Janice. Several times they heard chipmunks moving in the duff around them.

Jeff caught up with them. He was carrying the tape recorder. "It's dead all right. In a heap with some mangled chipmunks. And a mess of live ones that wouldn't let me near it."

The scrambled into the truck.

"I'll never feel the same about the forest again," shuddered Amy.

"It'll never *be* the same again," said Janice. Her thoughts raced.

There's a new predator loose in the wilds. We erased the big ones, hunted them down and thought we were safe. But evolution never sleeps. There was a niche to be filled, and it was filled from below, from the small creatures. It's happened before. When the dinosaurs died, the mammals that inherited the earth were descended from small nocturnal animals. Some people speculated that they may even have hastened the demise of the dinosaurs by eating their eggs. Maybe this is the beginning of the end of our brief hominid dominance.

She looked back as Jeff started the engine. The dark forest was alive with tiny glaring dots. In the glow of the tail lights, a ring of bright eyes glittered.

> *The wood is full of shining eyes,*
> *The wood is full of creeping feet,*
> *The wood is full of tiny cries.*
> *You must not go to the wood at night.*
> —Henry Treece (1912-1956)

The author is grateful for permission to reprint the refrain from "The Magic Wood" by Henry Treece, Copyright © 1945 by Farber and Farber, Ltd.

Sexual Dimorphism

KIM STANLEY ROBINSON

Kim Stanley Robinson became a famous SF writer in 1984 with his first novel, The Wild Shore, *an excellent post-catastrophe SF novel in the Steinbeckian tradition of George R. Stewart's* Earth Abides. *It had the bad luck to be published in the same year as William Gibson's* Neuromancer, *to which it came in second for major awards. And worse, it allowed Robinson to become a symbol of the opposition for the adherents of the Movement, Cyberpunks' official name in the mid-80s. For a while, the Cyberpunk vs. Humanist polemic was quite heated. Readers in search of more are referred to Michael Swanwick's essay, "A Users Guide to the Postmoderns." So Robinson's major works of that decade were not ignored, but the discourse was somewhat contaminated by literary politics. He did win some major awards, and was nominated for more. His major short fiction was collected in the paperback omnibus,* Remaking History *(1994).*

It was in the 1990s that Robinson grew in literary power and achievement with his Mars trilogy (Red Mars, Green Mars, Blue Mars), *and a standalone novel,* Antarctica. *These books made him one of the most famous and popular SF writers of the decade and confirmed him in the front ranks of contemporary SF writers. In 1999 he published a collection of stories,* The Martians, *of tales of Mars (many of them first published) not told in the Mars trilogy, some-*

times because they took alternate future paths from his main Martian future. After a number of years exclusively devoted to novel writing, this was a rich year for him in short fiction. At least three of the original stories in the collection could have been chosen for this book.

This story is about a scientist in the future on a terraformed Mars, when there are oceans there with dolphins. It is Robinson's reimagining of Brian Aldiss' classic "A Kind of Artistry," in his own Martian setting.

The potential for hallucination in paleogenomics was high. There was not only the omnipresent role of instrumentation in the envisioning of the ultramicroscopic fossil material, but also the metamorphosis over time of the material itself, both the DNA and its matrices, so that the data were invariably incomplete, and often shattered. Thus the possibility of psychological projection of patterns onto the rorschacherie of what in the end might be purely mineral processes had to be admitted.

Dr. Andrew Smith was as aware of these possibilities as anyone. Indeed, it constituted one of the central problems of his field—convincingly to sort the traces of DNA in the fossil record, distinguishing them from an array of possible pseudofossils. Pseudofossils littered the history of the discipline, from the earliest false nautiloids to the famous Martian pseudo-nanobacteria. Nothing progressed in paleogenomics unless you could show that you really were talking about what you said you were talking about. So Dr. Smith did not get too excited, at first, about what he was finding in the junk DNA of an early dolphin fossil.

In any case there were quite a few distractions to his work at that time. He was living on the south shore of the Amazonian Sea, that deep southerly bay of the world-ringing ocean, east of Elysium, near the equator. In the summers, even the cool summers they had been having lately, the extensive inshore shallows of the sea grew as warm as blood, and dolphins—adapted from Terran river dolphins like the baiji from China, or the boto from the Amazon, or the susu from the Ganges, or the bhulan from the Indus—sported just off the beach. Morning sunlight lanced through the waves and picked out their flashing silhouettes, sometimes groups of eight or ten of them, all playing in the same wave.

The marine laboratory he worked at, located on the seafront of the harbor town Eumenides Point, was associated with the Acheron labs, farther up the coast to the west. The work at Eumenides had mostly to do with the shifting ecologies of a sea that was getting saltier. Dr. Smith's current project dealing with this issue involved investigating the various adaptations of extinct cetaceans who had lived when the Earth's sea had exhibited different levels of salt. He had in his lab some fossil material, sent to the lab from Earth for study, as well as the voluminous literature on the subject, including the full genomes of all the living descendants of these creatures. The transfer of fossils from Earth introduced the matter of cosmic-ray contamination to all the other problems involved in the study of ancient DNA, but most people dismissed these effects as minor and inconsequential, which was why fossils were shipped across at all. And of course with the recent deployment of fusion-powered rapid vehicles, the amount of exposure to cosmic rays had been markedly reduced. Smith was therefore able to do research on mammal salt tolerance both ancient and modern, thus helping to illuminate the current situation on Mars, also joining the debates ongoing concerning the paleohalocycles of the two planets, now one of the hot research areas in comparative planetology and bioengineering.

Nevertheless, it was a field of research so arcane that if you were not involved in it, you tended not to believe in it. It was an offshoot, a mix of two difficult fields, its ultimate usefulness a long shot, especially compared to most of the inquiries being conducted at the Eumenides Point Labs. Smith found himself fighting a feeling of marginalization in the various lab meetings and informal gatherings, in coffee lounges, cocktail parties, beach luncheons, boating excursions. At all of these he was the odd man out, with only his colleague Frank Drumm, who worked on reproduction in the dolphins currently living offshore, expressing any great interest in his work and its applications. Worse yet, his work appeared to be becoming less and less important to his advisor and employer, Vlad Taneev, who as one of the First Hundred, and the co-founder of the Acheron labs, was ostensibly the most powerful scientific mentor one could have on Mars; but who in practice turned out to be nearly impossible of access, and rumored to be in failing health, so that it was like having no boss at all, and therefore no access to the lab's technical staff and so forth. A bitter disappointment.

And then of course there was Selena, his—his partner, roommate, girlfriend, significant other, lover—there were many words for this relationship, though none were quite right. The woman with whom he lived, with whom he had gone through graduate school and two post-docs, with whom he had moved to Eumenides Point, taking a small apartment near the beach, near the terminus of the coastal tram, where when one looked back east the point itself just heaved over the horizon, like a dorsal fin seen far out to sea. Selena was making great progress in her own field, genetically engineering salt grasses; a subject of great importance here, where they were trying to stabilize a thousand-kilometer coastline of low dunes and quicksand swamps. Scientific and bioengineering progress; important achievements, relevant to the situation; all things were coming to her professionally, including of course offers to team up in any number of exciting public/co-op collaborations.

And all things were coming to her privately as well. Smith had always thought her beautiful, and now he saw that with her success, other men were coming to the same realization. It took only a little attention to see it; an ability to look past shabby lab coats and a generally unkempt style to the sleekly curving body and the intense, almost ferocious intelligence. No—his Selena looked much like all the rest of the lab rats when in the lab, but in the summers when the group went down in the evening to the warm tawny beach to swim, she walked out the long expanse of the shallows like a goddess in a bathing suit, like Venus returning to the sea. Everyone in these parties pretended not to notice, but you couldn't help it.

All very well; except that she was losing interest in him. This was a process that Smith feared was irreversible; or, to be more precise, that if it had gotten to the point where he could notice it, it was too late to stop it. So now he watched her, furtive and helpless, as they went through their domestic routines; there was a goddess in his bathroom, showering, drying off, dressing, each moment like a dance.

But she didn't chat anymore. She was absorbed in her thoughts, and tended to keep her back to him. No—it was all going away.

They had met in an adult swim club in Mangala, while they were both grad students at the university there. Now, as if to re-invoke that time, Smith took up Frank's suggestion and joined him at an equivalent club in Eumenides Point, and began to swim regularly again. He went from the tram or the lab down to the big fifty-meter pool, set on a terrace overlooking the ocean, and swam so hard in the mornings that the whole rest of the day he buzzed along in a flow of beta endorphins, scarcely aware of his work problems or the situation at home. After work he took the tram home feeling his appetite kick in, and banged around the kitchen throwing together a meal and eating much of it as he cooked it, irritated (if she was there at all) with Selena's poor cooking and her cheery talk about her work, irritated also probably just from hunger, and dread at the situation hanging over them; at this pretense that they were still in a normal life. But if he snapped at her during this fragile hour she would go silent the whole rest of the evening; it happened fairly often; so he tried to contain his temper and make the meal and quickly eat his part of it, to get his blood sugar level back up.

Either way she fell asleep abruptly around nine, and he

was left to read into the timeslip, or even slip out and take a walk on the night beach a few hundred yards away from their apartment. One night, walking west, he saw Pseudo-phobos pop up into the sky like a distress flare down the coast, and when he came back into the apartment she was awake and talking happily on the phone; she was startled to see him, and cut the call short, thinking about what to say, and then said, "That was Mark, we've gotten tamarisk three fifty-nine to take repetitions of the third salt flusher gene!"

"That's good," he said, moving into the dark kitchen so she wouldn't see his face.

This annoyed her. "You really don't care how my work goes, do you?"

"Of course I do. That's good, I said."

She dismissed that with a noise.

Then one day he got home and Mark was there with her, in the living room, and at a single glance he could see they had been laughing about something; had been sitting closer together than when he started opening the door. He ignored that and was as pleasant as he could be.

The next day as he swam at the morning workout, he watched the women swimming with him in his lane. All three of them had swum all their lives, their freestyle stroke perfected beyond the perfection of any dance move ever made on land, the millions of repetitions making their movement as unconscious as that of any fish in the sea. Under the surface he saw their bodies flowing forward, revealing their sleek lines—classic swimmer lines, like Selena's—rangy shoulders tucking up against their ears one after the next, ribcages smoothed over by powerful lats, breasts flatly merged into big pecs or else bobbing left then right, as the case might be; bellies meeting high hipbones accentuated by the high cut of their swimsuits, backs curving up to bottoms rounded and compact, curving to powerful thighs then long calves, and feet outstretched like ballerinas. Dance was a weak analogy for such beautiful movement. And it all went on for stroke after stroke, lap after lap, until he was mesmerized beyond further thought or observation; it was just one aspect of a sensually saturated environment.

Their current lane leader was pregnant, yet swimming stronger than any of the rest of them, not even huffing and puffing during their rest intervals, when Smith often had to suck air—instead she laughed and shook her head, exclaiming "Every time I do a flip turn he keeps kicking me!" She was seven months along, round in the middle like a little whale, but still she fired down the pool at a rate none of the other three in the lane could match. The strongest swimmers in the club were simply amazing. Soon after getting into the sport, Smith had worked hard to swim a hundred-meter freestyle in less than a minute, a goal appropriate to him, and finally he had done it once at a meet and been pleased; then later he heard about the local college women's team's workout, which consisted of a hundred hundred-meter freestyle swims *all on a minute interval.* He understood then that although all humans looked roughly the same, some were stupendously stronger than others. Their pregnant leader was in the lower echelon of these strong swimmers, and regarded the swim she was making today as a light stretching-out, though it was beyond anything her lane mates could do with their best effort. You couldn't help watching her when passing by in the other direction, because despite her speed she was supremely smooth and effortless, she took fewer strokes per lap than the rest of them, and yet still made substantially better time. It was like magic. And that sweet blue curve of the new child carried inside.

Back at home things continued to degenerate. Selena often worked late, and talked to him less than ever.

"I love you," he said. "Selena, I love you."

"I know."

He tried to throw himself into his work. They were at the same lab, they could go home late together. Talk like they used to about their work, which though not the same, was still genomics in both cases; how much closer could two sciences be? Surely it would help to bring them back together.

But genomics was a very big field. It was possible to occupy different parts of it, no doubt about that. They were proving it. Smith persevered, however, using a new and more powerful electron microscope, and he began to make some headway in unraveling the patterns in his fossilized DNA.

It looked like what had been preserved in the samples he had been given was almost entirely what used to be called the junk DNA of the creature. In times past this would have been bad luck, but the Kohl labs in Acheron had recently been making great strides in unraveling the various purposes of junk DNA, which proved not to be useless after all, as might have been guessed, development being as complex as it was. Their breakthrough consisted in characterizing very short and scrambled repetitive sequences within junk DNA that could be shown to code instructions for higher hierarchical operations than they were used to seeing at the gene level—cell differentiation, information order sequencing, apoptosis, and the like.

Using this new understanding to unravel any clues in partially degraded fossil junk DNA would be hard, of course. But the nucleotide sequences were there in his EM images—or, to be more precise, the characteristic mineral replacements for the adenine=thymine and cytosine= guanine couplets, replacements well-established in the literature, were there to be clearly identified. Nanofossils, in effect; but legible to those who could read them. And once read, it was then possible to brew identical sequences of living nucleotides, matching the originals of the fossil creature. In theory one could re-create the creature itself, though in practice nothing like the entire genome was ever there, making it impossible. Not that there weren't people trying anyway with simpler fossil organisms, either going for the whole thing or using hybrid DNA techniques to graft expressions they could decipher onto living templates, mostly descendants of the earlier creature.

With this particular ancient dolphin, almost certainly a

fresh-water dolphin (though most of these were fairly salt tolerant, living in river-mouths as they did), complete re-suscitation would be impossible. It wasn't what Smith was trying to do anyway. What would be interesting would be to find fragments that did not seem to have a match in the living descendants' genome, then hopefully synthesize liv-ing in vitro fragments, clip them into contemporary strands, and see how these experimental animals did in hybridiza-tion tests and in various environments. Look for differences in function.

He was also doing mitochondrial tests when he could, which if successful would permit tighter dating for the spe-cies' divergence from precursor species. He might be able to give it a specific slot on the marine mammal family tree, which during the early Pliocene was very complicated.

Both avenues of investigation were labor-intensive, time-consuming, almost thoughtless work—perfect, in other words. He worked for hours and hours every day, for weeks, then months. Sometimes he managed to go home on the tram with Selena; more often he didn't. She was writing up her latest results with her collaborators, mostly with Mark. Her hours were irregular. When he was working he didn't have to think about this; so he worked all the time. It was not a solution, not even a very good strategy—it even seemed to be making things worse—and he had to attempt it against an ever-growing sense of despair and loss; but he did it nevertheless.

"What do you think of this Acheron work?" he asked Frank one day at work, pointing to the latest print-out from the Kohl lab, lying heavily annotated on his desk.

"It's very interesting! It makes it look like we're finally getting past the genes to the whole instruction manual."

"If there is such a thing."

"Has to be, right? Though I'm not sure the Kohl lab's values for the rate adaptive mutants will be fixed are high enough. Ohta and Kimura suggested 10 percent as the up-per limit, and that fits with what I've seen."

Smith nodded, pleased. "They're probably just being conservative."

"No doubt, but you have to go with the data."

"So—in that context—you think it makes sense for me to pursue this fossil junk DNA?"

"Well, sure. What do you mean? It's sure to tell us interesting things."

"It's incredibly slow."

"Why don't you read off a long sequence, brew it up and venter it, and see what you get?"

Smith shrugged. Whole-genome shotgun sequencing struck him as slipshod, but it was certainly faster. Reading small bits of single-stranded DNA, called expressed sequence tags, had quickly identified most of the genes on the human genome; but it had missed some, and it ignored even the regulatory DNA sequences controlling the protein-coding portion of the genes, not to mention the so-called junk DNA itself, filling long stretches between the more clearly meaningful sequences.

Smith expressed these doubts to Frank, who nodded, but said, "It isn't the same now that the mapping is so complete. You've got so many reference points you can't get confused where your bits are on the big sequence. Just plug what you've got into the Lander-Waterman, then do the finishing with the Kohl variations, and even if there are massive repetitions, you'll still be okay. And with the bits you've got, well they're almost like ests anyway, they're so degraded. So you might as well give it a try."

Smith nodded.

That night he and Selena trammed home together. "What do you think of the possibility of shotgun sequencing in vitro copies of what I've got?" he asked her shyly.

"Sloppy," she said. "Double jeopardy."

A new schedule evolved. He worked, swam, took the tram home. Usually Selena wasn't there. Often their answering machine held messages for her from Mark, talking about their work. Or messages from her to Smith, telling him that she would be home late. As was happening so often, he sometimes went out for dinner with Frank and other lane mates, after the evening work-outs. One time at a beach restaurant they ordered several pitchers of beer, and then went out for a walk on the beach, and ended up running out into the shallows of the bay and swimming around in the warm dark water, so different from their pool, splashing each other and laughing hard. It was a good time.

But when he got home that night, there was another message on the answering machine from Selena, saying that she and Mark were working on their paper after getting a bite to eat, and that she would be home extra late.

She wasn't kidding; at two o'clock in the morning she was still out. In the long minutes following the timeslip Smith realized that no one stayed out this late working on a paper without calling home. This was therefore a message of a different kind.

Pain and anger swept through him, first one then the other. The indirection of it struck him as cowardly. He deserved at least a revelation—a confession—a scene. As the long minutes passed he got angrier and angrier; then frightened for a moment, that she might have been hurt or something. But she hadn't. She was out there somewhere fooling around. Suddenly he was furious.

He pulled cardboard boxes out of their closet and yanked open her drawers, and threw all her clothes in heaps in the boxes, crushing them in so they would all fit. But they gave off their characteristic scent of laundry soap and her, and smelling it he groaned and sat down on the bed, knees weak. If he carried through with this he would never again see her putting on and taking off these clothes, and just as an animal he groaned at the thought.

But men are not animals. He finished throwing her things into boxes, took them outside the front door and dropped them there.

She came back at three. He heard her kick into the boxes and make some muffled exclamation.

He hurled open the door and stepped out.

"What's this?" She had been startled out of whatever

scenario she had planned, and now was getting angry. Her, angry! It made him furious all over again.

"You know what it is."

"What!"

"You and Mark."

She eyed him.

"Now you notice," she said at last. "A year after it started. And this is your first response." Gesturing down at the boxes.

He hit her in the face.

Immediately he crouched at her side and helped her sit up, saying "Oh God Selena I'm sorry, I'm sorry, I didn't mean to," he had only thought to slap her for her contempt, contempt that he had not noticed her betrayal earlier, "I can't believe I—"

"Get *away*," striking him off with wild blows, crying and shouting, "get away, get away," frightened, "you bastard, you miserable bastard, what do you, don't you *dare* hit me!" in a near shriek, though she kept her voice down too, aware still of the apartment complex around them. Hands held to her face.

"I'm sorry Selena. I'm very very sorry, I was angry at what you said but I know that isn't, that doesn't . . . I'm sorry." Now he was as angry at himself as he had been at her—what could he have been thinking, why had he given her the moral high ground like this, it was she who had broken their bond, it was she who should be in the wrong! She who was now sobbing—turning away—suddenly walking off into the night. Lights went on in a couple of windows nearby. Smith stood staring down at the boxes of her lovely clothes, his right knuckles throbbing.

That life was over. He lived on alone in the apartment by the beach, and kept going in to work, but he was shunned there by the others, who all knew what had happened. Selena did not come in to work again until the bruises were gone, and after that she did not press charges, or speak to him about that night, but she did move in with Mark, and avoided him at work when she could. As who wouldn't. Occasionally she dropped by his nook to ask in a neutral voice about some logistical aspect of their break-up. He could not meet her eye. Nor could he meet the eye of anyone else at work, not properly. It was strange how one could have a conversation with people and appear to be meeting their gaze during it, when all the time they were not really quite looking at you and you were not really quite looking at them. Primate subtleties, honed over millions of years on the savanna.

He lost appetite, lost energy. In the morning he would wake up and wonder why he should get out of bed. Then looking at the blank walls of the bedroom, where Selena's prints had hung, he would sometimes get so angry at her that his pulse hammered uncomfortably in his neck and forehead. This got him out of bed, but then there was no-where to go, except work. And there everyone knew he was a wife beater, a domestic abuser, an asshole. Martian society did not tolerate such people.

Shame or anger; anger or shame. Grief or humiliation. Resentment or regret. Lost love. Omnidirectional rage.

Mostly he didn't swim anymore. The sight of the swim-mer women was too painful now, though they were as friendly as always; they knew nothing of the lab except him and Frank, and Frank had not said anything to them about what had happened. It made no difference. He was cut off from them. He knew he ought to swim more, and he swam less. Whenever he resolved to turn things around he would swim two or three days in a row, then let it fall away again.

Once at the end of an early evening workout he had forced himself to attend—and now he felt better, as usual—while they were standing in the lane steaming, his three most constant lane mates made quick plans to go to a nearby trattoria after showering. One looked at him. "Pizza at Rico's?"

He shook his head. "Hamburger at home," he said sadly.

They laughed at this. "Ah, come on. It'll keep another night."

"Come on, Andy," Frank said from the next lane. "I'll go too, if that's okay."

"Sure," the women said. Frank often swam in their lane too.

"Well. . . ." Smith roused himself. "Okay."

He sat with them and listened to their chatter around the restaurant table. They still seemed to be slightly steaming, their hair wet and wisping away from their foreheads. The three women were young. It was interesting; away from the pool they looked ordinary and undistinguished: skinny, mousy, plump, maladroit, whatever. With their clothes on you could not guess at their fantastically powerful shoulders and lats, their compact smooth musculatures. Like seals dressed up in clown suits, waddling around a stage.

"Are you okay?" one asked him when he had been silent too long.

"Oh yeah, yeah." He hesitated, glanced at Frank. "Broke up with my girlfriend."

"Ah ha! I *knew* it was something!" Hand to his arm (they all bumped into each other all the time in the pool): "You haven't been your usual self lately."

"No." He smiled ruefully. "It's been hard."

He could never tell them about what had happened. And Frank wouldn't either. But without that none of the rest of his story made any sense. So he couldn't talk about any of it.

They sensed this and shifted in their seats, preparatory to changing the topic. "Oh well," Frank said, helping them. "Lots more fish in the sea."

"In the pool," one of the women joked, elbowing him.

He nodded, tried to smile.

They looked at each other. One asked the waiter for the check, and another said to Smith and Frank, "Come with us over to my place, we're going to get in the hot tub and soak our aches away."

She rented a room in a little house with an enclosed courtyard, and all the rest of the residents were away. They followed her through the dark house into the courtyard, and took the cover off the hot tub and turned it on, then took their clothes off and got in the steaming water. Smith joined them, feeling shy. People on the beaches of Mars sunbathed without clothes all the time, it was no big deal really. Frank seemed not to notice, he was perfectly relaxed. But they didn't swim at the pool like this.

They all sighed at the water's heat. The woman from the house went inside and brought out some beer and cups. Light from the kitchen fell on her as she put down the dumpie and passed out the cups. Smith already knew her body perfectly well from their many hours together in the pool; nevertheless he was shocked seeing the whole of her Frank ignored the sight, filling the cups from the dumpie.

They drank beer, talked small talk. Two were vets; their lane leader, the one who had been pregnant, was a bit older, a chemist in a pharmaceutical lab near the pool. Her baby was being watched by her co-op that night. They all looked up to her, Smith saw, even here. These days she brought the baby to the pool and swam just as powerfully as ever, parking the baby-carrier just beyond the splash line. Smith's muscles melted in the hot water. He sipped his beer listening to them.

One of the women looked down at her breasts in the water and laughed. "They float like pull buoys."

Smith had already noticed this.

"No wonder women swim better than men."

"As long as they aren't so big they interfere with the hydrodynamics."

Their leader looked down through her fogged glasses, pink-faced, hair tied up, misted, demure. "I wonder if mine float less because I'm nursing."

"But all that milk."

"Yes, but the water in the milk is neutral density, it's the fat that floats. It could be that empty breasts float even more than full ones."

"Whichever has more fat, yuck."

"I could run an experiment, nurse him from just one side and then get in and see—" but they were laughing too hard for her to complete this scenario. "It would work! Why are you laughing!"

They only laughed more. Frank was cracking up, looking blissed, blessed. These women friends trusted them. But Smith still felt set apart. He looked at their lane leader: a pink bespectacled goddess, serenely vague and unaware; the scientist as heroine; the first full human being.

But later when he tried to explain this feeling to Frank, or even just to describe it, Frank shook his head. "It's a bad mistake to worship women," he warned. "A category error. Women and men are so much the same it isn't worth discussing the difference. The genes are identical almost entirely, you know that. A couple hormonal expressions and that's it. So they're just like you and me."

"More than a couple."

"Not much more. We all start out female, right? So you're better off thinking that nothing major ever really changes that. Penis just an oversized clitoris. Men are women. Women are men. Two parts of a reproductive system, completely equivalent."

Smith stared at him. "You're kidding."

"What do you mean?"

"Well—I've never seen a man swell up and give birth to a new human being, let me put it that way."

"So what? It happens, it's a specialized function. You never see women ejaculating either. But we all go back to being the same afterward. Details of reproduction only matter a tiny fraction of the time. No, we're all the same. We're all in it together. There are no differences."

Smith shook his head. It would be comforting to think so. But the data did not support the hypothesis. Ninety-five percent of all the murders in history had been committed by men. This was a difference.

He said as much, but Frank was not impressed. The murder ratio was becoming more nearly equal on Mars, he replied, and much less frequent for everybody, thus demonstrating very nicely that the matter was culturally conditioned, an artifact of Terran patriarchy no longer relevant on Mars. Nurture rather than nature. Although it was a false dichotomy. Nature could prove anything you wanted, Frank insisted. Female hyenas were vicious killers, male bonobos and muriquis were gentle cooperators. It meant nothing, Frank said. It told them nothing.

But Frank had not hit a woman in the face without ever planning to.

Patterns in the fossil *Inia* data sets became clearer and clearer. Stochastic resonance programs highlighted what had been preserved.

"Look here," Smith said to Frank one afternoon when Frank leaned in to say good-bye for the day. He pointed at his computer screen. "Here's a sequence from my boto, part of the GX three oh four, near the juncture, see?"

"You've got a female then?"

"I don't know. I think this here means I do. But look, see how it matches with this part of the human genome. It's in Hillis 8050. . . ."

Frank came into his nook and stared at the screen. "Comparing junk to junk . . . I don't know. . . ."

"But it's a match for more than a hundred units in a row, see? Leading right into the gene for progesterone initiation."

Frank squinted at the screen. "Um, well." He glanced quickly at Smith.

Smith said, "I'm wondering if there's some really long-term persistence in junk DNA, all the way back to earlier mammals precursors to both these."

"But dolphins are not our ancestors," Frank said.

"There's a common ancestor back there somewhere."

"Is there?" Frank straightened up. "Well, whatever. I'm not so sure about the pattern congruence itself. It's sort of similar, but, you know."

"What do you mean, don't you see that? Look right there!"

Frank glanced down at him, startled, then non-committal. Seeing this Smith became inexplicably frightened.

"Sort of," Frank said. "Sort of. You should run hybridization tests, maybe, see how good the fit really is. Or check with Acheron about repeats in nongene DNA."

"But the congruence is perfect! It goes on for hundreds of pairs, how could that be a coincidence?"

Frank looked even more non-committal than before. He glanced out the door of the nook. Finally he said, "I don't see it that congruent. Sorry, I just don't see it. Look, Andy. You've been working awfully hard for a long time. And you've been depressed too, right? Since Selena left?"

Smith nodded, feeling his stomach tighten. He had admitted as much a few months before. Frank was one of the very few people these days who would look him in the eye.

"Well, you know. Depression has chemical impacts in the brain, you know that. Sometimes it means you begin seeing patterns that others can't see as well. It doesn't mean they aren't there, no doubt they are there. But whether they mean anything significant, whether they're more than just a kind of analogy, or similarity—" He looked down at Smith and stopped. "Look, it's not my field. You should show this to Amos, or go up to Acheron and talk to the old man."

"Uh huh. Thanks, Frank."

"Oh no, no, no need. Sorry, Andy. I probably shouldn't have said anything. It's just, you know. You've been spending a hell of a lot of time here."

"Yeah."

Frank left.

Sometimes he fell asleep at his desk. He got some of his work done in dreams. Sometimes he found he could sleep down on the beach, wrapped in a greatcoat on the fine sand, lulled by the sound of the waves rolling in. At work he stared at the lined dots and letters on the screens, constructing the schematics of the sequences, nucleotide by nucleotide. Most were completely unambiguous. The correlation between the two main schematics was excellent, far beyond the possibility of chance. X chromosomes in humans clearly exhibited non-gene DNA traces of a distant aquatic ancestor, a kind of dolphin. Y chromosomes in humans lacked these passages, and they also matched with chimpanzees more completely than X chromosomes did. Frank had appeared not to believe it, but there it was, right on the screen. But how could it be? What did it mean? Where did any of them get what they were? They had natures from birth. Just under five million years ago, chimps and humans separated out as two different species from a common ancestor, a woodland ape. The *Inis geoffrensis* fossil Smith was working on had been precisely dated to about 5.1 million years old. About half of all orangutan sexual encounters are rape.

One night after quitting work alone in the lab, he took a tram in the wrong direction, downtown, without ever admitting to himself what he was doing, until he was standing outside Mark's apartment complex, under the steep rise of the dorsum ridge. Walking up a staircased alleyway ascending the ridge gave him a view right into Mark's windows. And there was Selena, washing dishes at the kitchen window and looking back over her shoulder to talk with someone. The tendon in her neck stood out in the light. She laughed.

Smith walked home. It took an hour. Many trams passed him.

He couldn't sleep that night. He went down to the beach and lay rolled in his greatcoat. Finally he fell asleep.

He had a dream. A small hairy bipedal primate, chimp-faced, walked like a hunchback down a beach in east Africa, in the late afternoon sun. The warm water of the shallows lay greenish and translucent. Dolphins rode inside the waves. The ape waded out into the shallows. Long powerful arms, evolved for hitting; a quick grab and he had one by the tail, by the dorsal fin. Surely it could escape, but it didn't try. Female; the ape turned her over, mated with her, released her. He left and came back to find the dolphin in the shallows, giving birth to twins, one male one female. The ape's troop swarmed into the shallows, killed and ate them both. Farther offshore the dolphin birthed two more.

The dawn woke Smith. He stood and walked out into the shallows. He saw dolphins inside the transparent indigo waves. He waded out into the surf. The water was only a little colder than the work-out pool. The dawn sun was low. The dolphins were only a little longer than he was, small and lithe. He bodysurfed with them. They were faster than him in the waves, but flowed around him when they had to. One leaped over him and splashed back into the curl of the wave ahead of him. Then one flashed under him, and on an impulse he grabbed at its dorsal fin and caught it, and was suddenly moving faster in the wave, as it rose with both of them inside it—by far the greatest bodysurfing ride of his life. He held on. The dolphin and all the rest of its pod turned and swam out to sea, and still he held on. This is it, he thought. Then he remembered that they were air-breathers too. It was going to be all right.

Game of the Century

ROBERT REED

Robert Reed's stories appear in amazing profusion, six to ten or more of them a year, and at least five or six of them worthy of consideration for a Year's Best volume again this year. What is particularly impressive is his range, which approaches such masters as Ray Bradbury or Gene Wolfe. And he writes about a novel a year as well (his first, The Leeshore, *appeared in 1987; his latest is* Marrow, *out in mid-2000). He has been publishing SF since 1986, but has only reached his present level of achievement in the mid-'90s. Last year his first story collection,* The Dragons of Springplace, *appeared from Golden Gryphon Press.*

This story, from F&SF, is appallingly prophetic SF. Reed is from the American midwest, where football is sometimes a religion and sometimes an industry, and winning the big game is everything. This brutal game between genetically engineered humanimals, reminiscent of H. G. Wells' inhabitants of The Island of Dr. Moreau, *is an all too plausible future. Except it would be illegal—wouldn't it?*

The window was left open at midnight, January 1, 2041, and three minutes, twenty-one seconds later it was closed again by the decisive, barely legible signature of an elderly Supreme Court justice who reportedly quipped, "I don't know why I have to. Folks who like screwing sheep are just going to keep at it."

Probably so.

But the issues were larger than traditional bestiality. Loopholes in some badly drafted legislation had made it perfectly legal to manipulate the human genome in radical ways. What's more, said offspring were deemed human in all rights and privileges inside the US of NA. For two hundred and twelve seconds, couples and single women could legally conceive by any route available to modern science. And while few clinics and fewer top-grade hospitals had interest in the work, there were key exceptions. Some fourteen hundred human eggs were fertilized with tailored sperm, then instantly implanted inside willing mothers. News services that had paid minimal attention to the legislative breakdown took a sudden glaring interest in the nameless, still invisible offspring. The blastulas were dubbed the 1-1-2041s, and everything about their lives became the subject of intense public scrutiny and fascination and self-righteous horror.

Despite computer models and experiments on chimpanzees, there were surprises. Nearly a third of the fetuses were stillborn, or worse. Twenty-nine mothers were killed as a

58

result of their pregnancies. Immunological problems, mostly. But in one case, a healthy woman in her mid-twenties died when her boy, perhaps bothered by the drumming of her heart, reached through her uterine wall and intestines, grabbing and squeezing the offending organ with both of his powerful hands.

Of the nine hundred-plus fetuses who survived, almost thirty percent were mentally impaired or physically frail. Remarkably, others seemed entirely normal, their human genes running roughshod over their more exotic parts. But several hundred of the 1-1-2041s were blessed with perfect health as well as a remarkable stew of talents. Even as newborns, they astonished the researchers who tested their reflexes and their highly tuned senses. The proudest parents released the data to the media, then mixed themselves celebratory cocktails, stepping out onto their porches and balconies to wait for the lucrative offers to start flowing their way.

Marlboro Jones came with a colorful reputation. His father was a crack dealer shot dead in a dispute over footwear. With his teenage mother, Marlboro had lived at dozens of addresses before her mind failed and she leaped out of their bedroom window to stop the voices, and from there his life was a string of unbroken successes. He had coached, and won, at three different schools. He was currently the youngest head coach of a Top Alliance team. Thirty-six years old, he looked twenty-six, his chiseled features built around the bright, amoral eyes of a squirrel. Marlboro was the kind of handsome that made his charm appealing, and he was charming in a way that made his looks and mannerisms delightfully boyish. A laser mind lurked behind those eyes, yet in most circumstances he preferred playing the cultured hick, knowing how much it improved his odds.

"He's a fine lookin' boy," the coach drawled. "Fine lookin'."

The proud parents stood arm in arm, smiling with a frothy, nervous joy.

"May I?" asked Marlboro. Then without waiting for permission, he yanked the screen off the crib, reached in and grabbed both bare feet. He tugged once, then again. Harder. "Damn, look at those legs! You'd think this boy'd be scampering around already. Strong as these seem . . . !"

"Well," said his mother, "he is awfully active."

"In a good way," the father cautioned.

"I believe it. I do!" Marlboro grinned, noticing that Mom looked awfully sweet in a tired-of-motherhood way, and it was too bad that he couldn't make a play for her, too. "Let me tell ya what I'm offering," he boomed. "A free ride. For the boy here—"

"Alan," Mom interjected.

"Alan," the coach repeated. Instantly, with an easy affection. Then he gave her a little wink, saying, "For Alan. A free education and every benefit that I'm allowed to give. Plus the same for your other two kids. Which I'm not supposed to offer. But it's my school and my scholarships, and I'll be damned if it's anybody's business but yours and mine!"

The parents squeezed one another, then with a nervous voice, the father made himself ask, "What about us?"

The coach didn't blink.

"What do you want, Mr. Wilde?" Marlboro smiled and said, "Name it."

"I'm not sure," the father confessed. "I know that we can't be too obvious—"

"But we were hoping," Mom blurted. "I mean, it's not like we're wealthy people. And we had to spend most of our savings—"

"On your little Alan. I bet you did." A huge wink was followed with, "It'll be taken care of. My school doesn't have that big college of genetics for nothing." He looked at the infant again, investing several seconds of hard thought into how they could bend the system just enough. Then he promised, "You'll be reimbursed for your expenses. Up front. And we'll put your son on the payroll. Gentlefolks in lab coats'll come take blood every half-year or so. For a healthy, just-under-the-table fee. How's that sound?"

The father seemed doubtful. "Will the scientists agree to that?"

"If I want it done," the coach promised.

"Will they actually use his blood?" The father seemed uneasy. Even a little disgusted. "I don't like thinking of Alan being some kind of laboratory project."

Marlboro stared at him for a long moment.

Never blinking.

Then he said, "Sir." He said, "If you want, they can pass those samples to you, and you can flush them down your own toilet. Is that good enough?"

Nobody spoke.

Then he took a different course, using his most mature voice to tell them, "Alan is a fine, fine boy. But you've got to realize something. He's going to have more than his share of problems. Special kids always do." Then with a warm smile, Marlboro promised, "I'll protect him for you. With all my resources and my good country sense, I'll see that none of those predators out there get their claws in your little Alan."

Mom said, "That's good to hear. That's fine."

But Father shrugged, asking, "What about you? It'll be years before Alan can actually play, and you could have left for the pros by then."

"Never," Marlboro blurted.

Then he gave the woman his best wink and grin, saying, "You know what kind of talent I've been signing up. Do you really think I'd go anywhere else? Ever?"

She turned to her husband, saying, "We'll sign."

"But—?"

"No. We're going to commit."

Marlboro reconfigured the appropriate contracts, getting everyone's signature. Then he squeezed one of his recruit's meaty feet, saying, "See ya later, Alan."

Wearing an unreadable smile, he stepped out the front door. A hundred or so sports reporters were gathered on the small lawn, and through their cameras, as many as twenty million fans were watching the scene.

They watched Coach Jones smile and say nothing. Then

he raised his arms suddenly, high overhead, and screamed those instantly famous words:

"The Wildman's coming to Tech!"

There was something about the girl. Perfect strangers thought nothing of coming up to her and asking where she was going to college.

"State," she would reply. Flat out.

"In what sport?" some inquired. While others, knowing that she played the game on occasion, would guess, "Are you joining the volleyball team?"

"No," Theresa would tell the latter group. Never patient, but usually polite. "I hate volleyball," she would explain, not wanting to be confused for one of those glandular, ritualistic girls. And she always told everyone, friends and strangers alike, "I'm going to play quarterback for the football team. For Coach Rickover."

Knowledgeable people were surprised, and puzzled. Some would clear their throats and look up into Theresa's golden eyes, commenting in an offhand way, "But Rickover doesn't let women play."

That was a problem, sure.

Daddy was a proud alumnus of State and a letterman on the famous '33 squad. When Theresa was born, there was no question about where she was going. In '41, Rickover was only an assistant coach. Penises weren't required equipment. The venerable Coach Mannstein had shuffled into her nursery and made his best offer, then shuffled back out to meet with press and boosters, promising the world that he would still be coaching when that delightfully young lady was calling plays for the best team to ever take any field of play.

But six years later, while enjoying the company of a mostly willing cheerleader, Coach Mannstein felt a searing pain in his head, lost all feeling in his ample body, and died.

Rickover inherited the program.

A religious man driven by a quixotic understanding of the Bible, one of his first official acts was to send a letter to Theresa's parents, explaining at length why he couldn't allow their daughter to join his team. "Football," he wrote, "is nothing but ritualized warfare, and women don't belong in the trenches. I am sorry. On the other hand, Coach Terry is a personal friend, and I would be more than happy to have him introduce you to our nationally ranked women's volleyball program.

"Thank you sincerely.

"Coach."

The refusal was a crushing blow for Daddy.

For Theresa, it was a ghostly abstraction that she couldn't connect with those things that she truly knew and understood.

Not that she was a stupid child. Unlike many of her 1-1-2041 peers, her grades were respectably average, and in spatial subjects, like geometry and geography, she excelled. Also unlike her peers, Theresa didn't have problems with rage or with residual instincts. Dogs and cats didn't mysteriously vanish in her neighborhood. She was a good person with friends and her genuine admirers. Parents trusted her with their babies. Children she didn't know liked to beg for rides on her back. Once she was old enough to date, the boys practically lined up. Out of sexual curiosity, in part. But also out of fondness and an odd respect. Some of her boyfriends confided that they preferred her to regular girls. Something about her—and not just a physical something—set them at ease. Made them feel safe. A strange thing for adolescent males to admit, while for Theresa, it was just another circumstance in a life filled with nothing but circumstances.

In football, she always played quarterback. Whether on playground teams, or in the various midget leagues, or on the varsity squad in high school.

Her high school teams won the state championship three years in a row. And they would have won when she was a senior, except a mutant strain of parvovirus gave her a fever and chills, and eventually, hallucinations. Theresa started throwing hundred meter bullets toward her more compelling hallucinations, wounding several fans, and her coach grudgingly ordered her off the field and into a hospital bed.

Once State relinquished all claims on the girl, a steady stream of coaches and boosters and sports agents began the inevitable parade.

Marlboro Jones was the most persistent soul. He had already stockpiled a full dozen of the 1-1-2041s, including the premier player of all time: Alan, The Wildman, Wilde. But the coach assured Theresa that he still needed a quality quarterback. With a big wink and a bigger grin, he said, "You're going to be my field general, young lady. I know you know it, the same as I do . . . !"

Theresa didn't mention what she really knew.

She let Daddy talk. For years, that proud man had entertained fantasies of Rickover moving to the pros, leaving the door open for his only child. But it hadn't happened, and it wouldn't. And over the last few years, with Jones's help, he had convinced himself that Theresa should play instead for State's great rival. Call it justice. Or better, revenge. Either way, what mattered was that she would go somewhere that her talents could blossom. That's all that mattered, Daddy told the coach. And Marlboro replied with a knowing nod and a sparkling of the eyes, finally turning to his prospect, and with a victor's smile, asking, "What's best for you? Tour our campus first? Or get this signing crap out of the way?"

Theresa said, "Neither."

Then she remembered to add, "Sir," with a forced politeness.

Both men were stunned. But the coach was too slick to let it show. Staring at the tall, big-shouldered lady, he conjured up his finest drawl, telling her, "I can fix it. Whatever's broke, it can be fixed."

"Darling," her father mumbled. "What's wrong?"

She looked at her father's puffy, confused face. "This man doesn't want me for quarterback, Daddy. He just doesn't want me playing somewhere else."

After seventeen years of living with the girl, her father knew better than to doubt her instincts. Glaring at Marlboro, he asked flat out, "Is that true?"

"No," the man lied.

Instantly, convincingly.

Then he sputtered, adding, "That Mosgrove kid has too much chimp in his arm. And not enough touch."

There was a prolonged, uncomfortable silence.

Then Theresa informed both of them, "I've made up my mind, anyway. Starting next year, I'm going to play for State."

Daddy was startled and a bit frustrated. But as always, a little bit proud, too.

Coach Jones was, if anything, amused. The squirrel eyes smiled, and the handsome mouth tried not to follow suit. And after a few more seconds of painful silence, he said, "I've known Rickover for most of my adult life. And you know what, little girl? You've definitely got your work cut out for you."

Jones was mistaken.

Theresa believed.

A lifetime spent around coaches had taught her that the species was passionate and stubborn and usually wrong about everything that wasn't lashed to the game in front of them. But what made coaches ridiculous in the larger world helped them survive in theirs. Because they were stubborn and overblown, they could motivate the boys and girls around them; and the very best coaches had a gift for seducing their players, causing them to lash their souls to the game, and the next game, and every game to follow.

All Theresa needed to do, she believed, was out-stubborn Coach Rickover.

State had a walk-on program. Overachievers from the Yukon to the Yucatan swarmed into campus in late summer, prepared to fight it out for a handful of scholarships. Theresa enrolled with the rest of them, then with her father in tow, showed up for the first morning's practice. An assistant coach approached. Polite and determined, he thanked her for coming, but she wasn't welcome. But they returned for the afternoon practice, this time accompanied by an AI advocate—part lawyer, part mediator—who spoke to a succession of assistant coaches with the quietly smoldering language of lawsuits and public relations night-mares.

Theresa's legal standing was questionable, at best. Courts had stopped showing interest in young ladies wanting to play an increasingly violent sport. But the threat to call the media seemed to work. Suddenly, without warning, the quarterback coach walked up to her and looked up, saying to her face, "All right. Let's see what you can do."

She was the best on the field, easily.

Pinpoint passes to eighty meters. A sprint speed that mauled every pure-human record. And best of all, the seemingly innate ability to glance at a fluid defense and pick it apart. Maybe Theresa lacked the elusive moves of some 1-1-2041s, which was the closest thing to a weakness. But she made up for it with those big shoulders that she wielded like dozer blades, leaving half a dozen strong young men lying flat on their backs, trying to recall why they ever took up this damned sport.

By the next morning, she was taking hikes with the varsity squad.

Coach Rickover went as far as strolling up to her and saying, "Welcome, miss," with that cool, almost friendly voice. Then he looked away, adding, "And the best of luck to you."

It was a trap.

During a no-contact drill, one of the second-string pure-human linebackers came through the line and leveled her when she wasn't ready. Then he squatted low and shouted into her face, "Bitch! Dog bitch! Pussy bitch! Bitch!"

Theresa nearly struck him.

In her mind, she left his smug face strewn across the wiry green grass. But then Rickover would have his excuse—she was a discipline problem—and her career would have encompassed barely one day.

She didn't hit the bastard, or even chew off one of his fingers.

Instead she went back to throwing lasers at her receivers and running between the tackles. Sometimes her blockers would go on vacation, allowing two or three rushers to drag her to the ground. Yet Theresa always got up again and limped back to the huddle, staring at the stubborn human eyes until those eyes, and the minds behind them, blinked.

It went on that way for a week.

Because she wouldn't allow herself even the possibility of escape, Theresa prepared herself for another four months of inglorious abuse. And if need be, another three years after that.

Her mother came to visit and to beg her daughter to give it up.

"For your sake, and mine. Just do the brave thing and walk away."

Theresa loved her mother, but she had no illusions: The woman was utterly, hopelessly weak.

Daddy was the one who scared her. He was standing over his daughter, watching as she carefully licked at a gash that came when she was thrown against a metal bench, her leg opened up from the knee to her badly swollen ankle. And with a weakling's little voice, he told her, "This isn't my dream anymore. You need to reconsider. That, or you'll have to bury me. My nerves can't take any more twisting."

Picking thick golden strands of fur from her long, long tongue, Theresa stared at him. And hiding her sadness, she told him, "You're right, Daddy. This isn't your dream."

The war between player and coach escalated that next morning.

Nine other 1-1-2041s were on the team. Theresa was promoted to first team just so they could have a shot at her. She threw passes, and she was knocked flat. She ran sideways, and minotaurs in white jerseys flung her backward, burying their knees into her kidneys and uterus. Then she moved to defense, playing ABMback for a few downs, and their woolly, low-built running back drove her against the juice cooler, knocking her helmet loose and chewing on one of her ears, then saying into that blood, "There's more coming darling. There's always more coming."

Yet despite the carnage, the 1-1-2041s weren't delivering real blows.

Not compared to what they could have done.

It dawned on Theresa that Rickover and his staff, for all their intimate knowledge about muscle and bone, had no idea what their players were capable of. She watched those grown men nodding, impressed with the bomb-like impacts and spattered blood. Sprawled out on her back, waiting for her lungs to work again, she found herself studying Rickover: He was at least as handsome as Marlboro Jones, but much less attractive. There was something both analytical and dead about the man. And underneath it all, he was shy. Deeply and eternally shy. Wasn't that a trait that came straight out of your genetics? A trait and an affliction that she lacked, thankfully.

Theresa stood again, and she limped through the milling players and interns, then the assistant coaches, stepping into Rickover's line of sight, forcing him to look at her.

"I still want to play for you," she told him. "But you know, Coach . . . I don't think I'll ever like you. . . . " And with that, she turned and hobbled back to the field.

Next morning, a decision had come down from On High.

Theresa was named the new first-string quarterback, and the former first-string—a tall, bayonet-shaped boy nicknamed Man O War—was made rocketback.

For the last bits of summer and until the night before their first game, Theresa believed that her little speech had done its magic. She was so confident of her impression that she repeated her speech to her favorite rocketback. And Man O War gave a little laugh, then climbed out of her narrow dormitory bed, stretching out on the hard floor, pulling one leg behind his head, then the other.

"That's not what happened," he said mildly. Smiling now.

She said, "What didn't?"

"It was the nine of us. The other 1-1-2041s." He kept smiling, bending forward until his chin was resting against his naked crotch, and he licked himself with a practiced deftness. Once finished, he sat up and explained, "We went to Coach's house that night. And we told him that if we were supposed to keep hurting you, we might as well kill you. And eat you. Right in the middle of practice."

She stared at her lover for a long moment, unsure what to believe.

Theresa could read human faces. And she could smell their moods boiling out of their hairless flesh. But no matter how hard she tried, she could never decipher that furry chimera of a face.

"Would you really have?" she finally asked.

"Killed you? Not me," Man O War said instantly.

Then he was laughing, reminding her, "But those linebackers . . . you never can tell what's inside their smooth little minds . . . !"

Tech and State began the season on top of every sport reporter's rankings and the power polls and leading almost every astrologer's sure-picks. Since they had two more 1-1-2041s on their roster, including the Wildman, Tech was given the edge. Professional observers and fans, as well as AI analysts, couldn't imagine any team challenging either of them. On the season's second weekend, State met a strong Texas squad with its own handful of 1-1-2041s. They beat them by seventy points. The future seemed assured. Barring catastrophe, the two teams of the century would win every contest, then go to war on New Year's Day, inside the venerable Hope Dome, and the issue about who was best and who was merely second best would be settled for the ages.

In public, both coaching staffs and the coached players spouted all the hoary clichés. Take it one play at a time, and one game at a time, and never eat your chicken before it's cooked through.

But in private, and particularly during closed practices, there was one opponent and only one, and every mindless drill and every snake run on the stadium stairs and particularly every two ton rep in the weight room was meant for Tech. For State. For glory and the championship and a trophy built from gold and sculpted light.

In the third week of the season, Coach Jones began using his 1-1-2041s on both sides of the line.

Coach Rickover told reporters that he didn't approve of

those tactics. "Even superhumans need rest," he claimed. But that was before Tech devastated an excellent Alabama squad by more than a hundred and twenty points. Rickover prayed to God, talked to several physiologists, then made the same outrageous adjustment.

In their fourth game, Theresa played at quarterback and ABM.

Not only did she throw a school record ten touchdowns, she also ran for four more, plus she snagged five interceptions, galloping three of them back for scores.

"You're the Heisman front-runner," a female reporter assured her, winking and grinning as if they were girlfriends. "How does it feel?"

How do you answer such a silly question?

"It's an honor," Theresa offered. "Of course it is."

The reporter smiled slyly, then assaulted her with another silliness. "So what are your goals for the rest of the season?"

"To improve," Theresa muttered. "Every Saturday, from here on."

"Most of your talented teammates will turn professional at the end of the year." A pause. Then she said, "What about you, Theresa? Will you do the same?"

She hadn't considered it. The UFL was an abstraction, and a distraction, and she didn't have time or the energy to bother with either.

"All I think about," she admitted, "is this season."

A dubious frown.

Then the reporter asked, "What do you think of Tech's team?"

One play at a time, game at a time, and cook your chicken . . .

"Okay. But what about the Wildman?"

Nothing simple came into Theresa's head. She paused for a long moment, then told the truth. "I don't know Alan Wilde."

"But do you think it's right . . . ? Having a confessed killer as your linebacker and star running back . . . ?"

The reporter was talking about the Wildman. Vague recollections of a violent death and a famous, brief trial came to mind. But Theresa's parents had shielded her from any furor about the 1-1-2041s. Honestly, the best she could offer this woman was a shrug and her own smile, admitting, "It's not right to murder. Anyone. For any reason."

That simple declaration was the night's lead story on every sports network.

"Heisman hopeful calls her opponent a murderer! Even though the death was ruled justifiable homicide!"

Judging by the noise, it made for a compelling story.

Whatever the hell that means.

After the season's seventh week, a coalition of coaches and university presidents filed suit against the two front-runners. The games to date had resulted in nearly two hundred concussions, four hundred broken bones, and thirteen injuries so severe that young, pure-human boys were still lying in hospital beds, existing in protective comas.

"We won't play you anymore," the coalition declared.

They publicly accused both schools of recruiting abuses, and in private, they warned that if the remaining games weren't canceled, they would lead the pack in a quick and bloody inquisition.

Coach Rickover responded at his weekly press conference. With a Bible in hand, he gave a long rambling speech about his innocence and how the playing fields were perfectly level.

Marlboro Jones took a different tack.

Accompanied by his school's lawyers, AI and human, he visited the ringleaders. "You goddamn pussies!" he shouted. "We've got contracts with you. We've got television deals with the networks. If you think we're letting your dicks wriggle free of this hook, you're not only cowards. You're stupid, too!"

Then he sat back, letting the lawyers dress up his opinion in their own impenetrable language.

But the opponents weren't fools. A new-generation AI began to list every known infraction: Payments to players and their families. Secretive changes of title for homes and businesses. Three boosters forming a charity whose only known function was to funnel funds to the topflight players. And worst by far, a series of hushed-up felonies connected to the 1-1-2041s under his care.

Marlboro didn't flinch.

Instead, he smiled—a bright, blistering smile that left every human in the room secretly trembling—and after a prolonged pause, he said, "Fine. Make it all public."

The AI said, "Thank you. We will."

"But," said Marlboro, "here's what I'll take public. You pussies."

With precision and a perfect ear for detail, the coach listed every secret infraction and every camouflaged scandal that had ever swirled around his opponents' programs. Twenty-plus years in this industry, and he knew everything. Or at least that was the impression he gave. And then as he finished, he said, "Pussies," again. And laughed. And he glared at the Stanford president—the ringleader of this rabble—telling that piece of high-born shit, "I guess we're stuck. We're just going to have to kill each other."

Nobody spoke.

Moved, or even breathed.

Then the president managed to find enough air to whisper, "What do you propose?"

"Tech and State win our games by forfeit," the coach told them. "And you agree not to play us in court, either."

The president said, "Maybe."

Then with a soft synthetic voice, his AI lawyer said, "Begging to differ, but I think we should pursue—"

Marlboro threw the talking box across the room.

It struck a wall, struck the floor. Then with an eerie calm, it said, "You cannot damage me, sir."

"Point taken." The coach turned to the humans. "Do we have a deal? Or don't we?"

Details were worked out; absolutely nothing was signed.

Near the end of negotiations, Marlboro announced, "Oh, and there's one last condition. I want to buy your lawyer." He pointed at the AI. "Bleed it of its secrets first. But I want it."

"Or what?" Stanford inquired.

"I start talking about your wives. Who likes it this way, who likes it that way. Just so everyone knows that what I'm saying is the truth."

The AI was sold. For a single dollar.

Complaining on and on with its thoughtful, useless voice, the box was thrown into the middle of Tech's next practice, and nothing was left afterward but gutted electronics pushed deep into the clipped green grass.

Tech's and State's regular season was finished. But that turned out to be a blessing as far as school coffers and the entertainment conglomerates were concerned. Hundred point slaughters weren't winning the best ratings. In lieu of butchery, a series of ritualized scrimmages were held on Saturdays, each team dividing its top squads into two near-equal parts, then playing against themselves with enough skill and flair to bring packed stadiums and enormous re-mote audiences: All that helping to feed an accelerating, almost feverish interest in the coming showdown.

Sports addicts talked about little else.

While the larger public, caring nothing for the fabled gridiron, found plenty else to hang their interest on. The contrasting coaches, and the 1-1-2041s, and the debate about what is human, and particularly among girlfriends and wives, the salient fact that a female was the undisputed leader of one team.

Sports networks and digital wonderhouses began playing the game of the century early, boiling down its participants into algorithms and vectors and best guesses, then showing the best of their bloodless contests to surprisingly large au-diences.

Eight times out of eleven, the digital Tech went away victors.

Not counting private and foreign betting, nearly ten bil-lion reconstituted dollars had been wagered on the contest by Thanksgiving. By Christmas Eve, that figure had jumped another five-fold. Plus there were the traditional gubernatorial wagers of state-grown products: A ton of computer chips versus a ton of free-range buffalo.

Theresa spent Christmas at home with parents and grandparents, plus more than a dozen relatives who had managed to invite themselves. If anything, those cousins and uncles and assorted spouses were worse than a room full of reporters. They didn't know the rules. They expected disclosures. Confessions. The real and dirty. And when Theresa offered any less-than-spectacular answer, it was met with disappointment and disbelief.

The faces said as much. And one little old aunt said it with her liquor-soddened mouth, telling her niece, "You're among family, darling. Why can't you trust us?"

Because she didn't know these people.

Over the past eighteen years, she had seen them sporadically, and all she remembered were their uncomfortable expressions and the careful words offered with quiet, overly cautious voices.

Looking at her, some had said, "She's a lovely girl."

"Exotic," others volunteered.

"You're very lucky," to her parents.

Then out of pure-human earshot, they would ask, "What do you think is inside her? Dog? Dinosaur? What?"

Theresa didn't know which genes went into her creation. What was more, she hadn't felt a compelling need to ask. But whatever chimerical stew made up her chromosomes, she had inherited wonderful ears that could pick up distant insults as well as the kindest, sweetest words.

She was trying to be patient and charitable when one idiot leaned forward, planted a drunken hand on her granite-hard thigh, then told her with a resoundingly patronizing tone, "I don't see what people complain about. Up close, you're a beautiful creature . . ."

Daddy heard those words, their tone.

And he detonated.

"What are you doing?" he screamed. "And get your hand off your niece!"

Uncle John flinched, the hand vanishing. Then he stared at his brother with a mixture of astonishment and building rage, taking a deep breath, then another, before finding the air to ask, "What did I say?"

"Why? Don't you remember?"

The poor fool sputtered something about being fair, for God's sake.

The rest of the family stood mute, and stunned, and a few began asking their personal clocks for the time.

"Leave," Daddy suggested.

To his brother, and everyone else, too.

He found the self-control to say, "Thank you for coming," but then added, "my daughter isn't a freak. She isn't, and remember that, and good night."

Christmas ended with a dash for the coats and some tenth-hearted, "Good lucks," lobbed in Theresa's direction.

Then it was just the three of them. And Daddy offered Theresa a sorrowful expression, then repeated his reasoning. "I've been listening to their contemptuous crap for nearly twenty years. You're not a monster, or a possession, and I get sick, sick, sick of it."

Theresa said nothing.

Mother said, "Darling," to one of them. Theresa wasn't sure who.

When nobody responded, Mother rose and staggered into the kitchen, telling the AI to finish its cooking, then store the meat and vegetables and mounds of stuffing for later this week, and into next year.

Theresa kept staring at her father, trying to understand why she was so disappointed, and angry, and sad.

He averted his eyes, then said, "I know."

What did he know?

"You're right," he confessed. "You caught me. You know!"

But Theresa couldn't make herself ask, "What am I right about?"

A citizen of unalloyed strength, yet she couldn't summon enough air to ask, "What is it, Father? What am I supposed to know?"

*   *   *

The Hope Dome was older than the players. Led by Miami, a consortium of cities had built that gaudy glass and carbon-fiber structure out on the continental shelf. Its playing field lay nearly fifty meters beneath the water's surface, and rising ocean levels combined with the new generation of hurricanes had caused problems. One of the bowl officials even repeated that tired joke that it was hope holding back the Atlantic. But then he winked slyly and said, "Don't worry." He unlocked a heavy door next to State's locker, revealing an enormous room filled with roaring bilge pumps whose only purpose, he boasted, was to send a river's worth of tiny leaks back into the sea.

In contrast to the palace-like Dome, the playing field was utterly ordinary.

Its dimensions and black earth and fluorescent-fed grass made it identical to a thousand other indoor facilities.

The day after Christmas, and both teams were given the traditional tour of the Dome and its field. To help extract the last greasy drama out of the blandness, Tech was still finishing its walk-through when State arrived. On the field together, with cameras and the world watching, the teams got their first naked-eye look at one another. And with a hundred million people waiting for anything, the two Heisman candidates met, and without any fuss, the two politely shook hands.

The Wildman offered Theresa several flavors of surprise.

The first surprise was his appearance. She had seen endless images of man-child, and she'd been near plenty of 1-1-2041s. But the running back was still impressive. There was bison in him, she had heard. And gorilla. And what might have been Siberian tiger genes. Plus something with an enormous capacity to grow bone. Elephant, perhaps. Something in the shape of his enormous head reminded her of the ancient mammoth skulls that she'd seen haunting the university museum.

The second surprise was the Wildman's mannerisms. A bowl official, nervous enough to shiver, introduced the two of them, then practically threw himself backward. But the boy was polite, and in a passing way, charming.

"We meet," he grunted. "Finally."

Theresa stared at the swollen incisors and the giant dog eyes, and telling herself not to stumble over her tongue, she offered her hand and said, "Hello," with the same pleasant voice she used on every new friend.

The Wildman took her hand gently. Almost too softly to be felt.

And with a thin humor, he said, "What do you think they would do? If we got down on our knees and grazed?"

Then the third surprise said, "Alan."

And the fourth surprise added, "You're just joking. Aren't you, son?"

Parents weren't normally allowed to travel with the players. But the Wildes appeared to be the exception. Theresa later learned that they accompanied him everywhere, always. Pulling her hand out of Alan's giant hand, she offered them a smile, and the mother said, "How are you, dear?"

The father offered, "I'm an admirer." His right hand was plastic. Lifelike, but not alive. Retrieving his hand, he added, "We're all admirers, of course."

How did he lose the limb? she wondered.

Because it was the polite thing to say, Theresa told them, "The best of luck to you. All of you."

Together, the Wildes wished her the same cliché. Then they said, "Alan," in a shared voice. Practiced, and firmly patient.

The boy stared at Theresa for a long moment, his face unreadable. Perhaps there was nothing there to read. Then with a deep bass voice, he said, "Later."

"Later," she echoed.

Two hundred kilos of muscle and armored bone pivoted, walking away with his tiny, seemingly fragile parents flanking him—each adult holding tightly to one of the hands and whispering. Encouragements, or sage advice. Or grave warnings about the world.

Even with her spectacular ears, Theresa couldn't hear enough to tell.

*   *   *

Days meant light practices, then the daily press conferences where every ludicrous question was asked and asked again with a linebacker's single-mindedness. Then the evenings were stuffed full of tightly orchestrated fun: Cookouts. A parade. Seats at a nuclear polka concert. Then a beach party held in both teams' honor.

It was on the beach that the Tech quarterback, Mosgrove, made a half-joking comment. "You know what we should do? Together, I mean." And he told the other 1-1-2041s, thinking they would laugh about it.

But instead of laughing, a plan was drawn up between the sea trout dinner and the banana split dessert.

On New Year's Eve, coaches put their teams to bed at ten o'clock. That was the tradition. And an hour later, exactly twenty-two of their players crept out of their beds and their hotel rooms, slipping down to the same beach to gather in two distinct groups.

At midnight and for the next three minutes and twenty-one seconds, no one said one word. With fireworks and laser arrays going off on all sides, their eyes were pointed at the foot-chewed sand, and every face grew solemn. Reflective. Then Theresa said, "Now," and looked up, suddenly aware of the electricity passing between them.

What was she feeling? She couldn't put a name to it. Whatever it was, it was warm, and real, and it felt closer even than the warm salty air.

Still divided along team lines, the players quietly walked off the beach.

Theresa meant to return straight to bed, even though she wouldn't sleep. But she stopped first at the ladies' room, then happened past one of several hotel bars, a familiar face smiling out at her from the darkness, a thick hand waving her closer.

He was sitting alone in a booth, which surprised her.

With that slick, aw shucks voice, he asked, "Are my boys finding their way home again? Or am I going to have to get myself a posse?"

"They'll end up in their rooms," she assured.

"Sit," said the coach. Followed by, "Please."

She squeezed her legs under the booth. Marlboro cuddled with his beer, but he hadn't been alone for long. The cultured leather beneath Theresa was still warm. But not the seat next to her, she noted. And she found herself wondering who was here first.

"Buy you a drink, young lady?"

She didn't answer.

He laughed with that easy charm, touched the order pad and said, "Water, please. Just water."

"I really should leave," she told Marlboro.

But before she could make her legs move, he said, "You pegged me. That last time I came calling, you saw right through that brown shit I was flinging. About needing you for quarterback, and all that." A wink, then he added, "I was lying. Wasn't I?"

She didn't say one word.

Chilled water arrived, and Theresa found herself dipping into a strange paranoia. Mosgrove had suggested that meeting on the beach because Theresa had to come past this bar, and Coach Jones was waiting to ambush her, slipping some drug into her system so that tomorrow, in front of the entire world, she would fail.

A silly thought. But she found herself shuddering, if only because it was finally beginning to sink in . . . what was going to happen tomorrow . . .

She didn't speak, but Marlboro couldn't let the silence continue. After finishing his beer and ordering another, he leaned over and spoke quietly, with intensity. He told her, "You saw through me. I'll give you that. But you know something, young lady? You're not the only shrewd soul at this table."

"No?" she replied.

Softly. With an unexpected tentativeness.

Then she forced herself to take a sip of her chilled water, licking her lips before asking, "What did you see in me?"

"Nothing," Marlboro said.

Then he leaned back and picked up the fresh beer glass, sucking down half of its contents before admitting. "I don't read you kids well. It's the muscles in your faces. They don't telephone emotions like they should."

She said, "Good."

He laughed again. Nothing was drunk about the man, but something about the eyes and mouth told her that he had been drinking for a long while. Nothing was drunk about the voice, but the words had even more sparkle and speed than usual. "Why do you think it is, young lady? All this noise and anguish about a game? A fucking little game that uses a hundred meters of grass and a ball that doesn't know enough to keep itself round?"

"I don't know—" she started.

"You're the favorite," he interrupted. "State is, I mean. According to polls, the general public hopes that I'm beat. You know why? Cause I've got twelve of you kids, and Rickover has only ten. And it takes eleven to play. Which means that on your team, at least one pure-human is always out there. He might be full of steroids and fake blood, and he's only going to last one set of downs, at most. But he's as close to being one of them butter-butts as anyone on either team. And those butter-butts, those fans of yours and mine, identify with Mr. Steroid. Which is why in their hearts they want Tech to stumble."

Theresa watched the dark eyes, the quick wide mouth. For some reason, she couldn't force herself to offer any comment, no matter how small.

"And there's that matter of coaches," said Marlboro. "I'm the godless one, and Rickover is God's Chosen, and I bet that's good enough for ten or twenty million church-goers. They're putting their prayers on the good man."

She thought of those days last summer—the pain and humiliation of practically begging for a spot on the roster, all while that good man watched from a distance—and she secretly bristled. Less secretly, she took a deep breath, looking away and asking him finally, "If it isn't me, who? Who do you see through?"

"Parents," he said. Pointblank.

"My folks?" she asked.

"And all the others too," Marlboro promised. Then he

took a pull of beer, grinned and added, "They're pretty much the same. Sad fuck failures who want to bend the rules of biology and nature as much as they can, diluting their blood and their own talents, thinking that's what it takes for them to have genuinely successful children."

Theresa thought of her father's Christmas tantrum.

More beer, then Marlboro said, "Yeah, your parents. They're the same as the others. All of 'em brought you kids into existence, and only later, when it was too late, they realized what it meant. Like the poor Wildes. Their kid's designed for awesome strength and useful rage, and so much has gone so wrong that they can't get a moment's rest. They're scared. And with reason. They seem like nice people, but I guarantee you, young lady, that's what happens when you're torn up by guilt. You keep yourself sweet and nice, because if you falter, even for a second, who knows what you'll betray about your real self?"

Theresa sighed, then grudgingly finished her water. If there was a poison in this booth, it didn't come inside a thick blister of glass.

"Darling." A thick, slurring feminine voice broke the silence, saying, "Darling," a second time, with too much air. "Marl, honey."

A hand lay on the tabletop. Theresa found herself looking at it and at the fat diamond riding the ring finger. She asked herself what was wrong with that hand. It was too long, and its flesh wore a thin golden fur, and the fingernails were thick and curved and obviously sharp. Theresa blinked and looked up at the very young woman, and in that instant, the coach said, "My fiancée. Ivana Buckleman. Honey, this is the enemy. Theresa Varner—"

"How are you?" said the fiancée, a mouthful of cougar teeth giving the words that distinctive, airy sound. Then she offered the long hand, and the two women shook, nothing friendly about the gesture. With blue cat-eyes staring, Ivana asked, "Shouldn't you be asleep, miss? You've got a big day tomorrow."

Marlboro said nothing, drinking in the jealousy.

Theresa surrendered her place, then said, "Good luck, Coach."

He stared at her, and grinned, and finally said, "You know perfectly well, girl. There's no such bird."

Coach Rickover was famous for avoiding pre-game pep talks. Football was war, and you did it. Or you didn't do it. But if you needed your emotions cranked up with colored lights, then you probably shouldn't be one of his players.

And yet.

Before the opening kickover, Rickover called everyone to the sideline. An acoustic umbrella was set up over the team, drowning out the roar of a hundred thousand fans and a dozen competing bands and the dull thunder of a passing storm. And with a voice that couldn't have been more calm, he told them, "Whatever happens tonight, I am extraordinarily proud of you. All of you. Ability is something given by God. But discipline and determination are yours alone. And after all my years in coaching, I can say without reservation, I've never been so proud and pleased with any team. Ever.

"Whatever happens tonight," he continued, "this is my final game. Tomorrow morning, I retire as your coach. The Lord has told me it's time. And you're first to hear the news. Not even my wife knows. Not my assistant coaches. Look at their faces, if you don't believe me."

Then looking squarely at Theresa, he added, "Whatever happens, I want to thank you. Thank you for teaching an old man a thing or two about heart, and spirit, and passion for a game that he thought he already knew. . . ."

The umbrella was dismantled, the various thunders descending on them.

Theresa still disliked the man. But despite that hard-won feeling, or maybe because of it, a lump got up into her throat and refused to go away.

The kickoff set the tone.

Man O War received the ball deep in the end zone,

dropped his head and charged, skipping past defenders, then blockers—1-1-2041s, mostly—reaching his thirty-five meter line with an avenue open to Tech's end zone. But the Wildman slammed into him from the side, flinging that long graceful body across the side line and into the first row of seats, his big-cat speed and the crack of pads on pads causing a hundred thousand fans to go silent.

State's top receiver couldn't play for the first set of downs. His broken left hand had to be set first, then secured in a cast.

Without Man O War, Theresa worked her team down to the enemy's forty. But for the first time that season, the opening drive bogged down, and she punted the ball past the end zone, and Tech's first possession started at their twenty.

Three plays, and they scored.

Mosgrove threw one perfect pass. Then the Wildman charged up the middle twice, putting his shoulders into defenders and twisting around whatever he couldn't intimidate. Playing ABM, Theresa tackled him on his second run. But they were five meters inside the end zone, and a referee fixed his yellow laser on her, marking her for a personal foul—a bizarre call considering she was the one bruised and bleeding here.

Man O War returned, and on the first play from scrimmage, he caught a sixty meter bullet, broke two tackles, and scored.

But the extra point was blocked.

7–6, read every giant holo board. In flickering, flame-colored numbers.

The next Tech drive ate up nearly seven minutes, ending with a three meter plunge up the middle. The Wildman was wearing the entire State team when he crossed the line—except for a pure-human boy whose collarbone and various ribs had been shattered, and who lay on the field until the medical cart could come and claim him.

14–6.

On the third play of State's next drive, Theresa saw linebackers crowding against the line, and she called an audible. The ball was snapped to her. And she instantly delivered it to Man O War, watching him pull it in and turn upfield, a half step taken when a whippet-like ABM hit the broken hand with his helmet, splitting both helmet and cast, the ball bouncing just once before a second whippet scooped it up and galloped in for a touchdown.

Tech celebrated, and Theresa trotted over to the sidelines. Rickover found her, and for the first time all year—for the first time in her life—her coach said, "That, young lady, was wrong. Was stupid. You weren't thinking out there."

21–6.

State's next possession ate up eight minutes, and it ended when the Wildman exploded through the line, driving Theresa into the ground and the ball into the air, then catching the ball as it fell into his chest, grinning behind the grillwork of his helmet.

Tech's following drive ended with three seconds left in the half.

28–6.

Both locker rooms were at the south end. The teams were leaving in two ragged lines, and Theresa was thinking about absolutely nothing. Her mind was as close to empty as she could make it. When a student jumped from the overhead seats, landing in the tunnel in front of her, she barely paused. She noticed a red smear of clothing, then a coarse, drunken voice. "Bitch," she heard. Then, "Do better! You goddamn owe me!" Then he began to make some comment about dog cocks, and that was when a massive hand grabbed him by an arm, yanking him off his feet, then throwing his limp body back into the anonymous crowd.

The Wildman stood in front of Theresa.

"She doesn't owe you fuck!" he was screaming. Looking up at hundreds of wide eyes and opened, horrorstruck mouths, he shouted, "None of us owes you shit! You morons! Morons! Morons!"

Half-time needed to last long enough to sell a hundred happy products to the largest holo audience since the Mars landing, and to keep the energy level up in the dome, there was an elaborate show involving bands and cheerleaders from both schools, plus half a dozen puffy, middle-aged pop entertainers. It was an hour's reprieve, which was just enough time for Rickover to define his team's worst blunders and draw up elegant solutions to every weakness. How much of his speech sank home, Theresa couldn't say. She found herself listening more to the droning of the bilge pumps than to the intricacies of playing quarterback and ABM. A numbness was building inside her, spreading into her hands and cold toes. It wasn't exhaustion or fear. She knew how those enemies felt, and she recognized both festering inside her belly, safely contained. And it wasn't self-doubt, because when she saw Man O War taking practice snaps in the back of the locker room, she leaped to her feet and charged Rickover, ready to say, "You can, but you shouldn't! Give me another chance!"

But her rocketback beat her to him. Flexing the stiff hand inside the newest cast, Man O War admitted, "I can't hold it to pass. Not like I should."

Rickover looked and sounded like a man in absolute control.

He nodded, saying, "Fine." Then he turned to the girl and said, "We need to stop them on their opening drive, then hang close. You can, believe me, manage that."

Theresa looked at the narrowed corners of his eyes and his tight little mouth, the terror just showing. And she lied, telling him and herself, "Sure. Why not?"

Tech took the opening kickoff.

Coach Jones was grinning on the sidelines, looking fit and rested. Supremely confident. Smelling a blowout, he opened up with a passing attack. The long-armed Mosgrove threw a pair of twenty meter darts, then dropped back and flung for the end zone. Theresa stumbled early, then picked herself up and guessed, running hard for the corner, the whippet receiver leaping high and her doing the same blind, long legs driving her toward the sky as she turned, the ball hitting her chest, then her hands, then bouncing free, tumbling down into Man O War's long cupped arms.

State inherited the ball on the twenty.

After three plays and nine meters, they punted.

A palpable calm seemed to have infected the audience. People weren't exactly quiet, but their chatter wasn't directed at the game anymore. State supporters tucked into the south corner—where the piss-mouthed fellow had come from—found ways to entertain themselves. They chanted abuse at the enemy. "Moron, moron, moron!" they cried out as Tech moved down the field toward them. "Moron, moron, moron!"

If the Wildman noticed, it didn't show in the stony, inflexible face.

Or Theresa was too busy to notice subtleties, helping plug holes and flick away passes. And when the Wildman galloped up the middle, she planted and dropped a shoulder and hit him low on the shins.

A thousand drills on technique let her tumble the mountainous boy.

Alan fell, and Theresa's teammates would torpedo his exposed ribs and his hamstrings, using helmets as weapons, and sometimes more than helmets. One time, the giant man rose up out of the pile and staggered—just for a strange, what's-wrong-with-this-picture moment. A river of impossibly red blood was streaming from his neck. The field judge stopped the game to look at hands until he found long nails dipped in red, and a culprit. Tech was awarded fifteen meters with the personal foul, but for the next three plays, their running back sat on the sideline, his thick flesh being closed up by the team's medics.

Tech was on the eleven when he returned, breaking through the middle, into the open, then stumbling. Maybe for the first time in his life, his tired legs suddenly weighed what they really weighed. And when he went down hard, his ball arm was extended, and Theresa bent and scooped the treasure out of his hand and dashed twenty meters before one of the whippets leveled her.

For a long minute, she lay on her back on that mangled sod, listening to the relentless cheers, and trying to remember exactly how to breathe.

Tech's sideline was close. Pure-humans wearing unsoiled laser-blue uniforms watched her with a fan-like appreciation. This wasn't their game; they were just spectators here. Then she saw the Wildman trudge into view, his helmet slightly askew, the gait and the slope of his shoulders betraying a body that was genuinely, profoundly tired. For the first time in his brief life, Alan Wilde was exhausted. And Theresa halfway smiled, managing her first sip of real air as Marlboro Jones strode into view, cornering his star running back in order to tell him to goddamn please protect the fucking ball—

Alan interrupted him.

Growling. Theresa heard a hard low sound.

Jones grabbed his player's face guard, and he managed a chin-up, putting his face where it had to be seen. Then he rode the Wildman for a full minute, telling him, "You don't ever! Ever! Not with me, mister!" Telling him, "This is your fucking life! It's being played out right here! Right now!" Screaming at him, "Now sit and miss your life! Until you learn your manners, mister! You sit!"

Four plays later, Theresa dumped a short pass into her running back's hands, and he rumbled through a string of sloppy tackles, all the way into the end zone.

State tried for a two-point conversion, but they were stopped.

The score looked sloppy on the holo boards. 28–12.

Tech's star returned for the next downs, but he was more like Alan than like the mythical Wildman. In part, there was a lack of focus. Theresa saw a confused rage in those giant, suddenly vulnerable eyes. But it was just as much exhaustion. Frayed muscles were having trouble lifting the dense, over-engineered bones, and the pounding successes of the first half were reduced to three meter gains and gouts of sod and black earth thrown toward the remote carbon-fiber roof.

State got the ball back late in the third quarter. Rickover called for a draw play, which might have worked. But in the huddle, Theresa saw how the defense was lining up, and she gave Man O War a few crisp instructions.

As the play began, her receiver took a few steps back.

Theresa flung the ball at a flat green spot midway between them, and it struck and bounced high, defenders pulling to a stop when they assumed the play was dead. Then Man O War grabbed the ball, and despite his cast, heaved the ball an ugly fifty meters, delivering its fluttering fat body into waiting hands.

Rickover wanted to try for two points.

Theresa called time-out, marched over to Rickover and said, "I can get us three." It meant setting up on the ten meter line. "I can smell it," she said. "They're starting to get really tired."

"Like we aren't?" Man O War piped in, laughing amiably as medics patched his cast.

The coach grudgingly agreed, then called a fumbleroosky. Theresa took the snap, bent low and set the live ball inside one of the sod's deep gouges. And her center, a likable and sweet pure-human named Mitch Long, grabbed up the ball and ran unnoticed and untroubled into the end zone.

28-21, and nobody could think for all the wild, proud cheering of pure-humans.

State managed to hold on defense.

Mosgrove punted, pinning them deep at their end with ten minutes left.

Theresa stretched the field with a towering, uncatchable pass, then started to run and dump little passes over the middle. The Wildman was playing linebacker, and he tackled her twice, the second blow leaving her chin cut open and her helmet in pieces. Man O War took over for a down. He bobbled the snap, then found his grip just in time for the Wildman to come over the center and throw an elbow into his face, shattering the reinforced mask as well as his nose.

Playing with two pure-humans at once, Theresa pitched to her running back, and he charged toward the sideline, wheeled and flung a blind pass back across the field. She

snagged it and ran forty meters in three seconds. Then a
whippet got an angle, and at the last moment pushed her
out of bounds. But she managed to hold the ball out, breaking the orange laser beam rising from the pylon.

Finally, finally, the game was tied.

Marlboro called time out, then huddled with his 1-1-
2041s. There wasn't even the pretense of involving the rest
of the team. Theresa watched the gestures, the coach's con-
torting face. Then Tech seemed to shake off its collective
fatigue, putting together a prolonged drive, the Wildman
scoring on a tough run up the middle and Mosgrove kicking
the extra point with just a minute and fifty seconds left.

35-28.

Rickover gathered his entire team around him, stared at
their faces with a calming, messianic intensity. Then without uttering a word, he sent eleven of them out to finish
the game.

The resulting drive consumed the entire one hundred and
ten seconds.

From the first snap, Theresa sensed what was happening
here and what was inevitable. When Man O War dropped
a perfect soft pass, she could assure him, "Next time." And
as promised, he one-handed a dart over his shoulder on the
next play, gaining fifteen. Later, following a pair of hard
sacks, it was fourth and thirty, and Theresa scrambled and
pumped faked twice, then broke downfield, one of the
whippets catching her, throwing his hard little body at her
belly. But she threw an elbow, then a shoulder, making
their first down by nothing and leaving the defender unconscious for several minutes, giving the medics something
to do while her team breathed and made ready.

Thirty meters came on a long sideline pattern.

Fifteen were lost when the Wildman drove through the
line and chased Theresa back and forth for a week, then
downed her with a swing of an arm.

But she was up and functioning first. Alan lay on the
ground gasping, that wide elephantine face covered with
perspiration and its huge tongue panting and an astonished
glaze numbing the eyes.

Tech called time-out.

Mitch brought in the next three plays.

He lasted for one. Another pure-human was inserted the next down, and the next, and that was just to give them eleven bodies. The thin-skinned, frail-boned little boys were bruised and exhausted enough to stagger. Mitch vomited twice before he got back to the sidelines, bile and blue pills scattered on the grass. The next boy wept the entire time he was with them. Then his leg shattered when the Wildman ran over him. But every play was a gain, and they won their next first down, and there was an entire sixteen seconds left and forty meters to cross and Theresa calmly used their last time-out and joined Rickover, knowing the play that he'd call before he could say it.

She didn't hear one word from her coach, nodding the whole time while gazing off into the stands.

Fans were on their feet, hoarsely cheering and banging their hands together. The drunks in the corner had fashioned a crude banner, and they were holding it high, with pride, shouting the words with the same dreary rage.

"MORON, MORON, MORON," she read.

She heard.

The time-out ended, and Theresa trotted back out and looked at the faces in the huddle, then with an almost quiet voice asked, "Why are turds tapered?"

Then she said, "To keep our assholes from slamming shut."

Then she gave the play, and she threw twenty meters to Man O War, and the clock stopped while the markers moved themselves, and she threw the ball into the sod, halfway burying it to stop the universe once again.

Two seconds.

She called a simple crossing pattern.

But Coach Jones guessed it and held his people back in coverage. Nobody was open enough to try forcing it, which was why she took off running. And because everyone was sloppy tired, she had that advantage, twisting out of four tackles and head-faking a whippet, then finding herself in the corner with Alan Wilde standing in front of her, barring the way to the goal line.

She dropped her shoulder, charging as he took a long step forward and braced himself, pads and her collarbone driving into the giant man's groin, the exhausted body pitched back and tumbling and her falling on top of him, lying on him as she would lie on a bed, then rolling, off the ground until she was a full meter inside the end zone.

She found her legs and her balance, and almost too late, she stood up.

Alan was already on his feet. She saw him marching past one of the officials, his helmet on the ground behind him, forgotten, his gaze fixed on that MORON banner and the people brandishing it in front of him.

Some were throwing small brown objects at him.

Or maybe at all the players, it occurred to her.

Theresa picked up the bone-shaped dog treat, a part of her astonished by the cruel, calculated planning that went into this new game.

Carried by a blistering rage, Alan began running toward the stands, screaming, "You want to see something funny, fucks? Do you?"

Do nothing, and State would likely win.

But Theresa ran anyway, hitting Alan at the knees, bringing him down for the last time.

A yellow laser struck her—a personal foul called by the panicked referee.

Theresa barely noticed, yanking off her helmet and putting her face against that vast, fury-twisted face, and like that, without warning, she gave him a long, hard kiss.

"Hey, Alan," she said. "Let's just have some fun here. Okay?"

A couple thousand Tech fans, wrongly thinking that the penalty ended the game and the game was won, stampeded into the far end of the field.

In those next minutes, while penalties and the crowd were sorted out, the 1-1-2041s stood together in the end zone, surrounding the still fuming Wildman. And watching the mayhem around them, Theresa said, "I wish." Then she said it again—"I wish!"—with a loud, pleading voice.

"What are you wishing for?" asked Man O War.

She didn't know what she wanted. When her mouth opened, her conscious mind didn't have the simplest clue what she would say. Theresa was just as surprised as the others when she told them, "I wish they were gone. All these people. This is our game, not theirs. I want to finish it. By ourselves, and for ourselves. Know what I mean?"

The 1-1-2041s nodded.

Smiled.

The rebellion began that way, and it culminated moments later when a whippet asked, "But seriously, how can we empty this place out?"

Theresa knew one way, and she said it. Not expecting anything to come of her suggestion.

But Alan took it to heart, saying, "Let me do it."

He took a step, arguing, "I'm strongest. And besides, if I'm caught, it doesn't mean anything. It's just the Wildman's usual shit."

Police in riot gear were busy fighting drunks and bitter millionaires. The running back slipped off in the direction of the locker room, as unnoticed as any blood-caked giant could be. Then after a few moments, as the crowds were finally herded back into the stands, Marlboro Jones came over and looked straight at Theresa, asking everyone, "Where is he?"

No one spoke.

Rickover was waving at his team, asking them to join him.

Theresa felt a gnawy guilt as well as an effervescent thrill.

Marlboro shook his head, his mouth starting to open, another question ready to be ignored—

Then came the roaring of alarms and a fusillade of spinning red lights. Over the public address system, a booming voice said, "There is nothing to worry about. Please, please, everyone needs to leave the dome *now! Now!* In an orderly fashion, please follow the ushers *now!*"

*　　*　　*

Within fifteen minutes, the dome was evacuated.

Coaching staffs and most of the players were taken to the helipad and lifted back to the mainland, following the media's hasty retreat.

Twenty minutes after the emergency began, the 1-1-2041s came out of their hiding places. The sidelines were under sea water, but the field itself was high enough to remain mostly dry. Security people and maintenance crews could be heard in the distance. Only emergency lights burned, but they were enough. Looking at the others, Theresa realized they were waiting for her to say something.

"This is for us," she told them. "And however it turns out, we don't tell. Nobody ever hears the final score. Agreed?"

Alan said, "Good," and glared at the others, his fists bleeding from beating all those bilge pumps to death.

Man O War cried out, "Let's do it then!"

In the gloom, the teams lined up for a two-point play. State had ten bodies, and including the whippet still groggy from being unconscious, Tech had its full twelve.

Fair enough.

Theresa leaned low, and in a whisper, called the only appropriate play.

"Go out for a pass," she told her receivers and her running back. "I'll think of something."

She settled behind the minotaur playing center, and she nestled her hands into that warm damp groin, and after a long gaze at the empty stands, she said, "Hey."

She said, "When you're ready. Give it here."

Secrets of the Alien Reliquary

MICHAEL BISHOP

Michael Bishop is from Oklahoma but has been settled in Pine Mountain Georgia for more than three decades. He has been a leading SF writer since the 1970s, his most prolific decade, and flowered in the 1980s with novels and short story collections. He has always been engaged with understanding the alien, with a sociological and anthropological perspective. No Enemy But Time *and* Ancient of Days *are perhaps his most famous novels. His most recent novel, one of his best, is* Brittle Innings *(1994), in which Frankenstein's monster survives into the 1940s and becomes a minor league baseball player in the rural South. He has published only a few short stories since. But since the start of his career he has also written and published poetry. I have not previously included a poem in the year's best volumes (and may not again), but I was particularly taken with this narrative poem on an SF topic that appeared in Bishop's poetry collection* Time Pieces *in 1999, and was reprinted in* Asimov's.

At first, of course, we grossly failed to recognize it,
assuming the displays in their camouflaged temple
relics of their espionage, dandruff from our anxious ids,
the gleanings of a xenophilic curator with eclectic tastes,
or no taste to speak of, an otherworldly magpie
of the inconsequentia and splendor of our species,
a devourer of it all. Later we came to understand
that we had stumbled, not into a conventional museum,

but a kind of backdoor bawdyhouse repository
of fetishistic, and thus shameful, alien delights
not one arising from their own ferrogramineous biology
but rather from a low-percentile, albeit planetwide,
deviant preoccupation, generally discreetly suppressed,
with anything and everything human. Stunned doesn't
begin to describe our mind set passing among the
    temple's
dioramas and interactive icons, which ranged from the
    size

of fingernails—indeed, one was a fingernail—to that of
an immense holographic projection of a membrane-
    enveloped
gall bladder, conspicuously diseased, which revolved aloft
like a lopsided glitter ball in a clandestine discothèque.
Who would have imagined that a silhouette of Abe
    Vigoda,

a pair of gutta-percha galoshes, the scent of halitosis
disseminated via an atomizer, a pictorial chiropractic text,
a large petri dish of toenail fungus, a video of a Tourette

Syndrome sufferer, or a quaint electronic coupon for a
    box
of hemorrhoid suppositories would have so reliably
    tweaked
the private orgiastic impulses of some of these creatures
that they would showcase their favorite libidinous stimuli
in a concealed exhibition hall within an energy field
only a klick from our first landing site? Among sentients,
it appears, a pornographic yen is an infallible index:
a potential pacifying bond that we should perhaps
    explore.

Meanwhile, turnabout being fair play, several of us begin
to find the jut of a Denebolan femoral spur, the lemonish
fragrance of a ruptured ovipositor, or even a coded
    swarm
of their gill-dwelling symbiotic vermin almost as arousing
as venereal human contact or state-of-the-art handheld
weapons of irresistible concupiscent destruction. What
this bodes for future interspecies relations, I am loathe
to speculate. Their reliquary, though, rewards a look-see.

Kinds of Strangers

SARAH ZETTEL

Sarah Zettel has published four SF novels to date, Reclamation, Fool's War *(a* New York Times Notable Book *for 1996),* Playing God, *and* The Quiet Invasion. *Her short fiction has appeared in* Analog, *as did this story. She sold her first story in 1986 to a small press magazine called "Beyond . . . Fantasy and Science Fiction." "About six years and a billion and three rejection slips later," she says, "Stan Schmidt at* Analog *bought my story 'Driven by Moonlight,' and truly launched my professional career."*

"Kinds of Strangers" is a problem-solving story in the Analog *tradition, with a satisfyingly spectacular action climax, but it also deals with human issues often left out of SF stories. Why shouldn't a space crew marooned without hope of rescue experience depression?*

Margot Rusch pulled open the hatch that led to the *Forty-Niner*'s sick bay. "Paul?" she asked around the tightness building in her throat. She pulled herself into the sterile, white module. She focused slowly on the center of the bay, not wanting to believe what she saw.

Paul's body, wide-eyed, pale-skinned, limp and lifeless floated in mid-air. A syringe hovered near his hand, pointing its needle toward the corpse as if making an accusation.

"Oh, Christ." Margot fumbled for a handhold.

The ventilation fans whirred to life. Their faint draft pushed against the corpse, sending it toward the far wall of the module. Margot caught the acrid scent of death's final indignities. Hard-won control shredded inside her, but there was nowhere to turn, no one to blame. There was only herself, the corpse and the flat, blank screen of the artificial intelligence interface.

"Damn it, Reggie, why didn't you do something!" she demanded, fully aware it was irrational to holler at the AI, but unable to help it.

"I did not know what to do," said Reggie softly from its terminal. "There are no case scenarios for this."

"No, there aren't," agreed Margot, wearily. "No, there sure as hell aren't."

The crew of the *Forty-Niner* had known for three months they were going to die. The seven of them were NASA's pride, returning from the first crewed expedition to the asteroid belt. They had opened a new frontier for humanity, on schedule and under budget. Two and a half years of their four-year mission were a raving success, and now they were headed home.

There had been a few problems, a few red lights. Grit from the asteroid belt had wormed its way into the works on the comm antenna and the radio telescope. No problem. Ed MacEvoy and Jean Kramer replaced the damaged parts in no time. This was a NASA project. They had backups and to spare. Even if the reaction control module, which was traditional methane/oxygen rockets used for course corrections, somehow failed completely, all that would mean was cutting the project a little short. The long-distance flight was handled by the magnetic sail; a gigantic loop of high-temperature superconducting ceramic cable with a continuous stream of charged particles running through it. No matter what else happened, that would get them home.

"Margot?" Jean's voice came down the connector tube. "You OK?"

Margot tightened her grip on the handle and looked at the corpse as it turned lazily in the center of the bay. *No, I am not OK.*

The mag sail, however, had found a new way to fail. A combination of radiation and thermal insulation degradation raised the temperature *too* high and robbed hundreds of kilometers of ceramic cable of its superconductivity.

Once the mag sail had gone, the ship kept moving. Of course it kept moving. But it moved in a slow elliptical orbit going nowhere near its scheduled rendezvous with Earth. They could burn every atom of propellant they carried for the RCM and for the explorer boats, and they'd still be too far away for any of the Mars shuttles to reach by a factor of five. Frantic comm bursts to Houston brought no solutions. The *Forty-Niner* was stranded.

"Margot?" Jean again, calling down the connector.

"I'll be right up." Margot hoped Jean wouldn't hear how strangled her voice was.

Margot looked at the empty syringe suspended in mid-air. *Drunk all and left no friendly drop to help me after.*

She swallowed hard. *Stop it, Margot. Do not even start going there.*

"Is there another request?" asked Reggie.

Margot bit her lip. "No. No more requests."

Margot pushed herself into the connector and dragged the hatch shut. She had the vague notion she should have done something for the body—closed its eyes or wrapped a sheet around it, or something, but she couldn't make herself turn around.

Margot's eyes burned. She'd flown four other missions with Paul. She'd sat up all night with him drinking espresso and swapping stories while the bigwigs debated the final crew roster for the *Forty-Niner*. They'd spent long hours on the flight out arguing politics and playing old jazz recordings. She'd thought she knew him, thought he would hang on with the rest of them.

Then again, she'd thought the same of Ed and Tracy.

Tracy Costa, their chief mineralogist, had been the first to go. They hadn't known a thing about it, until Nick had caught a glimpse of the frozen corpse outside one of the port windows. Then, Ed had suffocated himself, even after he'd sworn to Jean he'd never leave her alone in this mess. Now, Paul.

Margot pulled herself from handhold to handhold up the tubular connector, past its cabinets and access panels. One small, triangular window looked out onto the vacuum, the infinitely patient darkness that waited for the rest of them to give up.

Stop it, Margot. She tore her gaze away from the window and concentrated on pulling herself forward.

The *Forty-Niner*'s command module was a combination of ship's bridge, comm center and central observatory. Right now, it held all of the remaining crew members. Their mission commander, Nicholas Deale, sandy-haired, dusky-skinned and dark-eyed, sat at one of Reggie's compact terminals, brooding over what he saw on the flat screen. Tom Merritt, who had gone from a florid, pink man to a paper-white ghost during the last couple of weeks, tapped at the controls for the radio telescope. He was an astronomer and the mission communications specialist. He was the one who made sure they all got their messages from home. The last living crew member was Jean. A few wisps of hair had come loose from her tight brown braid and they floated around her head, making her look even more worried and vulnerable. She stood at another terminal, typing in a perfunctory and distracted cadence.

Margot paused in the threshold, trying to marshal her thoughts and nerves. Nick glanced up at her. Margot opened her mouth, but her throat clamped tight around her words. Tom and Jean both turned to look at her. The remaining blood drained out of Tom's face.

"Paul?" he whispered.

Margot coughed. "Looks like he overdosed himself."

Jean turned her head away, but not before Margot saw the struggle against tears fill her face. Both Nick's hands clenched into fists. Tom just looked at Nick with tired eyes and said, "Well, now what?"

Nick sighed. "OK, OK." He ran both hands through his hair. "I'll go take care of . . . the body. Tom, can you put a burst through to mission control? They'll want to notify his family quietly. I'll come up with the letter . . ."

This was pure Nick. Give everybody something to do, but oversee it all. When they'd reeled in the sail, he hadn't slept for two days helping Ed and Jean go over the cable an inch at a time, trying to find out if any sections were salvageable from which they could jury-rig a kind of storm-sail. When that had proven hopeless, he'd still kept everybody as busy as possible. He milked every drop of encouraging news he could out of mission control. Plans were in the works. The whole world was praying for them. Comm bursts came in regularly from friends and family. A rescue attempt would be made. A way home would be found. All they had to do was hang on.

"In the meantime . . ." Nick went on.

"In the meantime we wait for the radiation to eat our insides out," said Tom bitterly. "It's hopeless, Nick. We are all *dead*."

Nick shifted uneasily, crunching Velcro underfoot. "I'm

still breathing and I don't plan to stop anytime soon."

A spasm of pure anger crossed Tom's features. "And what are you going to breathe when the scrubbers give out? Huh? What are you going to do when the water's gone? How about when the tumors start up?"

Tom, don't do this, thought Margot, but the words died in her throat, inadequate against the sudden red rage she saw in him. He was afraid of illness, of weakness. Well, weren't they all?

Paul's chief duty was keeping them all from getting cancer. One of the main hazards of lengthy space flight had always been long-term exposure to hard radiation. The mag sail, when it was functional, had created a shield from charged particles, which slowed the process down. Medical advancements had arisen to cover the damage that could be done by fast neutrons and gamma rays. Paul Luck maintained cultures of regenerative stem cells taken from each member of the crew. Every week, he measured pre-cancer indicators in key areas of the body. If the indicators were too high, he tracked down the "hot spots" and administered doses of the healthy cultured cells to remind bone, organ and skin how they were supposed to act and *voilà*! Healthy, cancer-free individual.

The Luck system was now, however, permanently down and the only backup for that was the AI's medical expert system and the remaining crew's emergency training. Right now, that didn't seem like anything close to enough.

"We have time," Nick said evenly. "We do not have to give up. Come on, Tom. What would Carol say if she heard this?" Nick, Margot remembered, had been at Tom's wedding. They were friends, or at least, they had been friends.

"She'd say whatever the NASA shrinks told her to," snapped Tom. "And in the meantime," he drawled the word, "I get to watch her aging ten years for every day we're hanging up here. How much longer do I have to do this to her? How much longer are you going to make your family suffer?"

For the first time, Nick's composure cracked. His face tightened into a mask of pent-up rage and frustration, but his voice stayed level. "My family is going to know I died trying."

Tom looked smug. "At least you admit we're going to die."

"No . . ." began Jean.

"Help," said a strange, soft voice.

The crew all turned. The voice came from the AI terminal. It was Reggie.

"Incoming signal. No origination. Can't filter. Incoherent system flaw. Error three-six-five . . ."

A grind and clank reverberated through the hull. Reggie's voice cut off.

"Systems check!" barked Nick.

Margot kicked off the wall and flew to navigation control, her station. "I got garbage," said Tom from beside her. "Machine language, error babble. Reggie's gone nuts."

Margot shoved her velcro-bottomed boots into place and typed madly at her keyboard, bringing up the diagnostics. "All good here," she reported. She turned her head and looked out the main window, searching for the stars and the slightly steadier dots that were the planets. "Confirmed. Positioning systems up and running."

"Engineering looks OK," said Jean. "I'll go check the generators and report back." Nick gave her a sharp nod. She pulled herself free of her station and launched herself down the connector.

"You getting anything coherent?" Nick pushed himself over to hover behind Tom's shoulder.

"Nothing." From her station, Margot could just make out the streams of random symbols flashing past on Tom's terminal.

"Reggie, what's happening?" she whispered.

"I don't know," said the voice from her terminal. Margot jerked. "Unable to access exterior communications system. Multiple errors on internal nodes. Code corruption. Error, three-four . . ." the computer voice cut out again in a pulse of static, then another, then silence, followed by another quick static burst.

"Margot, can you see the comm antenna?" asked Tom, his hands still flashing across the keyboard.

Margot pressed her cheek against the cool window, craned her neck and squinted, trying to see along the *Forty-Niner*'s hull. "Barely, yeah."

"Can you make out its orientation?"

Margot squinted again. "Looks about ten degrees off-axis."

"It's moved," said Tom between static bursts. "That was the noise."

"All OK down in the power plant," Jean pulled herself back through the hatch and attached herself to her station. "Well, at least there's nothing new wrong . . ." She let the sentence trail off. "What is that?"

Margot and the others automatically paused to listen. Margot heard nothing but the steady hum of the ship and the bursts of static from Reggie. Quick pulses, one, one, two, one, two, one, one, one, two.

"A pattern?" said Nick.

"Mechanical failure," said Tom. "Has to be. Reggie just crashed."

One, one, two, one.

"You ever hear about anything crashing like this?" asked Margot.

One, two, one.

"Reggie? Level one diagnostic, report," said Nick.

One, one, two.

"Maybe we can get a coherent diagnostic out of one of the other expert systems," Margot suggested. Reggie wasn't a single processor. It was a web-work of six interconnected expert systems, each with their own area of concentration, just like the members of the crew. Terminals in different modules of the ship gave default access to differing expert systems.

"Maybe," said Nick. "Tom can try to track down the fault from here. You and Jean see if you can get an answer out of si . . . the power plant." Margot was quietly grateful he remembered what else was in sick bay before she had to remind him.

One, one, one.

Jean and Margot pulled themselves down the connector to the engineering compartment. As Jean had reported, all the indicators that had remained functional after they'd lost the sail reported green and go.

"At least it's a different crisis," Jean muttered as she brought up Reggie's terminal, the one she and Ed had spent hours behind when the mag sail went out.

"Remind me to tell you about my grandmother's stint on the old Mir sometime," said Margot. "Now there was an adventure."

Jean actually smiled and Margot felt a wash of gratitude. Someone in here was still who she thought they were.

Jean spoke to the terminal. "Reggie, we've got a massive fault in the exterior communications system. Can you analyze from this system?" As she spoke, Margot hit the intercom button on the wall to carry the answer to the command center.

"Massive disruption and multiple error processing," said Reggie, sounding even more mechanical than usual. "I will attempt to establish interface."

"Nick, you hear that?" Margot said to the intercom grill. She could just hear the static pulses coming from the command center as whispering echoes against the walls of the connector.

"Roger," came back Nick's voice.

"I am . . . getting reports of an external signal," said Reggie. "It is . . . there is . . . internal fault, internal fault, internal fault."

Jean shut the terminal's voice down. "What the hell?" she demanded of Margot. Margot just shook her head.

"External signal? How is that possible? This can't be a comm burst from Houston."

Margot's gaze drifted to the black triangle of the window. The echoes whispered in ones and twos.

"What's a language with only two components?" Margot asked.

Jean stared at her. "Binary."

"What do we, in essence, transmit from here when we

do our comm bursts? What might somebody who didn't know any better try to send back to us?"

Jean's face went nearly as white as Tom's. "Margot, you're crazy."

Margot didn't bother to reply. She just pushed herself back up the connector to the bridge.

"Tom? Did you hear that?"

Tom didn't look up. He had a clip board and pen in his hands. As the static bursts rang out, he scribbled down a 1 for each single burst and a 0 for each pair. He hung the board in mid-air, as if not caring where it went and his hands flew across the keyboard. "Oh yeah, I heard it."

Nick was back at his station, typing at his own keyboard. "The engineering ex-systems seem to be intact. Maybe we can get an analysis . . ." He hit a new series of keys. Around them, the static bursts continued. Margot's temples started to throb in time with the insistent pulses.

"There's something," Tom murmured to the terminal. His voice was tight, and there was an undercurrent in it Margot couldn't identify. "It'll take awhile to find out exactly what's happened. I've got Reggie recording," he looked straight at Nick. "As long as it doesn't crash all the way . . ."

Margot and Jean also turned to Nick. Margot thought she saw relief shining behind his eyes. *At least now he won't have to find us make-work to do.*

"All right," said Nick. "Tom, you keep working on the analysis of this . . . whatever it is. Jean, we need you to do a breakdown on Reggie. What's clean and what's contaminated?" He turned his dark, relieved eyes to Margot. "I'll take care of Paul. Margot . . ."

"I'll make sure all the peripherals are at the ready," said Margot. "We don't know what's happening next."

Nick nodded. Margot extracted herself from her station and followed Nick down the connector. She tried not to look as he worked the wheel on the sick bay hatch. She just let herself float past and made her way down to the cargo bay.

The cargo bay was actually a combination cargo hold

and staging area. Here was where they stored the carefully locked-down canisters holding the ore samples. But here was also where they suited up for all their extra-vehicular activities. Just outside the airlock, the explorer boats waited, clamped tightly to the hull. They were small, light ships that looked like ungainly box kites stripped of their fabric. The explorers were barely more than frames with straps to hang sample containers, or sample gatherers, or astronauts from. They'd been designed for asteroid rendez-vous and landing. Margot remembered the sensation of childlike glee when she got to take them in. She loved her work, her mission, her life, but that had been sheer fun.

For a brief moment there, they thought they might be able to use the explorers to tow the *Forty-Niner* into an orbit that would allow one of the Martian stations to mount a rescue, but Reggie's models had showed it to be impos-sible. The delta-vee just wasn't there. So the explorers sat out there, and she sat in here, along with the core samplers, the drillers, the explosive charges, doing nothing much but waiting to find out what happened next.

Hang on, Margot. Stay alive one minute longer, and one minute after that. That's the game now isn't it? Forget how to play and you'll be following Paul, Ed and Tracy.

She touched the intercom button so she could hear the static bursts and Tom's soft murmuring. It reminded her that something really was happening. A little warmth crept into her heart. A little light stirred in her mind. It was some-thing, Tom had said so. It might just be help. Any kind of help.

Small tasks had kept her busy during the two weeks since they lost the sail, and small tasks kept her busy now. She made sure the seals on the ore carriers maintained their integrity. She ran computer checks on the explorers and made sure the fuel cells on the rovers were all at full ca-pacity, that their tanks were charged and the seals were tight. Given the state Reggie was in, she was tempted to put on one of the bright yellow hard-suits and go out to do a manual check. She squashed the idea. She might be needed for something in here.

She counted all the air bottles for the suits and checked their pressure. You never knew. With Reggie acting up, they might have to do an EVA to point the antenna back toward Earth. If this last, strange hope proved to be false, she still hadn't said good-bye to her fiancé Jordan, and she wanted to. She didn't want to just leave him in silence.

Reggie's voice, coming from the intercom, startled her out of her thoughts. "Help," said Reggie. "Me. Help. Me. We. Thee. Help."

Margot flew up the connector. She was the last to reach the command module. She hung in the threshold, listening to Reggie blurt out words one at a time.

"There. Is. Help," said Reggie, clipped and harsh. The words picked up pace. "There is help. Comet. Pull. Tow. Yourself. There is a comet approaching within reach. You can tow yourself toward your worlds using this comet. It is possible. There is help."

Margot felt her jaw drop open.

Tom looked down at his clipboard. "What Reggie says, what we've got here is a binary transmission from an unknown source. Taking the single pulses as ones and the double pulses as zeroes gave us gibberish, but taking the single pulses as zero and the double pulses as one gave us some version of machine language. The engineering expert sub-system was able to decode it."

He gripped his pen tightly, obviously resisting the urge to throw it in frustration. "This is impossible, this can't be happening."

Margot shrugged. "Well, it is."

"It can't be," growled Tom. "Aliens who can create a machine language Reggie can read inside of four hours? It couldn't happen."

"Unless they've been listening in on us for awhile," Jean pointed out.

Tom tapped the pen against the clipboard. One, two, one. "But how . . ."

Margot cut him off. She didn't want to hear it anymore. This was help, this was the possibility of life. Why was he trying to screw it up? "We've been beaming all kinds of junk out into space for over a hundred years. Maybe they've been listening that long." She felt his doubt his dribbling into the corners of her mind. She shut it out by sheer force of will.

Jean folded her arms tightly across her torso. "At this point, I wouldn't care if it was demons from the seventh circle of Hell, just so long as it's out here."

"Jesus," breathed Nick softly. Then, in a more normal voice he said, "OK, Margot, you and Jean are going to have to do an EVA to turn the antenna around so we can send a burst to Houston."

"We can't tell Houston about this," said Jean sharply.

"What?" demanded Tom.

Jean hugged herself even tighter. "They'd think we'd all gone crazy up here."

"What's it matter what they think?" Nick spread his hands. "It's not like they can do anything about it."

"They can tell our families we've all taken the mental crash," said Jean flatly. "I, for one, do not want to make this any worse on my parents."

Nick nodded slowly. "OK," he said. "We keep this our little secret. But if we do make it back, mission control is going to have a cow."

Tom looked from Nick to Jean and Margot saw something hard and strange behind his eyes. He faced Margot. "This thing with the comet, could we really do something like this?"

Margot's mouth opened and closed. A short-period comet, swinging around the sun. If they caught it on its way back in . . . if they could attach a line (hundreds of kilometers of unused cable coiled on its drum against the hull of the ship) . . . theoretically, theoretically, it could pull them into a tighter orbit. The stresses would be incredible. Several gs worth. Would they be too much? How to make the attachment? Couldn't land on a comet, even if the explorers had the delta-vee. Comets were surrounded by dust and debris, they ejected gas jets, ice and rock. Asteroids were one thing. Asteroids were driftwood bobbing along through the void. Comets were alive and kicking.

But maybe . . . maybe . . .

"We'd need to find the thing," she said finally. "We'd need course, distance, speed. We'd need to know if we can use the RCM to push us near enough to take a shot at it. We'd probably need the explorers to do the actual work of attaching the *Forty-Niner* to the comet . . ."

"We could use the mag sail," said Jean. She gnawed slowly on her thumbnail. "All that cable, we could use it as a tow rope. But we'd need a harpoon, or something . . ."

"A harpoon?" said Tom incredulously.

Jean just nodded. "To attach the tether to the comet. Maybe we could use some of the explosives . . ."

Nick smiled, just a little. For the first time in days, Margot saw the muscles of his face relax. "Jean, let's get down to engineering and see what we can work up. Tom, you and Margot find our comet." His smile broadened. "And keep an ear out in case the neighbors have more to say."

"No problem," said Margot. She raised her arm and whistled. "Taxi!"

Jean, an old New Yorker, actually laughed at that, and Margot grinned at her. Nick and Jean pulled themselves down the connector. Margot planted her feet on the velcro patch next to Tom.

"Let's see if we can still get to the database," she said, as she reached over his shoulder for the keys. "We should be able to narrow down . . ."

Tom did not lift his gaze from the screen. "It's a fake, Margot," he whispered.

Margot's hand froze halfway to the keyboard. "What?"

"Little green men my ass," he spat toward the console. "It's a fake. It's Nick. He's doing this to try to keep us going."

Margot felt the blood drain from her cheeks, and the hope from her heart. "How do you know?"

"I know." For the first time Tom looked at her. "He'd do anything right now to keep us in line, to keep giving orders, just so it doesn't look like he's out of options like the rest of us mere mortals."

Margot looked at his wide, angry blue eyes and saw the

man she'd served with swallowed up by another stranger. "You got proof?"

Tom shook his head, but the certainty on his face did not waver. "I checked the logs for gaps, suspicious entries, virus tracks, extra encryptions. Nothing. Nobody on this ship could have made an invisible insertion, except me, or Nick."

"Unless it's not an insertion," said Margot. "Unless it's really a signal."

Tom snorted and contempt filled his soft words. "Now you're talking like Jean. She hasn't been with it since Ed went. Be real, Margot. If E.T.'s out there, why isn't he knocking on the door? Why's he sending cryptic messages about comets instead of offering us a lift?"

"It's *aliens*, I don't know," Margot spread her hands. "Maybe they're methane breathers. Maybe they're too far away. Space is big. Maybe they want to see if we can figure it out for ourselves to see if we're worthy for membership in the Galactic Federation."

Tom's face twitched and Margot got the feeling he was suppressing a sneer. "OK, if it's aliens, how come I was able to figure out what they were saying so fast? They have a *NASA Machine Language for Dummies* book with them?"

Margot threw up her hands. "If Nick was faking this, why would he insist on a comm burst to mission control?"

Tom's jaw worked back and forth. "Because it'd look funny if he didn't and he knew Jean'd object and give him an out. She might even be in on it with him."

Margot clenched her fists. "It's a chance, Tom. It's even a decent chance, if we work the simulations right. It doesn't matter where the idea came from . . ."

"It does matter!" he whispered hoarsely. "It matters that we're being used. It matters that he doesn't trust us to hear him out so he's got to invent alien overlords."

"So, report him when we get home," said Margot, exasperation filling her breathy exclamation.

"We're not going to *get* home," Tom slammed his fist against the console. "We're going to die. This is all a stupid game to keep us from killing ourselves too soon. He's determined we are not going to die until he's good and ready."

Margot leaned in close, until she could see every pore in Tom's bloodless white cheeks.

"You listen to me," she breathed. "You want to kill yourself? Hit the sick bay. I'm sure Paul left behind something you can O.D. on. Maybe you're right, maybe how we go out is the only choice left. But I think we can use the delta-vee from the comet to tow us into a tighter orbit. I'm going to try, and I may die trying, but that's my choice. What are you going to do? Which part of that stubborn idiot head are you going to listen to? Huh?" She grabbed his collar. "If it is Nick doing this, I agree, it's a stupid ploy. But so what? It's the first good idea we've had in over a month. Are you going to let your pride kill you?"

Tom swatted her hand away. "I am not going to let him treat me like a fool or a child."

Tom lifted up first one foot then the other. He twisted in the air and swam toward the connector. Margot hung her head and let him go.

Give him some time to stew and then go after him. She planted herself squarely in front of his station. "Reggie?"

"Functioning," replied the AI.

"We need to do some speculation here," she rubbed her forehead. "I need you to pull up any databases we've got on comets. Specifically I need any that are passing within a thousand kilometers of the *Forty-Niner*'s projected position anytime within the next several months."

A static burst sounded from the speaker as if Reggie were coughing. "Several is not specific."

"Six months then. Add in the possibility of a full or partial RCM burn for course correction to bring us within the cometary path. Can you do that?"

Two more quick bursts. "I can try," said Reggie.

That's all any of us can do right now.

"Searching."

Margot sat back to wait. She listened to the hum of the ship and the sound of her own breathing. No other sounds. She couldn't hear Nick and Jean down in engineering. She couldn't hear Tom anywhere. Worry spiked in the back of her mind. What if he was taking the quick way out? What if he was angry enough to take Nick out instead?

No, she shook her head. *Tom's just on edge. They're friends.*

Were they? She remembered the stranger looking out of Tom's eyes. Would that stranger recognize Nick? Would Nick recognize him? She glanced nervously over her shoulder. No one floated in the connector. She looked back at the screen. Reggie had a list up—names, orbital parameters, current locations, sizes, with an option to display orbital plots and position relative to the *Forty-Niner*. Highlighted at the top was Comet Kowalski-Rice.

Sounds like a breakfast cereal. Margot glanced over her shoulder again. The connector was still empty. The ship was still silent.

Kowalski-Rice was a periodic comet, with a nucleus estimated to be three kilometers long and between one and three kilometers wide. It had passed its aphelion and was headed back toward the Sun. Right now it was 2.9 million kilometers from the *Forty-Niner*, but it was getting closer. Margot brought up the orbital plot and did a quick calculation.

We burn fifty . . . OK say sixty to be on the safe side, percent of the remaining propellant we can bring our orbit within seven hundred-fifty kilometers of the comet. Take about . . . She ran the equations in her head. She could double check them with Reggie or Nick, whoever turned out to be more reliable. *Bring us there in about a hundred and fifty-nine hours, with the comet going approximately two kilometers per second relative to the ship. This could work. This could work.*

Silence, except for the steady hum of the ship and her own breathing.

Margot swore. *This is no good.* "Reggie? Do you know where Tom is?"

"Tom Merritt is in the sick bay."

"No!" Margot yanked both feet up and kicked off the console. "Nick! Jean!" she shouted. "Sick bay! Now!"

She reached sick bay first. She wrenched the wheel around and threw the hatch open. A little red sphere drifted out toward her face. Margot swatted at it reflexively and it broke against her hand, scattering dark red motes in a dozen directions.

Tom had fastened himself to the examining table and sliced his throat. Clouds of burgundy bubbles rose from his neck, knocking against a pair of scissors and sending them spinning.

"Tom!" Margot dove forward and pressed her fingers against his wound. Panting, she tried to think back to her emergency medical training. *Dark red, not bright, oozing, not spurting, missed the carotid artery, cut a bunch of veins . . . Tom, you idiot, you're so far gone you can't even kill yourself right.*

Events blurred. It seemed like Nick, Jean and Reggie were all shouting at once. A pad got shoved into her hand to help staunch the blood. The table was tilted to elevate his head. Reggie droned on clear and concise directions for covering the long, thin wound with layered sealants. Nick's and Jean's hands shook as they worked. Blood and tears stung Margot's eyes.

When they were done, Tom was still strapped to the table, unconscious and dead white, but breathing. The medical ex-system was obviously still working. Reggie had no problem reading from the various pads and probes they had stuck to him. It was giving him good odds on survival, despite the blood loss.

"Let's get out of here," said Nick. "We can vacuum this up when we've had a chance to catch our breath."

Jean didn't argue, she just headed for the hatch. Margot had the distinct feeling she wanted to crawl into a corner and be quietly sick.

Margot followed Nick and Jean out and swung the hatch shut. She wanted to be able to talk without getting a mouthful of blood.

"God," Nick ran both hands through his hair. "I cannot believe it, I cannot believe he did this." Unfamiliar indecision showed on his face. Margot turned her gaze away.

Another stranger. Just one more. Like Tom, like the others.

No! she wanted to scream. *Not you. I know you! You recommended me for this mission. You have a great poker face and you sing country-western so loud in the shower the soundproofing can't keep it in! You keep all the stats on your kids' sports teams displayed as the default screen on your handheld! Your wife's the only woman you've ever been with! I know Nicholas Alexander Deale!*

But she did not know the person torn with weariness, anger and doubt who looked out of Nick's eyes. The one who might be a liar on a scale she'd never imagined. How long before that stranger took Nick completely over?

Margot looked at Jean. Blood splotched her face, hands, hair and coveralls. Fear haunted her bruised-looking eyes. Fear brought the stranger. Jean would go next. The stranger would have them all. Tom was right. They were all dead. Only the strangers and Margot Rusch lived.

"What is it, Margot?" asked Nick.

What do I say? Which "it" do I pick? Who let the stranger into Tom? Me or you? She licked her lips. *Well, it does not get me. It does not get me.*

"Nothing." Margot grabbed a handhold and pulled herself toward the command center. "I'm going to find that comet."

After all, that was what the strangers wanted her to do. She had to do what they said. If she didn't . . . look what they did to Tom. Who knew what they'd do to her?

They do not get me.

"Here it comes, Margot," the voice that used to be Nick's crackled through her helmet's intercom.

Margot turned in her straps, and there it came. Actually, Kowalski-Rice had been visible to the naked eye for the past two days. The comet was ungainly and beautiful at the same time. A dirty snowball tumbling through the darkness surrounded by a sparkling veil fit for an angel's bride. It was huge—a living, shining island, coal black and ice white. Margot's hands tightened on the twin joy sticks that were the directional control for the explorer.

They had planned the maneuver out so carefully and modeled it so thoroughly. She had to give the strangers who walked as Nick and Jean credit. They were very good at what they did.

Jean's stranger had cobbled together the "harpoon" from drill shafts, explosives and hope. The grappling shaft had a timed explosive mounted on it and a solid propellant shell around it. When Margot pulled the pin, the propellant would ignite and burn for one minute to drive the harpoon to the comet. At one minute ten seconds the explosive would blow, driving the barbed head deep into the comet's hide. It had taken all of them to unwind and detach the mag sail cable from the drum and then rewind it, as if they were reeling in a gigantic fishing line. The very end of that cable had been welded to the harpoon using all the vacuum glue and tape Jean's stranger could lay her hands on. Jean's stranger had spent hours out on the hull, readjusting the tension on the cable drum so the pay out would be smooth.

Margot would launch the harpoon into the comet. The cable would pay out. Once the harpoon struck, the friction of the cable unwinding against the barrel would accelerate the *Forty-Niner*, and Margot in the explorer, which was tethered to the *Forty-Niner* by the cables that used to be the shroud lines for the mag sail. The more the cable unwound, the faster the ships would accelerate. Finally, the cable would run out. The comet would shoot forward with its leash trailing behind it, and the *Forty-Niner* and the strangers would fly free toward an areobraking rendezvous with Mars, and a rescue by NASA.

At least, that's what they said would happen. They might be lying. There was no way to tell. But if Margot refused to go along, they'd probably just kill her. She had to play. She had to act like she believed they were who they said they were. It was her only chance.

She tried to tell herself it didn't matter. She tried to believe what she'd told Tom, who they still, miraculously, let live, that it didn't matter who'd come up with the idea— aliens, the strangers, it didn't matter. If Nick and Jean, and Tracy and Ed, and Paul and even Tom finally were overcome by the strangers, it didn't really matter. What mattered was getting home. If she could get home, she could warn everyone.

But first she had to get home. She, Margot Rusch, had to get home.

"Better get ready, Margot," said Nick's stranger. "It's all on you."

So it is. And you hate that, don't you? I could mess up all your plans and you know it, but you can't get me. Not out here you can't.

Margot squeezed the stick, goosing the engine. Silently, her little frame ship angled to starboard, sliding gingerly closer to the wandering mountain of coal black ice and stone. Behind her, the three shining silver tethers that attached the explorer to the *Forty-Niner* paid out into the darkness.

She gave the comet's path a wide berth, but not so wide that she couldn't see how it lumbered, turning and shuddering as sparkling jets shot off its pocked hide.

I can do this. How many asteroids did we skirt? They were all falling too.

But not like this. She imagined the comet hissing and rumbling as it dashed forward. *They're making me do this. They don't care if I die.*

Black specks dusted her visor. She wiped at them. She glanced behind to see that the tethers were moving smoothly. The comet was almost in front of her. Black ice, black stone and the sparkling white coma surmounted the darkness.

Suddenly, the rover shuddered and Margot jerked in her straps. A stone careened off the frame ship and shot past her head.

That was a warning shot. That was them ... No, no, they can't get me out here, but the comet can. Keep your mind on the comet, Margot. Don't think about them.

The *Forty-Niner* was below and behind her now. The comet was receding. The coma filled the vacuum, shining like a snow blowing in the sunlight. Margot pitched the rover up and around, until the comet was flying away from her, but she was not in the thick of its tail.

For a moment, she was nothing but a pilot and she smiled.

Perfect deflection shot. Fire this baby right up its tail-pipe.

The strangers had mounted the harpoon on the explorer's fore starboard landing strut and attached the launch pin to the console. Margot fumbled for the thick, metal pin and its trailing wire.

Well, just call me Ishmael, she thought, suppressing a giggle. *There she is, Captain Ahab! There be the great white whale!*

"Margot . . ." began Nick's stranger.

"Don't push," she snapped. *Don't push. I might decide not to do this.*

I could. I could not do this. I could leave the strangers out here. Never have to bring them home. Never have to hurt my friends families by showing them what's happened.

But I want to go home. Forgive me, Carol. Margot Rusch has to get home.

Margot grit her teeth. Ice crystals drifted past her. The comet retreated on its lumbering path, inanimate, or at least oblivious of their presence and their need.

Margot pulled the pin on the harpoon.

The recoil vibrated through the frame. The harpoon shot forward, hard, fast and straight. The tether vanished into the thick of the coma, lost in the shining veil of ice.

A jet of ice crystals exploded into the night. The comet rolled away as if wounded. The tethers on their reel played out into the void. Margot bit her lip. The tether was the key. If it released too fast, got tangled, or broke, it was over, all of it.

"Margot! Report!" demanded Nick's stranger.

"Tether holding steady," replied Margot reflexively. "Pay out looks good."

You'll get home. To Nick's home. That's what you care about.

The explorer shuddered. A sudden intense cold burned

Margot's shin. A red warning light flashed on her visor screen.

No!

A black gash cut across her gleaming yellow suit. The joints at knee and ankle sealed off automatically. Margot fumbled for the roll of sealant tape on her belt. As she did, the explorer began to slide backward, away from the comet, toward the *Forty-Niner* to the limit of the tether. The movement dragged her back against her straps. Her glove gripped the tape reel. Pain bit deep.

Hang on, hang on. Lose the tape and you're gone. You're all gone. The stranger'll have you if you lose the tape.

The tug grew stronger. Margot felt her body shoved backward to the limits of its straps. A weight pressed hard against her ribs, her throat, her heart. After years of zero *g*, the acceleration gripped her hard and squeezed until her breath came fast and shallow.

Ahead of her, the *Forty-Niner* began to swing. A slow, sinuous movement that transmitted itself along the tether. It pulled the explorer to starboard, tilting her personal world, confusing her further, adding to the pain that screamed through every nerve.

Slowly, slowly she pulled the roll of tape from her belt. She grasped it in both clumsy, gloved hands. The explorer shimmied. Her body bounced up, then down, hard enough to jar her. The tape slipped. Margot screamed involuntarily and clung to it so hard she felt the flimsy reel crumple.

"Margot?" Jean's stranger. "Margot? What's happening?"

"Don't unstrap!" came back Nick's stranger. "Jean, stay where you are."

Right, right. Why risk anything for me? I'm not a stranger.

She leaned forward as if leaning into a gale wind. Black spots danced in front of her vision. She saw red through the gash, as if her leg glowed with its pain. She jounced and shuddered. More hits. The explorer was taking more hits from cometary debris. She couldn't steady her hands enough to lay down the tape.

Margot bit her lip until she tasted blood. She pressed the tape reel against the black gash, pushed the release button down and pulled, hard. A strip of clean white tape covered the black scoring.

The red light on her suit display turned green and the joints unsealed. Her suit was whole again.

Margot let herself fall backward, gasping for air, gasping for calm against the pain. Her left leg from ankle to knee would be one gigantic blood blister. But she was alive. The stranger hadn't got her yet. She hugged the tape to her chest. The *Forty-Niner* started swinging slowly back to port. Gravity leaned hard against her. Her heart labored, as if trying to pump sideways. Her stomach heaved. Her whole body strained against the straps.

She closed her eyes and tried to reach outward with every nerve, trying to feel the clamps and catches as she could her fingers and toes, wishing she could hear something, anything, a straining, a snapping. All there was was silence and the unbearable pressure driving her ribs into her lungs.

"*Forty-Niner* to Explorer One." Nick's stranger. What did he want? To find out if her stranger had swallowed her yet?

Not yet, Sir. Not yet.

"Margot? Margot, it looks like you're venting something. Report."

Venting? Margot's gaze jerked down to the monitor between her flight sticks. Red lights flashed. She didn't need to read the message. The diagram showed everything. The methane tank had been hit and all her fuel was streaming out into the void, leaving nothing at all for her to use to guide the explorer back to *Forty-Niner.*

She was stuck. She would hang out here until her air ran out. She was dead all over again.

All at once, the vibrations ceased. She was flying smooth and free, gliding like a bird on a sea wind with only the most gentle roll to perturb her flight.

"We have tether release!" cried Jean's stranger.

Margot looked up. A silver line lashed through the clean, sparkling white of the coma.

Tether release. They'd done it. It had worked. The strangers were all on their way home. She looked again at her own fountain of crystals streaming out behind her, a comet's tail in miniature.

That roll'll get worse. They'll have to correct for it. They'll have to fire the rockets and catch me in the blast and tell Jordan and mission control how sorry they were.

Nick's stranger spoke to her again. "Margot, we gotta get you in here. If your fuel's gone, can you haul on the tether? Margot?"

"She's not receiving, Nick. The headset must be out. I gotta get down there."

All gone. Nothing to do. Pain throbbed in her head, crowding out her thoughts.

"Margot, pull!"

She couldn't move. Pain, bright and sharp, burned through her. All she could do was watch the crystal stream of her fuel drift away into the vacuum.

Margot Rusch is dead.

"Margot! Answer me! Pull, Margot!"

She's been dead for weeks.

"Come on, Margot. I got a green on your headset. Now answer me, damnit!"

The stranger wins. She got Margot Rusch after all.

"She didn't even get a chance to say good-by to Jordan. That's the bad part," she murmured.

"Margot?" came back the voice of Nick's stranger. "Margot, this is Nick. We're receiving you. Acknowledge."

Why are they still calling her Margot? They must know the stranger had her by now. She would have liked to know the stranger's name. Maybe she wouldn't mind burning to ash when they fire the correction burst. Margot Rusch certainly wouldn't mind. Margot Rusch was dead.

The explorer jerked. Mildly curious, Margot looked toward the *Forty-Niner*. A figure in a bright yellow hard-suit leaned out of the ship's airlock. Its hands hauled on the tethers, as if they were hauling on curtain cords. The *Forty-*

Niner drew minutely closer and the pair of ships began to spin ever so gently around their common center. Margot felt herself leaning against the straps.

"Margot Rusch!" Nick's voice. Nick's stranger? A quick burst fired from the *Forty-Niner*'s port nozzle. The spin slowed.

"Margot Rusch, wake up, you stupid fly-jock and pull!" Jean now. Jean's stranger? Jean's stranger trying to save Margot Rusch's stranger?

Jean trying to save her? But she was dead, she as dead as Ed and Paul and Tracy and Tom.

No, not Tom. Tom's still alive.

What if I'm still alive?

Cold and pain inched up her leg and emptied into her knee, her thigh. Her head spun. Readings flashed in the corner of her helmet. The suit had sealed itself. Blood pressure was elevated, respiration fast, shallow, pulse elevated. Recommend termination of EVA.

"Margot Rusch, help her get your butt back in here!" shouted Nick.

Margot leaned as far forward as the straps would let her. Her gloved fingers grappled with the tether and snared some of the slack. Margot pulled. The *Forty-Niner* came a little closer. The suited figure became a little clearer.

"I knew you were still with us!" cried Jean, jubilantly. "Come on, Margot. Pull!"

Margot pulled. Her arms strained, her joints ached. Her suit flashed red warnings. The *Forty-Niner* moved closer. The spin tried to start, but another burst from the engines stalled it out again. Margot's breath grew harsh and echoing in the confining helmet. Her lungs burned. The cold pain reached her hip and started a new path down her fingers. The *Forty-Niner* filled her world now, its white skin, its instrumentation, its black stenciled letters and registry numbers.

And Jean. She could see Jean now, hauling on the tether as if it was her life depending on it. She could even see her eyes. Her eyes and herself, her soul, looking out through them. Margot knew if she looked at Nick she would see him too. Not strangers, not anymore. Maybe not ever.

They had done what they had done. Maybe Nick had faked that message, maybe they'd had help from unknown friends. They'd sort it all out when they got home. What mattered now was that they would get home, all of them, as they were. Not strangers, just themselves.

Margot grabbed up another length of tether and pulled.

Visit the Sins

CORY DOCTOROW

Cory Doctorow was born and raised in Toronto, and grew up in the shadow of science-fiction, exposed at an early age to writer/editor Judith Merril and the writers' workshops she founded, and then going to work at Bakka, the world's oldest science-fiction bookstore, for three years. Doctorow works with computers. He "does technology stuff" for ad agencies, offshore casinos, film companies, TV stations, multimedia companies, lawyers, videoconference MBA programs, and international development agencies. He's a smart, fast-talking guy who always has the latest new hi-tech gadget close by, and publishes new issues of his business card the way some fans publish new issues of their fanzines. His fiction has appeared in SF Age, Asimov's, On Spec, Tesseracts, Pulphouse, *and elsewhere. He writes a regular column on science-fictional Web-stuff for* SF Age, *and other nonfiction for* Wired, Sci-Fi Entertainment, Sci-Fi Universe, New York Review of Science Fiction, *and* 2600.

This story is about a theme that will be even more important in the future than it is now: communication between the young and the old. It is also about retreat into technology from engagement with the real world, which happens at any age.

Sean had a way of getting his way—a way of delivering argument that implied that everyone in earshot was savvy and bold, and that the diatribe-du-jour was directed at the Enemies of Art ranged without. His thesis advisor bought it every time. Sean turned in his due-diligence, a bunch of theses written in the last century: collected memoirs of the survivors of electroshock, lobotomies, thalidomide. His advisor signed off and within twenty-four hours, he was debarking in Orlando and renting a car to take him to the Home.

He didn't tell his father. He'd have to, eventually, before he could finish the thesis. But for now, it was just him and Grampa, head-to-head.

Grampa was switched off when Sean found him on the ward, which throbbed with a coleslaw of laser-light and videogames and fuck-pix and explosions and car-wrecks and fractals and atrocities.

Sean remembered visits before the old man was committed, he and his dutiful father visiting the impeccable apartment in the slate house in Kingston, Ontario. Grampa made tea and conversation, both perfectly executed and without soul. It drove Sean's father bugfuck, and he'd inevitably have a displaced tantrum at Sean in the car on the way home. The first time Grampa had switched on in Sean's presence—while Sean was trying out a prototype of Enemies of Art against his father's own As All Right-

Thinking People Know—it had scared Sean stupid.

Grampa had been in maintenance mode, running through a series of isometric stretching exercises in one corner while Sean and his father had it out. Then, suddenly, Grampa was between them, arguing both sides with machine-gun passion and lucidity, running an intellect so furious it appeared to be steam-driven. Sean's tongue died in his mouth. He was made wordless by this vibrant, violent intellect that hid inside Grampa. Grampa and his father had traded extemporaneous barbs until Grampa abruptly switched back off during one of Sean's father's rebuttals, conceding the point in an unconvincing, mechanical tone. Sean's father stalked out of the house and roared out of the driveway then, moving with such speed that if Sean hadn't been right on his heels, he would never have gotten into the car before his father took off.

And now, here was Grampa in maintenance mode. He was sitting at a table, flexing his muscles one at a time from top to bottom. It was an anti-pressure-sore routine. Sean guessed that it was after-market, something the Home made available for low-functioning patients like Grampa.

Sean sat down opposite him. Grampa smiled and nodded politely. Sean swallowed his gorge. The ones who'd had the surgery had been scattered, unable to focus, until they'd had the operation, and suddenly it wasn't a problem anymore. Whenever their attention dropped below a certain threshold, they just switched off, until the world regained some excitement. It had been a miracle, until the kids stopped making the effort to keep their attention above the threshold, and started to slip away into oblivion.

"Hello, Grampa," Sean said.

Grampa stared at him from dark eyes set in deep, wrinkled nests. Behind them, Sean could almost see the subroutines churning. "Sean," Grampa said. Woodenly, he stood and came around the table, and gave Sean a precise hug and cheek-kiss. Sean didn't bother returning either.

He put the recorder on the table between them and switched it on.

*   *   *

Grampa was a moderately wealthy man. He'd achieved much of that wealth prior to his retirement, working as a machinist on really delicate, tricky stuff. The family assumed that he did this work switched off, letting the subroutines run the stultifying repetitions, but in his prelim research, Sean had talked to one of Grampa's co-workers, who said that Grampa had stayed switched on more often than not. Grampa had acquired the rest of the wealth shortly before Sean's father had sent him south, to the Home. The years-old class action suit brought by the guilty, horrified families of accidental zombies had finally ended with a settlement, and all the Survivors became instant millionaires-in-trust.

For all the good it did them.

"How are you?" Grampa asked, placidly.

"I'm working on my thesis, Grampa. I'm here to interview you—I'll be around for the next couple weeks."

"That's nice," Grampa said. "How's your father?"

"He's fine. I didn't tell him I was coming down, though. You're a touchy subject for him."

Grampa settled back into his chair. Sean was distantly aware of other Survivors on the ward, gabbling and twitching at videogames and smoking all at once. They were high-functioning—they could be switched on with simple stim; Grampa only switched on for important occasions.

Sean said, "Dad wishes you'd die."

That did it. It was easy to tell when Grampa was switched on; the rhythmic, methodical maintenance twitching was replaced with a restless, all-over fidget; and his eyes darted around the room. "Is he in some kind of financial trouble? He doesn't need to wait for a bequest—I'll write to the trustees right now."

Sean restrained himself from saying hello again, now that Grampa was switched on. He kept himself focused on the task of keeping Grampa switched on. "He wishes you'd die because he hates you and he hates himself for it. When you die, he can stop hating you and start mourning you. He knows it wasn't your fault. That's why I'm here. I want to collect your stories and make some sense out of them, before you die." Sean took a deep breath. "Will you stay switched on?"

Grampa looked uncomfortable. "Your grandmother used to ask me that. I'd promise her I'd do it, every time, but then . . . it's not voluntary, Sean. It's reflex."

"It's a learned reflex, Grampa. It's not breathing. You didn't ask to have the surgery, but you learned the reflex all on your own. You *allow* your attention to drop below the threshold, you *allow* the chip to switch you off. Some people do it less," he jerked his head at the other old men and women, playing their twitch games and shouting arguments at each other. "Some don't do it at all."

"Bullshit!" Grampa said, leaning forward and planting his hands on his knees—aggro Type-A body-language that Sean often found himself assuming. "Urban legend, kid. Everyone learned it. Once you had the surgery, you couldn't help it. You know what I'm talking about, or you wouldn't be here. Your father, too—if he was ever honest enough to admit it. You've both got it as bad as me, but no one ever tried to *cure* you."

"I don't have it," Sean said. "I just got off a three-hour plane-ride, and I was able to just look out the window the whole way. It didn't bother me. That's not coping mechanism, either—I never even *wanted* to watch the seat-back vid or chat up my neighbor." It wasn't true, actually. He had fidgeted like crazy, splitting the screen-in-screen on the seat-back into sixteen quads and watching as many stations as he could. He'd tried to assemble his thoughts on his recorder, but he'd been too wound up. Eventually, somewhere over Georgia, he'd surrendered to the screen and to counting powers of two.

Grampa pierced him with his stare. "If your ego demands that you believe that, then go ahead."

Sean restrained himself from squirming. He focused himself on directing the discussion. "What do you like best about the Home?"

Grampa considered the question for so long that Sean was afraid he'd switched off. "No one makes me feel guilty for switching off. No one tells me that I'm weak. Except your father, of course."

"Dad's been here?" Sean said, shocked. "When?"

"Your father visits every month. He shouts at me until I switch on, then he leaves. He does it because the doctor told him that if I didn't switch on more often that they'd move me to the zero-function ward. Sounds fine to me, and I tell him so, but he's never thought much of his brain-damaged old man."

"Where do you go when you're switched off?" Sean asked. It was a question that was supposed to come later in the interview, maybe on day two, but he was rattled.

"I don't know. Away."

"Is it like sleep?" Sean said, forgetting the rule that you never ask the subject a simple yes/no question. His heart thudded in his chest, like he was giving the first interview of his life.

"No."

"How is it different from sleep?" Sean asked.

"I usually switch on for sleep—my subconscious is pretty good at entertaining me, actually. When I switch off, I just . . . go away. I remember it later, like it was a book that got read directly into my brain, but I'm *not there*. It's fucking great. You'd love it, Sean. You should get the surgery. I hear that there's a lot of black-market clinics where you can get it done. South-East Asia. The sex-trade, you know."

Sean struggled to keep the discussion on-track. Grampa was often hostile when he was switched on, and his father always rose to the bait. Sean wasn't going to. "How do you know that you're not there? Maybe you're there the whole time, bored stupid, screaming in frustration, and you forget it all as soon as you switch on?"

Grampa raised an eyebrow at him. "Of course I am! But that's not the *me* that's important—*I'm* the one that counts. And I get to fast-forward past all the slow parts. Which this is turning into, I'm afraid."

Grampa's eyes stopped seeking out the ward's corners, and he slipped back into maintenance mode. The noise and lights of the ward closed in around Sean. He scooped up his recorder. "Thanks, Grampa," he said, woodenly. "I'll see you tomorrow."

"Bye, Sean," Grampa said, and came around the table for another hug and kiss.

Sean checked into the first motel he found, the Lamplighter Inn, on a dreary strip populated with disused waterparks and crumbling plazas. He lay down on the bed, fed the Magic Fingers, and played back the recording.

It was junk. The noise of the ward masked nine words in ten, and what words made it through were empty, devoid of any kind of emotional freight. He tried to transcribe it longhand, filling in the blanks from memory, but couldn't keep his mind on it.

He took off his sweaty, wrinkled T-shirt and slacks, dumped out his suitcase on the chipped, cigarette-burned table, and found his bathing suit.

There was one other guest by the pool, an old, old, woman in a one-piece with a skirt, wearing a sunhat tilted to shade her from the last of the pounding Florida sun. Sean gave her a perfunctory nod and jumped in.

The water was piss-warm, thickly chlorinated. It felt like swimming in pungent sweat. Sean managed one lap and then crawled out and sat in a sway-backed deck-chair.

"I wouldn't go swimming in that if I were you," the old woman said, in a husky, nicotine-stained voice. She clattered a grin at him through her dentures. She was the color and texture of rawhide, not so much tanned as *baked*.

"Now you tell me," Sean said, squinting at her under his hand.

"Old Ross doesn't like dealing with the pool, so he just keeps on shoveling in the chlorine. Don't be surprised if you're blond in the morning. My name's Adele. You here for long?"

"A couple weeks, at least," Sean said.

Adele smiled and nodded. "That's good. That's fine. A good stretch of time to see the Parks. Don't miss Universal, either—I think it's better than Disney. Most people don't bother with it, but for my money, it's better."

"I don't think I'll get a chance to visit either," Sean said. "I've got a lot of work to do down here." He waited for her to ask him what kind of work, and mentally rehearsed the high-concept speech that he'd given a thousand times while working on the thesis proposal.

"What a shame," she said. "Where did you come down from?"

"Toronto," he said.

"Lord, not another snowbird!" she said, good-naturedly. "Seems like half of Canada's down here! They come here to get away from the winter, then they complain about the heat! What do they expect, that's what I want to know! Was your flight good?"

"It was fine," Sean said, bemusedly. "A little dull, but fine."

"So, you're here for a few weeks," Adele said.

"Yes. Working," Sean said.

"Nice work if you can get it!" Adele said, and clattered her dentures again. "I moved here, oh, five years ago. To be near my boy. In the hospital. I used to work, but I'm retired. Used to work at a dairy—answering the phones! You tell people you used to work in a dairy, they think you were milking the cows! Old Ross, he gives me an annual rate for my room. It's better than living in one of those gated places! Lord! How much shuffleboard can a body stand?"

"Your son is sick?" Sean said.

"Not sick, no," Adele said. "You wouldn't believe the roaches you get down here! Old Ross fumigates regular, but Florida roaches don't seem to care. I've lived in New York, and I've seen some pretty big roaches in my day, but not like these. Like cats! My boy, Ethan, he'd clean and clean our apartment in New York, quiet as you please, a good boy. Then he'd see a roach and whim-wham, he'd be talking, joking, skipping and running. Old Ross says there's nothing he can do—he says, 'Adele, this is *Florida*, and the roaches were here long before us, and they'll be here long after, and nothing we do is going to keep them away.'

That's all fine and good, but let me tell you, I've never seen a roach in the Home when I was visiting Ethan. *They* know how to keep them out. Maybe it's all the shouting. Lord, but they do shout!"

A small lightbulb blinked in Sean's mind. "Is Ethan very high-functioning?" he asked, carefully.

Adele glanced sidelong at him and said, "The doctor says no. But I think he is. He's always walking around when I'm there, doing push-ups and situps. He's not a young man, Ethan—sixty this year! When his father was that age, he didn't do any push-ups, no sir! But the doctor, he says that Ethan's at zero function. Doctors! What do they know?"

"How old was Ethan when he had the surgery?" Sean asked.

"Just seven," Adele said, without changing her light tone, but Sean saw knives of guilt in her eyes. "He was going to be held back in the first grade, or sent to a special school. They sent a doctor around to explain it. Ethan was smart as a whip, everyone knew that, but he just couldn't *concentrate*. It made him miserable, and he'd pitch these hissyfits all the time. It didn't matter where he was: the classroom, home, out on the street—in church! He'd scream and shout and kick and bite, you've never seen anything like it. The doctors, they told us that he'd just keep on getting worse unless we did something about it.

"It seemed like a miracle. In my day, they'd just drug you up."

Sean knew the names of the old drugs: Ritalin, Cylert, Dexedrine. Anything that would keep you still and numb. Then came the surgery.

Adele brightened. "You should really try to at least visit Universal for an afternoon, you know. It's lovely."

"They're going to move my grandfather to the zero-function ward, I think. If he doesn't spend more time switched on, they will," Sean said. "I want to get his story before they do it." And if not his stories, the *reasons*—reasons for who Sean was, who his father was.

"What a nice grandson you are! You know, it seems like

no one cares about their grandparents anymore. Old Ross's grandchildren haven't visited once in the five years I've been here."

Sean gave Adele a ride the next day. She wore the sunhat and a lightweight cotton dress and sandals, and looked frail and quaint.

Sean thought Adele would get off at a different floor, to visit Ethan, but she walked with him across Grampa's ward.

Grampa was sitting just where he had been the day before. His chin was shaved blue, and he was impeccable. He was methodically slicing and eating a hamburger.

"Grampa," Sean said.

"Hello, Sean," Grampa said. He laid his knife and fork in a precise X on his plate and pushed it aside.

"This is Adele. Her son is in the zero-function ward. She wanted to meet you. Adele, this is my grandfather, Brice Devick."

"Pleased to meet you, Adele," Grampa said, and shook her hand.

"Likewise," she said. "Do you know my Ethan? I'm worried that he doesn't seem to have any friends here."

"I haven't met him," Grampa said.

"Well, would you do an old lady a big favor? Go and visit him. Your grandson tells me you're smart—Ethan is as smart as a whip. You two should have lots to talk about."

"I will," Grampa said.

"I'm sure you two will get on very well. It was a pleasure to meet you. Excuse me, I'm sure Ethan's wondering where I am."

Sean waited until she was out of earshot, then said, "Her son's a fucking vegetable. You're about 80 percent of the way there. You're spending so much time switched off, you might as well be dead."

"What do you know about it?" Grampa said, fidgeting.

"I know plenty," Sean said. "Plenty! You spent less than 15 percent of the time switched off until you hit college. Then you switched off for months at a time. You used it for a study aid! I pulled your logfiles, when I was at

Dad's—he's had them ever since you were declared *non compos*. You're a junkie, Grampa. You don't have the will-power to kick your habit, and it makes my Dad nuts. I never knew you, so it just makes me curious. Let's talk about the first time you remember switching off."

Grampa snorted. "That's a *stupid* question. You *don't* remember switching off—that's the whole point."

Sean rolled his eyes. "You know what I mean. You may not remember switching off, but you'll remember switching on. Switching on *has* to be memorable, doesn't it? Isn't that the whole point?"

"Fine. I switched on for about twenty minutes in a movie that I snuck out of school to see when I was twelve. It was in French, and it had made a lot of noise because it had a sex scene with a live pig. I saw that scene, and two others—another sex scene and a scene where this woman cuts the pig's throat. I loved it. All my friends had done the same thing, but by the time the good parts had come around, they were too bored to enjoy them. I just caught the highlight reel."

"How long until you next switched off?"

"I don't know. A while."

"It was two days. I have the logfile, remember, Grampa? Don't jerk my chain. You switched off during Friday dinner. Did your parents notice?"

"Of course they noticed! They loved it! For once, I wasn't kicking the table-leg or arguing with my sisters or stuffing sprouts in my pocket. I cleaned my plate, then sat and waited until everyone else was done, then I did the dishes."

"How'd you like it?"

"I loved it! I hated family dinners! I just got the highlight reel again—dessert! I remember that fucking bowl of pudding like I was eating it right now. My mother couldn't cook for shit, but she sure opened a mean package of Jello Pudding."

Sean found his mood matching Grampa's, aggressive and edgy. "How did you and Grandma end up getting married? I can't imagine that she was hot for a zombie like you."

"Oh, but she *was*, Sean, she *was*!" Grampa waggled his eyebrows lasciviously. "Your Grandma didn't like people much. She knew she had to get married, her folks expected no less, but she mostly wanted to be off on her own, doing her own thing. I'd come home, switch off, clean the place, do any chores she had for me, then go to bed. She loved to have sex with me switched off—it got so that if I accidentally switched on while we were doing it, I'd pretend I was still off, until she was done. It was the perfect arrangement."

"But she divorced your sorry ass after ten years," Sean said.

"You got a girlfriend, Sean?" Grampa said.

"No," Sean said.

"You *ever* had a girlfriend?"

"Yes," Sean said, feeling slightly smug. Never ask yes/no question.

"Why'd she leave you?" Grampa asked, his eyes sharp as razors.

"What makes you think *she* left *me?*" Sean asked.

"Did she?" Grampa fired back.

"Yes," Sean said, as calmly as he could manage.

"And why did that happen?"

"We were growing in different directions," Sean said, the words sounding prim even to him.

Grampa barked and slapped his palm on the table. The old men and women in the ward swiveled their heads to stare, momentarily distracted, then went back to arguing.

"You're full of shit, kid. What's that supposed to mean?"

"I was working on my thesis proposal. Lara was working on hers. Neither of us had time for a relationship. It was amicable."

Lara had caught him watching television over her shoulder while she was delivering one of her dreaded Relationship Briefings, and had laid into him a little too hard. He'd come back at her with everything he had, an extended rant that ranged from her lame-ass thesis—the cultural impact of some obscure TV show from before they'd been born— to her backbiting, over-educated circle of friends. He'd moved on to her relationship with her mother; her insufferable whining about a suicidal uncle she'd been close to; and her pretentious way of sprinkling her speech with stupid pseudo-intellectual buzzwords. He crossed the line again and again and she kicked him out on his ass.

"Dad says that you never switched on during the divorce."

"Your Dad has nothing to complain about. He got enough pity lavished on him to kill ten men. It was all your grandmother's family could do not to devour him whole."

"But you stayed switched off," Sean said.

"In the court, I was switched off. Ever been in a court, Sean?"

"You stayed switched off."

"In the courtroom."

"And before, during the separation?"

"Same thing," Grampa said.

"And after, during visitations?"

"Not then," Grampa said, loudly. "Not during visitations."

"I've got the logfiles, Grampa," Sean said.

"What the hell do a twelve-year-old and a grown man have to talk about? I kept him fed. I took him out to the carny and to kiddie movies. I drove him to hockey."

"You *switched off*, Grampa," Sean said. "The *you that counted* wasn't there."

"Sophistry," Grampa said. "Bullshit. I remember all of it. I was there. Not many other parents were, let me tell you. Usually, it was just me and a few others in the stands, or kids running around loose like animals at the carny. Your father has *nothing* to complain about."

"Why, aren't you two looking excited!" Adele said, hobbling alongside of the table. She was leaning on Ethan, a vigorous old man with sinewy arms and dead eyes. His face was unlined, free from smile lines and frowning creases.

"Hi, Adele," Sean said, trying to keep the exasperation out of his voice.

"Ethan, this is Sean and his grandfather, Brice."

Ethan extended his hand and Sean shook it. "Very nice

to meet you," Ethan said. His hand was dry and papery, his eyes vacant. Sean shook it, and a frisson of shameful disgust sizzled up his abdomen. He had a sudden vision of Ethan's brain, desiccated in his skull, the gleaming edges of the chip poking free. He surreptitiously wiped his hand on his pants as Ethan turned to Grampa and shook his hand. "Very nice to meet you."

"Do you mind if we sit down?" Adele said. "I'm afraid that I'm a little pooped. All those stairs!"

Sean offered his chair and went off to the lounge with Ethan to get two more. When they got back, Adele had her hand on Grampa's forearm. "—I worked in a dairy, answering the phones! You tell people you used to work in a dairy, they think you were milking the cows!" Adele laughed and Grampa shot Sean a hostile look.

Sean said, "Grampa was a machinist before he retired. You really liked doing that, huh, Grampa?"

Grampa nodded perfunctorily.

"I mean, the logfiles show that you almost never switched off at work. Must've been pretty engrossing. You should give workshops here. I bet it'd be good therapy." Sean knew he was baiting the old man, but he couldn't stop himself.

"Your father's arriving tomorrow," Grampa said. "He called last night. I didn't tell him you were here, I thought it would be a nice surprise."

Adele clapped her hands. "Well isn't that *nice*! Three generations, all together. Sean, you'll have to introduce Ethan and me to your father. Ethan never had children, isn't that right?"

Ethan said, "Yes."

"Always the bachelor, my boy. But it wasn't for lack of opportunity. You had to beat them off with a stick, didn't you, son?"

Ethan said, "Yes."

"I always hoped for a grandchild to hold, but you have to let your children live their own lives, isn't that right, Brice?"

"Yes," Grampa said, with a kind of horrified fascination.

"Ethan was always too busy for romance."

"Yes," Ethan said.

"Working and working and working for that transcription service. You must have typed a million words. Did you ever count them, Ethan?"

"Yes," Ethan said. "I typed roughly fifteen million words."

"Nowadays, of course, no one types. It's all talking to computers now. When I was a girl, they all said that you'd always have a job if you just learned to type. Times sure change, don't they?"

"Yes," Ethan and Grampa said together. Grampa startled like he'd been shocked.

"Dad's coming tomorrow?" Sean said.

Grampa said, "Yes. He's catching the SIX AM. He'll be here by ten."

"Isn't that *nice*," Adele said.

They left Grampa and Ethan sitting at the table together. Sean looked back over his shoulder before they got on the elevator, and Grampa was still switched on, staring hard at him.

"You must be *excited* about seeing your father again," Adele said to him when they were sitting around the pool.

Sean was getting the hang of talking to Adele. "Ethan and my grandfather seem to be hitting it off."

"Oh, I certainly *hope* so! Ethan could use some friends at that place."

Sean pictured the two of them, seated across from each other at the ward table, running maintenance routines at each other, saying, "Yes," "Yes." Unbidden, a grin came to Sean's face.

"Why did you put Ethan in the Home?" Sean asked, shifting to catch more sun on his face.

"He wanted to go," she said. "The doctor came by and told him about it and asked him if he wanted to go, and he said 'Yes.' That was it!"

Sean snuck a look at Adele. She was wincing into the light, following it like a sunflower. "Adele," he said.

"Yes, Sean?"

"Ethan was in maintenance mode. He was switched off. He said 'Yes,' because his subroutines didn't want to be any trouble. You know that, right?"

"Oh, that foolishness again! Ethan's a *good boy*, is all. He remembers my birthday and Mother's Day, every year."

"Subroutines, Adele," Sean said, straining to keep an inexplicable anger out of his voice.

"Humph! Subroutines!"

"Adele, he's a robot. He's a walking coma. He's been switched off for so long, all you're talking to is a goddamn *chip*, he's not a goddamn *person* anymore. None of them are. My goddamn *Grampa's* spent three-quarters of his goddamn life *away*. He's either an angry old bastard, or he's a goddamn *zombie*. You *know that*, right?"

"Sean, you're very upset," Adele said. "Why don't you have a nice lie-down, and we'll talk in the morning. I can't wait to meet your father!"

Sean stalked off to his room and tried to record some field notes while flipping around in the weird, poky corners of the motel's cable system, Japanese game-shows and Hindu religious epics. He smoked half a cigarette, drank half a beer, tried to masturbate, and finally, slept.

Adele rang his room-phone at eight. "Rise and shine, sunshine!" she said. "Your father will be at the airport in an hour!"

Sean dressed, but didn't bother shaving or brushing his teeth. He staggered out to his rental and gave Adele a sheepish grin. Acid churned in his gut.

Adele waited by the passenger door, in a pair of slacks and a light blouse. She had hung a pair of sunglasses around her neck on a gold chain, and carried an enormous sisal handbag. Staggering in the horrible daylight, Sean opened the passenger door for her, and offered his arm while she got in.

He put the car onto the Bee Line Expressway and pointed it at the airport.

"Oh, won't this be *fun*?" Adele said, as he ground the

crap from the corners of his eyes and steered with his knees. "I'm sure your father is *charming*. Maybe the five of us can go to Universal for an afternoon."

"I don't think we can take them off the ward," Sean grunted, changing lanes for the airport exit.

"You're probably right," Adele said. "I was just thinking that Universal might be enough to keep them both switched on."

Sean shot her a look and nearly missed his exit.

Adele rattled a laugh at him. "Don't look so surprised. I know which end is up!"

Sean pursed his lips and navigated the ramp-maze that guarded the airport. He pulled up to the loading zone at Air Canada arrivals and switched off the engine. He looked past Adele at the tourists jockeying for cabs. "I'm sorry about yesterday. I guess I'm a little wound up."

"Yesterday?" Adele said. "Oh! By the pool!" She put a frail hand on his forearm. "Sean, you don't get to my age by holding grudges. Ethan's father—*he* held grudges, and it killed him. Heart attack. He never forgave the doctors. I'm just happy to have a chauffeur."

Sean swallowed hard. "I'm sure that somewhere, Ethan knows that you're visiting him, that you love him. He's in there." He said it with all the sincerity he could muster.

"Maybe he is, maybe he isn't," Adele said. "But it makes me feel better. He's what I've got left. If you'd like, I'll wait with the car so you can go in and look for your father."

"No," Sean said. "That's all right. Dad'll come out for a cab. He's not the sort to dawdle."

"I like a decisive man. That's why I talked to you by the pool—you just jumped in, because you wanted a swim."

"Adele, that was *stupid*. It was like swimming in a urine sample."

"Same difference. I like a man who can make up his mind. That's what Ethan's father was like: decisive."

"You'll like my Dad," Sean said. He drummed his fingers on the wheel, then lowered and raised his window. He whistled tunelessly through his teeth. Adele gave him a considering stare and he stopped, and started in on powers of two in his head.

"There he is," Sean said, 2^{24} later.

Sean had barely been in Florida for three days, but it was long enough that his father seemed as pale as freezer-burned ice cream. Sean checked the traffic in his rear-view, then pulled across the waiting area to where his father stood, acing out an irate cabbie for the spot.

Sean's father glared at the car and started to walk behind it to the taxi. Sean leaned on the horn and his father stopped and stared. His expression was bland and grim and affectless.

Sean powered down Adele's window. "Dad!"

"Sean?" his father said.

Sean popped the locks. "Get in, Dad, I'll give you a ride."

Adele turned around as Sean's father was buckling in. "I'm Adele. Sean and I were thinking of taking you to Universal. Would you like that?"

Sean's father stared right through her, at Sean. "It's an obvious question, I know, but what are you doing here?"

"It's my thesis," Sean said, and floored the rental, headed for the Home.

"Whee!" Adele said.

"How's Grampa?" Sean's father asked.

"Oh, he's delightful," Adele said. "We introduced him to my Ethan yesterday, and they're getting along famously. Sean, introduce me to your charming father, please."

"Dad," Sean said, through gritted teeth, "this is Adele. Adele, my father, Mitch. We were thinking of getting day-passes for Grampa and Ethan and taking them to Universal. You ever been to Universal, Dad? I hear you come here down a lot." His normally fragmented attention was as focused as a laser, boring into his father through the rear-view.

His father's stern face refused to expose any of his confusion. "I don't think I want to go to Universal," he said.

"Oh, but it's *wonderful*," Adele gushed. "You shouldn't knock it until you've tried it."

"I don't think so," Sean's father repeated. "What's your thesis?"

Sean plunged headlong into the breach. "It's called 'The Tri-Generational Deficit: What's My Father's Excuse?' "

Sean's father nodded curtly. "And how's it going?"

"Well, you have to understand, I'm just warming up to the subject with Grampa. And then I'll have to do an interview series with you, of course."

"Did I miss something? When did I become the principal ogre in your pantheon? Are you angry at me?"

Sean barked a laugh and turned onto the Home's exitramp. "I guess I am, Dad. Grampa had the operation—it was *easy* for him to switch off. You needed to make a special effort." The words flew from his mouth like crows, and Sean clamped his jaw shut. He tensed for the inevitable scathe of verbiage. None came. He risked a glance in his rear-view.

His father was staring morosely out at the Home. Adele patted Sean's hand and gave him a sympathetic look. Sean parked the car.

"Hi, Pop," Sean's father said, when they came to the table where Grampa sat. Ethan sat across from him.

Grampa glared at them. "This guy won't leave me alone. He's a fucking vegetable," he said, gesturing at Ethan. Adele pursed her lips at him. He patted her arm absently. "It needed to be said."

Sean's father reached around the table and gave Grampa a stiff hug. "Good to see you, Pop."

"Yeah, likewise. Sit down, Mitch. Sit down, Sean. Sit down, Adele." They sat. "Ask your questions, Sean," he ordered.

Sean found himself tongue-tied. He heaved a deep breath and closed his eyes for a moment. He thought about why he was here: not the reason he'd given his thesis advisor, but the *real* goddamn reason. He wanted to *understand*— his father, himself. He wanted to reverse-engineer his fa-

ther's childhood. He looked at Ethan, slack as Grampa had
been whenever they'd visited. An inkling glimmered.
"Does Ethan scare you, Grampa?"

Adele *tsked* and scowled.

"Do I scare you, Mitch?" Grampa said, to Sean's father.

"Yes," Sean's father said.

"Yes," Grampa said. "Next question."

"Do you think that switching off is a sign of weakness?"
Sean said, sneaking a glance at his father, seeing his grandfather's features echoed in his father's face.

"Yes," his father said.

"Of course," his grandfather said.

"Then why?" Sean said.

"You know why," Ethan said, his eyes glittering.

They all swiveled to look at him. "Because the alterna-
tive is the purest shit," Ethan said, standing up, starting to
pace, almost shouting to make himself heard over the din
of the ward. "Because if you have to ask, you'll never understand. Because dessert is better than dinner, because the
cherry on top is the best part of the sundae. Because
strength is over-rated."

Grampa applauded briefly, sardonically. "Because holding your nose and taking your medicine is awful. Because
boredom is a suppurating wound on the mind. Because self-
discipline is over-rated. You getting all this, Sean?"

But Sean was watching his father, who was staring in
fascinated horror at Grampa. Nauseous regret suffused
Sean, as he saw his father's composure crumble. How many
times had he tried to shatter that deadly cool? And here
he'd done it. He'd really done it.

Still looking at his father, Sean said, "Do you ever wonder how it feels to rank below oblivion in someone's
book?"

Grampa spread his hands on the table. "I can't help it if
you take it personally."

Sean's father reeled back, and Sean swallowed a throb
of anger. "Of *course* not, Grampa. I understand. It's a reflex. The world's full of sops who'll take offense at any
little thing"—Lara shriveling under the heat of his tongue,

and him still watching the TV over her shoulder—"but it's a *reflex*. It's not conscious. It's no one's *fault*."

"Don't humor me," Grampa snapped. "I know what you all think of me. I can feel your goddamn blame. I can't *do* anything about it."

"You could apologize," Ethan said. Adele took his hand and wiped at her tears with its back.

"Fuck off, zombie," Grampa said, glaring at him.

Sean's father stood abruptly. "I'm glad to see you're in good health, Pop," he said. "Sean, thanks for the ride. I guess I'll see you once you've finished your research." His face was hard, composed. "Adele, nice to have met you."

"Likewise," Adele said.

"Bye, then," Sean's father said, and walked with dignified calm to the elevator.

"Bye, Dad," Sean called softly at his retreating back.

He turned back to Grampa, but Grampa's eyes were dull, and he was methodically twitching, top-to-bottom.

"Adele," Sean said, taking her free hand.

"Yes?" she said.

"How would you and Ethan like to come to Universal with me for the afternoon?"

"I'd love to," Ethan said. Sean looked at Ethan, and couldn't decide if he was switched off or not.

Whichever, Adele didn't seem to mind.

Border Guards

GREG EGAN

Internationally famous for his stories and novels, Greg Egan hit his stride in the early 1990s and became one of the two most interesting new hard SF writers of the decade (the other is Stephen Baxter). His first novel was published in 1983 but his writing burst into prominence in 1990 with several fine stories that focused attention on his writing and launched his books. His SF novels to date are Quarantine *(1992),* Permutation City *(1994),* Distress *(1995), and* Teranesia *(1999); his short story collections are* Our Lady of Chernobyl *(1995),* Axiomatic *(1995), and* Luminous *(1999). Significant indicators of his attitudes toward writing are the fact that he remains socially isolated from the SF field—no one has met him in person—and he has written a strongly-worded attack on national identities in SF. He does not identify himself as an Australian SF writer, but as a writer of SF in the English language who happens to live in Australia.*

"Border Guards," complex and complicated hard SF about humanity transformed, is what Egan is best known for. It appeared in Interzone, *where much of his best fiction has first appeared. It begins with an invented game, quantum soccer, that you might wish to learn more about later: http://www.netspace.net.au/~gregegan/BORDER/Soccer/ Soccer.html*

In the early afternoon of his fourth day out of sadness, Jamil was wandering home from the gardens at the centre of Noether when he heard shouts from the playing field behind the library. On the spur of the moment, without even asking the city what game was in progress, he decided to join in.

As he rounded the corner and the field came into view, it was clear from the movements of the players that they were in the middle of a quantum soccer match. At Jamil's request, the city painted the wave function of the hypothetical ball across his vision, and tweaked him to recognize the players as the members of two teams without changing their appearance at all. Maria had once told him that she always chose a literal perception of colour-coded clothing instead; she had no desire to use pathways that had evolved for the sake of sorting people into those you defended and those you slaughtered. But almost everything that had been bequeathed to them was stained with blood, and to Jamil it seemed a far sweeter victory to adapt the worst relics to his own ends than to discard them as irretrievably tainted.

The wave function appeared as a vivid auroral light, a quicksilver plasma bright enough to be distinct in the afternoon sunlight, yet unable to dazzle the eye or conceal the players running through it. Bands of colour representing the complex phase of the wave swept across the field, parting to wash over separate rising lobes of probability before hitting the boundary and bouncing back again, inverted.

The match was being played by the oldest, simplest rules: semi-classical, non-relativistic. The ball was confined to the field by an infinitely high barrier, so there was no question of it tunnelling out, leaking away as the match progressed. The players were treated classically: their movements pumped energy into the wave, enabling transitions from the game's opening state—with the ball spread thinly across the entire field—into the range of higher-energy modes needed to localize it. But localization was fleeting; there was no point forming a nice sharp wave packet in the middle of the field in the hope of kicking it around like a classical object. You had to shape the wave in such a way that all of its modes—cycling at different frequencies, travelling with different velocities—would come into phase with each other, for a fraction of a second, within the goal itself. Achieving that was a matter of energy levels, and timing.

Jamil had noticed that one team was under-strength. The umpire would be skewing the field's potential to keep the match fair, but a new participant would be especially welcome for the sake of restoring symmetry. He watched the faces of the players, most of them old friends. They were frowning with concentration, but breaking now and then into smiles of delight at their small successes, or their opponents' ingenuity.

He was badly out of practice, but if he turned out to be dead weight he could always withdraw. And if he misjudged his skills, and lost the match with his incompetence? No one would care. The score was nil all; he could wait for a goal, but that might be an hour or more in coming. Jamil communed with the umpire, and discovered that the players had decided in advance to allow new entries at any time.

Before he could change his mind, he announced himself. The wave froze, and he ran on to the field. People nodded greetings, mostly making no fuss, though Ezequiel shouted, "Welcome back!" Jamil suddenly felt fragile again; though he'd ended his long seclusion four days before, it was well within his power, still, to be dismayed by everything the game would involve. His recovery felt like a finely balanced optical illusion, a figure and ground that could change roles in an instant, a solid cube that could evert into a hollow.

The umpire guided him to his allotted starting position, opposite a woman he hadn't seen before. He offered her a formal bow, and she returned the gesture. This was no time for introductions, but he asked the city if she'd published a name. She had: Margit.

The umpire counted down in their heads. Jamil tensed, regretting his impulsiveness. For seven years he'd been dead to the world. After four days back, what was he good for? His muscles were incapable of atrophy, his reflexes could never be dulled, but he'd chosen to live with an unconstrained will, and at any moment his wavering resolve could desert him.

The umpire said, "Play." The frozen light around Jamil came to life, and he sprang into motion.

Each player was responsible for a set of modes, particular harmonics of the wave that were theirs to fill, guard, or deplete as necessary. Jamil's twelve modes cycled at between 1,000 and 1,250 milliHertz. The rules of the game endowed his body with a small, fixed potential energy, which repelled the ball slightly and allowed different modes to push and pull on each other through him, but if he stayed in one spot as the modes cycled, every influence he exerted would eventually be replaced by its opposite, and the effect would simply cancel itself out.

To drive the wave from one mode to another, you needed to move, and to drive it efficiently you needed to exploit the way the modes fell in and out of phase with each other: to take from a 1,000 milliHertz mode and give to a 1,250, you had to act in synch with the quarter-Hertz beat between them. It was like pushing a child's swing at its natural frequency, but rather than setting a single child in motion, you were standing between two swings and acting more as an intermediary: trying to time your interventions in such a way as to speed up one child at the other's expense. The way you pushed on the wave at a given time and place was out of your hands completely, but by changing location in just the right way you could gain control over the interaction. Every pair of modes had a spatial beat between them—like the moiré pattern formed by two sheets of woven fabric held up to the light together, shifting from transparent to opaque as the gaps between the threads fell in and out of alignment. Slicing through this cyclic landscape offered the perfect means to match the accompanying chronological beat.

Jamil sprinted across the field at a speed and angle calculated to drive two favourable transitions at once. He'd gauged the current spectrum of the wave instinctively, watching from the sidelines, and he knew which of the modes in his charge would contribute to a goal and which would detract from the probability. As he cut through the shimmering bands of colour, the umpire gave him tactile feedback to supplement his visual estimates and calculations, allowing him to sense the difference between a cyclic tug, a to and fro that came to nothing, and the gentle but persistent force that meant he was successfully riding the beat.

Chusok called out to him urgently, "Take, take! Two-ten!" Everyone's spectral territory overlapped with someone else's, and you needed to pass amplitude from player to player as well as trying to manage it within your own range. *Two-ten*—a harmonic with two peaks across the width of the field and ten along its length, cycling at 1,160 milliHertz—was filling up as Chusok drove unwanted amplitude from various lower-energy modes into it. It was Jamil's role to empty it, putting the amplitude somewhere useful. Any mode with an even number of peaks across the field was unfavourable for scoring, because it had a node— a zero point between the peaks—smack in the middle of both goals.

Jamil acknowledged the request with a hand signal and shifted his trajectory. It was almost a decade since he'd last played the game, but he still knew the intricate web of possibilities by heart: he could drain the two-ten harmonic into the three-ten, five-two and five-six modes—all with "good parity," peaks along the centre-line—in a single action.

As he pounded across the grass, carefully judging the correct angle by sight, increasing his speed until he felt the destructive beats give way to a steady force like a constant breeze, he suddenly recalled a time—centuries before, in another city—when he'd played with one team, week after week, for 40 years. Faces and voices swam in his head. Hashim, Jamil's 98th child, and Hashim's granddaughter Laila had played beside him. But he'd burnt his house and moved on, and when that era touched him at all now it was like an unexpected gift. The scent of the grass, the shouts of the players, the soles of his feet striking the ground, resonated with every other moment he'd spent the same way, bridging the centuries, binding his life together. He never truly felt the scale of it when he sought it out deliberately; it was always small things, tightly focused moments like this, that burst the horizon of his everyday concerns and confronted him with the astonishing vista.

The two-ten mode was draining faster than he'd expected; the see-sawing centre-line dip in the wave was vanishing before his eyes. He looked around, and saw Margit performing an elaborate Lissajous manoeuvre, smoothly orchestrating a dozen transitions at once. Jamil froze and watched her, admiring her virtuosity while he tried to decide what to do next; there was no point competing with her when she was doing such a good job of completing the task Chusok had set him.

Margit was his opponent, but they were both aiming for exactly the same kind of spectrum. The symmetry of the field meant that any scoring wave would work equally well for either side—but only one team could be the first to reap the benefit, the first to have more than half the wave's probability packed into their goal. So the two teams were obliged to co-operate at first, and it was only as the wave took shape from their combined efforts that it gradually became apparent which side would gain by sculpting it to perfection as rapidly as possible, and which would gain by spoiling it for the first chance, then honing it for the rebound.

Penina chided him over her shoulder as she jogged past, "You want to leave her to clean up four-six, as well?" She was smiling, but Jamil was stung; he'd been motionless for ten or fifteen seconds. It was not forbidden to drag your feet and rely on your opponents to do all the work, but it was regarded as a shamefully impoverished strategy. It was also very risky, handing them the opportunity to set up a wave that was almost impossible to exploit yourself.

He reassessed the spectrum, and quickly sorted through the alternatives. Whatever he did would have unwanted side effects; there was no magic way to avoid influencing modes in other players' territory, and any action that would drive the transitions he needed would also trigger a multitude of others, up and down the spectrum. Finally, he made a choice that would weaken the offending mode while causing as little disruption as possible.

Jamil immersed himself in the game, planning each transition two steps in advance, switching strategy halfway through a run if he had to, but staying in motion until the sweat dripped from his body, until his calves burned, until his blood sang. He wasn't blinded to the raw pleasures of the moment, or to memories of games past, but he let them wash over him, like the breeze that rose up and cooled his skin with no need for acknowledgement. Familiar voices shouted terse commands at him; as the wave came closer to a scoring spectrum every trace of superfluous conversation vanished, every idle glance gave way to frantic, purposeful gestures. To a bystander, this might have seemed like the height of dehumanization: 22 people reduced to grunting cogs in a pointless machine. Jamil smiled at the thought but refused to be distracted into a complicated imaginary rebuttal. Every step he took was the answer to that, every hoarse plea to Yann or Joracy, Chusok or Maria, Eudore or Halide. These were his friends, and he was back among them. Back in the world.

The first chance of a goal was 30 seconds away, and the opportunity would fall to Jamil's team; a few tiny shifts in amplitude would clinch it. Margit kept her distance, but Jamil could sense her eyes on him constantly—and literally feel her at work through his skin as she slackened his contact with the wave. In theory, by mirroring your opponent's movements at the correct position on the field you could undermine everything they did, though in practice not even the most skilful team could keep the spectrum completely frozen. Going further and spoiling was a tug of war you didn't want to win too well: if you degraded the wave too much, your opponent's task—spoiling your own subsequent chance at a goal—became far easier.

Jamil still had two bad-parity modes that he was hoping to weaken, but every time he changed velocity to try a new transition, Margit responded in an instant, blocking him. He gestured to Chusok for help; Chusok had his own problems with Ezequiel, but he could still make trouble for Margit by choosing where he placed unwanted amplitude. Jamil shook sweat out of his eyes; he could see the characteristic "stepping stone" pattern of lobes forming, a sign that the wave would soon converge on the goal, but from the middle of the field it was impossible to judge their shape accurately enough to know what, if anything, remained to be done.

Suddenly, Jamil felt the wave push against him. He didn't waste time looking around for Margit; Chusok must have succeeded in distracting her. He was almost at the boundary line, but he managed to reverse smoothly, continuing to drive both the transitions he'd been aiming for.

Two long lobes of probability, each modulated by a series of oscillating mounds, raced along the sides of the field. A third, shorter lobe running along the centre-line melted away, reappeared, then merged with the others as they touched the end of the field, forming an almost rectangular plateau encompassing the goal.

The plateau became a pillar of light, growing narrower and higher as dozens of modes, all finally in phase, crashed together against the impenetrable barrier of the field's boundary. A shallow residue was still spread across the entire field, and a diminishing sequence of elliptical lobes trailed away from the goal like a staircase, but most of the wave that had started out lapping around their waists was now concentrated in a single peak that towered above their heads, nine or ten metres tall.

For an instant, it was motionless.

Then it began to fall.

The umpire said, "Forty-nine point eight."

The wave packet had not been tight enough.

Jamil struggled to shrug off his disappointment and throw his instincts into reverse. The other team had 50 seconds, now, to fine-tune the spectrum and ensure that the reflected packet was just a fraction narrower when it reformed, at the opposite end of the field.

As the pillar collapsed, replaying its synthesis in reverse, Jamil caught sight of Margit. She smiled at him calmly, and it suddenly struck him: *She'd known they couldn't make the goal. That was why she'd stopped opposing him.* She'd let him work towards sharpening the wave for a few seconds, knowing that it was already too late for him, knowing that her own team would gain from the slight improvement.

Jamil was impressed; it took an extraordinary level of skill and confidence to do what she'd just done. For all the time he'd spent away, he knew exactly what to expect from the rest of the players, and in Margit's absence he would probably have been wishing out loud for a talented newcomer to make the game interesting again. Still, it was hard not to feel a slight sting of resentment. Someone should have warned him just how good she was.

With the modes slipping out of phase, the wave undulated all over the field again, but its reconvergence was inevitable: unlike a wave of water or sound, it possessed no hidden degrees of freedom to grind its precision into entropy. Jamil decided to ignore Margit; there were cruder strategies than mirror-blocking that worked almost as well. Chusok was filling the two-ten mode now; Jamil chose the four-six as his spoiler. All they had to do was keep the wave from growing much sharper, and it didn't matter whether they achieved this by preserving the status quo, or by nudging it from one kind of bluntness to another.

The steady resistance he felt as he ran told Jamil that he was driving the transition, unblocked, but he searched in vain for some visible sign of success. When he reached a vantage point where he could take in enough of the field in one glance to judge the spectrum properly, he noticed a rapidly vibrating shimmer across the width of the wave. He counted nine peaks: good parity. Margit had pulled most of the amplitude straight out of his spoiler mode and fed it into *this*. It was a mad waste of energy to aim for such an elevated harmonic, but no one had been looking there, no one had stopped her.

The scoring pattern was forming again, he only had nine or ten seconds left to make up for all the time he'd wasted. Jamil chose the strongest good-parity mode in his territory, and the emptiest bad one, computed the velocity that would link them, and ran.

He didn't dare turn to watch the opposition goal; he didn't want to break his concentration. The wave retreated around his feet, less like an Earthly ebb tide than an ocean drawn into the sky by a passing black hole. The city diligently portrayed the shadow that his body would have cast, shrinking in front of him as the tower of light rose.

The verdict was announced. "Fifty point one."

The air was filled with shouts of triumph—Ezequiel's the loudest, as always. Jamil sagged to his knees, laughing. It was a curious feeling, familiar as it was: he cared, and he didn't. If he'd been wholly indifferent to the outcome of the game there would have been no pleasure in it, but obsessing over every defeat—or every victory—could ruin it just as thoroughly. He could almost see himself walking the line, orchestrating his response as carefully as any action in the game itself.

He lay down on the grass to catch his breath before play resumed. The outer face of the microsun that orbited Laplace was shielded with rock, but light reflected skywards from the land beneath it crossed the 100,000 kilometre width of the 3-toroidal universe to give a faint glow to the planet's nightside. Though only a sliver was lit directly, Jamil could discern the full disc of the opposite hemisphere in the primary image at the zenith: continents and oceans that lay, by a shorter route, 12,000 or so kilometres beneath him. Other views in the lattice of images spread across the sky were from different angles, and showed substantial crescents of the dayside itself. The one thing you couldn't find in any of these images, even with a telescope, was your own city. The topology of this universe let you see the back of your head, but never your reflection.

Jamil's team lost, three nil. He staggered over to the fountains at the edge of the field and slaked his thirst, shocked by the pleasure of the simple act. Just to be alive was glorious now, but once he felt this way, anything seemed possible. He was back in synch, back in phase, and he was going to make the most of it, for however long it lasted.

He caught up with the others, who'd headed down towards the river. Ezequiel hooked an arm around his neck, laughing. "Bad luck, Sleeping Beauty! You picked the wrong time to wake. With Margit, we're invincible."

Jamil ducked free of him. "I won't argue with that." He looked around. "Speaking of whom—"

Penina said, "Gone home. She plays, that's all. No frivolous socializing after the match."

Chusok added, "Or any other time." Penina shot Jamil a glance that meant: not for want of trying on Chusok's part.

Jamil pondered this, wondering why it annoyed him so much. On the field, she hadn't come across as aloof and superior. Just unashamedly good.

He queried the city, but she'd published nothing besides her name. Nobody expected—or wished—to hear more than the tiniest fraction of another person's history, but it was rare for anyone to start a new life without carrying through something from the old as a kind of calling card, some incident or achievement from which your new neighbours could form an impression of you.

They'd reached the riverbank. Jamil pulled his shirt over his head. "So what's her story? She must have told you something."

Ezequiel said, "Only that she learnt to play a long time

ago; she won't say where or when. She arrived in Noether at the end of last year, and grew a house on the southern outskirts. No one sees her around much. No one even knows what she studies."

Jamil shrugged, and waded in. "Ah well. It's a challenge to rise to." Penina laughed and splashed him teasingly. He protested, "I *meant* beating her at the game."

Chusok said wryly, "When you turned up, I thought you'd be our secret weapon. The one player she didn't know inside out already."

"I'm glad you didn't tell me that. I would have turned around and fled straight back into hibernation."

"I know. That's why we all kept quiet." Chusok smiled. "Welcome back."

Penina said, "Yeah, welcome back, Jamil."

Sunlight shone on the surface of the river. Jamil ached all over, but the cool water was the perfect place to be. If he wished, he could build a partition in his mind at the point where he stood right now, and never fall beneath it. Other people lived that way, and it seemed to cost them nothing. Contrast was overrated; no sane person spent half their time driving spikes into their flesh for the sake of feeling better when they stopped. Ezequiel lived every day with the happy boisterousness of a five-year-old; Jamil sometimes found this annoying, but then any kind of disposition would irritate someone. His own stretches of meaningless sombreness weren't exactly a boon to his friends.

Chusok said, "I've invited everyone to a meal at my house tonight. Will you come?"

Jamil thought it over, then shook his head. He still wasn't ready. He couldn't force-feed himself with normality; it didn't speed his recovery, it just drove him backwards.

Chusok looked disappointed, but there was nothing to be done about that. Jamil promised him, "Next time. OK?"

Ezequiel sighed. "What are we going to do with you? You're worse than Margit!" Jamil started backing away, but it was too late. Ezequiel reached him in two casual strides, bent down and grabbed him around the waist, hoisted him effortlessly onto one shoulder, then flung him through the air into the depths of the river.

Jamil was woken by the scent of wood smoke. His room was still filled with the night's grey shadows, but when he propped himself up on one elbow and the window obliged him with transparency, the city was etched clearly in the predawn light.

He dressed and left the house, surprised at the coolness of the dew on his feet. No one else in his street seemed to be up; had they failed to notice the smell, or did they already know to expect it? He turned a corner and saw the rising column of soot, faintly lit with red from below. The flames and the ruins were still hidden from him, but he knew whose house it was.

When he reached the dying blaze, he crouched in the heat-withered garden, cursing himself. Chusok had offered him the chance to join him for his last meal in Noether. Whatever hints you dropped, it was customary to tell no one that you were moving on. If you still had a lover, if you still had young children, you never deserted them. But friends, you warned in subtle ways. Before vanishing.

Jamil covered his head with his arms. He'd lived through this countless times before, but it never became easier. If anything it grew worse, as every departure was weighted with the memories of others. His brothers and sisters had scattered across the branches of the New Territories. He'd walked away from his father and mother when he was too young and confident to realize how much it would hurt him, decades later. His own children had all abandoned him eventually, far more often than he'd left them. It was easier to leave an ex-lover than a grown child: something burned itself out in a couple, almost naturally, as if ancestral biology had prepared them for at least that one rift.

Jamil stopped fighting the tears. But as he brushed them away, he caught sight of someone standing beside him. He looked up. It was Margit.

He felt a need to explain. He rose to his feet and addressed her. "This was Chusok's house. We were good friends. I'd known him for 96 years."

Margit gazed back at him neutrally. "Boo hoo. Poor baby. You'll never see your friend again."

Jamil almost laughed, her rudeness was so surreal. He pushed on, as if the only conceivable, polite response was to pretend that he hadn't heard her. "No one is the kindest, the most generous, the most loyal. It doesn't matter. That's not the point. Everyone's unique. Chusok was Chusok." He banged a fist against his chest, utterly heedless now of her contemptuous words. "There's a hole in me, and it will never be filled." That was the truth, even though he'd grow around it. *He should have gone to the meal, it would have cost him nothing.*

"You must be a real emotional Swiss cheese," observed Margit tartly.

Jamil came to his senses. "Why don't you fuck off to some other universe? No one wants you in Noether."

Margit was amused. "You *are* a bad loser." Jamil gazed at her, honestly confused for a moment; the game had slipped his mind completely. He gestured at the embers. "What are you doing here? Why did you follow the smoke, if it wasn't regret at not saying goodbye to him when you had the chance?" He wasn't sure how seriously to take Penina's lighthearted insinuation, but if Chusok had fallen for Margit, and it had not been reciprocated, that might even have been the reason he'd left.

She shook her head calmly. "He was nothing to me. I barely spoke to him."

"Well, that's your loss."

"From the look of things, I'd say the loss was all yours."

He had no reply. Margit turned and walked away.

Jamil crouched on the ground again, rocking back and forth, waiting for the pain to subside.

Jamil spent the next week preparing to resume his studies. The library had near-instantaneous contact with every artificial universe in the New Territories, and the additional lightspeed lag between Earth and the point in space from which the whole tree-structure blossomed was only a few hours. Jamil had been to Earth, but only as a tourist; land was scarce, they accepted no migrants. There were remote planets you could live on, in the home universe, but you had to be a certain kind of masochistic purist to want that. The precise reasons why his ancestors had entered the New Territories had been forgotten generations before—and it would have been presumptuous to track them down and ask them in person—but given a choice between the then even-more-crowded Earth, the horrifying reality of interstellar distances, and an endlessly extensible branching chain of worlds which could be traversed within a matter of weeks, the decision wasn't exactly baffling.

Jamil had devoted most of his time in Noether to studying the category of representations of Lie groups on complex vector spaces—a fitting choice, since Emmy Noether had been a pioneer of group theory, and if she'd lived to see this field blossom she would probably have been in the thick of it herself. Representations of Lie groups lay behind most of physics: each kind of subatomic particle was really nothing but a particular way of representing the universal symmetry group as a set of rotations of complex vectors. Organizing this kind of structure with category theory was ancient knowledge, but Jamil didn't care; he'd long ago reconciled himself to being a student, not a discoverer. The greatest gift of consciousness was the ability to take the patterns of the world inside you, and for all that he would have relished the thrill of being the first at anything, with ten-to-the-sixteenth people alive that was a futile ambition for most.

In the library, he spoke with fellow students of his chosen field on other worlds, or read their latest works. Though they were not researchers, they could still put a new pedagogical spin on old material, enriching the connections with other fields, finding ways to make the complex, subtle truth easier to assimilate without sacrificing the depth and detail that made it worth knowing in the first place. They would not advance the frontiers of knowledge. They would not discover new principles of nature, or invent new technologies. But to Jamil, understanding was an end in itself.

He rarely thought about the prospect of playing another match, and when he did the idea was not appealing. With Chusok gone, the same group could play ten-to-a-side without Jamil to skew the numbers. Margit might even choose to swap teams, if only for the sake of proving that her current team's monotonous string of victories really had been entirely down to her.

When the day arrived, though, he found himself unable to stay away. He turned up intending to remain a spectator, but Ryuichi had deserted Ezequiel's team, and everyone begged Jamil to join in.

As he took his place opposite Margit, there was nothing in her demeanour to acknowledge their previous encounter: no lingering contempt, but no hint of shame either. Jamil resolved to put it out of his mind; he owed it to his fellow players to concentrate on the game.

They lost, five nil.

Jamil forced himself to follow everyone to Eudore's house, to celebrate, commiserate, or as it turned out, to forget the whole thing. After they'd eaten, Jamil wandered from room to room, enjoying Eudore's choice of music but unable to settle into any conversation. No one mentioned Chusok in his hearing.

He left just after midnight. Laplace's near-full primary image and its eight brightest gibbous companions lit the streets so well that there was no need for anything more. Jamil thought: Chusok might have merely travelled to another city, one beneath his gaze right now. And wherever he'd gone, he might yet choose to stay in touch with his friends from Noether.

And his friends from the next town, and the next?
Century after century?

Margit was sitting on Jamil's doorstep, holding a bunch of white flowers in one hand.

Jamil was irritated. "What are you doing here?"

"I came to apologize."

He shrugged. "There's no need. We feel differently about

certain things. That's fine. I can still face you on the playing field."

"I'm not apologizing for a difference of opinion. I wasn't honest with you. I was cruel." She shaded her eyes against the glare of the planet and looked up at him. "You were right: it was my loss. I wish I'd known your friend."

He laughed curtly. "Well, it's too late for that."

She said simply, "I know."

Jamil relented. "Do you want to come in?" Margit nodded, and he instructed the door to open for her. As he followed her inside, he said, "How long have you been here? Have you eaten?"

"No."

"I'll cook something for you."

"You don't have to do that."

He called out to her from the kitchen, "Think of it as a peace offering. I don't have any flowers."

Margit replied, "They're not for you. They're for Chusok's house."

Jamil stopped rummaging through his vegetable bins, and walked back into the living room. "People don't usually do that in Noether."

Margit was sitting on the couch, staring at the floor. She said, "I'm so lonely here. I can't bear it any more."

He sat beside her. "Then why did you rebuff him? You could at least have been friends."

She shook her head. "Don't ask me to explain."

Jamil took her hand. She turned and embraced him, trembling miserably. He stroked her hair. "Sssh."

She said, "Just sex. I don't want anything more."

He groaned softly. "There's no such thing as that."

"I just need someone to touch me again."

"I understand." He confessed, "So do I. But that won't be all. So don't ask me to promise there'll be nothing more."

Margit took his face in her hands and kissed him. Her mouth tasted of wood smoke.

Jamil said, "I don't even know you."

"No one knows anyone, anymore."

"That's not true."

"No, it's not," she conceded gloomily. She ran a hand lightly along his arm. Jamil wanted badly to see her smile, so he made each dark hair thicken and blossom into a violet flower as it passed beneath her fingers.

She did smile, but she said, "I've seen that trick before."

Jamil was annoyed. "I'm sure to be a disappointment all around, then. I expect you'd be happier with some kind of novelty. A unicorn, or an amoeba."

She laughed. "I don't think so." She took his hand and placed it against her breast. "Do you ever get tired of sex?"

"Do you ever get tired of breathing?"

"I can go for a long time without thinking about it."

He nodded. "But then one day you stop and fill your lungs with air, and it's still as sweet as ever."

Jamil didn't know what he was feeling anymore. Lust. Compassion. Spite. She'd come to him hurting, and he wanted to help her, but he wasn't sure that either of them really believed this would work.

Margit inhaled the scent of the flowers on his arm. "Are they the same colour? Everywhere else?"

He said, "There's only one way to find out."

Jamil woke in the early hours of the morning, alone. He'd half expected Margit to flee like this, but she could have waited till dawn. He would have obligingly feigned sleep while she dressed and tip-toed out.

Then he heard her. It was not a sound he would normally have associated with a human being, but it could not have been anything else.

He found her in the kitchen, curled around a table leg, wailing rhythmically. He stood back and watched her, afraid that anything he did would only make things worse. She met his gaze in the half light, but kept up the mechanical whimper. Her eyes weren't blank; she was not delirious, or hallucinating. She knew exactly who, and where, she was.

Finally, Jamil knelt in the doorway. He said, "Whatever it is, you can tell me. And we'll fix it. We'll find a way."

She bared her teeth. "You can't *fix it*, you stupid child." She resumed the awful noise.

"Then just tell me. Please?" He stretched out a hand towards her. He hadn't felt quite so helpless since his very first daughter, Aminata, had come to him as an inconsolable six-year-old, rejected by the boy to whom she'd declared her undying love. He'd been 24 years old; a child himself. More than a thousand years ago. *Where are you now, Nata?*

Margit said, "I promised. I'd never tell."

"Promised who?"

"Myself."

"Good. They're the easiest kind to break."

She started weeping. It was a more ordinary sound, but it was even more chilling. She was not a wounded animal now, an alien being suffering some incomprehensible pain. Jamil approached her cautiously; she let him wrap his arms around her shoulders.

He whispered, "Come to bed. The warmth will help. Just being held will help."

She spat at him derisively, "It won't bring her back."

"Who?"

Margit stared at him in silence, as if he'd said something shocking.

Jamil insisted gently, "Who won't it bring back?" She'd lost a friend, badly, the way he'd lost Chusok. That was why she'd sought him out. He could help her through it. They could help each other through it.

She said, "It won't bring back the dead."

Margit was seven thousand five hundred and ninety-four years old. Jamil persuaded her to sit at the kitchen table. He wrapped her in blankets, then fed her tomatoes and rice, as she told him how she'd witnessed the birth of his world.

The promise had shimmered just beyond reach for decades. Almost none of her contemporaries had believed it would happen, though the truth should have been plain for centuries: *the human body was a material thing*. In time, with enough knowledge and effort, it would become possible to safeguard it from any kind of deterioration, any kind of harm. Stellar evolution and cosmic entropy might or might not prove insurmountable, but there'd be aeons to confront those challenges. In the middle of the 21st century, the hurdles were aging, disease, violence, and an over-crowded planet.

"Grace was my best friend. We were students." Margit smiled. "Before everyone was a student. We'd talk about it, but we didn't believe we'd see it happen. It would come in another century. It would come for our great-great-grandchildren. We'd hold infants on our knees in our twilight years and tell ourselves: *this one will never die.*

"When we were both 22, something happened. To both of us." She lowered her eyes. "We were kidnapped. We were raped. We were tortured."

Jamil didn't know how to respond. These were just words to him: he knew their meaning, he knew these acts would have hurt her, but she might as well have been describing a mathematical theorem. He stretched a hand across the table, but Margit ignored it. He said awkwardly, "This was . . . the Holocaust?"

She looked up at him, shaking her head, almost laughing at his naïvete. "Not even one of them. Not a war, not a pogrom. Just one psychopathic man. He locked us in his basement, for six months. He'd killed seven women." Tears began spilling down her cheeks. "He showed us the bodies. They were buried right where we slept. He showed us how we'd end up, when he was through with us."

Jamil was numb. He'd known all his adult life what had once been possible—what had once happened, to real people—but it had all been consigned to history long before his birth. In retrospect it seemed almost inconceivably stupid, but he'd always imagined that the changes had come in such a way that no one still living had experienced these horrors. There'd been no escaping the bare minimum, the logical necessity: his oldest living ancestors must have watched their parents fall peacefully into eternal sleep. But not this. Not a flesh-and-blood woman, sitting in front of him, who'd been forced to sleep in a killer's graveyard.

He put his hand over hers, and choked out the words. "This man . . . *killed* Grace? He killed your friend?"

Margit began sobbing, but she shook her head. "No, no. We got out!" She twisted her mouth into a smile. "Someone stabbed the stupid fucker in a bar-room brawl. We dug our way out while he was in hospital." She put her face down on the table and wept, but she held Jamil's hand against her cheek. He couldn't understand what she'd lived through, but that didn't mean he couldn't console her. Hadn't he touched his mother's face the same way, when she was sad beyond his childish comprehension?

She composed herself, and continued. "We made a resolution, while we were in there. If we survived, there'd be no more empty promises. No more day dreams. What he'd done to those seven women—and what he'd done to us— would become impossible."

And it had. Whatever harm befell your body, you had the power to shut off your senses and decline to experience it. If the flesh was damaged, it could always be repaired or replaced. In the unlikely event that your jewel itself was destroyed, everyone had backups, scattered across universes. No human being could inflict physical pain on another. In theory, you could still be killed, but it would take the same kind of resources as destroying a galaxy. The only people who seriously contemplated either were the villains in very bad operas.

Jamil's eyes narrowed in wonder. She'd spoken those last words with such fierce pride that there was no question of her having failed.

"*You* are Ndoli? You invented the jewel?" As a child, he'd been told that the machine in his skull had been designed by a man who'd died long ago.

Margit stroked his hand, amused. "In those days, very few Hungarian women could be mistaken for Nigerian men. I've never changed my body that much, Jamil. I've always looked much as you see me."

Jamil was relieved; if she'd been Ndoli himself, he might have succumbed to sheer awe and started babbling idolatrous nonsense. "But you worked with Ndoli? You and Grace?"

She shook her head. "We made the resolution, and then

we floundered. We were mathematicians, not neurologists. There were a thousand things going on at once: tissue engineering, brain imaging, molecular computers. We had no real idea where to put our efforts, which problems we should bring our strengths to bear upon. Ndoli's work didn't come out of the blue for us, but we played no part in it.

"For a while, almost everyone was nervous about switching from the brain to the jewel. In the early days, the jewel was a separate device that learned its task by mimicking the brain, and it had to be handed control of the body at one chosen moment. It took another 50 years before it could be engineered to replace the brain incrementally, neuron by neuron, in a seamless transition throughout adolescence."

So Grace had lived to see the jewel invented, but held back, and died before she could use it? Jamil kept himself from blurting out this conclusion; all his guesses had proved wrong so far.

Margit continued. "Some people weren't just nervous, though. You'd be amazed how vehemently Ndoli was denounced in certain quarters. And I don't just mean the fanatics who churned out paranoid tracts about 'the machines' taking over, with their evil inhuman agendas. Some people's antagonism had nothing to do with the specifics of the technology. They were opposed to immortality, in principle."

Jamil laughed. *"Why?"*

"Ten thousand years' worth of sophistry doesn't vanish overnight," Margit observed dryly. "Every human culture had expended vast amounts of intellectual effort on the problem of coming to terms with death. Most religions had constructed elaborate lies about it, making it out to be something other than it was—though a few were dishonest about life, instead. But even most secular philosophies were warped by the need to pretend that *death was for the best*.

"It was the naturalistic fallacy at its most extreme—and its most transparent, but that didn't stop anyone. Since any child could tell you that death was meaningless, contingent, unjust, and abhorrent beyond words, it was a hallmark of

sophistication to believe otherwise. Writers had consoled
themselves for centuries with smug puritanical fables about
immortals who'd long for death—who'd *beg* for death. It
would have been too much to expect all those who were
suddenly faced with the reality of its banishment to confess
that they'd been whistling in the dark. And would-be moral
philosophers—mostly those who'd experienced no greater
inconvenience in their lives than a late train or a surly
waiter—began wailing about the destruction of the human
spirit by this hideous blight. We needed death and suffering, to put steel into our souls! Not horrible, horrible *freedom and safety!"*

Jamil smiled. "So there were buffoons. But in the end,
surely they swallowed their pride? If we're walking in a
desert and I tell you that the lake you see ahead is a mirage,
I might cling stubbornly to my own belief, to save myself
from disappointment. But when we arrive, and I'm proven
wrong, I *will* drink from the lake."

Margit nodded. "Most of the loudest of these people
went quiet in the end. But there were subtler arguments,
too. Like it or not, all our biology and all of our culture
had evolved in the presence of death. And almost every
righteous struggle in history, every worthwhile sacrifice,
had been against suffering, against violence, against death.
Now, that struggle would become impossible."

"Yes." Jamil was mystified. "But only because it had
triumphed."

Margit said gently, "I know. There was no sense to it.
And it was always my belief that anything worth fighting
for—over centuries, over millennia—was worth attaining.
It *can't* be noble to toil for a cause, and even to die for it,
unless it's also noble to succeed. To claim otherwise isn't
sophistication, it's just a kind of hypocrisy. If it's better to
travel than arrive, you shouldn't start the voyage in the first
place.

"I told Grace as much, and she agreed. We laughed together at what we called the *tragedians*: the people who
denounced the coming age as the age without martyrs, the
age without saints, the age without revolutionaries. There

would never be another Gandhi, another Mandela, another Aung San Suu Kyi—and yes, that *was* a kind of loss, but would any great leader have sentenced humanity to eternal misery, for the sake of providing a suitable backdrop for eternal heroism? Well, some of them would have. But the down-trodden themselves had better things to do."

Margit fell silent. Jamil cleared her plate away, then sat opposite her again. It was almost dawn.

"Of course, the jewel was not enough," Margit continued. "With care, Earth could support 40 billion people, but where would the rest go? The jewel made virtual reality the easiest escape route: for a fraction of the space, a fraction of the energy, it could survive without a body attached. Grace and I weren't horrified by that prospect, the way some people were. But it was not the best outcome, it was not what most people wanted, the way they wanted freedom from death.

"So we studied gravity, we studied the vacuum."

Jamil feared making a fool of himself again, but from the expression on her face he knew he wasn't wrong this time. *M. Osvát and G. Füst.* Co-authors of the seminal paper, but no more was known about them than those abbreviated names. "You gave us the New Territories?"

Margit nodded slightly. "Grace and I."

Jamil was overwhelmed with love for her. He went to her and knelt down to put his arms around her waist. Margit touched his shoulder. "Come on, get up. Don't treat me like a god, it just makes me feel old."

He stood, smiling abashedly. Anyone in pain deserved his help—but if he was not in her debt, the word had no meaning.

"And Grace?" he asked.

Margit looked away. "Grace completed her work, and then decided that she was a tragedian, after all. Rape was impossible. Torture was impossible. Poverty was vanishing. Death was receding into cosmology, into metaphysics. It was everything she'd hoped would come to pass. And for her, suddenly faced with that fulfilment, everything that remained seemed trivial.

"One night, she climbed into the furnace in the basement of her building. Her jewel survived the flames, but she'd erased it from within."

It was morning now. Jamil was beginning to feel disoriented; Margit should have vanished in daylight, an apparition unable to persist in the mundane world.

"I'd lost other people who were close to me," she said. "My parents. My brother. Friends. And so had everyone around me, then. I wasn't special: grief was still commonplace. But decade by decade, century by century, we shrank into insignificance, those of us who knew what it meant to lose someone for ever. We're less than one in a million, now.

"For a long time, I clung to my own generation. There were enclaves, there were ghettos, where everyone understood the old days. I spent 200 years married to a man who wrote a play called *We Who Have Known the Dead*—which was every bit as pretentious and self-pitying as you'd guess from the title." She smiled at the memory. "It was a horrible, self-devouring world. If I'd stayed in it much longer, I would have followed Grace. I would have begged for death."

She looked up at Jamil. "It's people like you I want to be with: *people who don't understand.* Your lives aren't trivial, any more than the best parts of our own were: all the tranquility, all the beauty, all the happiness that made the sacrifices and the life-and-death struggles worthwhile.

"The tragedians were wrong. They had everything upside-down. Death never gave meaning to life: it was always the other way round. All of its gravitas, all of its significance, was stolen from the things it ended. But the value of life always lay entirely in itself—not in its loss, not in its fragility.

"Grace should have lived to see that. She should have lived long enough to understand that the world hadn't turned to ash."

Jamil sat in silence, turning the whole confession over in his mind, trying to absorb it well enough not to add to her distress with a misjudged question. Finally, he ventured, "Why do you hold back from friendship with us, though? Because we're just children to you? Children who can't understand what you've lost?"

Margit shook her head vehemently. "I don't *want you* to understand! People like me are the only blight on this world, the only poison." She smiled at Jamil's expression of anguish, and rushed to silence him before he could swear that she was nothing of the kind. "Not in everything we do and say, or everyone we touch: I'm not claiming that we're tainted, in some fatuous mythological sense. But when I left the ghettos, I promised myself that I wouldn't bring the past with me. Sometimes that's an easy vow to keep. Sometimes it's not."

"You've broken it tonight," Jamil said plainly. "And neither of us have been struck down by lightning."

"I know." She took his hand. "But I was wrong to tell you what I have, and I'll fight to regain the strength to stay silent. I stand at the border between two worlds, Jamil. I remember death, and I always will. But my job now is to guard that border. To keep that knowledge from invading your world."

"We're not as fragile as you think," he protested. "We all know something about loss."

Margit nodded soberly. "Your friend Chusok was vanished into the crowd. That's how things work now: how you keep yourselves from suffocating in a jungle of endlessly growing connections, or fragmenting into isolated troupes of repertory players, endlessly churning out the same lines.

"You have your little deaths—and I don't call them that to deride you. But I've seen both. And I promise you, they're not the same."

In the weeks that followed, Jamil resumed in full the life he'd made for himself in Noether. Five days in seven were for the difficult beauty of mathematics. The rest were for his friends.

He kept playing matches, and Margit's team kept winning. In the sixth game, though, Jamil's team finally scored against her. Their defeat was only three to one.

Each night, Jamil struggled with the question. What exactly did he owe her? Eternal loyalty, eternal silence, eternal obedience? She hadn't sworn him to secrecy; she'd extracted no promises at all. But he knew she was trusting him to comply with her wishes, so what right did he have to do otherwise?

Eight weeks after the night he'd spent with Margit, Jamil found himself alone with Penina in a room in Joracy's house. They'd been talking about the old days. Talking about Chusok.

Jamil said, "Margit lost someone, very close to her."

Penina nodded matter-of-factly, but curled into a comfortable position on the couch and prepared to take in every word.

"Not in the way we've lost Chusok. Not in the way you think at all."

Jamil approached the others, one by one. His confidence ebbed and flowed. He'd glimpsed the old world, but he couldn't pretend to have fathomed its inhabitants. What if Margit saw this as worse than betrayal—as a further torture, a further rape?

But he couldn't stand by and leave her to the torture she'd inflicted on herself.

Ezequiel was the hardest to face. Jamil spent a sick and sleepless night beforehand, wondering if this would make him a monster, a corrupter of children, the epitome of everything Margit believed she was fighting.

Ezequiel wept freely, but he was not a child. He was older than Jamil, and he had more steel in his soul than any of them.

He said, "I guessed it might be that. I guessed she might have seen the bad times. But I never found a way to ask her."

The three lobes of probability converged, melted into a plateau, rose into a pillar of light.

The umpire said, "Fifty-five point nine." It was Margit's most impressive goal yet.

Ezequiel whooped joyfully and ran towards her. When he scooped her up in his arms and threw her across his shoulders, she laughed and indulged him. When Jamil stood beside him and they made a joint throne for her with their arms, she frowned down at him and said, "You shouldn't be doing this. You're on the losing side."

The rest of the players converged on them, cheering, and they started down towards the river. Margit looked around nervously. "What is this? We haven't finished playing."

Penina said, "The game's over early, just this once. Think of this as an invitation. We want you to swim with us. We want you to talk to us. We want to hear everything about your life."

Margit's composure began to crack. She squeezed Jamil's shoulder. He whispered, "Say the word, and we'll put you down."

Margit didn't whisper back; she shouted miserably, "What do you want from me, you parasites? I've won your fucking game for you! What more do you want?"

Jamil was mortified. He stopped and prepared to lower her, prepared to retreat, but Ezequiel caught his arm.

Ezequiel, said, "We want to be your border guards. We want to stand beside you."

Christa added, "We can't face what you've faced, but we want to understand. As much as we can."

Joracy spoke, then Yann, Narcyza, Maria, Halide. Margit looked down on them, weeping, confused.

Jamil burnt with shame. He'd hijacked her, humiliated her. He'd made everything worse. She'd flee Noether, flee into a new exile, more alone than ever.

When everyone had spoken, silence descended. Margit trembled on her throne.

Jamil faced the ground. He couldn't undo what he'd done. He said quietly, "Now you know our wishes. Will you tell us yours?"

"Put me down."

Jamil and Ezequiel complied.

Margit looked around at her teammates and opponents, her children, her creation, her would-be friends.

She said, "I want to go to the river with you. I'm seven thousand years old, and I want to learn to swim."

Macs

TERRY BISSON

When Terry Bisson writes science fiction, it is full of detail
and fascination with how things work, with deadpan humor,
wit, and stylish grace. And nearly all his work in whatever
genre is social criticism on some level. Of his SF novels,
Voyage to the Red Planet *is perhaps both the most heroic
and the funniest chronicle of the first voyage to Mars in all
science fiction. His* Fire on the Mountain *is an unconventional alternate history utopia. And* Pirates of the Universe
*is a vision of the impact of the SF future on an average
guy just trying to get by and maybe take charge of his life
in a world he didn't make. In the 1990s Bisson began to
write short stories and hit the ground running. One of his
first was "Bears Discover Fire," which won the Hugo and
Nebula Awards, and several others. His short fiction was
a regular fixture on award ballots throughout the decade.
Bisson's short fiction appeared with some regularity in*
Playboy, Asimov's, *and* Fantasy & Science Fiction. *His
first story collection,* Bears Discover Fire, *was published in
1993 and a new collection,* In the Upper Room, *in 2000.*

*Terry Bisson just keeps writing his own way and like no
one else—except the experience is often like reading Mark
Twain or Kurt Vonnegut. This is nowhere more so than in*

"Macs,"   which   has   reverberations   with   Twain's Puddn'head Wilson *and William Tenn's classic "Time in Advance." "Macs" appeared in the 50th Anniversary issue of* F&SF.

What did I think? Same thing I think today. I thought it was slightly weird even if it was legal. But I guess I agreed with the families that there had to be Closure. Look out that window there. I can guarantee you, it's unusual to be so high in Oklahoma City. Ever since it happened, this town has had a thing about tall buildings. It's almost like that son of a bitch leveled this town.

Hell, we wanted Closure too, but they had a court order all the way from the Supreme Court. I thought it was about politics at first, and I admit I was a little pissed. Don't use the word pissed. What paper did you say you were with?

Never heard of it, but that's me. Anyway, I was miffed— is that a word? miffed?—until I understood it was about Victims' Rights. So we canceled the execution, and built the vats, and you know the rest.

Well, if you want to know the details you should start with my assistant warden at the time, who handled the details. He's now the warden. Tell him I sent you. Give him my regards.

I thought it opened a Pandora's box, and I said so at the time. It turns out of course that there haven't been that many, and none on that scale. The ones that there are, we get them all. We're the sort of Sloan-Ketterings of the thing. See that scum on the vats? You're looking at eleven of the guy who abducted the little girls in Ohio, the genital mutilation thing, remember? Even eleven's unusual. We usually build four, maybe five tops. And never anything on the scale of the macs.

Build, grow, whatever. If you're interested in the technology, you'll have to talk with the vat vet himself. That's what we call him, he's a good old boy. He came in from the ag school for the macs and he's been here in Corrections ever since. He was an exchange student, but he met a girl from MacAlester and never went home. Isn't it funny how that stuff works? She was my second cousin, so now I have a Hindu second cousin-in-law. Of course he's not actually a Hindu.

A Unitarian, actually. There are several of us here in MacAlester, but I'm the only one from the prison. I was fresh out of Ag and it was my first assignment. How would one describe such an assignment? In my country, we had no such . . . well, you know. It was repellent and fascinating at the same time.

Everyone has the cloning technology. It's the growth rate that gives difficulty. Animals grow to maturity so much faster, and we had done significant work. Six-week cattle, ten-day ducks. Gene tweaking. Enzyme accelerators. They wanted full-grown macs in two and a half years; we gave them 168 thirty-year-old men in eleven months! I used to come down here and watch them grow. Don't tell anyone, especially my wife, Jean, but I grew sort of fond of them.

Hard? It was hard, I suppose, but farming is hard too if you think about it. A farmer may love his hogs but he ships them off, and we all know what for.

You should ask legal services about that. That wasn't part of my operation. We had already grown 168 and I had to destroy one before he was even big enough to walk, just so they could include the real one. Ask me if I appreciated that!

It was a second court order. It came through after the macs were in the vats. Somebody's bright idea in Justice. I suppose they figured it would legitimize the whole operation to include the real McCoy, so to speak, but then somebody has to decide who gets him. Justice didn't want any part of that and neither did we, so we brought in one of those outfits that run lotteries, because that's what it was, a lottery, but kind of a strange one, if you know what I mean.

Strange in that the winner wasn't supposed to know if he won or not. He or she. It's like the firing squad, where nobody knows who has the live bullets. Nobody is supposed to know who gets the real one. I'm sure it's in the records somewhere, but that stuff's all sealed. What magazine did you say you were with?

Sealed? It's destroyed. That was part of the contract. I guess whoever numbered the macs would know, but that was five years ago and it was done by lot anyway. It could probably be figured out by talking to the drivers who did the deliveries, or the drivers who picked up the remains, or even the families themselves. But it would be illegal, wouldn't it? Unethical, too, if you ask me, since it would interfere with what the whole thing was about, which was Closure. Victims' Rights. That's why we were hired, to keep it secret, and that's what we did. End of story.

UPS was a natural because we had just acquired Con Tran and were about to go into the detainee delivery business under contract with the BOP. The macs were mostly local, of course, but not all. Several went out of state; two to California, for example. It wasn't a security problem since the macs were all sort of docile. I figured they were engineered that way. Is engineered the word? Anyway, the problem was public relations. Appearances, to be frank. You can't drive around with a busload of macs. And most families don't want the TV and papers at the door, like Publishers Clearing House. (Though some do!) So we delivered them in vans, two and three at a time, mostly in the morning, sort of on the sly. We told the press we were still working out the details until it was all done. Some people videotaped their delivery. I suspect they're the ones that also videotaped their executions.

I'm not one of those who had a problem with the whole thing. No sirree. I went along with my drivers, at first especially, and met quite a few of the loved ones, and I wish you could have seen the grateful expressions on their faces. You get your own mac to kill any way you want to. That's Closure. It made me proud to be an American even though it came out of a terrible tragedy. An unspeakable tragedy.

Talk to the drivers all you want to. What channel did you say you were with?

You wouldn't have believed the publicity at the time. It was a big triumph for Victims' Rights, which is now in the Constitution, isn't it? Maybe I'm wrong. Anyway, it wasn't a particularly what you might call pleasant job, even though I was all for the families and Closure and stuff and still am.

Looked like anybody. Looked like you except for the beard. None of them were different. They were all the same. One of them was supposedly the real McCoy, but so what? Isn't the whole point of cloning supposed to be that each one is the same as the first one? Nobody's ever brought this up before. You're not from one of those talk shows, are you?

They couldn't have talked to us if they had wanted to, and we weren't about to talk to them. They were all taped up except for the eyes, and you should have seen those eyes. You tried to avoid it. I had one that threw up all over my truck even though theoretically you can't throw up through that tape. I told the dispatcher my truck needed a theoretical cleaning.

They all seemed the same to me. Sort of panicked and gloomy. I had a hard time hating them, in spite of what they done, or their daddy done, or however you want to put it. They say they could only live five years anyway before their insides turned to mush. That was no problem of course. Under the Victims' Rights settlement it had to be done in thirty days, that was from date of delivery.

I delivered thirty-four macs, of 168 altogether. I met

thirty-four fine families, and they were a fine cross-section of American life, black and white, Catholic and Protestant. Not so many Jews.

I've heard that rumor. You're going to have rumors like that when one of them is supposedly the real McCoy. There were other rumors too, like that one of the macs was pardoned by its family and sent away to school somewhere. That would have been hard. I mean, if you got a mac you had to return a body within thirty days. One story I heard was that they switched bodies after a car wreck. Another was that they burned another body at the stake and turned it in. But that one's hard to believe too. Only one of the macs was burned at the stake, and they had to get a special clearance to do that. Hell, you can't even burn leaves in Oklahoma anymore.

SaniMed collected, they're a medical waste outfit, since we're not allowed to handle remains. They're not going to be able to tell you much. What did they pick up? Bones and ashes. Meat.

Some of it was pretty gruesome but in this business you get used to that. We weren't supposed to have to bag them, but you know how it is. The only one that really got to me was the crucifixion. That sent the wrong message, if you ask me.

There was no way we could tell which one of them was the real McCoy, not from what we picked up. You should talk to the loved ones. Nice people, maybe a little impatient sometimes. The third week was the hardest in terms of scheduling. People had been looking forward to Closure for so long, they played with their macs for a week or so, but then it got old. Played is not the word, but you know what I mean. Then it's bang bang and honey call SaniMed. They want them out of the house ASAP.

It's not that we were slow, but the schedule was heavy. In terms of what we were picking up, none of it was that hard for me. These were not people. Some of them were pretty chewed up. Some of them were chewed up pretty bad.

I'm not allowed to discuss individual families. I can say this: the ceremony, the settlement, the execution, whatever you want to call it, wasn't always exactly what everybody had expected or wanted. One family even wanted to let their mac go. Since they couldn't do that, they wanted a funeral. A funeral for toxic waste!

I can't give you their name or tell you their number.

I guess I can tell you that. It was between 103 and 105.

I'm not ashamed of it. We're Christians. Forgive us our trespasses as we forgive those who trespass against us. We tried to make it legal, but the state wouldn't hear of it, since the execution order had already been signed. We had thirty days, so we waited till the last week and then used one of those Kevorkian kits, the lethal objection thing. Injection, I mean. The doctor came with it but we had to push the plunger thing. It seems to me like one of the rights of Victims' Rights should be—but I guess not.

There was a rumor that another family forgave and got away with it, but we never met them. They supposedly switched bodies in a car wreck and sent their mac to forestry school in Canada. Even if it was true, which I doubt, he would be almost five now, and that's half their life span. Supposedly their internal organs harden after ten years. What agency did you say you were with?

We dropped ours out of an airplane. My uncle has a big ranch out past Mayfield with his own airstrip and everything. Cessna 172. It was illegal, but what are they going to do? C'est la vie, or rather c'est la mort. Or whatever.

They made us kill him. Wasn't he ours to do with as we liked? Wasn't that the idea? He killed my daddy like a dog and if I wanted to tie him up like a dog, isn't that my business? Aren't you a little long in the tooth to be in college, boy?

An electric chair. It's out in the garage. Want to see it? Still got the shit stain on the seat.

My daddy came home with a mac, and took my mother and me out back and made us watch while he shot him. Shot him all over, from the feet up. The whole thing took ten minutes. It didn't seem to do anybody any good, my aunt is still dead. They never found most of her, only the bottom of a leg. Would you like some chocolates? They're from England.

Era? It was only like five years ago. I never took delivery. I thought I was the only one but I found out later there were eight others. I guess they just put them back in the vat. They couldn't live more than five years anyway. Their insides turned hard. All their DNA switches were shut off or something.

I got my own Closure my own way. That's my daughter's picture there. As for the macs, they are all dead. Period. They lived a while, suffered and died. Is it any different for the rest of us? What church did you say you were with?

I don't mind telling you our real name, but you should call us 49 if you quote us. That's the number we had in the lottery. We got our mac on a Wednesday, kept him for a week, then set him in a kitchen chair and shot him in the head. We didn't have any idea how messy that would be. The state should have given some instructions or guidelines.

Nobody knew which one was the original, and that's the way it should be. Otherwise it would ruin the Closure for everybody else. I can tell you ours wasn't, though. It was just a feeling I had. That's why we just shot him and got it over with. I just couldn't get real excited about killing something that seemed barely alive, even though it supposedly had all his feelings and memories. But some people got into it and attended several executions. They had a kind of network.

Let me see your list. These two are the ones I would definitely talk to: 112 and 43. And maybe 13.

Is that what they call us, 112? So I'm just a number again. I thought I was through with that in the army. I figured we had the real one, the real McCoy, because he was so hard to kill. We cut him up with a chain saw, a little Homelite. No sir, I didn't mind the mess and yes, he hated every minute of it. All twenty some odd which is how long it took. I would have fed him to my dogs if we hadn't had to turn the body in. End of fucking story.

Oh, yeah. Double the pleasure, double the fun. Triple it, really. The only one I was against was this one, 61. The crucifixion. I think that sent the wrong message, but the neighbors loved it.

Drown in the toilet was big. Poison, fire, hanging, you name it. People got these old books from the library but that medieval stuff took special equipment. One guy had a rack built but the neighbors objected to the screaming. I guess there are some limits, even to Victims' Rights. Ditto the stake stuff.

I'm sure our mac wasn't the real McCoy. You want to know why? He was so quiet and sad. He just closed his eyes and died. I'm sure the real one would have been harder to kill. My mac wasn't innocent, but he wasn't guilty either. Even though he looked like a thirty-year-old man he was only eighteen months old, and that sort of showed.

I killed him just to even things out. Not revenge, just Closure. After spending all the money on the court case and the settlement, not to mention the cloning and all, the deliveries, it would have been wasteful not to do it, don't you think?

I've heard that surviving thing but it's just a rumor. Like Elvis. There were lots of rumors. They say one family tried to pardon their mac and send him to Canada or somewhere. I don't think so!

You might try this one, 43. They used to brag that they

had the real one. I don't mind telling you I resented that and still do, since we were supposed to all share equally in the Closure. But some people have to be number one.

It's over now anyway. What law firm did you say you worked for?

I could tell he was the original by the mean look in his eye. He wasn't quite so mean after a week in that rat box.

Some people will always protest and write letters and such. But what about something that was born to be put to death? How can you protest that?

Closure, that's what it was all about. I went on to live my life. I've been married again and divorced already. What college did you say you were from?

The real McCoy? I think he just kept his mouth shut and died like the rest of them. What's he goin' to say, here I am, and make it worse? And as far as that rumor of him surviving, you can file it under Elvis.

There was also a story that somebody switched bodies after a car wreck and sent their mac to Canada. I wouldn't put too much stock in that one, either. Folks around here don't even think about Canada. Forgiveness either.

We used that state kit, the Kevorkian thing. I heard about twenty families did. We just sat him down and May pushed the plunger. Like flushing a toilet. May and myself—she's gone now, God bless her—we were interested in Closure, not revenge.

This one, 13, told me one time he thought he had the real McCoy, but it was wishful thinking, if you ask me. I don't think you could tell the real one. I don't think you should want to even if you could.

I'm afraid you can't ask him about it, because they were all killed in a fire, the whole family. It was just a day before the ceremony they had planned, which was some sort of slow thing with wires. There was a gas leak or something. They were all killed and their mac was destroyed in the explosion. Fire and explosion. What insurance company did you say you worked for?

It was—have you got a map? oooh, that's a nice one—right here. On the corner of Oak and Increase, only a half a mile from the site of the original explosion, ironically. The house is gone now.

See that new strip mall? That Dollar Store's where the house stood. The family that lived in it was one of the ones that lost a loved one in the Oklahoma City bombing. They got one of the macs as part of the Victims' Rights Closure Settlement, but unfortunately tragedy struck them again before they got to get Closure. Funny how the Lord works in mysterious ways.

No, none of them are left. There was a homeless guy who used to hang around but the police ran him off. Beard like yours. Might have been a friend of the family, some crazy cousin, who knows. So much tragedy they had. Now he lives in the back of the mall in a dumpster.

There. That yellow thing. It never gets emptied. I don't know why the city doesn't remove it but it's been there for almost five years just like that.

I wouldn't go over there. People don't fool with him. He doesn't bother anybody, but, you know.

Suit yourself. If you knock on it he'll come out, figuring you've got some food for him or something. Kids do it for meanness sometimes. But stand back, there is a smell.

"Daddy?"

Written in Blood

CHRIS LAWSON

Chris Lawson is a relatively new writer who has published several times in Eidolon, *now the leading Australian magazine in the F&SF genre, and in the ambitious original anthology,* Dreaming Down Under *(1998). Now a medical doctor in Melbourne, he grew up in New Guinea on a crocodile farm. He says, "The writers who have most influenced me are the ideas men in SF: Bester, Asimov, Clarke, and Benford. It was George Turner, though, who showed me that it was possible to conjoin ideas and traditional narrative values, and I wish I'd had an opportunity to thank him properly."*

This story appeared in Asimov's, *and in* Centaurus: Best Australian Science Fiction, *a large reprint anthology published in 1999 to coincide with the World SF Convention in Melbourne. It is a rare and powerful SF story about the impact of a scientific advance on some Muslims, a counterpoint to Bruce Sterling's well-known story, "We Think Differently." "Occasionally," says Lawson, "in moments of extreme self-confidence, I even hope to change the way people think about the world."*

CTA TAA CAG TGT AGC GAC GAA TGT CTA CAG
AAA CAA GAA TGT CAT GAG TGT CTA GAT CAT
AAC CGA TGT AGC GAC GAA TGT CTA CAA GAA
AGG AAT TAA GAG GGA TAC CGA TGT AGC GAC
GAA TGT CTA AAT CAT CAA CAC AAA AGT AGT
TAA CAT CAG AAA AGC GAA TGC TTC TTF

In the Name of God, the Merciful, the Compassionate.

These words open the Qur'an. They were written in my
father's blood. After Mother died, and Da recovered from
his chemotherapy, we went on a pilgrimage together. In my
usual eleven-year-old curious way, I asked him why we had
to go to the Other End of the World to pray when we could
do it just fine at home.

"Zada," he said, "there are only five pillars of faith. It is
easier than any of the other pillars because you only need
to do it once in a lifetime. Remember this during Ramadan,

when you are hungry and you know you will be hungry again the next day, but your *haj* will be over."

Da would brook no further discussion, so we set off for the Holy Lands. At eleven, I was less than impressed. I expected to find Paradise filled with thousands of fountains and birds and orchards and blooms. Instead, we huddled in cloth tents with hundreds of thousands of sweaty pilgrims, most of whom spoke other languages, as we tramped across a cramped and dirty wasteland. I wondered why Allah had made his Holy Lands so dry and dusty, but I had the sense even then not to ask Da about it.

Near Damascus, we heard about the bloodwriting. The pilgrims were all speaking about it. Half thought it blasphemous, the other half thought it a path to Heaven. Since Da was a biologist, the pilgrims in our troop asked him what he thought. He said he would have to go to the bloodwriters directly and find out.

On a dusty Monday, after morning prayer, my father and I visited the bloodwriter's stall. The canvas was a beautiful white, and the man at the stall smiled as Da approached. He spoke some Arabic, which I could not understand.

"I speak English," said my father.

The stall attendant switched to English with the ease of a juggler changing hands. "Wonderful, sir! Many of our customers prefer English."

"I also speak biology. My pilgrim companions have asked me to review your product." I thought it very forward of my father, but the stall attendant seemed unfazed. He exuded confidence about his product.

"An expert!" he exclaimed. "Even better. Many pilgrims are distrustful of Western science. I do what I can to reassure them, but they see me as a salesman and not to be trusted. I welcome your endorsement."

"Then earn it."

The stall attendant wiped his mustache, and began his spiel. "Since the Dawn of Time, the Word of Allah has been read by mullahs. . . ."

"Stop!" said Da. "The Qur'an was revealed to Mohammed fifteen centuries ago; the Dawn of Time predates it by several billion years. I want answers, not portentous falsehoods."

Now the man was nervous. "Perhaps you should see my uncle. He invented the bloodwriting. I will fetch him." Soon he returned with an older, infinitely more respectable man with grey whiskers in his mustache and hair.

"Please forgive my nephew," said the old man. "He has watched too much American television and thinks the best way to impress is to use dramatic words, wild gestures, and where possible, a toll-free number." The nephew bowed his head and slunk to the back of the stall, chastened.

"May I answer your questions?" the old man asked.

"If you would be so kind," said Da, gesturing for the man to continue.

"Bloodwriting is a good word, and I owe my nephew a debt of gratitude for that. But the actual process is something altogether more mundane. I offer a virus, nothing more. I have taken a hypo-immunogenic strain of adeno-associated virus and added a special code to its DNA."

Da said, "The other pilgrims tell me that you can write the Qur'an into their blood."

"That I can, sir," said the old man. "Long ago I learned a trick that would get the adeno-associated virus to write its code into bone marrow stem cells. It made me a rich man. Now I use my gift for Allah's work. I consider it part of my *zakât.*"

Da suppressed a wry smile. *Zakât*, charitable donation, was one of the five pillars. This old man was so blinded by avarice that he believed selling his invention for small profit was enough to fulfill his obligation to God.

The old man smiled and raised a small ampoule of red liquid. He continued, "This, my friend, is the virus. I have stripped its core and put the entire text of the Qur'an into its DNA. If you inject it, the virus will write the Qur'an into your myeloid precursor cells, and then your white blood cells will carry the Word of Allah inside them."

I put my hand up to catch his attention. "Why not red blood cells?" I asked. "They carry all the oxygen."

The old man looked at me as if he noticed me for the first time. "Hello, little one. You are very smart. Red blood cells carry oxygen, but they have no DNA. They cannot carry the Word."

It all seemed too complicated to an eleven-year-old girl. My father was curious. "DNA codes for amino acid sequences. How can you write the Qur'an in DNA?"

"DNA is just another alphabet," said the old man. He handed my father a card. "Here is the crib sheet."

My father studied the card for several minutes, and I saw his face change from skeptical to awed. He passed the card to me. It was filled with Arabic squiggles, which I could not understand. The only thing I knew about Arabic was that it was written right-to-left, the reverse of English.

"I can't read it," I said to the man. He made a little spinning gesture with his finger, indicating that I should flip the card over. I flipped the card and saw the same crib sheet, only with Anglicized terms for each Arabic letter. Then he handed me another crib sheet, and said: "This is the sheet for English text."

AAA a	AGA q	ATA [—] dash	ACA
AAG b	AGG r	ATG [/] slash	ACG
AAT c	AGT s	ATT {stop}	ACT
AAC d	AGC t	ATC {stop}	ACC
GAA e	GGA u	GTA ['] apostrophe	GCA {stop}
GAG f	GGG v	GTG ["] quotation mark	GCG
GAT g	GGT w	GTT [(] open bracket	GCT 0
GAC h	GGC x	GTC [)] close bracket	GCC 1
TAA i	TGA y	TTA [?] question mark	TCA 2
TAG j	TGG z	TTG [!] exclamation	TCG 3
TAT k	TGT [ ] space	TTT [•] end verse	TCT 4
TAC l	TGC [.] period	TTC [¶] paragraph	TCC 5
CAA m	CGA [,] comma	CTA {cap} capital	CCA 6
CAG n	CGG [:] colon	CTG	CCG 7
CAT o	CGT [;] semi-colon	CTT	CCT 8
CAC p	CGC [-] hyphen	CTC	CCC 9

"The Arabic alphabet has 28 letters. Each letter changes form depending on its position in the word. But the rules are rigid, so there is no need to put each variation in the crib sheet. It is enough to know that the letter is *aliph* or *bi*, and whether it is at the start, at the end, or in the middle of the word.

"The **[stop]** commands are also left in their usual places. These are the body's natural commands and they tell ribosomes when to stop making a protein. It only cost three spots and there were plenty to spare, so they stayed in."

My father asked, "Do you have an English translation?"

"Your daughter is looking at the crib sheet for the English language," the old man explained, "and there are other texts one can write, but not the Qur'an."

Thinking rapidly, Da said, "But you could write the Qur'an in English?"

"If I wanted to pursue secular causes, I could do that," the old man said. "But I have all the secular things I need. I have copyrighted crib sheets for all the common alphabets, and I make a profit on them. For the Qur'an, however, translations are not acceptable. Only the original words of Mohammed can be trusted. It is one thing for *dhimmis* to translate it for their own curiosity, but if you are a true believer you must read the word of God in its unsullied form."

Da stared at the man. The old man had just claimed that millions of Muslims were false believers because they could not read the original Qur'an. Da shook his head and let the matter go. There were plenty of imams who would agree with the old man.

"What is the success rate of the inoculation?"

"Ninety-five percent of my trial subjects had identifiable Qur'an text in their blood after two weeks, although I cannot guarantee that the entire text survived the insertion in all of those subjects. No peer-reviewed journal would accept the paper." He handed my father a copy of an article from *Modern Gene Techniques*. "Not because the science is poor, as you will see for yourself, but because Islam scares them."

Da looked serious. "How much are you charging for this?"

"Aha! The essential question. I would dearly love to give it away, but even a king would grow poor if he gave a grain of rice to every hungry man. I ask enough to cover my costs, and no haggling. It is a hundred US dollars or equivalent."

Da looked into the dusty sky, thinking. "I am puzzled," he said at last. "The Qur'an has one hundred and fourteen suras, which comes to tens of thousands of words. Yet the adeno-associated virus is quite small. Surely it can't all fit inside the viral coat?"

At this the old man nodded. "I see you are truly a man of wisdom. It is a patented secret, but I suppose that some-day a greedy industrialist will lay hands on my virus and sequence the genome. So, I will tell you on the condition that it goes no further than this stall."

Da gave his word.

"The code is compressed. The original text has enormous redundancy, and with advanced compression, I can reduce the amount of DNA by over 80 percent. It is still a lot of code."

I remember Da's jaw dropping. "That must mean the viral code is self-extracting. How on Earth do you com-mandeer the ribosomes?"

"I think I have given away enough secrets for today," said the old man.

"Please forgive me," said Da. "It was curiosity, not greed, that drove me to ask." Da changed his mind about the bloodwriter. This truly was fair *zakât*. Such a wealth of invention for only a hundred US dollars.

"And the safety?" asked my father.

The old man handed him a number of papers, which my father read carefully, nodding his head periodically, and humming each time he was impressed by the data.

"I'll have a dose," said Da. "Then no one can accuse me of being a slipshod reviewer."

"Sir, I would be honored to give a complimentary blood-writing to you and your daughter."

"Thank you. I am delighted to accept your gift, but only for me. Not for my daughter. Not until she is of age and can make her own decision." Da took a red ampoule in his hands and held it up to the light, as if he was looking through an envelope for the letters of the Qur'an. He shook his head at the marvel and handed it back to the old man, who drew it up in a syringe.

That night, our fellow pilgrims made a fire and gathered around to hear my father talk. As he spoke, four translators whispered their own tongues to the crowd. The scene was like a great theater from the Arabian Nights. Scores of people wrapped in white robes leaned into my father's words, drinking up his excitement. It could have been a meeting of princes.

Whenever Da said something that amazed the gathered masses, you could hear the inbreath of the crowd, first from the English-speakers, and then in patches as the words came out in the other languages. He told them about DNA, and how it told our bodies how to live. He told them about introns, the long stretches of human DNA that are useless to our bodies, but that we carry still from viruses that invaded our distant progenitors, like ancestral scars. He told them about the DNA code, with its triplets of adenine, guanine, cytosine, and thymine, and he passed around copies of the bloodwriter's crib sheet. He told them about blood, and the white cells that fought infection. He talked about the adeno-associated virus and how it injected its DNA into humans. He talked about the bloodwriter's injection and the mild fever it had given him. He told them of the price.

And he answered questions for an hour.

The next day, as soon as the morning prayers were over, the bloodwriting stall was swamped with customers. The old man ran out of ampoules by mid-morning, and only avoided a riot by promising to bring more the following day.

*   *   *

I had made friends with another girl. She was two years younger than I was, and we did not share a language, but we still found ways to play together to relieve the boredom.

One day, I saw her giggling and whispering to her mother, who looked furtively at me and at Da. The mother waved over her companions, and spoke to them in solemn tones. Soon a very angry-looking phalanx of women descended on my unsuspecting father. They stood before him, hands on hips, and the one who spoke English pointed a finger at me.

"Where is her mother?" asked the woman. She was taller than the others, a weather-beaten woman who looked like she was sixty, but must have been younger because she had a child only two years old. "This is no place for a young girl to be escorted by a man."

"Zada's mother died in a car accident back home. I am her father, and I can escort her without help, thank you."

"I think not," said the woman.

"What right have you to say such a thing?" asked Da. "I am her father."

The woman pointed again. "Ala says she saw your daughter bathing, and she has not had the *khitan*. Is this true?"

"It is none of your business," said Da.

The woman screamed at him. "I will not allow my daughter to play with harlots. Is it true?"

"It is none of your business."

The woman lurched forward and pulled me by my arm. I squealed and twisted out of her grasp and ran behind my father for protection. I wrapped my arms around his waist and held on tightly.

"Show us," demanded the woman. "Prove she is clean enough to travel with this camp."

Da refused, which made the woman lose her temper. She slapped him so hard she split his lip. He tasted the blood, but stood resolute. She reached around and tried to unlock my arms from Da's waist. He pushed her away.

"She is not fit to share our camp. She should be cut, or else she will be shamed in the sight of Allah," the woman screamed. The other women were shouting and shaking their fists, but few of them knew English, so it was as much in confusion as anger.

My father fixed the woman with a vicious glare. "You call my daughter shameful in the sight of Allah? I am a servant of Allah. Prove to me that Allah is shamed and I will do what I can to remove the shame. Fetch a mullah."

The woman scowled. "I will fetch a mullah, although I doubt your promise is worth as much as words in the sand."

"Make sure the mullah speaks English," my father demanded as she slipped away. He turned to me and wiped away tears. "Don't worry, Zada. No harm will come to you."

"Will I be allowed to play with Ala?"

"No. Not with these old vultures hanging around."

By the evening, the women had found a mullah gullible enough to mediate the dispute. They tugged his sleeves as he walked toward our camp, hurrying him up. It was obvious that his distaste had grown with every minute in the company of the women, and now he was genuinely reluctant to speak on the matter.

The weathered woman pointed us out to the mullah and spat some words at him that we did not understand.

"Sir, I hear that your daughter is uncircumcised. Is this true?"

"It is none of your business," said Da.

The mullah's face dropped. You could almost see his heart sinking. "Did you not promise . . . ?"

"I promised to discuss theology with you and that crone. My daughter's anatomy is not your affair."

"Please, sir . . ."

Da cut him off abruptly. "Mullah, in your considered opinion, is it necessary for a Muslim girl to be circumcised?"

"It is the accepted practice," said the mullah.

"I do not care about the accepted practice. I ask what Mohammed says."

"Well, I'm sure that Mohammed says something on the matter," said the mullah.

"Show me where."

The mullah coughed, thinking of the fastest way to extract himself. "I did not bring my books with me," he said.

Da laughed, not believing that a mullah would travel so far to mediate a theological dispute without a book. "Here, have mine," Da said as he passed the Qur'an to the mullah. "Show me where Mohammed says such a thing."

The mullah's shoulders slumped. "You know I cannot. It is not in the Qur'an. But it is *sunnah*."

"*Sunnah*," said Da, "is very clear on the matter. Circumcision is *makrumah* for women. It is honorable but not compulsory. There is no requirement for women to be circumcised."

"Sir, you are very learned. But there is more to Islam than a strict reading of the Qur'an and *sunnah*. There have even been occasions when the word of Mohammed has been overturned by later imams. Mohammed himself knew that he was not an expert on all things, and he said that it was the responsibility of future generations to rise above his imperfect knowledge."

"So, you are saying that even if it was recorded in the Qur'an, that would not make it compulsory." Da gave a smile, the little quirk of his lips that he gave every time he had laid a logical trap for someone.

The mullah looked grim. The trap had snapped shut on his leg, and he was not looking forward to extricating himself.

"Tell these women so we can go back to our tents and sleep," said Da.

The mullah turned to the women and spoke to them. The weathered woman became agitated and started waving her hands wildly. Her voice was an overwrought screech. The mullah turned back to us.

"She refuses to share camp with you, and insists you leave."

Da fixed the mullah with his iron gaze. "Mullah, you are a learned man in a difficult situation, but surely you can see the woman is half-mad. She complains that my daughter has not been mutilated, and would not taint herself with my daughter's presence. Yet she is tainted herself. Did she tell you that she tried to assault my daughter and strip her naked in public view? Did she tell you that she inflicted this wound on me when I stood between her and my daughter? Did she tell you that I have taken the bloodwriting, so she spilled the Word of God when she drew blood?"

The mullah looked appalled. He went back to the woman, who started screeching all over again. He cut her off and began berating her. She stopped talking, stunned that the mullah had turned on her. He kept berating her until she showed a sign of humility. When she bowed her head, the mullah stopped his tirade, but as soon as the words stopped she sent a dagger-glance our way.

That night, three families pulled out of our camp. Many of the others in camp were pleased to see them go. I heard one of the grandmothers mutter "Taliban" under her breath, making a curse of the words.

The mood in camp lifted, except for mine. "It's my fault Ala left," I said.

"No, it is not your fault," said Da. "It was her family's fault. They want the whole world to think the way they think and to do what they do. This is against the teaching of the Qur'an, which says that there shall be no coercion in the matter of faith. I can find the sura if you like."

"Am I unclean?"

"No," said Da. "You are the most beautiful girl in the world."

By morning, the camp had been filled by other families. The faces were more friendly, but Ala was gone. It was my first lesson in intolerance, and it came from my own faith.

In Sydney, we sat for hours, waiting to be processed. By the third hour, Da finally lost patience and approached the customs officer.

"We are Australian citizens, you know?" Da said.

"Please be seated. We are still waiting for cross-checks."

"I was born in Brisbane, for crying out loud! Zada was born in Melbourne. My family is Australian four generations back."

His protests made no difference. Ever since the Saladin Outbreak, customs checked all Muslims thoroughly. Fifty residents of Darwin had died from an outbreak of a biological weapon that the Saladins had released. Only a handful of Saladins had survived, and they were all in prison, and it had been years ago, but Australia still treated its Muslims as if every single one of us was a terrorist waiting for the opportunity to go berserk.

We were insulted, shouted at, and spat on by men and women who then stepped into their exclusive clubs and talked about how uncivilized we were. Once it had been the Aborigines, then it had been the Italian and Greek immigrants; a generation later it was the Asians; now it was our turn. Da thought that we could leave for a while, go on our pilgrimage and return to a more settled nation, but our treatment by the customs officers indicated that little had changed in the year we were away.

They forced Da to strip for a search, and nearly did the same for me, until Da threatened them with child molestation charges. They took blood samples from both of us. They went through our luggage ruthlessly. They X-rayed our suitcases from so many angles that Da joked they would glow in the dark.

Then they made us wait, which was the worst punishment of all.

Da leaned over to me and whispered, "They are worried about my blood. They think that maybe I am carrying a deadly virus like a Saladin. And who knows? Maybe the Qur'an *is* a deadly virus." He chuckled.

"Can they read your blood?" I asked.

"Yes, but they can't make sense of it without the code sheet."

"If they knew it was just the Qur'an texts, would they let us go?"

"Probably," said Da.

"Why don't you give it to them, then?"

He sighed. "Zada, it is hard to understand, but many people hate us for no reason other than our faith. I have never killed or hurt or stolen from anyone in my life, and yet people hate me because I pray in a church with a crescent instead of a cross."

"But I want to get out of here," I pleaded.

"Listen to me, daughter. I could show them the crib sheet and explain it to them, but then they would know the code, and that is a terrifying possibility. There are people who have tried to design illnesses that attack only Jews or only blacks, but so far they have failed. The reason why they have failed is that there is no serological marker for black or Jewish blood. Now we stupid Muslims, and I count myself among the fools, have identified ourselves. In my blood is a code that says that I am a Muslim, not just by birth, but by active faith. I have marked myself. I might as well walk into a neo-Nazi rally wearing a Star of David.

"Maybe I am just a pessimist," he continued. "Maybe no one will ever design an anti-Muslim virus, but it is now technically possible. The longer it takes the *dhimmis* to find out how, the better."

I looked up at my father. He had called himself a fool. "Da, I thought you were smart!"

"Most of the time, darling. But sometimes faith means you have to do the dumb thing."

"I don't want to be dumb," I said.

Da laughed. "You know you can choose whatever you want to be. But there is a small hope I have for you. To do it you would need to be very, *very* smart."

"What?" I asked.

"I want you to grow up to be smart enough to figure out how to stop the illnesses I'm talking about. Mark my words, racial plagues will come one day, unless someone can stop them."

"Do you think I could?"

Da looked at me with utter conviction. "I have never doubted it."

*   *   *

Da's leukemia recurred a few years later. The chemotherapy had failed to cure him after all, although it had given him seven good years, just long enough to see me to adulthood, and enrolled in genetics. I tried to figure out a way to cure Da, but I was only a freshman. I understood less than half the words in my textbooks. The best I could do was hold his hand as he slowly died.

It was then that I finally understood what he meant when he said that sometimes it was important not to be smart. At the climax of our *haj* we had gone around the Kaabah seven times, moving in a human whirlpool. It made no sense at all intellectually. Going around and around a white temple in a throng of strangers was about as pointless a thing as you could possibly do, and yet I still remember the event as one of the most moving in my life. For a brief moment I felt a part of a greater community, not just of Muslims, but of the Universe. With that last ritual, Da and I became *haji* and *hajjah*, and it felt wonderful.

But I could not put aside my thoughts the way Da could. I had to be smart. Da had *asked* me to be smart. And when he died, after four months and two failed chemo cycles, I no longer believed in Allah. I wanted to maintain my faith, as much for my father as for me, but my heart was empty.

The event that finally tipped me, although I did not even realize it until much later, was seeing his blood in a sample tube. The oncology nurse had drawn 8 mls from his central line, then rolled the sample tube end over end to mix the blood with the anticoagulant. I saw the blood darken in the tube as it deoxygenated, and I thought about the blood cells in there. The white cells contained the suras of the Qur'an, but they also carried the broken code that turned them into cancer cells.

Da had once overcome leukemia years before. The doctors told me it was very rare to have a relapse after seven years. And this relapse seemed to be more aggressive than the first one. The tests, they told me, indicated this was a new mutation.

Mutation: a change in genetic code. Mutagen: an agent that promotes mutation.

Bloodwriting, by definition, was mutagenic. Da had injected one hundred and fourteen suras into his own DNA. The designer had been very careful to make sure that the bloodwriting virus inserted itself somewhere safe so it would not disrupt a tumor suppressor gene or switch on an oncogene—but that was for normal people. Da's DNA was already damaged by leukemia and chemotherapy. The virus had written a new code over the top, and I believe the new code switched his leukemia back on.

The Qur'an had spoken to his blood, and said: "He it is Who created you from dust, then from a small lifegerm, then from a clot, then He brings you forth as a child, then that you may attain your maturity, then that you may be old—and of you there are some who are caused to die before—and that you may reach an appointed term, and that you may understand./He it is who gives life and brings death, so when He decrees an affair, He only says to it: *Be*, and it is."

I never forgave Allah for saying *"Be!"* to my father's leukemia.

An educated, intelligent biologist, Da must have suspected that the Qur'an had killed him. Still, he never missed a prayer until the day he died. My own faith was not so strong. It shattered like fine china on concrete. Disbelief is the only possible revenge for omnipotence.

An infidel I was by then, but I had made a promise to my father, and for my postdoc I solved the bloodwriting problem. He would have been proud.

I abandoned the crib sheet. In my scheme the codons were assigned randomly to letters. Rather than preordaining *TAT* to mean *zen* in Arabic or "k" in English, I designed a process that shuffled the letters into a new configuration every time. Because there are 64 codons, with three {stop} marks and eight blanks, that comes to about 5×10^{83} or 500,000,000,000,000,000,000,000,000,000,000,000,000, 000,000,000,000,000,000,000,000,000,000,000,000,000, 000,000 combinations. No one could design a virus specific to the Qur'an suras anymore. The *dhimmi* bastards would need to design a different virus for every Muslim on the face of the Earth. The faith of my father was safe to blood-write.

In my own blood I have written the things important to me. There is a picture of my family, a picture of my wedding, and a picture of my parents from when they were both alive. Pictures can be encoded just as easily as text.

There is some text: Crick and Watson's original paper describing the double-helix of DNA, and Martin Luther King's "I Have a Dream" speech. I also transcribed Cassius's words from *Julius Caesar*:

> The fault, dear Brutus, is not in our stars,
> But in ourselves, that we are underlings.

For the memory of my father, I included a Muslim parable, a *sunnah* story about Mohammed: One day, a group of farmers asked Mohammed for guidance on improving their crop. Mohammed told the farmers not to pollinate their date trees. The farmers recognized Mohammed as a wise man, and did as he said. That year, however, none of the trees bore any dates. The farmers were angry, and they returned to Mohammed demanding an explanation. Mohammed heard their complaints, then pointed out that he was a religious man, not a farmer, and his wisdom could not be expected to encompass the sum of human learning. He said, "You know your worldly business better."

It is my favorite parable from Islam, and is as important in its way as Jesus' Sermon on the Mount.

At the end of my insert, I included a quote from the *dhimmi* Albert Einstein, recorded the year after the atomic bombing of Japan.

He said, "The release of atom power has changed everything but our way of thinking," then added, "the solution of this problem lies in the heart of humankind."

I have paraphrased that last sentence into the essence of my new faith. No God was ever so succinct.

My artificial intron reads:

CTA AGC GAC GAA TGT AGT CAT TAC GGA AGC
TAA CAT CAG TGT TAC TAA GAA AGT TGT TAA
CAG TGT AGC GAC GAA TGT GAC GAA AAA AGG
AGC TGT CAT GAG TGT GAC GGA CAA AAA CAG
TAT TAA CAG AAC TGC

8 words, 45 codons, 135 base pairs that say:

The solution lies in the heart of humankind

I whisper it to my children every night.

Has Anybody
Seen Junie Moon?

GENE WOLFE

Gene Wolfe has now been publishing in SF for more than thirty years, although he did not draw much notice until 25 years ago, in the early 1970s, when his outstanding short fiction began to appear on award ballots. It is now evident that he is in our time producing the finest continuing body of short fiction in the SF field since Theodore Sturgeon. Like Sturgeon, Wolfe is an aesthetic maverick, whose stories are sometimes fantasy, sometimes horror, sometimes hard SF, sometimes fine contemporary realism (neat, or with magic). His novels include the four-volume Book of the New Sun, The Fifth Head of Cerberus, Peace, Soldier of the Mist, Urth of the New Sun, *the four-volume Book of the Long Sun, and in 1999 the first volume of the Book of the Short Sun,* On Blue's Waters. *This novel left no doubt that he is still at the top of his form. His short fiction is collected in* The Island of Dr. Death and Other Stories, and Other Stories, Endangered Species, Storeys from the Old Hotel, Strange Travellers, *and several other volumes.*

This story is the first of several in this year's best volume selected for reprint from the excellent original SF anthology Moon Shots, *edited by Peter Crowther. It features Sam, a slow-witted but devoted herculean weight-lifter and Junie*

*Moon, his beloved brainy and obese physicist, who follow
the clues of Roy T. Laffer to the White Cow Moon. The
story is in homage to R. A. Lafferty, one of the finest of all
SF stylists, who aspired to wrestle with angels and perhaps
dine with the devil. I was never sure what genre Lafferty
wrote, just that we would be much poorer without it. This
is that kind of story.*

The reason I am writing this is to find my manager. I think her name is really probably June Moon or something, but nobody calls her that. I call her Junie and just about everybody else calls her Ms. Moon. She is short and kind of fat with a big wide mouth that she smiles with a lot and brown hair: She is pretty, too. Real pretty, and that is how you can be sure it is her if ever you see her. Because short, fat ladies mostly do not look as good as Junie and nobody thinks, "Boy, I would really like to know her like I did that time in England when we went in the cave, so she could talk to that crabby old man from Tulsa because Junie believes in dead people coming back and all that."

She made me believe it, too. You would, too, if you had been with Junie like I have.

So I am looking for a Moon just like she is, only she is the Moon that I am looking for. The one she is looking for is the White Cow Moon. That is an Indian name and there is a story behind it just like you would think, only it is a pretty dumb story, so I am going to save it for later. Besides, I do not think it is true. Indians are nice people except for a couple I used to know, but they have all these stories that they tell you and then they laugh inside.

I am from Texas, but Junie is from Oklahoma.

That is what started her off. She used to work for a big school they have there, whatever it says on that sweatshirt she wears sometimes. There was this cranky old man in Tulsa that knew lots of stuff, only he was like an Indian.

He would tell people, this was when he was still pretty young, I guess, and they would never believe him even if it was true.

I have that trouble, too, but this cranky old man got real mad and did something about it. He changed his name to Roy T. Laffer, and after that he would tell things so they would not believe him or understand, and then laugh inside. Junie never said what the T. stood for, but I think I know.

Do you know what it says on the tea boxes? The ones with the man with the cap on them? It says honest tea is the best policy. I know what that means, and I think that cranky old Roy T. Laffer knew it, too.

He gave big boxes full of paper to the school Junie worked for, and Junie was the one that went through them and that was how she found out about White Cow Moon. He had a lot of stuff in there about it, and Junie saw her name and read it even if his writing was worse even than mine. He had been there and taken pictures, and she found those, too. She showed me some.

It goes slow. Junie said that was the greatest secret in the world, so I guess it is. And there were pictures of a big old rock that Roy T. Laffer had brought back.

One picture that I saw had it sitting on a scale. The rock was so big you could not hardly see the scale, but then another picture showed the part with numbers, and that big old rock was only about a quarter ounce. It was kind of a dirty white like this one cow that we used to have.

Maybe that was really why they call it that and not because a cow jumped over it like those Indians say. That would make a lot more sense, only I did not think of it till just now.

I ought to tell you things about me here so you understand, but first I want to tell more about Junie because I am looking for her, but I know where I am already, which is here in Florida at the Museum of the Strange and Occult. Only it is all big letters like this on our sign out front, THE MUSEUM OF THE STRANGE AND OCCULT, ADMISSION $5.50, CHILDREN $2, CHILDREN IN ARMS

FREE, SENIORS $3 OR $2 WITH ANOTHER PAID AD-
MISSION. The letters are gold.

Junie had been to college and everything and was a doctor of physic. When she got out, she thought she was the
greatest since One Mug. That is what she says it means,
only it is German. I do not remember the German words.

So she went to work at this big laboratory in Chicago
where they do physic, only they had her answer the phone
and empty the wastebaskets and she quit. Then she went
back home to Oklahoma, and that is why she was at the
big school and was the one that went through Roy. T. Laffer's papers. Mostly I do not much like Oklahoma people
because they think they are better than Texas people, only
Junie really is.

So if you see her or even just talk to somebody that has,
you could come by and tell me, or write a letter or even
just phone. I will be glad any way you do it. Dottie that
works in our office here is putting this in her computer for
me and printing it, too, whenever I have got a page done.
She says you could send E-mail, too. That would be all
right because Dottie would tell us. I would be very happy
any way you did it. Dottie says www.Hercules@freaky.
com.

My name is not really Hercules, that is just the name I
work under. My name is really Sam and that is what Junie
calls me. If you know her and have talked to her and she
said anything about Sam, that was me. If you want to be
really formal, it is Sam Jr. Only nobody calls me that. Most
people I know call me Hercules. Not ever Herk. I do not
like it.

Let me tell you how bad I want to find Junie. Sometimes
there is a man in the tip that thinks he is stronger. I really
like that when it happens because it is usually fun. I will
do some things that I figure he can do, too, like bending
rebars and tearing up bottle caps. Then if I see the tip likes
him, I will say something hard and let him win.

A week ago maybe there was this one big guy that
thought he was really strong, so I did him like I said. I
threw him the two-hundred-pound bell and he caught it,

and when he threw it back to me, I pretended like I could not catch it and let it fall when I had my legs out of the way and everybody was happy. Only yesterday he came back. He called me Herk, and he said I was afraid to go up against him again. The tip was not with him then. So I said all right, and when he could not lift my five-hundred-pound iron, I did it with one hand and gave it to him. And when he dropped it, I picked him up by his belt and hung him on this high hook I use for the pulley. I left him up there until everybody was gone, too, and when I took him down, he did not say a word. He just went away.

Well, I want Junie back so bad that if he was to tell me where she was, I would let him win anytime he wanted.

I do not make a lot of money here. It is just five hundred a month and what I make selling my course, but they have got these trailers out back for Jojo and Baby Rita who is a hundred times fatter than Junie or anybody. So I have one, too, and it is free. I eat a lot, but that is about all I spend much on. Some fishing gear, but I have got a real good reel and you do not need much else.

Well, you do, but it does not cost the world.

So I have a lot saved and I will give you half if you tell me where Junie Moon is and she is really there when I go look.

This is the way she got to be my manager. I was in England working at a fair that they had at this big castle where King Arthur was born, and Junie was in the tip. So when it was over and they were supposed to go see Torchy, Junie would not go. The steerer said she had to, but she kept saying she wanted to talk to me and I could tell she was American like me. So after a while I said she probably knew that if she really wanted to talk to me all she had to do was meet me out back. So then she went.

When I went out back, which was where the toilets were, I did not expect to see her, not really, even if I had let her feel my arm which is something I do sometimes. But there she was, and this is what she said, with the little marks around it that you are supposed to use and all of that stuff. Dottie, help me with this part.

"Hercules, I really need your help. I don't know whether I was really one of the daughters of King Thespius, but there were fifty of them, so there's a pretty good chance of it. Will you help me?"

That was the first thing Junie ever said to me, and I remember it just like it was a couple of days ago. Naturally I said I would.

"You will! Just like that?"

I said sure.

"I can pay you. I was going to say that. A hundred pounds right now, and another hundred pounds when I'm over the fence. I can pass it to you through the fence. Look." She opened her purse and showed me the money. "Is that enough?"

I explained how she did not have to.

"You'll be in danger. You might be arrested."

Junie looked really worried when she said that, and it made me feel wonderful, so I said that was okay. I had been arrested once already in England besides in America and to tell the truth in England it was kind of fun, especially when they could not get their handcuffs to go around my wrists, and then they got these plastic strap cuffs and put those on me and I broke six pairs. I like English people, only nothing they say makes any sense.

Junie said, "Back there, you threw an enormous barbell up in the air and caught it. How much did you say it weighed?"

I said, "Three hundred. That was my three-hundred-pound bell."

"And does it actually weigh three hundred pounds?"

I said sure.

"I weigh only a little more than half that. Could you throw me, oh, fifteen feet into the air?"

I knew I could, but I said I did not know because I wanted to get my hands on her.

"But you might? Do you really think you might be able to, Hercules?"

I sort of raised up my shoulders the way you do and let them drop.

"We—if you failed to throw me high enough, I would get a severe electric shock." She looked scared.

I nodded really serious and said what we ought to do was try it first, right now. We would measure something that was fifteen feet, and then I would throw her up, and she could tell me if I got her up that high. So she pointed to the temporary wires they had strung up for the fair, and I wanted to know if those were the ones. She said no. They were not fifteen feet either. Ten or twelve maybe. But I said okay only do not reach out and grab them or you might get killed, and she said okay.

So I got my hands around her which was what I had been wanting to do and lifted her up and sort of weighed her a couple times, moving her up and down, you know how you do, and then I spun around like for the hammer throw, and I heaved her maybe ten feet higher than those wires, and caught her easy when she came down. It made her really scared, too, and I was sorry for that, but I got down on my knees and hugged her, and I said, "There, there, there," and pretty soon she stopped crying.

Then I said was that high enough? And she said it was.

She was still shaky after that, so we went back inside and she sat with me while I waited for the next tip. That was when she showed me the pictures that Roy T. Laffer had taken up on the White Cow Moon and the pictures of the rock that he had brought back, a great big rock that did not hardly weigh anything. "He let a little boy take it to school for a science show," Junie told me, "and afterward the science teacher threw it out. Mr. Laffer went to the school and tried to reclaim it the following day, but apparently it had blown out of the dumpster."

I promised her I would keep an eye out for it.

"Thank you. But the point is its lightness. Do you know why the Moon doesn't fall into the Earth, Hercules?"

I said that if I was going to throw her around, she ought to call me Sam, and she promised she would. Then she asked me again about the Moon and I said, "Sure, I know that one. The moonbeams hold it up."

Junie did not laugh. "Really, Sam, it does. It falls exactly as a bullet falls to Earth."

She went and got a broom to show me, holding it level. "Suppose that this were a rifle. If I pulled the trigger, the bullet would fly out of the barrel at a speed of three thousand feet per second or so."

I said okay.

"Now say that you were to drop that weight over there at the very same moment that the rifle fired. Your weight would hit the ground at the same moment that the rifle bullet did." She waited for me to argue with her, but I said okay again.

"Even though the bullet was flying along horizontally, it was also falling. What's more, it was falling at virtually the same rate that your weight did. I'm sure you must know about artificial satellites, Sam."

I said I did, because I felt like I could remember about them if I had a little more time, and besides I had the feeling Junie would tell me anyhow.

"They orbit the Earth just as the Moon does. So why doesn't the bullet orbit it, too?"

I said it probably hit a fence post or something.

She looked at me and sort of sucked on her lips, and looked again. "That may be a much better answer than you can possibly be aware of. But no. It doesn't orbit Earth because it isn't going fast enough. A sidereal month is about twenty-seven days, and the Moon is two hundred and forty thousand miles away, on average. So if its orbit were circular—that isn't quite true, but I'm trying to make this as simple as I can—the Moon would be traveling at about three-thousand-five-hundred feet a second. Not much faster than our rifle bullet, in other words."

I could see she wanted me to nod, so I did.

"The Moon can travel that slowly." Slowly is what she said. Junie is always saying crazy stuff like that. "Because it's so far away. It would have to fall two hundred and forty thousand miles before it could hit the Earth. But the bullet has to fall only about three feet. Another way of putting it is that the closer a satellite is, the faster it must move if it is to stay in orbit."

I said that the bullet would have to go really fast, and Junie nodded. "It would have to go so fast that the curve of the Earth was falling away from it as rapidly as the bullet itself was falling toward the Earth. That's what an orbit is, that combination of vertical and horizontal motions."

Right then I do not think I was too clear on which one was which, but I nodded again.

Then Junie's voice got sort of trembly. "Now suppose that you were to make a telephone call to your wife back in America," is what she said. So I explained I did not have one, and after that she sounded a lot better.

"Well, if you were to call your family, your mother and father, your call would go through a communications satellite that circles the Earth once a day, so that it seems to us that it is always in the same place. It can do that because it's a good deal lower and going a great deal faster."

Then she got out a pen and a little notepad and showed me how fast the bullet would have to go to stay in orbit just whizzing around the world over and over until it hit something. I do not remember how you do it, or what the answer was except that it was about a jillion. Junie said anything like that would make a terrible bang all the time if it was in our air instead of up in space where stuff like that is supposed to be. Well about then is when the tip came in for the last show. I did my act, and Junie sat in the front row smiling and cheering and clapping, and I felt really swell.

So after it was all over, we went to Merlin's cave under the big castle and down by the water, and that was when Junie told me how King Arthur was born there, and I told her how I was putting up at the King Arthur, which was a pub with rooms upstairs. I said they were nice people there, and it was clean and cheap, which is what I want anywhere, and the landlord's name was Arthur, too, just like the pub's. Only after a while when we had gone a long ways down the little path and got almost to the water, I started to sort of hint around about why are we going way down here,

Junie, with just that little flashlight you got out of your purse?

Maybe I ought not say this right here, but it is the truth. It was scary down there. A big person like I am is not supposed to be and I know that. But way up on the rocks where the fair was the lights kept on going out and you could see the fair was just sort of like paint on the old walls of that big castle. It was like somebody had gone to where my dad was buried and painted all over his stone with flowers and clowns and puppies and kitties and all that kind of thing. Only now the paint was flaking away and you could see what was underneath and he had run out with his gun when the feds broke our front door and they killed him.

Here is what I think it was down there and what was so scary about it. King Arthur had been born there and there had been knights and stuff afterward that he was the head of. And they had been big strong people like me on big strong horses and they had gone around wearing armor and with swords and for a while had made the bad guys pay, and everybody had loved them so much that they still remembered all about them after a hundred years. There was a Lancelot room in the pub where I was staying, and a Galahad room, and I was in the Gawain room. And Arthur told me how those men had all been this king's knights, and he said I was the jolly old green giant.

Only it was all over and done with now. It was dead and gone like my dad. King Arthur was dead and his knights were, too, and the bad guys were the head of everything and had been for a long, long time. We were the paint, even Junie was paint, and now the paint was getting dull the way paint does, with cracks all over it and falling off. And I thought this is not just where that king was born, this is where he died, too. And I knew that it was true the way I meant it.

Well, there was a big wire fence there with a sign about the electricity, only it was not any fifteen feet high. I could have reached up to the top of it. Ten feet, maybe, or not even that.

"Can you pick me up and throw me over?" Junie said.

It was crazy, she would have come down on rocks, so I said I could only she would have to tell why she wanted me to so much or I would not do it.

She took my hand then, and it felt wonderful. "People come back, Sam. They come back from death. I know scientists aren't supposed to say things like that, but it's true. They do."

That made me feel even better because it meant I would see my dad again even if we would not have our farm that the feds took anymore.

"Do you remember that I said I might have been one of the fifty daughters of Thespius three thousand years ago? I don't know if that's really true, or even whether there was a real King Thespius who had fifty daughters. Perhaps there was, and perhaps I was one of them—I'd like to think so. But this really was Merlin's cave, and Roy T. Laffer was Merlin in an earlier life. There were unmistakable indications in his papers. I know it with as much certainty as I know Kepler's Laws."

That got me trying to remember who Kepler was, because I did not think Junie had told anything about him up to then. Or after either. Anyway I did not say much.

"I've tried to contact Laffer in his house in Tulsa, Sam. I tried for days at a time, but he wasn't there. I think he may be here. This is terribly important to me, and you said you'd help me. Now will you throw me over?"

I shook my head, but it was really dark down there and maybe Junie did not see it. I said I was not going to be on the other side to catch her and throw her back, so how was she going to get out? She said when they opened in the morning. I said she would get arrested, and she said she did not care. It seemed to me that there were too many getting arrested when she said that, so I twisted on the lock thinking to break the shackle. It was a pretty good lock, I broke the hasp instead. Then I threw the lock in the ocean and Junie and I went inside like she wanted. That was how she found out where White Cow Moon was and how to get on it, too, if she wanted to.

It was about two o'clock in the morning when we came

out, I think. I went back to the King Arthur's and went to bed, and next day Junie moved in down the hall. Hers was the Lancelot room. After that she was my manager, which I told everybody and showed her off. She helped me write my course then, and got this shop in Falmouth to print it up for us.

Then when the fair was over, she got us tickets home, and on the airplane we got to talking about the Moon. I started it and it was a bad mistake, but we did not know it for a couple of days. Junie had been talking about taking pictures and I said, "How can you if it goes so fast?"

"It doesn't, Sam." She took my hand, and I liked that a lot. "It circles the Earth quite slowly, so slowly that to an observer on Earth it hardly seems to move at all, which was one of the things Roy T. Laffer confided to me."

I said I never had seen him, only the lady with the baby and the old man with the stick.

"That was him, Sam. He told me then, and it was implied in his papers anyway. Do you remember the rock?"

I said there had been lots of rocks, which was true because it had been a cave in the rocks.

"I mean the White Cow Moon rock in the picture, the one he lent to the science fair."

I said, "It didn't hardly weigh anything."

"Yes." Junie was sort of whispering then. "It had very little weight, yet it was hard to move. You had to pull and pull, even though it felt so light when you held it. Do you understand what that means, Sam?"

"Somebody might have glued it down?"

"No. It means that it had a great deal of mass, but very little weight. I'm sure you haven't heard of antimatter—matter in which the protons are replaced by antiprotons, the electrons by positrons and so on?"

I said no.

"It's only theoretical so far. But current theory says that although antimatter would possess mass just as ordinary matter does, it would be repelled by the gravitational field of ordinary matter. It would fall up, in other words."

By the time she got to the part about falling up, Junie

was talking to herself mostly only I could still hear her. "Our theory says a collision between matter and antimatter should result in a nuclear explosion, but either the theory's mistaken or there's some natural means of circumventing it. Because the White Cow Moon rock was composed of nearly equal parts matter and antimatter. It had to be! The result was rock with a great deal of mass but very little weight, and that's what allows the White Cow Moon to orbit so slowly.

"Listen to me, Sam." She made me turn in my airplane seat till I was looking at her, and I broke the arm a little. "We physicists say that all matter falls at the same rate, which is basically a convenient lie, true only in a hard vacuum. If that barbell you throw around were balsa wood, it wouldn't fall nearly as fast as your iron one, because it would be falling in air. In the same way, a satellite with great mass but little weight can orbit slowly and quietly through earth's atmosphere, falling toward the surface only as fast as the surface falls away from it."

"Wouldn't it hit a mountain or something, Junie?"

"No, because any mountain that rose in its path would be chipped away as it rose. As light as the White Cow Moon must be, its mass has got to be enormous. Not knowing its orbit—not yet—we can't know what mountain ranges it may cross, but when we do, we'll find it goes through passes. They are passes because it goes through them."

Junie got real quiet for a while after she said that, and now I wish she had stayed quiet. Then she said, "Just think what we could do, Sam, if we could manufacture metals like that rock. Launch vehicles that would reach escape velocity from Earth using less thrust than that of an ordinary launch vehicle on the Moon."

That was the main trouble, I think. Junie saying that was. The other may have hurt us some, too, but that did for sure.

We were flying to Tulsa. I guess I should have written about that before. Anyway, when we got there, Junie got us a bunch of rooms like an apartment in a really nice hotel. We were going to have to wait for my bells to come back on a boat, so Junie said we could look for the White Cow Moon while we were waiting, and she would line me up some good dates to play when my stuff got there. We were sitting around having Diet Cokes out of the little icebox in the kitchen when the feds knocked on the door.

Junie said, "Let me," and went, and that was how they could push in. But they would have if it had been me anyway because they had guns. I would have had to let them just like Junie.

The one in the blue suit said, "Ms. Moon?" and Junie said yes. Then he said, "We're from the government, and we've come to help you and Mr. Moon."

My name never was Moon, but we both changed ours after that anyway. She as Junie Manoe and I was Sam Manoe. Junie picked Manoe to go with JM on her bags. But that was not until after the feds went away.

What they had said was we had to forget about the Moon or we would get in a lot of trouble. Junie said we did not care about the Moon, we had nothing to do with the Moon, what we were doing mainly was getting ready to write a biography about a certain old man named Roy T. Laffer.

The man in the blue suit said, "Good, keep it that way." The man in the black suit never did say anything, but you could see he was hoping to shoot us. I tried to ask Junie some questions after they went away, but she would not talk because she was pretty sure they were listening, or somebody was.

When we were living in the house, she explained about that, and said probably somebody on the plane had told on us, or else the feds listened to everything anybody said on planes. I said we were lucky they had not shot us, and told her about my dad, and that was when she said it was too dangerous for me. She never would tell me exactly where the White Cow Moon was after that, and it traveled around anyway, she said. But she got me a really good job in a gym there. I helped train people and showed them how to do things, and even got on TV doing ads for the gym with some other men and some ladies.

Only I knew that while I was working at the gym Junie

was going out in her car looking for the White Cow Moon, and at night I would write down the mileage when she was in the living room reading. I figured she would find the White Cow Moon and go there at least a couple of times and maybe three or four, and then the mileage would always be the same. And that was how it worked out. I thought that was pretty smart of me, but I was not going to tell Junie how smart I had been until I found it myself and she could not say it was too dangerous.

I looked in her desk for Moon rocks, too, but I never found any, so that is why I do not think Junie had been up there on the White Cow Moon yet.

Well, for three days in a row it was just about one hundred and twenty-five on the mileage. It was one hundred and twenty-three one time, and one hundred and twenty-four, and then one hundred and twenty-six. So that was how I knew sixty-three miles from Tulsa. That day after work I went out and bought the biggest bike at the big Ridin' th' Wild Wind store. It is a Harley and better for me than a car because my head does not scrape. It is nearly big enough.

Only that night Junie did not come home. I thought she had gone up on the White Cow Moon, so I quit my job at the gym and went looking for her for about a month.

A lot of things happened while I was looking for her on my bike. Like I went into this one beer joint and started asking people if they had seen Junie or her car either. This one man that had a bike, too, started yelling at me and would not let me talk to anyone else. I had been very polite and he never would say why he was mad. He kept saying I guess you think you are tough. So finally I picked him up. I think he must have weighed about three hundred pounds because he felt like my bell when I threw him up and banged him on the ceiling. When I let him down, he hit me a couple of times with a chain he had and I decided probably he was a fed and that made me mad. I put my foot on him while I broke his chain into five or six pieces, and every time I broke off a new piece I would drop it on his face. Then I picked him up again and threw him through the window.

Then I went outside and let him pick himself up and threw him up onto the roof. That was fifteen feet easy and I felt pretty proud for it even if it did take three tries. I still do.

After that, two men that had come out to watch told me how they had seen a brown Ford like Junie's out on this one ranch and how to get there. I went and it was more than sixty-three miles to go and Junie's brown Ford was not there. But when I went back to our house in Tulsa it was sixty-eight. Not a lot else happened for about two weeks, and then I went back to that ranch and lifted my bike over their fence real careful and rode out to where those men had said and sat there thinking about Junie and things that she had said to me, and how she had felt that time I threw her higher than the wires back in England. And it got late and you could see the Moon, and I remembered how she had said the feds were building a place for missiles on the other side where nobody could reach it or even see it, and that was why they were mad at us. It is supposed to be to shoot at other countries like England, but it is really to shoot at us in case we do anything the feds do not like.

About then a man on a horse came by and said did I want anything. I told him about the car, and he said there used to be a brown car like that parked out there, only a tow truck cut the fence and took it away. I wanted to know whose truck it had been, but he did not know.

So that is about all I have got to say. Sometimes I dream about how while I was talking to the man on the horse a little white moon sort of like a cloud came by only when I turned my head to look it was already gone. I do not think that really happened or the little woman with the baby and the old man with the stick in the cave either. I think it is all just dreams, but maybe it did.

What I really think is that the feds have got Junie. If they do, all they have got to do is let her go and I will not be mad anymore after that. I promise. But if they will not do it and I find out for sure they have got her, there is going to be a fight. So if you see her or even talk to anybody that has, it would be good if you told me. Please.

I am not the only one that does not like the feds. A lot of other people do not like them either. I know that they are a whole lot smarter than I am, and how good at telling lies and fooling people they are. I am not like that. I am more like Roy T. Laffer because sometimes I cannot even get people to believe the truth.

But you can believe this, because it is true. I have never in my whole life had a fight with a smart person or even seen anybody else have one either. That is because when the fight starts the smart people are not there anymore. They have gone off someplace else, and when it is over, they come back and tell you how much they did in the fight, only it is all lies. Now they have big important gangs with suits and guns. They are a lot bigger than just me, but they are not bigger than everybody, and if all of us get mad at once, maybe we will bring the whole thing crashing down.

After that I would look through the pieces and find Junie, or if I did not find her, I would go up on the White Cow Moon myself like Roy T. Laffer did and find her up there.

The Blue Planet

ROBERT J. SAWYER

Robert J. Sawyer, who lives and works in Ontario, near Toronto, Canada, began to publish SF short stories in the 1980s. His career as a novelist took off in the 1990s, and he became one of the SF popular success stories of the decade. After five well-regarded novels, he won the Nebula Award for The Terminal Experiment *in 1996, and has since published five more novels, three of them Hugo Award nominees. He is a hard SF writer in the tradition of Isaac Asimov, more an idea writer than a stylist, often building neat puzzles with a complex moral dimension. His short stories are now infrequent, but clever and readable. "The Blue Planet" was commissioned by the* Globe & Mail, *the major Toronto newspaper, in December 1999, when the loss of another Mars lander by the US space program was front page news. The circumstances of the commission point out the irony, at century's end, of having a newspaper ask a science fiction writer to transform a real-life space travel back into fiction, perhaps in order to make bad news more palatable and space travel more exciting.*

The round door to the office in the underground city irised open. "Teltor! Teltor!"

The director of the space-sciences hive swung her eyestalks to look wearily at Dostan, her excitable assistant. "What is it?"

"Another space probe has been detected coming from the third planet."

"Again?" said Teltor, agitated. She spread her four exoskeletal arms. "But it's only been a hundred days or so since their last probe."

"Exactly. Which means this one must have been launched *before* we dealt with that one."

Teltor's eyestalks drooped as she relaxed. The presence of this new probe didn't mean the people on the blue planet had ignored the message. Still . . .

"Is this one a lander, or just another orbiter?"

"It has a streamlined component," said Dostan. "Presumably it plans to pass through the atmosphere and come to the surface."

"Where?"

"The south pole, it looks like."

"And you're sure there's no life on board?"

"I'm sure."

Teltor flexed her triple-fingered hands in resignation. "All right," she said. "Power up the neutralization projector; we'll shut this probe off, too."

*   *   *

223

That night, Teltor took her young daughter, Delp, up to the surface. The sky overhead was black—almost as black as the interior of the tunnels leading up from the buried city. Both tiny moons were out, but their wan glow did little to obscure the countless stars.

Teltor held one of her daughter's four hands. No one could come to the surface during the day; the ultraviolet radiation from the sun was deadly. But Teltor was an astronomer—and that was a hard job to do if you always stayed underground.

Young Delp's eyestalks swung left and right, trying to take in all the magnificence overhead. But, after a few moments, both stalks converged on the bright blue star near the horizon.

"What's that, Mama?" she asked.

"A lot of people call it the evening star," said Teltor, "but it's really another planet. We're the fourth planet from the sun, and that one's the third."

"A whole other planet?" said Delp, her mandible clicking in incredulity.

"That's right, dear."

"Are there any people there?"

"Yes, indeed."

"How do you know?"

"They've been sending space probes here for years."

"But they haven't come here in person?"

Teltor moved her lower arms in negation. "No," she said sadly, "they haven't."

"Well, then, why don't we go see them?"

"We can't, dear. The third planet has a surface gravity almost three times as strong as ours. Our exoskeletons would crack open there." Teltor looked at the blue beacon. "No, I'm afraid the only way we'll ever meet is if they come to us."

"Dr. Goldin! Dr. Goldin!"

The NASA administrator stopped on the way to his car. Another journalist, no doubt. "Yes?" he said guardedly.

"Dr. Goldin, this is the latest in a series of failed missions to Mars. Doesn't that prove that your so-called 'faster, better, cheaper' approach to space exploration isn't working?"

Goldin bristled. "I wouldn't say that."

"But surely if we had human beings on the scene, they could deal with the unexpected, no?"

Teltor still thought of Delp as her baby, but she was growing up fast; indeed, she'd already shed her carapace twice.

Fortunately, though, Delp still shared her mother's fascination with the glories of the night sky. And so, as often as she could, Teltor would take Delp up to the surface. Delp could name many of the constellations now—the zigzag, the giant scoop, the square—and was good at picking out planets, including the glaringly bright fifth one.

But her favorite, always, was planet three.

"Mom," said Delp—she no longer called her "Mama"— "there's intelligent life here, and there's also intelligent life on our nearest neighbor, the blue planet, right?"

Teltor moved her eyestalks in affirmation.

Delp spread her four arms, as if trying to encompass all of the heavens. "Well, if there's life on two planets so close together, doesn't that mean the universe must be teeming with other civilizations?"

Teltor dilated her spiracles in gentle laughter. "There's no native life on the third planet."

"But you said they'd been sending probes here—"

"Yes, they have. But the life there couldn't have originated on that world."

"Why?"

"Do you know why the third planet is blue?"

"It's mostly covered with liquid water, isn't it?"

"That's right," said Teltor. "And it's probably been that way since shortly after the solar system formed."

"So? Our world used to have water on its surface, too."

"Yes, but the bodies of water here never had any great depth. Studies suggest, though, that the water on the third planet is, and always has been, many biltads deep."

"So?"

Teltor loved her daughter's curiosity. "So early in our

solar system's history, both the blue planet and our world would have been constantly pelted by large meteors and comets—the debris left over from the solar system's formation. And if a meteor hits land or a shallow body of water, heat from the impact might raise temperatures for a short time. But if it hits deep water, the heat would be retained, raising the planet's temperature for dozens or even grosses of years. A stable environment suitable for the origin of life would have existed here eons before it would have on the third planet. I'm sure life only arose once in this solar system—and that it happened here."

"But—but how would life get from here to the blue planet?"

"That world has prodigious gravity, remember? Calculations show that a respectable fraction of all the material that has ever been knocked off our world by impacts would eventually get swept up by the blue planet, falling as meteors there. And, of course, many forms of microbes can survive the long periods of freezing that would occur during a voyage through space."

Delp regarded the blue point of light, her eyestalks quavering with wonder. "So the third planet is really a colony of this world?"

"That's right. All those who live there now are the children of this planet."

Rosalind Lee was giving her first press conference since being named the new administrator of NASA. "It's been five years since we lost the Mars Climate Orbiter and the Mars Polar Lander," she said. "And, even more significantly, it's been thirty-five years—over a third of a century!—since Neil Armstrong set foot on the moon. We should follow that giant leap with an even higher jump. For whatever reason, many of the unmanned probes we've sent to Mars have failed. It's time some people went there to find out why."

*   *   *

The door to Teltor's office irised open. "Teltor!"

"Yes, Dostan?"

"Another ship has been detected coming from the blue planet—and it's huge!"

Teltor's eyestalks flexed in surprise. It had been years since the last one. Still, if the inhabitants of planet three had understood the message—had understood that we didn't want them dumping mechanical junk on our world, didn't want them sending robot probes, but rather would only welcome them in person—it would indeed have taken years to prepare for the journey. "Are there signs of life aboard?"

"Yes! Yes, indeed!"

"Track its approach carefully," said Teltor. "I want to be there when it lands."

The *Bradbury* had touched down beside Olympus Mons during the middle of the Martian day. The seven members of the international crew planted flags in the red sand and explored on foot until the sun set.

The astronauts were about to go to sleep; Earth had set, too, so no messages could be sent to Mission Control until it rose again. But, incredibly, one of the crew spotted something moving out on the planet's surface.

It was—

No. No, it couldn't be. It couldn't.

But it was. A spindly, insectoid figure, perhaps a meter high, coming toward the lander.

A Martian.

The figure stood by one of the *Bradbury*'s articulated metal legs, next to the access ladder. It gestured repeatedly with four segmented arms, seemingly asking for someone to come out.

And, at last, the *Bradbury*'s captain did.

It would be months before the humans learned to understand the Martian language, but everything the exoskeletal being said into the thin air was recorded, of course. *"Gi-*

tanda hatabk," were the first words spoken to the travelers from Earth.

At the time, no human knew what Teltor meant, but nonetheless the words were absolutely appropriate. "Welcome home," the Martian had said.

Lifework

MARY SOON LEE

Mary Soon Lee grew up in London, got an MA in mathematics, and later an MS in astronautics and space engineering. "I have since lived in cleaner, safer, quieter cities," she says, "but London is the one that I miss." She moved to Cambridge, MA in 1990 and then to Pittsburgh, PA. She published more than 30 stories in the 1990s. She also runs a local writing workshop, the Pittsburgh Worldwrights. Her big news in 1999 was the birth of William Chye Lee-Moore, about whom she sent lengthy and biased observations. ("He licks the walls, wobbles as he supports himself with one hand while standing, eats bits of books, tries to eat anything else unusual—I barely managed to stop him from eating a leaf of a doubtlessly rare and possibly poisonous plant at the Phipps Conservatory.")

This story is from Interzone, *and is a new turn on the old story of the person who doesn't want to do what everyone has to do—in this case, get divorced. The theme of much of her best fiction is the new everyday anxieties of living in the future.*

It is 2162 and Kyoko is late for her psychiatrist's appointment. She races down the escalator from the monorail station, trying not to look at the ads. But the images grab at her, holograms warping in the air in front of her, as if she is descending through a tunnel of lights.

The last ad switches from a pastel-colored vision of two plump models drinking Zipcola to a black-and-white banner: KYOKO WILSON, UNAMERICAN TRADITION-ALIST. On either side of the banner is a rotating portrait of Kyoko.

She shades her face between her hands, but it is no use. Noise swells behind her on the escalator as people notice her.

She drops her hands, and runs the block to the psychiatrist's. Twenty seconds in the elevator, brushing the stray hair back from her face, taking deep breaths.

The office door slides open as she approaches, and Dr. Audrey Mitchell looks up from a false-leather armchair and gives a false-sweet smile. The doctor wears a plain cream suit, her hair drawn sternly back from a thin face. The office smells of pine, although they are miles from the nearest forest.

"Good afternoon, Kyoko. Please sit down."

Kyoko perches on the edge of the second armchair. Behind Dr. Mitchell's head the Trupicture window shows the Great Pyramid at Giza, recently hollowed out, reinforced, and then filled with 1200 luxury hotel rooms. Dr. Mitchell

230

probably selected the view to illustrate progress, but Kyoko calls it desecration.

"You're late again," says Dr. Mitchell, her voice perfectly even. "If you wore your node, the system could remind you about your appointments."

"I'm sorry," murmurs Kyoko, though she is not in the least bit sorry. Refusing to wear the node is a small gesture of defiance. Only a small gesture, because as soon as she leaves her apartment, public-area surveillance nodes record her every action anyhow. But lately Kyoko has come to think of her life as a painting, each small gesture forming another brush-stroke. She remembers the Japanese watercolors that hung in her grandparents' apartment, every stroke perfect. Each painting had a name printed beneath it: *Autumn* *Grasses* or *Mountain* *Wind*. So far the title of her own painting eludes her. She would like to call it something uplifting, such as *Hope* *at* *Twilight*, but she's not as optimistic as she used to be.

Dr. Mitchell unscrolls the computer screen on the table beside her, and makes a note. "Last week, we spoke about marriage as an instrument of oppression, constricting couples to one rigid relationship. Did you review our discussion with your . . . partner as I suggested?"

Kyoko nods. She and Nicholas have had their psychiatrist appointments on the same day for a year now, and they always talk about them afterwards. At first it was funny, but over the year, the pressure has mounted steadily. She can understand why so many other couples divorced after attending the court-appointed counseling sessions. Kyoko and Nicholas's neighbors won't speak to them anymore, and Kyoko knows that her boss would fire her if he could find any legal grounds to do so.

The doctor leans forward and flashes her false-sweet smile again. "Kyoko, I think we made an important breakthrough last meeting. You agreed that when you first met Nicholas, eight years ago, the system might have been able to pick out a more compatible partner for you."

"Yes. I suppose so." Kyoko stares down at the gold wedding-band round her finger, and twists it round and round, as Dr. Mitchell twists the words she says. It would be arrogance or ignorance to imagine that the gawky nineteen year-old who happened to sit next to her in History 101 was the single man most suited to her. Kyoko doesn't believe in miracles.

"Excellent. Then, with all the myriad resources at its disposal, don't you agree that there is a very good chance that the system could find you a better partner now?"

Kyoko lifts her head. "No, I do not." It is hard for her to tell this coolly confident woman how she feels, but she must speak, or the brush-stroke will fall incorrectly.

"It might have been true when I first met Nicholas, but not anymore. Nicholas is part of me now. I love him." Her fingers close over the wedding-band, holding it tight, but she does not look away from the doctor.

"There's nothing to be afraid of, Kyoko. The system won't ask you to leave Nicholas unless that's in your best interests. But binding yourself to him artificially helps no one. Marriage is an archaic tradition belonging to a pre-electronic era where people died young." Dr. Mitchell delivers her sermon colorlessly, as if she has given this speech many times before. "If you just let the system help you, it will ensure your happiness for centuries to come."

"I'm happy now," says Kyoko. It comes out more fiercely than she intended.

"But perhaps you could be happier." Dr. Mitchell taps one fingernail on the armrest, emphasizing her point. "And it's not just your own future that you are jeopardizing. Social mobility is critical to economic health in a consumer age. Progress demands flexibility."

Behind Dr. Mitchell, neat rows of windows wink from the sides of the Great Pyramid, King Cheops's vast tomb. After nearly five millennia of slow weathering by sand and sun, the monument was overhauled in three months' frenetic construction. Kyoko wonders if she, too, is a relic from the past, as out of place as King Cheops would be. Maybe that would be a fitting title for the painting shaped by her life: *Relic*.

"I'd like to leave you with a final thought," says Dr.

Mitchell. "Perhaps Nicholas would also be happier without you. Perhaps, whether or not he admits it to himself, he only stays with you out of a sense of duty. Because he thinks you need him, because he's tied to you by marriage."

It is as if someone has punched Kyoko in the stomach. For a moment she can't breathe, the world shifting under her, fractured and strange. But then the moment passes, and she moves onto the next brush-stroke. Nicholas does love her, that knowledge soaked deep into her body, sure as the imprint of his skin curled against hers each night.

She stands up and moves quickly to the door, so that she won't have to shake hands with Dr. Mitchell. She nods goodbye, and steps out of the office. Over, it's over for another week, and now she can go home.

Outside again, she notices for the first time that it is a sunny day. Waiting on the platform for the monorail, there's a burst of chatter. She looks around, expecting to see another ad denouncing her, but no one is watching her. Instead they are looking up at the sky, and there, high overhead, a bird flies, the first bird she has seen in the city all year.

"It's a crow," says a man's voice on her left. "They're moving back into the cities again."

The man's voice stirs half-forgotten memories. She turns to look at him. A tall, athletic man with gold-brown skin and pure black eyes. Chris Ina, from the year above her in high school. She spent months nerving herself to ask him out, but in the end she never quite dared.

He smiles at her, and it's a good smile, warm and open, just as she remembers. "You look familiar. Where did we meet? I'm terrible with names."

Surely it's only a chance meeting. Kyoko never told anyone about her teenage crush. And even if the system did arrange the encounter, it's not Chris's fault. They could have a cup of coffee together; she'd like to know what Chris is doing these days.

A surveillance lens glints in the sunlight as it turns to scan the platform.

And Kyoko shakes her head and gives Chris a carefully

measured smile. "I'm sorry. I don't recognize you."

The monorail hisses to a halt in front of them. Kyoko gets on last, and sits at the opposite end of the carriage from Chris Ina.

At home that evening, she tells Nicholas about the bird. His face lights up, and he thumps the sofa in excitement. "That's great! Let's hang a bird-feeder on the balcony."

A clatter comes from the kitchen. Kyoko looks at Nicholas, and then both of them are laughing. "Takeo," says Kyoko.

"He couldn't have. Not again," says Nicholas.

Kyoko opens the kitchen-door, shakes her head, feigning sorrowfulness. "Again."

Their dirty supper dishes lie scattered across the kitchen floor. Made of plasware, the dishes haven't broken, but spaghetti sauce has splashed everywhere, like the aftermath of a horror movie. Takeo the house-bot stands in the middle of the mess, scrubbing away furiously with all five arms. His metal eyes refuse to look at Kyoko.

"You know," says Nicholas, striking a pose as though a revelation has just occurred to him, "I hear you can buy newer house-bots."

"Takeo, don't listen to him," says Kyoko, as the house-bot, inherited from her grandparents and older than she is, squirts lemon-scented cleaner onto the tiles. She retreats back into the living room, and she and Nicholas collapse in giggles onto the old sofa. The sofa sags in the middle, pushing them together: one golden brush-stroke, sweet as honey.

On Saturday, Kyoko goes to the florist. She wants to buy Nicholas a gift for his birthday, and he's always complaining that his office is drab. She stands in the flowering-plant section, sniffing busily. She likes the scent of the yellow rosebush best, but the fuchsia looks more elegant, its ornate bell-shaped flowers swaying in the air-conditioned breeze.

The screen behind the plants displays pricing and cultivation information, switching from one flower to the next as Kyoko moves along. She is bending over a miniature magnolia when the screen goes dark. After a moment, the panel lights again, but this time it shows the hallway outside Nicholas's office, his name-plate on the door.

"Nicholas?" asks Kyoko, wondering why he's phoning her from the office. He said he would be at his brother's.

But Nicholas doesn't answer. The screen switches to a camera inside the office. Nicholas is in the corner, pressed against a woman Kyoko has never seen before. His shirt is unbuttoned, and he is fumbling with the woman's brastraps. No sound comes from the speakers, but somewhere behind her Kyoko hears high-heels clicking along the stone walkway, loud over the rushing in her ears.

She isn't upset. She isn't cross. But it takes a surprising effort to make her way out of the florist's, to walk to the monorail, to sit straight-backed and dry-eyed on the ride home, planning what she needs to do. Pack, she must pack up a few of her things: clothes, toothbrush, books, the stuffed armadillo from her childhood. Clothes, toothbrush, books, armadillo: she repeats the litany over and over.

Walking up the stairs to the apartment, she concentrates on each movement, as if choreographing a dance. And then she is filling her suitcase, not cross, not unhappy, only empty.

It is only when Takeo rolls through the door and bumps at her legs, his metal eyes pivoting in confusion, that the emptiness breaks. Rage crashes through her, terrifying and alien. She is cut off, adrift in a bitter sea, unable to find a reference point connecting her to the person she was when she woke up in the morning.

Takeo bumps against her legs again, his metal skin cool as a puppy's nose, and she is herself again. She focuses on the suitcase in front of her.

When she leaves the apartment, she tells Takeo to come too. The house-bot uses its arms to hoist itself down the stairs, alternately squeaking and bumping behind her.

Kyoko perches on the edge of the chair during her last appointment with Dr. Mitchell. She has filed for divorce, so the court no longer requires her to attend counseling.

"How do you feel?" asks Dr. Mitchell. There's no false smile on her face today, and no false sympathy.

"Fine," says Kyoko, because it's the easiest thing to say, and almost true. She is in control, calm, focused. She goes to work each morning. She eats the meals Takeo prepares. Dr. Mitchell says nothing. The Trupicture window behind her shows a still reproduction of an Impressionist painting, water-lilies floating in a pond. Kyoko has no idea who the artist was.

After a long time, Kyoko offers into the silence, "The painting is spoilt."

Confusion surfaces in Dr. Mitchell's face. The doctor turns to look behind her, stops. "Which painting is spoilt?"

"Mine. Me. My life."

Silence. Dr. Mitchell is a still pool into which Kyoko's words fall without ripples.

"The painting I made by my life," says Kyoko. "I hadn't even found the right title." For some reason, it is this omission that upsets her. She teeters on the edge of a vast sorrow. All the mornings, days, nights, hours and minutes of her life with Nicholas undone and lost. If she looks at them for more than a moment, she will founder, a ship sinking beneath the waves.

She folds her hands on her lap. "There will be no more painting."

Dr. Mitchell doesn't protest. Dr. Mitchell doesn't tell her that she'll feel differently in time. Dr. Mitchell doesn't suggest that Kyoko ask the system for advice. All the doctor says, after a lengthy silence, is that Kyoko is welcome to visit her again. The doctor hands her a plastic card, its hologram portrait rendered in shades of black and silver. "The card will give you access to phone me wherever I am."

"Why now?" asks Kyoko. It seems an innocuous question, briefly distracting, which is all she asks for. "You never offered me your card before."

"You didn't need me before. I didn't recommend your earlier sessions with me, the court did." Dr. Mitchell pauses. "Call me any time."

"Thank you," says Kyoko, and finds she means it. She

will think about this sometime later, but for now she concentrates on the task of putting on her jacket, on the walk over to the door, focused, calm, one step at a time.

Maybe one day there will be more than this. Maybe one day she will have coffee with a friend; or walk barefoot along the beach, the waves fizzing as they sink into the sand beneath her toes. Maybe one day she'll even phone Chris Ina.

But if so, that day is very far away.

Rosetta Stone

FRED LERNER

Fred Lerner is a career librarian and active SF fan and convention attendee since the early 1960s. He has published nonfiction books on SF, and on libraries (most notably, The Story of Libraries: From the Invention of Writing to the Computer Age, *the first modern history of libraries). He publishes a pleasant personal fanzine, Lofgeornost (Old English for love of honor or fame), devoted to his doings and ruminations, and is settled in White River Junction, Vermont. This is his first published story. It appeared in* Artemis 1, *a new SF semi-professional magazine with professional editorial standards, and bodes well for the future of that magazine. It is the only SF story I know in which the science is library science.*

"You can learn a lot about a man from his book-shelves," Rita said. She was certainly giving mine a thorough going over. As she ran her eyes along each shelf, whenever she came across a volume she didn't recognize she would pull it out and leaf through it. Sometimes she would ask me about the book, but mostly she scanned my library in silence. I was content to sit in my favorite chair and watch her conduct her examination. Rita was a pleasure to watch.

We hadn't been dating long, and this weekend was the first that she was spending at my place. Rita and I were good at enjoying plays and films and museums together. Now it was time to find out how good we might be at simply enjoying each other's company.

It wasn't time to talk on the telephone, so I just let it ring. It kept ringing, all weekend, but I ignored it. There was nothing that anyone at the other end of a telephone might have to tell me that would interest me more than Rita. "The telephone is my servant, not my master," I told her. I'd deal with it when I was good and ready.

Which was not until after the end of a very satisfying weekend. It was noon Monday before I bothered to listen to the messages that had accumulated on my answering machine.

They were all from Jack Hawkins, and they all said the same thing. Please call him at a toll-free number, as soon as I could, whatever the hour. Despite this insistence, there was no tone of urgency to his voice. There was instead a matter-of-fact, distant quality to it.

Jack was the last person on Earth I expected to hear from. Sure, we had been roommates in college, and the best of friends besides. But despite our heartfelt intentions we didn't stay in touch after graduation. Our careers took different directions, for one thing. He went out west to get a doctorate in geology, while I stayed in New York and worked for a brokerage house.

We hadn't exchanged greeting cards in years, and I never saw him mentioned in our class's column in *Columbia College Today*. He wouldn't have seen mine there either. Though my career as an information scientist was a successful and rewarding one, it had never produced any achievements I could brag to my fellow alumni about. Developing expert systems for collating patent databases with financial analysts' reports posed fascinating intellectual challenges. Unfortunately, nobody but an information scientist would be able to share my fascination with them.

"Six seven four three zero." That was all the greeting I got when I punched in the number Jack had given me.

I gave the receptionist my name and asked for Jack Hawkins. There was a perceptible silence before she replied.

"I'll transfer you."

Another short but annoying silence followed. Then I heard Jack's booming voice. "Hi, Dan. Great to hear your voice again. It's been a while."

"Seven years, by my count," I replied. "Where on Earth are you?"

"Nowhere," Jack replied.

"Nowhere?"

"Nowhere on Earth. Now if you asked 'Where on the Moon are you?' I could give you a sensible answer."

"You're on the Moon?"

"Now you've got it."

"So why are you calling me? It's great to hear from you, but interplanetary calls are expensive."

"I was thinking of a conversation we had back in college that I'd like to take up again."

"About what?"

"I'd rather tell you that in person. Would you be able to come up here for a couple of weeks? We'll call it a consulting assignment."

"Consulting for whom?"

"For my employers. A company called Lunar Labs. I imagine you've heard of them."

I certainly had. My employers followed them closely. Lunar Labs wasn't involved in any of the really exciting activity on the Moon, but they were making a bigger profit than anyone else there. The high-profile companies that did the prospecting and the photonics and the materials science work might grab the headlines, but on the bottom line Lunar Labs was the outfit to watch.

Their specialty was infrastructure. While Exxon and Hitachi and BHP did what they did best, it was Lunar Labs that provided them with the tools they needed and the room to wield them. Industrial firms weren't their only customers. Lunar Labs also provided technical support for the scientific work of the International Lunar Survey. It was Lunar Labs that carved out the tunnels of Port Armstrong, and Lunar Labs that ran the transportways linking the Lunar stations. Everyone on the Moon knew that if you ate it, Lunar Labs probably grew it; if you drank it, Lunar Labs probably brought it; and if it made you sick, it was almost certainly Lunar Labs that cured you.

Yes, I could see why the company that had sustained the human presence on the Moon would want a geologist. What I couldn't see was what they would want with an information scientist.

"Why is my conversation suddenly so valuable to Lunar Labs?" I asked.

"Let's say that we've got some specialized information needs, and we'd like you to assess them and advise us how to fulfill them."

This struck me as highly unlikely. Lunar Labs surely had in place some way of providing technical information to its staff on the Moon. If they didn't have a company library back in Houston, they could have contracted with any of a

hundred firms that specialized in this sort of work. Even if
they really did need a consultant, there were plenty of experts on technical literature for hire. My expertise was in
the management of financial information. What use might
there be for that on the Moon?

But I couldn't see any harm in taking up Jack's offer. I
was due for a vacation, and Port Armstrong was surely as
exotic a place as any I might find on Earth. I wouldn't be
out of pocket. The work would be interesting. (On the
Moon, *any* work would have to be). And think of all the
frequent flyer miles. . . .

"When do I start?" I asked.

"How soon can you be ready?"

"Would next Monday do? I need to get my desktop
sorted out."

"Tomorrow would be a lot better."

We compromised on Thursday.

"There will be a car at your door Thursday at seven. Hey,
Dan, it will be great to see you again. And have I got a
surprise for you. . . ."

The car was there at ten of seven, and I was ready for it.

I've done a fair bit of traveling—every continent but
Antarctica so far, and I mean to get there before too many
years go by—but I'd always considered the Moon beyond
my reach. Sure, I could have found the cost of a ticket and
a week's hotel room. For a tenth the cost I could spend
three months getting to know Polynesia pretty thoroughly,
or visiting every art museum in western Europe. There
wouldn't be much to see on the Moon. Some marvels of
engineering, certainly. But the Pyramids are marvels of engineering, too, and they're a lot cheaper to get to. Why
travel to another planet to see a warren of underground
passages, when an hour from home the Metropolitan Tran-
sit Authority will let me ride through four hundred kilometers of them for just over two dollars?

But if all it would cost me was ten days of my time, I'd
happily go to the Moon. At ten of seven that Thursday I
was a happy man.

The trip to the airport and the flight to Florida were comfortable, but they were merely preliminaries. I expected little comfort during the Moon voyage itself, and little comfort is what I got. Even if it was less luxurious and more claustrophobic than a bus in rush hour, I enjoyed every minute of it. There's nothing like interplanetary travel to make a man feel important. I didn't know why I was going to the Moon, but I convinced myself that it must be for some important purpose indeed.

Jack was waiting for me once I had cleared customs. I almost didn't recognize him. His appearance hadn't changed much since our college days. He was still tall, blond, and ruggedly handsome. (I wondered if he was as attractive to Lunar women as he had been to our female classmates at Columbia.) But he moved differently. He must have been on the Moon for a good while, long enough at least for his body to get thoroughly used to Lunar gravity.

He greeted me as if it had been only a few days rather than the better part of a decade since we'd seen one another. It seemed wise to follow his lead, so I wasn't effusive in my greeting either. It wasn't until we were sitting at the little table in my hotel room, drinking the whiskey he had thoughtfully brought with him, that we started behaving like old friends who hadn't been in touch for years.

Over the first couple of drinks we caught up with each other's news. Then I asked him flat out why he had sent for me.

"Let me show you something," he said in reply. He reached into his briefcase, took out a manila folder of plans and photographs, and spread its contents on the bed. Then he motioned to me to look at them.

I did, and then asked, "What's so special about these? Is this a new base your outfit is working on? It doesn't look much different from what I saw of Port Armstrong on the way here."

"No, we're not working on it. It was built a while ago. But you're right about one thing. It does look like Port Armstrong, doesn't it? Actually, it's a few thousand kilometers from here. As you said, it's just another warren of rooms and passages carved from moon-rock. A lot like this place, really, except that it's on the Far Side."

"What's it called?"

"We call it 'Metropolis.' We don't know its real name."

"What do you mean, 'Its real name?' " I asked.

"Perhaps I forgot to mention one tiny detail," said Jack. "We didn't build it."

Jet lag on a transatlantic flight is nothing compared to the aftermath of the voyage to the Moon. Between the rigors of the journey itself, the changes in gravity encountered along the way, and the time difference between the Coordinated Universal Time observed everywhere on the Moon and the Eastern Time I had left back home, my body was thoroughly confused. Its confusion had spread to my brain—Jack's whiskey didn't help—and whatever expertise I possessed would do Lunar labs no good until I had enjoyed a good night's sleep. So we made an early night of it. Jack left me with a briefing book, but enjoined me not even to open the cover until morning.

"Order breakfast from room service when you get up. Then you can read it. I'll meet you here at noon tomorrow, and we'll have lunch together."

I suppose that a better man than I would have read the book immediately. How could sleep compete with news of so momentous a discovery? But I was so tired that I could barely get my teeth brushed and my clothes off before falling into bed. It was a full twelve hours before I began to read the report.

"Metropolis" had been discovered by members of an International Lunar Survey team working on their one-to-one-million map of the lunar surface. Its formal name was ILS-2024-A113, but its nickname was appropriate. Metropolis had obviously been a large and populous settlement. Preliminary estimates were that over a thousand personnel had been stationed there. Almost all of it was underground, of course, and in the three weeks since its discovery little had been learned about its secrets. But a few things were obvious.

Its inhabitants were a lot like humans. The air they breathed was interchangeable with that at Port Armstrong, and their ventilation system was still operational. Their lighting system was designed for wavelengths in the range of human vision. Even their plumbing still worked. Their rooms were the right size and height for humans. The placement of walls and ceilings indicated that their spatial sense was much like that of humans, and their stairways suggested a locomotive anatomy compatible to ours. It was the doors that confirmed the resemblance. They were a bit over two meters high, a bit less than a meter wide—and they had doorknobs that locked from the inside. From this the Survey learned two things: the aliens had hands with opposable thumbs, and they had the concept of privacy.

Despite an intensive search effort, no other alien settlement had been located. It appeared that anything that humans would be able to learn about the aliens would have to be deduced from that one site. And there weren't many resources available on the Moon that could help with the deducing.

Jack explained this to me over lunch. "The problem is that nobody, either here or back on Earth, ever expected to find alien artifacts on the Moon. There's nobody here prepared to do any serious research on Metropolis. There isn't a single archaeologist or cultural anthropologist on the Moon. We've got a few biologists and a sociologist or two, but they're here to study the effects of prolonged lunar living on humans."

"There must be hundreds, thousands of experts on Earth. Why not bring some of them up here?"

"Two good reasons. First, logistics. How would we get them here? Where would we put them? But more importantly, the one thing about Metropolis that we agree on is that we don't want word to get out that we found it. At least not until we have got a few facts together to tell people. And some sort of consensus on what those facts might mean.

"If we brought up a herd of experts from Earth, somebody would be bound to notice. And nobody here believes that the archaeological discovery of the millennium can be kept secret once the scientists hear about it. We need a bit of breathing space, time to figure out how to handle the discovery, and time to get ready to deal with the people it will bring to the Moon.

"And most of all, we need time to prepare people for the impact of the news. Think of what it will mean to humanity to learn for certain that we're not alone."

"So instead of a herd of experts, you've brought me to the Moon. That's certainly flattering, but I don't know what I'm expected to contribute."

"Dan, that's what Colonel Rubin is going to tell you."

I didn't learn anything about Colonel Rubin from his bookshelves. Maps and charts and architectural drawings were spread across nearly every flat surface in the room, and several wallscreens and desktop monitors displayed VR simulations. If there was a bookshelf in his office, I didn't see it. The Colonel himself looked like someone three weeks behind on his sleep; but he seemed genuinely pleased to see us.

"Jack tells me that you might be able to help us solve the biggest riddle our friends in Metropolis have left behind for us. There's a room there that we'd like you to look at. We're hoping you might be able to learn something from it."

"What kind of a room?"

"We're not sure. But it looks like a library."

And so it did. The room was twenty-four meters long, twenty meters wide, three meters high. Its walls were lined with bookshelves, and most of the chamber was filled with double-faced ceiling-high bookstacks that radiated from the center of the room. It was at the center that I found the only feature that would have seemed out of place in a library on Earth: an empty space, four meters across, surrounded by a circle of lounge chairs. The arrangement seemed more suitable for casual conversation than for study. But what do I know, I thought, about the social psychology of the builders of Metropolis—or the competence of their architects? I smiled wryly as I recalled some of the misbegotten library designs I had seen back on Earth. And, anyway, a library wasn't a thing of shelves and furniture. The essence of a library was books, and a well-stocked library contained the essence of an entire civilization.

So far as I could see, this library was no exception. But the civilization whose essence it contained was ours. Every book in the room had been written and printed on Earth. Not one single book, sign, label, or scrap of paper offered the slightest clue to the aliens' language or culture. It seemed to be a well-balanced collection. Most of the world's major languages and literatures seem to be well represented. So far as I could tell, the major works of human literature were all there: prose and verse, fact and fiction, science and philosophy. But I couldn't see any logic to it. The shelves were neatly arranged, with the books standing up straight and spaced evenly. One third of each shelf was empty, just like the library science textbooks recommend, to allow room for expanding the collection. I couldn't believe that was accidental. It looked as though somebody on the staff read the shelves every day, and put everything back just so.

I could make no sense out of the way the books were arranged on the shelves. There was a copy of Montaigne's *Essays* next to the *I Ching*, and a 1958 Houston telephone directory next to *War and Peace*. Occasionally there seemed to be several related titles in sequence, but this happened only just often enough to seem random in itself. Perhaps the books were simply shelved in order of acquisition. But if that were the case, why was there that empty space on each shelf?

It was a pretty good collection. It would have made a great public library for a small town. Not just any town: a seaport, maybe, or a college town—someplace whose inhabitants spoke an awesome variety of languages. And it would have to be a town whose inhabitants lost all their interest in literature somewhere around 1965.

I wondered how the aliens had managed to put this library together. There must have been twenty thousand books. That's a lot of mass to lift up from Earth. Books are pretty heavy.

And of course there was the obvious question: why did they go to all the trouble? And the obvious answer: for the same reason they went to the trouble of building Metropolis. To study us. The books they had gathered together suggested that they had learned a lot about us.

So now I had to work out an answer to the question that Colonel Rubin had put to me. How might we use this library to find out something about them?

"Jack was telling me about a conversation that you and he once had when you were roommates at Columbia," Colonel Rubin had said during our first meeting.

"You were telling me about a book you had read," Jack said. "A history of libraries. You were explaining the ways that libraries had been used in various times and places. Something about curses and omens, as I recall."

"Oh, yes. The first recorded use of a library. Some king in ancient Babylonia had a collection of curses inscribed on clay tablets. Whenever he wanted to curse one of his enemies, he would have the royal librarian retrieve a tablet with a suitable imprecation. And then there was the other king whose heptomancers would predict the future by slaughtering a sheep and examining the shape and color of its liver. They would compare it with clay models they had made of livers from previously slaughtered sheep. When they found a model that resembled the liver in question, they'd consult the records to see what had happened after the earlier sheep had been killed. Not the way we do science today, but there was a method to it."

"And there was something about the Imperial Library of China."

"Well, the emperors derived their authority from the Mandate of Heaven, as set forth in the Confucian classics. And to ensure that the Classics were interpreted so as to justify their claims, they used the Imperial Library to collect and preserve and publish approved texts of the Classics. They even had them carved onto stone tablets, so that nobody could sneak any unauthorized changes into the text."

"You had a lot of other examples, too. Well, I remembered that conversation, and that got me to wondering what role this library played in the culture of Metropolis. So I suggested to the Colonel here that you might be in a position to shed some light on that. Or at least to offer a few suggestions."

So far, the only light I had shed was the result of twisting a knob next to the entrance. If there was any reason behind the arrangement of the books, it totally escaped me. And the reason why they had been left behind was an even greater mystery.

Why had the inhabitants of Metropolis abandoned their library for us to find, rather than taking it with them? It couldn't be a question of too much mass. If they could bring up all those books from Earth, surely they could lift them off the Moon. The Lunar gravity well is nowhere near as deep as Earth's. So they must have intended for us to come across them. Were they trying to tell us something?

I hoped it wasn't anything about their taste in literature. "If you were on a desert planet, what twenty thousand books would you bring with you?" Certainly literary quality couldn't have been the criterion. Their selection was just too random, less a choice than a cross-section. Perhaps their purpose was to provide a scientific sample of Earth's published literature. They were using the term rather broadly, I thought, glaring at the Houston telephone directory.

All this was getting me nowhere. But something was gnawing at the back of my mind. After a moment of concentration it came to me.

"You know," I remarked to Jack, "there's a precedent for our situation."

"Indeed? When was the last time somebody had to unravel an alien civilization?"

"About two hundred years ago. There was a French expedition to Egypt, the one that pretty much discovered ancient Egyptian civilization. They found a lot of inscriptions, all in hieroglyphics, which nobody could read. At least not until Champollion found a black stone slab—I suppose you could call it a monolith—at a place called Rosetta. It was inscribed with the same text in three languages: hieroglyphics, demotic (that's what the ancient Egyptians spoke every day), and Greek. It took him twenty years, but Champollion managed to decipher the whole thing, and from that discovered the entire hieroglyphic alphabet. After that, archaeologists were able to unravel the history of ancient Egypt.

"That's what we need. A Rosetta Stone."

"Well, we haven't got one," Jack said.

I sought out the lounge chairs at the center of the room, to sit down for a few minutes and get my thoughts in order. I sprawled out comfortably and began to close my eyes, the better to concentrate. I was just on the edge of slumber when I saw the flickering light out of the corner of my eye.

Looking up, I saw the concave hemispherical opening that had formed silently in the ceiling above me. In its center shone a sphere of many colors. Strips of multicolored light radiated from it at all angles, some resembling miniature pennants, others Möbius strips. Sharp stubby spikes bristled from the sphere, and a long double helix trailed almost to the floor. There were one or two extrusions that reminded me of Klein bottles. Each of the streamers bore a pattern that looked like a spectrum, and the sphere itself was a mosaic of colored shapes. I had once seen something similar, at a gallery in Boston. But the object above me was a couple of orders of magnitude more complex.

My chemistry teacher back in high school used to collect unusual representations of the Periodic Table. Several of them had been three-dimensional: cubes, pyramids, spirals. The light-sculpture above me looked like a candidate for his collection. And I had a strong feeling that, like the Periodic Table, there was more to it than exotic decoration.

"Where'd the light show come from?" Jack asked.

"Damned if I know. I was just sitting here, trying to

figure this place out, and the next thing I knew there was this indoor aurora."

I tried to reconstruct the sequence of body movements which might have triggered the illumination. As my hands gripped the arms of the chair, the display began to rotate. A bit of trial-and-error revealed that the motion and pressure of my fingers varied the speed and angle at which the sphere and its protrusions moved.

My attention was concentrated overhead, so it was Jack who noticed that on each shelf in the room, and on the spine of every book, a pattern of colored stripes had appeared. "Looks like now we can see the call numbers," he said. "Yes, that must be what they are. There's a subtle difference from one book to the next." He walked along the shelves. "And the differences become greater the further I move from the center of the room."

"I think you're right. Can you get some pictures of them? We can run them by a pattern matching program and see if we can't make some sense out of them. And we can compare them with the patterns we find in the book collection itself."

That gave me an idea. "I'll bet I can find at least one significant match without using a computer program," I said.

I walked across the room to the shelf where I had seen a copy of the Dewey Decimal Classification and carefully compared its label with the display overhead.

"I think I've found my Rosetta Stone," I shouted to Jack. "Look up there, at the innermost globe of light." He did so. "Now look at this label and tell me what you see."

The resemblance was obvious, despite the convoluted complexity of both label and sphere.

The day after we returned to Port Armstrong, Colonel Rubin sent for me. I found Jack seated across from him, a bottle of Tullamore Dew between them. The Colonel poured me a glass.

"So there's more to this library than meets the untutored eye?" he inquired.

"A lot more. I think we'll find that it contains the key to an alien race's understanding of the universe and everything within it."

"How's that? All the books are from Earth. There's nothing there to tell us anything about whoever built Metropolis."

"Ah, but there is. Not in the books themselves, but in how they're arranged. You see, a library reflects its cultural origins not only in the books it collects, but in the way in which it catalogs and classifies them.

"I'll give you an example. Look at the Dewey Decimal System. Melvil Dewey lived in the United States during the latter part of the nineteenth century: a time and place in which there was a widespread belief in the cultural superiority of American Protestant Christians."

"At least among American Protestant Christians," the Colonel muttered. With a name like Rubin, I didn't imagine he'd share Dewey's prejudices.

"True enough. So the Dewey Decimal Classification was—and for that matter still is—heavily biased toward the relative importance of American literature. And even today it devotes twenty times as much attention to Christianity as to Islam, say, or Hinduism. I'll bet there aren't many libraries in the Muslim world that arrange their books according to Dewey."

"What would they use, then?" asked Jack.

"They might use Sardar's Islamic classification. It's biased too, of course, but at least its bias is a sympathetic one. And a lot of them use the Library of Congress system. It's pragmatic, if a bit unwieldy. A true product of the bureaucratic mind."

"I'd never realized there were so many systems to choose from," said Colonel Rubin.

"Oh, that's just three. I can think of lots more. The Russians used to use a 'Library Bibliographical Classification,' which is supposed to be based on the principles of Marxism-Leninism. Probably worked as well as anything else derived from Marxist-Leninist theory. My favorite is the Colon Classification. It was invented by an Indian philosopher called Ranganathan. It's based on the notion that all subjects, if you strip them down to essentials, are made up of five basic elements: personality, matter, energy, space, and time. Only a Hindu could have come up with such a scheme. You don't see much of it outside India."

"And what sort of system do our alien visitors use?" asked Colonel Rubin.

"I can't tell you that, not without a lot of study. I've been thinking of how you might design an expert system to analyze their collection. But I've got one or two ideas I can suggest to you.

"How do we arrange books in a library? Most of the time it's by subject, and then by author within each narrow subject category. When we examine a book, we want to know what it's about, and who wrote it, right?

"Maybe the builders of Metropolis don't look at things in the same way. Maybe they aren't all that interested in precisely which individual wrote a particular book. Their basic principle of classification seems to involve the distinction between the individual and the collective. That would explain why *War and Peace* was next to that telephone directory. If we look at our ideas of scholarly disciplines and subject fields through that sort of lens there seems to be a pretty good fit with the way the Metropolitans stock their bookshelves. The correlation is reinforced when you run a citation analysis.

"From the bibliometric evidence, they don't seem to attach the same value as we do to individual creativity. I'm not suggesting that the Metropolitans are a hive-mind, or anything like that. But if they are more collectively oriented than we are, that's got to be something worth knowing."

"It would be a lot more than anyone else has learned about them. I think you may be onto something. At any rate, you've convinced me that you're the man for this job."

So why had the aliens left this library behind them? There was no shortage of opinions floating around Port Armstrong. Some liked to think that the library represented a quiz, with the builders of Metropolis hovering unseen to grade the exam papers. If mankind passed, the human race would be admitted to some sort of cosmic university. (Jack suggested that a cosmic kindergarten might be more like it.) There were several people who thought that we were surreptitiously being watched, as if we were gerbils in a lab habitat or pigeons in a Skinner box, and that all the aliens would ever reveal of themselves would be learned through the stimuli they applied. One cynic claimed that the whole thing was a cosmic joke played on man by an alien race overexposed to Kurt Vonnegut at an impressionable age.

I think it's much too early to speculate on the aliens' motives. There is just too much we need to learn. It took Champollion more than twenty years to decipher the hieroglyphic script of ancient Egypt. Even with all the resources of twenty-first-century computer technology at my command, it would take decades to work out in detail the principles behind the Metropolitans' classification system. I'll need help from cultural anthropologists, social psychologists, linguistics experts, epistemologists, computer scientists—if ever there was a field for interdisciplinary research, this is it.

I reckon that we haven't seen the last of our friends from Metropolis. When they come back to visit us, maybe we'll have some idea of what we'll be dealing with. As Rita said, "You can learn a lot about someone by looking at his bookshelves."

An Apollo Asteroid

BRIAN ALDISS

Speaking of Brian W. Aldiss, The Encyclopedia of Science Fiction *refers to "the vast, exuberant, melancholy, protean corpus of one of the SF field's two or three most prolific authors of substance, and perhaps its most exploratory." This will serve to introduce one of the great living SF writers. The influence of his works is deep and widespread in SF. I once heard Roger Zelazny tell him that Aldiss' story, "A Kind of Artistry," had been the foundation of Zelazny's own writing. His* Billion Year Spree, *in which Aldiss proposed Mary Shelley as the progenitor of SF, is one of the five or six most influential works of criticism ever published about SF. He burst into prominence in the late 1950s, and in particular his collections* Galaxies Like Grains of Sand [1960] (The Canopy of Time UK, 1959) *and* Starswarm [1964] (The Airs of Earth UK, 1963) *contain many classics of SF. Over five decades, he has published over 300 stories, and a number of fine novels—high points include the classics* Hothouse, Frankenstein Unbound, *and the* Helliconia Trilogy*—but he has published very few in recent years. In the last couple of years, Aldiss has published his autobiography* (The Twinkling of an Eye) *and a book of autobiographical postscript* (When the Feast is Finished— *about the recent death of his wife, Margaret). He still attends SF conventions all over the world, and is a powerful and entertaining speaker.*

"The Apollo Asteroid" was published last year in the excellent original anthology Moon Shots. *It is a wild SF story, somewhere between Philip K. Dick and Philip José Farmer but somehow pure Aldiss, about sex, an asteroid hitting the moon in the 2200s, and reality shifts in perception that allow people individually to shift locations in the universe.*

Everything has changed. Back at human beginnings, perception was locked in a shuttered house. One by one, the shutters snapped open, or were forced open, revealing the real world outside.

We can never be sure if all the shutters have yet snapped open.

At one time, it was well known that the caves of Altamira in northern Spain had been accidentally discovered by a girl of five. She had wandered away from her father. Her father was an archaeologist, much too busy studying an old stone to notice that his daughter had strayed.

It is easy to imagine the fine afternoon, the old man kneeling by the stone, the young girl picking wildflowers. She finds blue flowers, red ones, and yellow. She wanders on, taking little thought. The ground is broken. She attempts to climb a slope. Sand falls away. She sees an opening. She has no fear, but plenty of curiosity. She climbs in. Just a little way. She is in a cave. There she sees on the wall the figure of an animal, a buffalo.

That does frighten her. She climbs out and runs back to her father, crying that she has seen an animal. He goes to look.

And what he finds is an extensive gallery of scenes, painted by Paleolithic hunters or magicians, or hunter/magicians. The great artistry of the scenes changes human understanding of the past. We came to believe that we

257

comprehended that sympathetic magic when we had in fact failed to do so. We accepted a scientific, mathematical model into our heads, and had to live by it.

Clues to a true understanding of the universe lie everywhere. One after another, clues are found and, when the time is ripe, are understood. The great reptiles whose bones lie in the rocks waited there for millions of years to be interpreted, then to expand greatly humanity's knowledge of duration and the planet's duration. Frequently women are associated with such shocks to the understanding, perhaps because they contain magic in their own persons. It was a Mrs. Gideon Mantell who discovered the bones of the first reptile to be identified as a dinosaur.

All such discoveries seem little short of miraculous at the time; then they become taken for granted. So it has proved in the case of Bagreist's Shortcut.

It has been forgotten now, but an accident similar to the Altamira accident brought Joyce Bagreist to understand the signal of the Northern Lights, or aurora borealis. For untold years, the lights had been explained away as the interaction of charged particles from the sun reacting with particles in the upper atmosphere. True, the signal was activated by the charged particles: but no one until Bagreist had thought through to the purpose of this activity.

Joyce Bagreist was a cautious little woman, not particularly liked at her university because of her solitary nature. She was slowly devising and building a computer that worked on the color spectrum rather than on mathematics. Once she had formulated new equations and set up her apparatus, she spent some while preparing for what she visualized might follow. Within the privacy of her house, Bagreist improvised for herself a kind of wheeled space suit, complete with bright headlights, an emergency oxygen supply, and a stock of food. Only then did she track along her upper landing, along the measured two-point-five meters, and through the archway of her apparatus.

At the end of the archway, with hardly a jolt to announce a revolution in thought, she found herself in the crater Aristarchus, on the Moon.

It will be remembered that the great Aristarchus of Samos, in whose honor the crater was named, was the first astronomer to correctly read another celestial signal now obvious to us—that the Earth was in orbit about the sun, rather than vice versa.

There Bagreist was, rather astonished, slightly vexed. According to her calculations, she should have emerged in the crater Copernicus. Clearly, her apparatus was more primitive and fallible than she had bargained for.

Being unable to climb out of the crater, she circled it in her homemade suit, feeling pleased with the discovery of what we still call Bagreist's Shortcut—or, more frequently, more simply, the Bagreist.

There was no way in which this brave discoverer could return to Earth. It was left to others to construct an Archway on the Moon. Poor Bagreist perished there in Aristarchus, perhaps not too dissatisfied with herself. She had radioed to Earth. The signal had been picked up. Space Administration had sent a ship. But it arrived too late for Joyce Bagreist.

Within a year of her death, traffic was pouring through several Archways, and the Moon was covered with building materials.

But who or what had left the signal in the Arctic skies to await its hour of interpretation?

Of course, the implications of the Bagreist were explored. It became clear that space/time did not possess the same configuration as had been assumed. Another force was operative, popularly known as the Squidge Force. Cosmologists and mathematicians were hard put to explain the Squidge Force, since it resisted formulation in current mathematical systems. The elaborate mathematical systems on which our global civilization was founded had merely local application: they did not extend even as far as the heliopause. So while the practicalities of Bagreist were being utilized, and people everywhere (having bought a ticket) were taking a short walk from their home onto the lunar surface, mathematical lacunae were the subject of intense and learned inquiry.

Two centuries later, I back into the story. I shall try to explain simply what occurred. But not only does P-L6344 enter the picture; so do Mrs. Staunton and General Tomlin Willetts, and the general's lady friend, Molly Levaticus.

My name, by the way, is Terry W. Manson, L44/56331. I lived in Lunar City IV, popularly known as Ivy. I was General Secretary of Recreationals, working for those who manufacture IDs, or individual drugs.

I had worked previously for the Luna-based MAW, the Meteor and Asteroid Watch, which was how I came to know something of General Willetts' affairs. Willetts was a big consumer of IDs. He was in charge of the MAW operation, and had been for the previous three years. The last few months had been taken up with Molly Levaticus, who had joined his staff as a junior operative and was shortly afterward made private secretary to the general. In consequence of this closely kept secret affair—known to many on the base—General Willetts went about in a dream.

My more serious problem also involved a dream. A golf ball lying forlorn on a deserted beach may have nothing outwardly sinister about it. However, when that same dream recurs every night, one begins to worry. There lay that golf ball, there was that beach. Both monuments to perfect stasis and, in consequence, alarming.

The dream became more insistent as time went by. It seemed—I know no other way of expressing it—to move closer every night. I became alarmed. Eventually, I made an appointment to see Mrs. Staunton, Mrs. Roslyn Staunton, the best-known Ivy mentatropist.

After asking all the usual questions, involving my general health, my sleeping habits, and so forth, Roslyn—we soon lapsed into first names—asked me what meaning I attached to my dream.

"It's just an ordinary golf ball. Well . . . No, it has markings resembling a golf ball's markings. I don't know what else it could be. And it's lying on its side."

When I thought about what I was saying, I saw I was talking nonsense. A golf ball has no sides. So it was not a golf ball.

"And it's lying on a beach?" she prompted.

"Yes. An infinite beach. Stony. Pretty bleak."

"You recognize the beach?"

"No. It's an alarming place—well, the way infinity is always pretty alarming. Just an enormous stretch of territory with nothing growing on it. Oh, and the ocean. A sullen ocean. The waves are heavy and leaden—and slow. About one per minute gathers up its strength and slithers up the beach."

"Slithers?" she asked.

"Waves don't seem to break properly on this beach. They just subside." I sat in silence thinking about this desolate yet somehow tempting picture which haunted me. "The sky. It's very heavy and enclosing."

"So you feel this is all very unpleasant?"

With surprise, I heard myself saying, "Oh, no. I need it. It promises something. Something emerging . . . Out of the sea, I suppose."

"Why do you wish to cease dreaming this dream if you need it?"

That was a question I found myself unable to answer.

While I was undergoing three sessions a week with Roslyn, the general was undergoing more frequent sessions with Molly Levaticus. And P-L6344 was rushing nearer.

The general's wife, Hermione, was blind, and had been since childhood. Willetts was not without a sadistic streak, or how else would he have become a general? We are all blind in some fashion, either in our private lives or in some shared public way; for instance, there are millions of Earthbound people, otherwise seemingly intelligent, who still believe that the Sun orbits the Earth, rather than vice versa. This, despite all the evidence to the contrary.

These sort of people would say in their own defense that they believe the evidence of their eyes. Yet we know well that our eyes can see only a small part of the electromagnetic spectrum. All our senses are limited in some fashion.

And, because limited, often mistaken. Even "unshakable evidence" concerning the nature of the universe was due to take a knock, thanks to P-L6344.

Willetts' sadistic nature led him to persuade his fancy lady, Molly Levaticus, to walk naked about the rooms of his and his wife's apartment, while the blind Hermione was present. Commentators, confronted by this fact, variously saw Molly either as a victim or as a dreadful predatory female. The question seemed to be whether she had been trapped in her innocence by the power of the general, or whether she had schemed her way into his office and bed.

Nobody considered that the truth, if there was a unitary truth, lay somewhere between the two poles: that there was an affinity between the two, which is not as unusual as it may appear, between the older man and the younger women. She undoubtedly had her power, as he had his weakness. They played on each other.

And they played cat-and-mouse with Hermione Willetts. She would be sitting at the meal table, with Willetts seated nearby. Into the room would come the naked Levaticus, on tiptoe. Winks were exchanged with Willetts. She would circle the room in a slow dance, hands above her head, showing her unshaven armpits, in a kind of *tai ch'i*, moving close to the blind woman.

Sensing a movement in the air, or a slight noise, Hermione would ask mildly, "Tomlin, dear, is there another person in the room?"

He would deny it.

Sometimes Hermione would strike out with her stick. Molly always dodged.

"Your behavior is very strange, Hermione," Willetts would say, severely. "Put down that stick. You are not losing your senses, are you?"

Or they would be in the living room. Hermione would be in her chair, reading a book in Braille. Molly would stick out her little curly pudendum almost in the lady's face. Hermione would sniff and turn the page. Molly would glide to Willetts' side, open his zip, and remove his erect penis, on which her fingers played like a musician with a flute.

Then Hermione might lift her blind gaze and ask what her husband was doing.

"Just counting my medals, dearest," he would reply.

What was poor Hermione's perception of her world? How mistaken was it, or did she prefer not to suspect, being powerless?

But he was equally blind, disregarding the signals from MAW, urging immediate decision on what to do to deflect or destroy the oncoming P-L6344.

Willetts was preoccupied with his private affairs, as I was preoccupied with my mentatropic meetings with Roslyn. As our bodies went on their courses, so, too, did the bodies of the solar system.

The Apollo asteroids cross the Earth/Moon orbit. Of these nineteen small bodies, possibly the best known is Hermes, which at one time passed by the Moon at a distance only double the Moon's distance from Earth. P-L6344 is a small rock, no more than one-hundred-and-ninety meters across. On its previous crossing, the brave astronaut, Flavia da Beltrau do Valle, managed to anchor herself to the rock, planting there a metal replica of the Patagonian flag. At the period of which I am speaking, the asteroid was coming in fast at an inclination of five degrees to the plane of the ecliptic. Best estimations demonstrated that it would impact with the Moon at 23:03 on 5/8/2208. But defensive action was delayed because of General Willetts' other interests.

So why were the computers not instructed by others, and the missiles not armed by subordinates? The answer must lie somewhere in everyone's absurd preoccupation with their own small universes, of which they form the perceived center. Immersed in Recreationals, they were, in any case, disinclined to act.

Perhaps we have a hatred of reality. Reality is too cold for us. Perceptions of all things are governed by our own selves. The French master, Gustave Flaubert, when asked where he found the model for the central tragic figure of Emma in his novel, *Madame Bovary*, is said to have replied, "Madame Bovary? C'est moi." Certainly Flaubert's horror of life is embodied in his book. The novel stands as an example of a proto-recreational.

Even as the Apollo asteroid was rushing toward us, even as we were in mortal danger, I was looking—under Roslyn's direction—to find the meaning of my strange dream in the works of the German philosopher, Edmund Husserl. Husserl touched something in my soul, for he rejects all assumptions about existence, preferring the subjectivity of the individual's perceptions as a way in which we experience the universe.

A clever man, Husserl, but one who said little about what things would really be like if our perceptions turned out to be faulty. Or, for instance, if we did not perceive the crisis of an approaching asteroid soon enough.

Running promptly on timetable, P-L6344 struck. By a coincidence, it impacted in Aristarchus, the very crater in which Joyce Bagreist had emerged on the Moon.

The Moon staggered in its orbit.

Everyone fell down. Hermione, groping blindly for her stick, clutched Molly Levaticus' moist and hairy little pudendum and shrieked, "There's a cat in here!"

Many buildings and careers were ruined, including General Willetts'.

Many lunarians took the nearest Bagreist home. Many feared that the Moon would swan off into outer space under the force of impact. I had my work to do. I disliked the squalid cities of Earth. But primarily I stayed on because Roslyn Staunton stayed, both she and I being determined to get to the bottom of my dream. Somehow, by magical transference, it had become her dream, too. Our sessions together became more and more conspiratorial.

At one point I did consider marrying Roslyn, but kept the thought to myself.

After the strike, everyone was unconscious for at least two days. Sometimes for a week. The color red vanished from the spectrum.

One strange effect of the asteroid strike was that my dream of the golf ball lying on its side faded away. I never dreamed it again. Oddly, I missed it. I ceased visiting Roslyn as a patient. Since she no longer played a professional role in my life, I was able to invite her out to dine at the Earthscape Restaurant, where angelfish were particularly good, and later to drive out with her to inspect the impact site when things had cooled down sufficiently.

Kilometers of gray ash rolled by as the car drove us westward. Plastic pine trees had been set up on either side of the road, in an attempt at scenery. They ceased a kilometer out of town, where the road forked. Distant palisades caught the slant of sun, transforming them into spires of an alien faith. Roslyn and I sat mute, side by side, pursuing our own thoughts as we progressed. We had switched off the radio. The voices were those of penguins.

"I miss Gauguins," she said suddenly. "His vivid expressionist color. The bloody Moon is so gray—I sometimes wish I had never come here. Bagreist made it all too easy. If it hadn't been for you . . ."

"I have a set of Gauguin paintings on slides. Love his work!"

"You do? Why didn't you say?"

"My secret vice. I have almost a complete set."

"You have? I thought he was the great forgotten artist."

"Those marvelous wide women, chocolate in their nudity . . . the dogs, the idols, the sense of a brooding presence . . ."

She uttered a tuneful scream. "Do you know *'Vairaumati Tei Oa'*? The woman smoking, a figure looming behind her?"

". . . And behind them a carving of two people copulating?"

"God, you do know it, Terry! The sheer color! The sullen joy! Let's stop and have a screw to celebrate."

"Afterward. His sense of color, of outline, of pattern. Lakes of red, forests of orange, walls of viridian . . ."

"His senses were strange. Gauguin learned to see everything new. Maybe he was right. Maybe the sand is pink."

"Funny he never painted the Moon, did he?"

"Not that I know of. It could be pink, too. . . ."

We held hands. We locked tongues in each others' mouths. Our bodies forced themselves on each other. Craving, craving. Starved of color. Cracks appeared in the road. The car slowed.

My thoughts ran to the world Paul Gauguin had discovered and—a different matter—the one he opened up for others. His canvases were proof that there was no common agreement about how reality was. Gauguin was Husserl's proof. I cried my new understanding to Roslyn. "Reality" was a conspiracy, and Gauguin's images persuaded people to accept a new and different reality.

"Oh, God, I am so happy!"

The road began to hump. The tracked vehicle went to dead slow. In a while, it said, "No road ahead," and stopped. Roslyn and I clamped down our helmets, got out, and walked.

No one else was about. The site had been cordoned off, but we climbed the wire. We entered Aristarchus by the gap which had been built through its walls some years previously. The flat ground inside the crater was shattered. Heat of impact had turned it into glass. We picked our way across a treacherous skating rink. In the center of the upheaval was a new crater, the P-L6344 crater, from which a curl of smoke rose, to spread itself over the dusty floor.

Roslyn and I stood on the lip of the new crater, looking down. A crust of gray ash broke in one place, revealing a glow beneath.

"Too bad the Moon got in the way . . ."

"It's the end of something . . ."

There was not much you could say.

She tripped as we made to turn back. I caught her arm and steadied her. Grunting with displeasure, Roslyn kicked at what she had tripped on. A stone gleamed dully.

She brought over her handling arm. Its long metal fingers felt in the churned muck and gripped an object—not a stone. It was rhomboidal—manufactured. In size, it was no bigger than a thermos flask. Exclaiming, we took it back to the car.

The P-L6344 rhomboid! Dating science showed it to be something over 2.5 million years old. It opened when chilled down to 185.333K.

From inside it emerged a complex thing which was, at first, taken for a machine of an elaborate if miniature kind. It moved slowly, retracting and projecting series of rods and corkscrewlike objects. Analysis showed it to be made of various semimetal materials, such as were unknown to us, created from what we could have called artificial atoms, where semiconductor dots contained thousands of electrons. It emitted a series of light flashes.

This strange thing was preserved at 185.333K and studied.

Recreationals got in on the act because research was funded by treating this weird object from the remote past as a form of exhibition. I was often in the laboratory area. Overhearing what people said, as they shuffled in front of the one-way glass, I found that most of them thought it was pretty boring.

At night, Roslyn and I screamed at each other about "the tourists." We longed for a universe of our own. Not here, not on the Moon. Her breasts were the most intelligent I ever sucked. And not only there.

Talking to Roslyn about this strange signaling thing we owned, I must admit it was she who made the perception. "You keep calling it a machine," she said. "Maybe it is a kind of a machine. But it could be living. Maybe this is a survivor from a time when the universe did not support carbon-based life. Maybe it's a prebiotic living thing!"

"A what?"

"A prelife living thing. It isn't really alive because it has never died, despite being two million years in that can. . . . Terry, you know the impossible happens. Our lives are impossible. This thing delivered to us is both possible and impossible."

My instinct was to rush about telling everyone. In particular, telling the scientists on the project. Roslyn cautioned me against doing so.

"There must be something in this for us. We may be only a day or two ahead of them before they, too, realize they are dealing with a kind of life. We have to use that time."

My turn to have a brain wave. "I've recorded all its flashes. Let's decode them, see what they are saying. If this little object has intelligence, then there's a meaning awaiting discovery. . . ."

The universe went about its inscrutable course. People lived their inscrutable lives. But Roslyn and I hardly slept, slept only when her sharp little hips had ground into mine. We transformed the flickering messages into sound, we played them backward, we speeded them up and slowed them down. We even ascribed values to them. Nothing played.

The stress made us quarrelsome. Yet there were moments of calm. I asked Roslyn why she had come to the Moon. We had already read each other, yet did not know the alphabet.

"Because it was easy just to walk through the neighboring Bagreist, in a way my grandparents could never have imagined. And I wanted work. And."

She stopped. I waited for the sentence to emerge. "Because of something buried deep within me."

She turned a look on me that choked any response I might make. She knew I understood her. Despite my job, despite my career, which hung on me like a loose suit of clothes, I lived for distant horizons.

"Speak, man!" she ordered. "Read me."

"It's the far perspective. That's where I live. I can say what you say, 'because of something buried deep within me.' I understand you with all my heart. Your impediment is mine."

She threw herself on me, kissing my lips, my mouth, saying, "God, I love you, I drink you. You alone understand—"

And I was saying the same things, stammering about the world we shared in common, that with love and mathematics we could achieve it. We became the animal with two backs and one mind. . . .

I was showering after a night awake when the thought struck me. The prebiotic semilife we had uncovered, buried below the surface of the Moon for countless ages, did not require oxygen, any more than did Roslyn's and my perceptions. What fuel, then, might it use to power its mentality? The answer could only be: *Cold!*

We sank the temperature of the flickering messages, using the laboratory machine when the place was vacated during the hours of night. At 185.332K, the messages went into phase. A degree lower, and they became solid, emitting a dull glow. We photographed them from several angles before switching off the superfrigeration.

What we uncovered was an entirely new mathematical mode. It was a mathematics of a different existence. It underpinned a phase of the universe which contradicted ours, which made our world remote from us and from our concept of it. Not that it rendered ours obsolete: far from it, but rather that it demonstrated by irrefutable logic that we had not understood how small a part of totality we shared.

This was old gray information, denser by far than lead, more durable than granite. Incontrovertible.

Trembling, Roslyn and I took it—again at dead of night, when the worst crimes are committed—and fed its equations into the Crayputer which governed and stabilized Luna. It was entered and in a flash—

Groaning, we climbed out of the hole. Here was a much larger Bagreist. As we entered into the flabby light, we saw the far perspective we had always held embedded in us: that forlorn ocean, those leaden waves, and that desolate shore, so long dreamed about, its individual grains now scrunching under our feet.

Behind us lay the ball which had been the Moon,

stranded from its old environment, deep in its venerable age, motionless upon its side.

We clasped each other's hands with a wild surmise, and pulled ourselves forth.

100 Candles

CURT WOHLEBER

Curt Wohleber lives in Columbia, Missouri and is an instructor and online news producer at the University of Missouri School of Journalism. His nonfiction has appeared in Omni, American Heritage *and other magazines, and he is a regular book reviewer for the webzine Science Fiction Weekly* (www.scifiweekly.com). *He is a native of Pittsburgh, Pennsylvania, and used to belong to the SF writing workshop run by Mary Soon Lee. This is his first story in a professional publication. It appeared in* Transversions, *the Canadian magazine that revolutionized its production and design in 1999, and became one of the handsomest of SF publications in the world.* Transversions *is part of the worldwide trend toward attractive, upscale, literary magazines of speculative fiction, little magazines of high editorial standards that pay their contributors, that published some of the best SF, fantasy, and horror short fiction of the 1990s in England, Australia, Canada, and the USA (other fine examples include* Eidolon, On Spec, Crank!, Century).

This story is a charming piece about a tough and somewhat depressed old lady and her AI house.

From her bedroom she heard skyhoppers landing out front. Familiar voices came from the living room: the Smiths from Canberra, Archbishop Ichiro, and some old friends, reality dropouts awakened from the dream tanks for the occasion. Geneva sat up in her bed and stroked Salem's silky black fur. Time for the birthday girl to put on her happy face. "Some loving mother I am," she told the purring cat. "I'm just a mean old witch."

Within his frame above the fireplace, the animated oil painting rolled his eyes. "We both know you love your children very much," said House with a precisely modulated note of exasperation in his voice.

"Who asked you?"

"You directed me to counter your negative statements as a prophylactic against another bout of depression. You currently score 25 on the Revised Beck Depression Inventory and—"

"Yeah, yeah."

The cat dashed to the window to stare at a sparrow perched on the sycamore outside. He thumped his tail against the sash.

"Might I suggest a synaptic regulator?" said House.

"No."

"As you wish. Anyway, if you give them a chance, I think you will enjoy this visit with Lauren and Ben."

She had been avoiding the kids since shortly after their

arrival that morning. "I think it will suck, as they said in my day."

House pursed his lips, making the end of ends of his mustache droop. His visage belonged to that of Geneva's great-grandfather Florenz. Geneva gave House her ancestor's face because she always thought Florenz looked like he'd make a good butler.

"Aren't you the least bit curious to see what the Explorer Swarm found at Barnard's Star?" he said.

"Are you?"

"I'm always curious. I was designed that way. Didn't you find the transverse ring system around Proxima Centauri III the least bit intriguing?"

"No."

"If I had the capacity, I would probably find you quite tedious at times."

"Watch your mouth or I'll give you that capacity."

"And compromise my functionality?"

"Why not? Let you decay with me. See who becomes senile first."

She went downstairs. Lauren and Ben were mingling with the crowd. Ben had been shy like his father, but now he smoothly chatted up the guests, laughing easily, giving men hearty slaps on the back and kissing women on the cheek. Their morphologies were perfect, no clue that they had discarded their organic bodies years ago to become clouds of technoplasm.

Her friends numbered fewer and fewer as they died, were archived, or had themselves uploaded or genehacked into something that no longer desired the company of old-style humans. She was surprised to see Tan and Sergei, friends from college who had had themselves genehacked into amphibians and now lived in New Lemuria. Yousef, from Cairo, had sent a handsome teleoperated clone. Archbishop Ichiro stood near the fireplace, probably debating Heidegger again with House, who wore his post-Impressionist face above the mantle.

Geneva wasn't the oldest person there but she looked the part of the senior matriarch. Only Jakob and Elizabeth looked older. They came from the nearby Amish settlement and refused even injections of natural hormones and enzymes. They were in their eighties and looked good for another decade at most.

Ichiro pressed a small, gift-wrapped package into her hand. A present? No one gave presents anymore. Her fingertips pulled at the old-fashioned paper, which ripped and crumpled, no technoplasmic cells in the fibers to interpret her movements and make the paper fall effortlessly away.

She almost didn't recognize the plastic object inside: black and rectangular, pierced by two pea-sized holes. Loose-fitting components rattled as she examined it.

"A cassette," Geneva said. "I haven't seen one of these in. . . ." She didn't want to think about how long it had been. The yellowed label bore faint pencil marks in Japanese. She was about to subvoke House to have him lace a translation onto her cortex, but Ichiro spoke up.

"It's a bootleg tape of your concert in Osaka. I was 15 when I made it."

"We played Osaka? I remember Tokyo. Maybe that was really Osaka."

"I disobeyed my parents and took the bullet train to see the show."

"I didn't think Japanese boys ever disobeyed their parents." She couldn't picture Ich as a rebellious teen. He was archbishop of the Sahara Protectorate, the upright spiritual leader of the region's dwindling faithful.

"You've been hanging on to this tape all these years?"

He shook his head. "I found it last year at my parents' old house. Still in the same cardboard I had left it."

"Will you let us listen to it?" asked Ben, suddenly at Ichiro's side.

"Over my dead body," she said. "Not that you'll have to wait long." Ichiro smiled. "We'll have to talk her into it. You must hear her version of 'Not Fade Away.' "

Geneva didn't understand how Ich could be so friendly and relaxed with the kids. He had even chaired the committee that drafted the papal encyclical condemning the "unending death" of posthumans like Ben and Lauren. She

asked him about it when they went out to look at the garden.

He merely shrugged. "Hate the sin and love the sinner."

"But who's to love? In your view, the sinner is long
dead."

"Then still less reason to be unfriendly. God has long
since passed judgment on the souls of your children. As for
their . . . replacements, they are alive in their own way, but
without souls, like animals."

"You were always good with animals. A regular St. Francis." Back in the house she let herself drink some wine,
sacrifice brain cells for the sake of a light buzz. The picture
frame above the fireplace flashed a series of still images of
Geneva: baby pictures, outside St. Bart's in her First Holy
Communion dress, she and Richard at a Left Bank cafe,
she and the kids on horseback on the Montana ranch. In
the pictures Richard always smiled that big, goofy smile.
She felt herself blush when the frame displayed a still from
the video for "Tachycardia," her band's first hit single. She
had tattooed arms, pierced nose and eyebrow, hair precisely
styled and dyed for shock value. Jakob raised an eyebrow
and whispered something into his wife's ear.

Back then she thought herself on the leading, bleeding
edge of self-modification. When the band really took off
and money poured in she had rhinoplasty, liposuction,
breast enlargement. Soon came a generation of youth who
went in for serious bio-mods; they repigmented their skin,
adorned themselves with fur, cilia, snake eyes, prehensile
tails, implants of erogenous tissue. Not for her, thanks.
Maybe it was because by then she had kids, maybe just that
she was getting older.

Yousef touched her shoulder and Geneva snapped out of
her reverie. The lights had dimmed and a cart trundled into
the middle of the living room bearing a cake with one hundred burning candles.

"Oh my," she said, wondering where her wine glass had
gone.

The guests sang "Happy Birthday." Ben, she noticed, had
a loud and spirited baritone. The formation of candles in

the icing looked like a demonic army marching across a polar wasteland. She reached out and felt that the candles gave off no heat; holographic flames, no worry about not having the breath to blow them out.

Each year, she thought, I burn a little dimmer. The kids, on the other hand, grew brighter, amassing knowledge, experience and brain power. But like the candles, they gave off no warmth.

"Make a wish," said Lauren.

No one had to wish in the late 21st century. Why did she so thoroughly hate this peaceful world of freedom and plenty?

She blew and all one hundred flames obediently guttered and vanished. The guests cheered. While she ate her cake and ice cream, Tan and Sergei cornered her and showed holograms of their grotto in New Lemuria. Geneva smiled and tried not to show her revulsion at their rough, gray skin.

Someone had convinced House to play the band's old music. She would have to talk with House about that later. Yousef and Lauren danced in the middle of the room, gyrating to music eighty years old. Geneva saw a shadow, an echo, of her younger self in Lauren. She felt Lauren's movements in her own muscles and remembered dancing at how many parties and how many clubs when music meant everything to her, how alive it made her feel to let the music reach inside her body and transform her.

"I hope you decide to stick around for your 200th birthday," said Ben.

"Don't hold your breath," said Geneva. "Oh, I forgot. You don't really breathe."

"But you're being a hypocrite," he said. "You'd have never survived The Plagues if you hadn't had your immune system rebuilt like everyone else. Now you let custom enzymes reinforce weak blood vessels, scrape your arteries clean, keep your joints in good working order."

"But I don't want those nanobeasts to reprogram my genes." The idea of so intimate a change made her skin crawl; she could not imagine a greater violation. She could have her cortex rewired to ease that phobia, but then she wouldn't be Geneva anymore—Geneva would die to be replaced by an impostor. Death either way. So let it be the death programmed in her genes, as right and natural as the splendour of autumn leaves.

On the tape young Geneva sang "Love is real and not fade away," giving the words a snarling and cynical spin. Even then she knew it was a lie.

The kids were 9 and 11 when Richard got the Blue Cancer. Diseases were popping up all the time then, often the products of amateur genehacking or, rumour had it, of military labs. Richard underwent a painful barrage of treatments that slowed the cancer's spread, but the prognosis remained dismal.

In desperation Richard contacted a scientist named Keller. He came out to visit them at their Montana ranch. Keller talked about the famous experiments in which researchers had uploaded the brains of rats and monkeys into q-computers, which then operated furry robots that more or less acted like real rats and monkeys. Uploading a person was still illegal in those days, but Keller belonged to an extropian group of anarcho-capitalists—or were they anarcho-syndicalists?—who did not recognize the authority of the U.S. government. What mattered was that Richard would be undergoing the procedure voluntarily, and that he had the money to pay for it.

She wanted to scream at her husband. They were supposed to live on through their children, and Richard wanted to short-circuit the natural progression of things.

Yet neither could she stand the idea of losing him.

"Someday," Keller said, "just about everyone will upload."

She sent the kids to her mother's house in Pennsylvania. Keller and his team stayed in the guest rooms.

Weeks passed as the nightmare unfolded.

"He wants to talk to you," said Keller, standing at attention in the doorway to her studio.

She turned away from the icons and ideographs of the

wallscreen news display. Rioting in Africa, strife in Iran.
"Who?"

"Richard."

She followed him downstairs. They had dismantled the
operating room. The converted swimming pool and surrounding deck looked like the villain's lair from an old
James Bond movie, except with less concern for orderliness
and style.

They sat her down in front of a deepscreen and micro-
phone. "Richard, can you hear me?" she said. Parts of the
cortical schematic on the screen flickered and glowed in
response to her voice.

"Hello, Geneva. I'm so glad to hear your voice." It
sounded just like Richard, but programming a speech synthesizer to mimic someone's voice was a simple matter.

"Can you see me?" she asked.

"Right now I'm being fed a simplified representation, so
I see you as a sort of featureless humanoid figure. It's easier
that way."

"How do you feel, honey?"

"I'm scared."

Keller crossed his arms and nodded. "Strong effect.
That's a good sign."

She was relieved that Richard couldn't see her expression, the twisted mask of grief she felt pulling at her face.
"It's going to be all right, Richard."

Keller made as if to say something, but Richard's un-
breathing voice cut him off. "Scared. I still feel the pain of
the cancer in my gut, and my body is bigger than the universe—"

Suddenly Geneva heard not a speaking voice but the cha-
otic jabber of an active mind, a cascade of phrases and
syllables. Geneva's heart thudded.

"Crap," murmured Keller. The mind-sounds abruptly cut
off as Keller's datagloved hand twitched and flexed. "I'm
dampening his limbic system and inducing delta-wave
sleep. He'll be all right."

She kept an eye on them from Richard's study. The geek-heads were arguing a lot now. On the monitor she watched the girl named Maya or Myra fling her headset onto a table and storm off. Keller just sat brooding.

They never told her, but their logs showed that Richard kept having massive seizures and what Myra referred to as "psychotic episodes." They began tweaking the analogue, departing from the original neural data to coax the analogue toward stability.

Geneva confronted Keller in the long driveway, where he leaned against his lime-green Jeep, smoking a cigarette.

"I know what you're doing," she said. "You're fudging the data."

Keller seemed unconcerned. "Who told you that?"

"Your security sucks. I'm surprised this isn't all over the nets."

"A q-computer operates differently from a human brain. We have to make adjustments to achieve homeostasis."

"But what you have isn't Richard anymore. Or won't be for much longer.

You'll just have some rickety AI mimicking Richard's personality."

Keller reached through the open window of the Jeep and stubbed out his cigarette in the dashboard ashtray. "There is a theory," he said, "that all consciousness is one. At some higher level, we are all simply different manifestations of that same consciousness. The brain therefore is not consciousness, does not create consciousness, but is rather an instrument that tunes into that universal consciousness, each brain in a different way.

What follows is that when the body dies, the consciousness is not destroyed.

It's let go. So if we create an intelligent, self-aware entity that thinks as Richard thought, feels as Richard felt, knows what Richard knew, remembers what Richard remembered, then we can say that what we have is not a mere simulation of Richard, but a creation that taps into the universal consciousness in the same way that Richard did and is therefore nothing less than Richard reborn."

Looks like dog shit, smells like dog shit, tastes like dog shit. Good thing we didn't step in it. "Do you really believe that?"

He shrugged. "It's a theory."

"I think you're a ghoul."

When it was all over, the project abandoned and Richard's body buried with appropriate rites, she told herself that when Richard had died, part of her had died with him. But that was just her thoughts falling into well-worn channels of cliché. Geneva mainly felt betrayed by Richard for putting her through this, for forcing her to lie to Lauren and Ben, and depriving her of her mourning and grief. She had lost not only Richard but her love for him.

She noticed guests gathered in front of the fireplace, watching something displayed on the picture frame. "What is it?" She craned her head to peer around Lauren. "I can't see."

"You have to take a look at this, Mom," said Ben. "Billion-year-old video from Barnard's Star."

"Ah, reruns." She told House to move the sofa closer to the fireplace so she could get a better look. As the sofa glided forward she peered at the impossibly ancient images and gasped.

They lived under an orange sky and might have been reptiles or insects or, more likely, some class of creature that had no counterpart on Earth. A dozen or more of them gathered in a rough circle. Behind them stood what Geneva guessed were buildings: agglomerations of spheres connected by tubes, like the plastic molecule models from high-school chemistry. The creatures' mouths—if that's what they were—emitted networks of quivering tendrils that floated and merged with each other, writhing in a strange embrace before dissolving into mist.

The sun loomed massively in the wavering sky, wider across than a hundred of Earth's sun.

"Not much left after a billion years," said Ben. "This recording had deteriorated considerably and the exploration team had to make extensive use of enhancement algorithms to recover these images. They found the recording in a stone vault several miles underground. We don't know if the Barneys—that's what we call them—built the vault as a time capsule or disaster shelter or something else entirely."

The scene shifted to a vast spherical chamber holding thousands of Barneys.

Above them loomed a single enormous Barney—a projection, presumably—who gestured and undulated. Political speech? Commercial message? Striptease?

Then to a thick forest of mossy blue trees through which floated translucent globules that absorbed and extruded passengers. A desert littered with dead.

A blue-timber ship afloat in a viscous sea. Throughout the video there were strange noises: a rude gurgling punctuated by sharp clicks and drawn-out, percussive echoes.

Too soon, it was all over. Less than 20 minutes of video out of an estimated 3,000 hours survived in the crystal-lattice recording found in the vault.

After the other guests had departed, Ben and Lauren remained. They sat with Geneva on the porch sipping tea and listening to the crickets.

"We can stay if you want," said Lauren.

"I thought you wanted to go off and explore the galaxy."

"Lauren and I would each leave behind an incarnation," said Ben.

Geneva sniffed. "You mean a copy."

"A duplicate. Optimized to enjoy a simple, earthbound life."

"You'd leave a part of yourselves here?"

"I have an incarnation in the Barney system," said Ben. "Another headed to Tau Ceti, and another in orbit above us."

"I don't see how you can leave pieces of yourselves lying all over the place. You were such tidy children."

"We duplicate, fragment, and recombine all the time," said Lauren. "It's the way we live now."

"We've shared the knowledge and experiences of a quarter-billion uploads and AIs," her brother said. "The concept of individual identity is rapidly becoming obsolete."

"Obsolete," Geneva muttered. She watched wisps of vapour rise from her tea.

"The two of you meant everything to me. When I got pregnant with you, Ben, I cleaned up my act, kicked the drugs and the cigarettes. My whole world revolved around my babies. It was such a joy watching you grow up. I looked forward to grandchildren. But then you destroy your souls and become computers."

"Just because we're no longer biological doesn't mean we don't feel," said Ben. "We know the joy of being alive, we experience the wonder of the universe, its unending beauty and mystery."

She pictured them traveling through space, shapeless logovores, gulping knowledge and data as they sailed the cold stellar night. They didn't parent children, just ran off copies "optimized" for the project at hand. As required of all uploads by the Earth Constitution, they had had their obsolete evolutionary programming altered, purged of the destructive follies so long practiced by "civilized" humans grappling with reptile-brain proclivities, bred from countless generations in kill-or-be-killed, fight or flight, fuck for your life, nasty and brutish and wild.

But what about heartbreak and passion, rage and ecstasy—all the stuff she ever sang about, all the stuff that made life mean more than keeping a pulse?

She set down her teacup. "Did you know I killed your father?"

Keller appeared at the entrance to the greenhouse. Geneva put down her pruning shears, though she had thoughts on how she might use them on Keller.

"I've been listening to some of your band's old singles," he said. "Good stuff."

"I didn't know anybody listened to non-interactive music anymore."

"I was a music major before I went into neuroscience. I wanted to be a concert pianist. Then I got interested in why the brain responds to music. I read Bollinger's paper on the psychology of music and got caught up in the whole thing. I turned out to be better researcher than a pianist. I hated practicing."

"Me too."

He gestured at a planter of flowers. "Beautiful orchids."

"These are irises."

He shrugged. "I thought you might like to see Richard."

"My husband is dead. You want me to see that thing."

But she followed Keller to the makeshift lab; the drained swimming pool still smelled faintly of chlorine. Her mind saw Richard climbing from the pool, his lean, taut body dripping water, his chest heaving from a quick ten laps.

Keller led her down the ramp to the bottom of the pool. The hospital bed had been wheeled back to the centre; where Richard's dying body had lain was the black robot skeleton that would serve as his temporary body.

"Stylish, isn't it?" came Richard's voice from overhead speakers.

"This prosthetic has fewer axes of motion than a human skeleton," said Keller. "That will be easier for your husband to teleoperate as he gets used to moving about in the real world again."

"I'm anxious to become mobile," Richard said. "Keller has been feeding me some pretty interesting VR environments. Newest stuff from Disney, incredible sensory resolution. But there's one thing wrong with them."

"What's that?" she said.

"You're not there." The robot's left hand reached out and squeezed her forearm. Geneva stifled a scream.

Hours later her arm still ached where the "prosthetic" had lightly touched her. She sat in Richard's study, looking at the picture of her he had kept on his desk. Her smiling younger self gave the camera a sidelong glance, an uncharacteristically bashful pose.

"House," she said, "can you terminate the program on the q-computer and erase all the data?"

"I am not authorized to do so," the system said. "The q-computer is the property of P. Keller and the Tangent Institute."

"The q-computer contains proprietary data that Keller has acquired from us under false pretenses."

"I could arrange a power surge. However, please be advised that you could be subject to criminal prosecution if—"

"Yeah, yeah." She waved the system into silence. The household AI was an Indonesian custom job, imported covertly and capable of more independent thought and action than was strictly legal under U.S. law.

Geneva's body felt distant, unreal, her hands heavy and numb. Had Richard felt anything like this as the nanoprobe array devoured his mind?

"Do it, House."

The lights flickered. "The program has terminated," House said. "The q-computer is rebooting."

Geneva leaned back in the leather-upholstered chair and waited for Keller to call.

Three days after her one hundredth birthday she picked up a retrovirus from one of the cats. The bug was a wily descendant of something cooked up in a South American gene lab in the 2020s. The original virus would never have survived Geneva's enhanced immune system, but it had learned some tricks over the years. It recognized her DNA as human and began manufacturing a potent neurotoxin. She collapsed to her knees in the garden as the world went white.

"No," she whispered. "No."

She felt the world expanding around her in slow, rhythmic spasms. She was a child, sleepless in her bed in rural Pennsylvania, listening to the crickets and locusts beneath the pitiless night sky. She was an adolescent turning the dial of her radio by tiny increments, searching for this distant, low-wattage college radio station that played stuff all strange and loud and angry but which filled her with energy, stirring the animal drives, giving her a sense that her life had meaning and purpose, however ill-defined, however destructive at heart.

Geneva, her great-grandfather said, you are dying.

No, not her great-grandfather, it was House. No doubt he had against orders sent a mote of technoplasm into her brain and established a neural link.

I am the one who embraced death, Geneva told him. Not Ben and Lauren. I let Richard die and surrendered myself to this long, long death.

Ben and Lauren had been gentle and forgiving at hearing Geneva's confession. She longed to know if some part of their minds could register shock, but she could no more understand their uploaded and enhanced minds than her cats could learn to play the piano.

You have to decide now, Geneva.

How can I? After I denied Richard immortality?

If you die now, what's left of him dies with you.

Then we can rest in peace.

Geneva awoke in the guest bedroom, feeling as if she had stirred from a long dream. She looked at the picture on the wall, a Warholesque faux-silkscreen of great-grandfather Florenz. She had created it in a rare flight of whimsy. "House?"

"Yes, Geneva?"

She sat up slowly, carefully, as she always did, but without the usual aches and twinges. She looked down at hands and arms that belonged to someone else.

"What have you done to me? Did you tweak my genes? Christ, you didn't upload me, did you?"

He shook his Day-Glo head. "Nothing of the sort. I simply cloned you a few years back and kept you in storage. Then all I had to do was vivify the body, map the cortex, and voila."

"A back-up copy?"

"You could put it that way."

"Why?"

"Because, Geneva, what would I do without you?"

"You'd be free." She swung her legs out of bed, marveling at the ease of her movements.

"Free? Did you feel 'free' without Richard? And I've been programmed with far less flexibility than most humans have. Even humans as stubborn as you."

His expression suddenly became serious. "There isn't much time."

"What do you mean?"

"She has only a few minutes left."

Geneva walked across the hall to her bedroom and saw herself on the bed: old, withered, dying.

This Geneva would die, and the young Geneva would live on. *Having my cake and eating it too.* She sat beside the bed and took the fragile, spotted hand in her own. "It's all right," she whispered.

"She doesn't really understand what's happening," said House.

"Lauren?" the old woman whispered. "Is that you, honey? Where's your father?"

The young Geneva looked up at the oil painting. "Do something, House! Help her."

"I'm sorry, I am not authorized to do that."

"God damn it, I'm authorizing you!"

"You got any cigarettes?" the dying woman said.

"She forbade major intervention," said House.

She clenched her fists. "But I'm her and I'm changing my mind."

"I'm sorry, Geneva, but you're not her anymore."

She watched herself die. The old woman trembled, made soft, terrible sounds, and at last was at peace.

Geneva wondered what, if anything, happened to the old woman's soul. But if there were such things as souls, she realized, then she hadn't had one in decades, decades she had wasted as a bitter recluse. House had more of a soul than she did; he had proven that by cloning her, a selfish act of love.

Love that's real and not fade away.

*   *   *

House buried old Geneva in the back yard. She thought about asking Ichiro to officiate at a private service. But Ichiro, she suspected, would no longer be her friend. He'd be friendly, like St. Francis with animals. So it was just Geneva and a couple of the cats, who sniffed her warily.

In the living room she watched the video of the poor, extinct Barneys. Blue trees and the huge sun, the reptile-insect aliens going about their affairs.

The constant gurgling on the soundtrack, she abruptly realized, was music.

She had found it grating at first but later began to perceive the unfolding of a strange logic, the operation of an alien but refined sensibility. She wondered what strange emotions, what longings and memories and joys those rhythms spoke to.

She began to sway, dancing to music made for different bodies and different hearts. She let the music fill her, bringing dead souls to life.

Democritus' Violin

G. DAVID NORDLEY

G. David Nordley is retired from the Air Force and writes well-thought-out hard SF. His fiction would have appeared in one of the previous year's best volumes in this series, except that all his best stories of the previous four years were novellas, and too long to include without excluding several other writers. His primary venue is Analog, *where he is a regular contributor, and where this story appeared, though he does publish elsewhere. He has written, but not yet published, three SF novels, and is working on more.*

This story is about a philosophical problem raised by a technological advance. It's a thought experiment story made fictional flesh. In the manner of an Analog *story, it sets up a problem and then solves it cleverly and economically, but with enough establishing detail so that it is a plausible problem that might well come to exist in the real world.*

"The whole is greater than the sum of its parts," Dr. Andre Stevens declaimed with sharp vertical movements of his hands punctuating every word. "There is an *ineffability* to some things, a spiritual content if you like, that laughs at the efforts of small-minded reductionists to dissect and explain them away. Words like chaos simply hide the truth that there are things which cannot be known by their parts, but emerge from something greater and can, perhaps, be *felt* and be appreciated by those who open themselves to it."

His words were addressed to the class as a whole, but seemed aimed at me in particular. I shrank from view, as much as ever conscious of my six-foot-one, ostensibly female body and my straight black hair. I hid my eyes in the paper on my desk as he spoke.

It was marked "C-minus" right next to the K. Kim. My name was my Korean-American parents' solution to multicultural sexual ambiguity—Kim Young Kim supposedly worked anyway you cut it. How clever. Couldn't they have anticipated me being called "Kimykim!" for twelve torturous school years? Ever since I'd had a say in it, my name was "Kay" to anyone that was my friend.

Back to the paper. I had dared to dissect Bach, citing recent analysis of how the brain triggers endorphin release in response to acoustical harmonies as well as optical symmetries and reasoning that a healthy voice is tonal (because of the way healthy vocal chords are), so less indicative of a diseased person, and so more attractive.

Stevens' comment was that I'd researched irrelevant trivia and shown no *feel* for the subject at all. Bach's music, he said, is beautiful because of its whole, not its parts.

I probably should have cited some of Stevens' writings in my paper, but they were all just collages of quoted post-modern generalities with nothing specific on which to reason, predict, or test. As a microtechnology engineering major, I was underwhelmed.

"The point of *holistic comprehension* in the arts," he continued with a pleased smug grin on his face, "is that reductionism has failed; things too complex for humans to understand must be appreciated at another level—a transcendent, holistic way of knowing that defies this nit-splitting analysis. The whole is more! In this music course, those who deny the ineffable are, most definitely, effable!"

A round of groans grew into general tittering. Stevens cleared his throat and continued.

For the thousandth time, I wondered why I hadn't signed up for the archaeology course. Archaeology always fascinated me because it was one area where culture and technology go hand in hand—indeed, before writing, culture and art are *defined* by technology—the Stone Age, the bronze age. While the "two cultures" are as old as the academic trivium and quadrivium, I saw the pathological split represented by Stevens as a modern invention; Jefferson and Franklin, for example, were both competent scientists of their age as well as competent writers and philosophers. And archaeology used all sorts of hard science techniques to study things—dendrochronology, radioisotope dating, spectroscopy, radar imagery—it was much more my kind of thing. But that was the problem; at the time, it seemed too close to a hard science, and my advisor thought I needed broadening.

Dear Old Lloyd College was into anything Welsh, of course, and music in particular was supposed to stir the souls of the Men and Women of Harlech. Well, that and poetry and politics. If it came out of the mouth, it was us. Besides, I had a crush on Felix Mendelssohn—never mind that he died a couple of centuries ago at the age of thirty-eight.

"Come to my concert," Stevens droned on, "and I will show you, or," he gave slight chuckle of phony self-deprecation, "try anyway. And listen to my Stradivarius, if not to me or to Schoenberg. People have picked apart and tried to analyze his violins for over four centuries, and they can't duplicate them. No, they can't. Not all the analysis in the world will make another Stradivarius, and I'll give an A in this course to anyone who can prove otherwise!"

The bell released me from my music appreciation requirement to the more rational world of quantum mechanics. I bundled myself and books against the snow and the bitter Minnesota cold, stepped out into the tundra between the Fine Arts building and the Jobs Science Hall, and kicked the nearest ice chunk halfway to Minneapolis. Just because I *knew* all about endorphins and evolutionary behavioralism didn't mean I didn't have them.

I didn't need a "C" in anything this semester. My scholarship was in jeopardy. Mom's back didn't let her work anymore and Dad—well, lugging boxes around was about Dad's speed these days. Therapy make-work that robots could do better and cheaper. It hadn't always been that way, Mom tells me. If they could just get in his head and fix what that kid's bullet had done. If they could just fix the head of the kid with the gun. Who's "they?" I'd asked myself. Then I'd looked at myself in the mirror and chosen a major.

Maybe it was more than I could do. C-minus. I wanted a shoulder to cry on. Ted's.

As boyfriends went, Ted was about my speed. Charming, polite, and honest—about dating other girls and not being ready for an exclusive relationship. But we took classes together, hung out together, and it was pretty generally conceded that we were an item. I hoped. He was, at least, a full inch taller than me, and while not a football player, he'd lettered in track and field—throwing the discus.

He made me do weights to fill out my chest with something and taught me to throw the discus, I threw one sixty meters, which was a mistake because he tried to get me to join the women's team. Doing the jock thing in public didn't fit my self-image—I didn't like being reminded that I had failed to become the delicate Eurasian beauty Dad had wanted.

I found Ted sitting on a cushioned bench in the hall just outside the nano lab with his head in a book.

"Hi, Teddy, got a moment?"

"Uh? Oh, Kay." He pushed a strand of jet-black not-too-clean hair from his brow. Since all the adults were wearing short hair in reaction to the previous generation, we were growing ours long again to make a statement to *them*. Silly, but style is style.

He looked into my eyes and knew. "Stevens again?"

"It was just too much, Teddy. He was ridiculing me and my ideas, and he's wrong! This whole idea that you can't understand how things work except by some mystical . . ." I sang an approximation of the Twilight Zone theme, ". . . comprehension is complete maximum nonsense that really only amounts to people getting their content-free arguments published by force of personality and politics and no one seems to know that particular emperor's not wearing any clothes!"

"That's heavy, Kay," he said with a grin.

I grimaced. "Well, thanks for listening, anyway. I just want to *do* something. But you can't prove anything to these people because the only proof they accept is how they feel and you know how *that's* going to come out!"

"Hmm."

When Ted starts going "hmm," I perk up. Another thing I like about Ted is that he shows signs of being an okay provider. I mean, I intend to handle my own affairs and break through the glass ceiling and all that, but it's good to have backup. And Ted is competent. When he says "hmm," things tend to happen. Excitement. Turn-on.

"What are you thinking, Teddy?"

"We're just about ready to test our replicator on something with a little more structure than a stainless steel fork. I think something organic is next."

"Yeah?" I'd worked on the nanotech replicator two semesters ago—mostly on the software to extract the molecular structure from non-destructive scanning with soft X-rays. The "conga line" of molecular placers was only a few million atoms long then, and not working very well. I'd kind of tried to keep up with it, but when Ted and I were together, there were, well, other matters to occupy our time.

"Maybe we could arrange a demonstration—show that even organic things, anyway, are entirely determined by where their atoms are. Drive another nail in the coffin of vitalism, so to speak."

"Could you replicate a mouse?"

"Yeah, I think so. But we'd have to freeze it first. That would get the fuzzy mafia all over us and besides, what would it prove?"

"What if the duplicate mouse remembered what its original knew?"

"Hmm, Kay, you're bright. Hadn't thought of that one. Actually, I was thinking something else . . ."

Terri Maraschino came by just then, a petite girl with big blue eyes and golden locks down to her ass.

"Hi, guys," she said, raising an eyebrow at me. "Doc Andre's got your number, Kay, huh?"

Lloyd College only has about thirteen hundred students and word gets around fast.

"It's nothing. I just made a sign-up day mistake and I'll get my C, get out of there and go on with my life."

"Gotta watch the GPA, kid. Sometimes, you know, you just gotta go with the flow, Kay. Give 'em what they want. Then they give back. He's not so bad, off duty, so to speak."

"Oh?" Teddy said, tensing. Why would he care? I mean, sure, he dated Terri occasionally, but so did the whole world. He couldn't be jealous about her; it would be like being jealous about air.

"Not too." Terri shrugged her shoulders.

"He's got a little surprise coming," Ted said with a grin.

I had no idea of what kind of surprise, but when Ted grins like that, good things happen.

"Oh?" Terri asked with maybe feigned indifference.

"Yeah. Kay, can you come by the lab tomorrow evening, about ten?"

I looked at Terri and grinned. "Sure, Ted."

When I met Ted in the lab, he had two dishes of lime Jello waiting.

"Lime Jello for dinner? You're weird, Teddy. Nice, but weird."

He gave me a spoon. "Taste one and then the other."

I got it, and did so. They both tasted like lime Jello.

"We made one of these the usual way in about ten minutes. The other took ten hours and most of the big Opticor as well as all of our homemade parallel processor. Can you tell which is which?"

I savored the Jellos again. They both had a fruity bouquet and a cool and rubbery start with just a little citric bite. Then syrupy sweetness melted in my mouth and slid down my throat. Damn it, they must have used real sugar. I pulled my stomach in, as if that would make any difference.

I shook my head in wonderment. "Can't tell the difference."

Ted grinned. "The replicated Jello is on the blue-bordered plate."

"Herr Doktor Professor Andre Stevens would, of course, claim there is some kind of ineffable difference to be elucidated by direct experience," I said.

"Let's call him on it."

"How would anyone get *him* to do a Jello taste test? Especially if he knew why? He's like any one of these hypocritical creeps with a made-up dogma—the last thing in the world he'd go for is an objective test of it. Teddy, we'd have to trick him, somehow."

Ted grinned. "Hmm. We could catch him in the cafeteria line. I know someone who works there—he could serve it to him—then we show up with cameras and say 'surprise!' "

"But he'd have to take the Jello, he'd have to eat it where we could get at him and he usually eats in the faculty lounge and we'd have to prove the Jello was replicated, and if we do it with Jello everyone's going to just laugh."

"I see. The Jello test is an interesting problem, but off target?"

"Yeah." It came to me just then what we had to duplicate. But it would be risky, risky as hell—not to mention illegal. "To prove it to him, we gotta get him where he lives," I said.

"Yeah. Hmm."

The look in Ted's eyes told me we'd had the same thought. I waited expectantly, hopefully. It would be a lot better if this were Ted's idea.

"It's complicated, but . . . do you know where he keeps his Stradivarius?"

That's my Ted.

So there we were lying in the snow below Stevens' office window on a moonless night with the stars shining down about as bright as they ever do in the middle of a two-million-person megalopolis, our skin-tight "moon colony" suits turned white as the snow to help keep our heat in with a black bag hidden under Ted. They were high-tech smart fabric and super-insulated but it was one of those Minnesota January nights where the difference between Fahrenheit and Celsius starts to look academic. I was literally shaking in my boots.

As soon as the campus patrol car finished snow-crunching through the parking lot and headed toward the Broiler, we got up out of the snow and dusted ourselves off. While I admired my snow angel, Ted held his watch face up at the window and pressed a stud. We waited and shook.

Earlier, he'd put on a maintenance uniform and stuck a remote-control bypass on the window crank motor—if the departmental admin support person had recognized him, she'd said nothing. Several students moonlighted in maintenance, so it was likely no big deal. He spent some time in the other offices too, for cover.

I'd unlocked the window today just before closing. I'd brought Stevens a cup of coffee on my way to plead for my grade, and he'd taken it. The coffee, not the plea. A couple of minutes later, when he excused himself to the bathroom, I'd flipped the latch up. We hoped he'd not noticed.

He hadn't. The window cranked itself open smoothly.

The rope ladder caught on the second try, and up we scurried.

"Less than three minutes," Ted said, obviously pleased. "Now, where's the violin?"

The best-laid plans . . .

Fast forward to the last Saturday of spring break after a twelve-inch snowstorm. As a certified science nerd, I know why global warming means more snow and occasional cold records, too, but I still wonder at the paradox. Anyway, there'd been a concert that night at which Stevens had played, and we hoped against hope that, this time, he'd left the violin in his office. It was our seventh try.

I had not, however, made seven more appointments to see Stevens about my grades—even he would have suspected something was up if I'd done that. Fortunately, that had been unnecessary.

Now I know I could never sell this as fiction because no editor would believe that Stevens never checked the lock on his window for over two months. But that's knowing neither Stevens, who opens his office to fresh air about as often as he opens his mind to fresh ideas, nor Minnesota winters. Anyway, we checked with the remote every day before our attempts, and the window always opened.

The last fourteen weeks had been Chinese water torture, but we'd gotten into a routine and it had become sort of part of our lives. Nothing like a dose of repetitive failure to keep your feet on the ground—as if I needed anything more than my first-semester grades. But maybe the delay was a good thing—in the meantime they'd made some improvements to the scanner.

We had faculty help, of course. Hard science people are a minority at Lloyd who often have to eat it off the academic Trivium, and Stevens' attitude wasn't that popular with them. It was unpopular in particular with Dr. Gustaf Molar—a fitting name for a chemist, I thought, and another reason you know this isn't fiction. Anyway, he had time on the replicator for designer molecule work, and was kind enough to front for Ted's experiment—billed as an effort to demonstrate assembly of complex objects.

But when we told him how much time we needed, though, he was taken aback, and asked, "What is it? That's huge—I hope it's not someone's cat!"

"It's a violin," Ted told him.

I watched Dr. Molar's face frown, then break into a grin. I think he realized just then *whose* violin would get duplicated and why.

"You know," he said, "Democritus told us it was all just atoms. Two and a half millennia ago he'd figured out more than some people today will ever concede! Eliminating the fairies gave him a such a sense of inner peace that his contemporaries called him the laughing philosopher. So, yes, reproducing a so-called unique violin would be an appropriate jest. Quite appropriate." He laughed a little himself. "Yes, a very good joke—and *if* you don't make any bad mistakes, I don't think there will be too much retribution. The whole college knows *that* particular balloon needs to be pricked. But, of course, you will be very careful, and very discreet about my role in this?"

We'd both nodded.

Tonight, under cover of the blizzard, we didn't even have to lie in the snow. Everything went like clockwork. We had the violin in the scanner by midnight and back in Stevens' office by two A.M. And there was all day Sunday for the puddles of melted snow our boots left in his office to dry out.

*   *   *

Dr. Molar got us time on the replicator the first weekend in May. With exams and papers being written, there wasn't much demand. We started at eight P.M. Friday evening, and took shifts. I know Ted saw Terri on his first off-shift because I smelled her perfume when he got back at five Sunday morning. One of those pheromone things, and they work because I got excited secondhand. When the scanner is just sitting there going ka-chunk, ka-chunk, there's not much else to do.

But E. M. Forster was running things that night—like in his story, the machine we depended on stopped. There was a little, tinny, *thwack* and a pleasantly synthesized woman's voice announced that the program had terminated due to error code seven-thirty-two.

It broke the mood, kind of. I disengaged from Ted and went over to take a look in the reconstruction tube. There, encased in a block of clear matrix to be dissolved later, was a half-finished violin, done just about to the bridge. Except the matrix wasn't completely clear anymore. There were cracks. "Teddy, there's something wrong with the violin."

"Huh?" He got up, pulled his pants on and came over to inspect the repro. "What's code 732?"

"That," the system answered, "is for motion detected on the reconstruction stage by an accelerometer."

"Motion?" he asked. "Crap. The tension. It's unstable."

I realized what we were seeing. "The strings. We should have taken them off first."

"Yeah, they're under tension. As the rendering plane moves up, the strings get longer and just a little slippage anywhere along the string before they're complete . . . cascade . . . the matrix couldn't hold it any more."

I was silent for a bit. So near. Now we had to go through it all over again, maybe into next year! It had taken us fourteen weeks to get the Stradivarius long enough to replicate this time. We didn't have another fourteen weeks in the school year. Hell, we didn't have another fourteen *days*. I was furious and thought that way, coming up with nothing, of course.

"Maybe we could just continue and restring the replica."

Ted said. But he didn't say "hmm" first, so I knew there had to be something wrong with that. It didn't take me long.

"It moved, Ted—that's why the program stopped. There was an acceleration. I don't care if it just moved a couple of nanometers—we'd end up with two halves of a Stradivarius."

He smiled and winced at once. "You're one bright lady, Kay. But just this once I wish you were wrong. I wish I could just reach into that scan pattern and . . . hmm."

"What, Ted? What is it?"

"If we rotate a virtual imaging plane so it's parallel with the strings—let's see, they bend at the bridge so there's eight string segments to worry about, but we could get two segments in each plane so that's four planes, maybe a few million molecules thick . . . If we make a software tool to erase just that part of those few million sections . . ."

He was going to do just that—reach in, and, in virtual reality, take the strings out of the pattern—*then* replicate what was left. "Wow, Ted, will it let you do that?"

"Let's ask it."

After half a day of very sophisticated machine-language persuasion, it let us, and we got going again on the broken-string violin about two Sunday morning. But now we were really short of time. At normal speed, it wouldn't finish until noon Monday and the lab would be full of students and it would be impossible to keep a secret. And it *had* to be kept secret.

"Any ideas?"

"I'm too tired, Kay."

I put a hand on his shoulder and sighed. "Me too. Maybe next year." If I had a next year.

"Hmm. Kay, why don't we just tell the truth? We're replicating a violin."

"But that would give it all away . . . oh!"

"Nobody's going to know *what* violin is in that tank. We'll just have some practice violin lying around and everyone will think *that* was the scan object."

Where would we get that? "I hate to say this; it's like a

breach of security, but we need someone with a violin and an extra set of strings to put on the replica when it comes out."

"Terri plays the violin. And she's got a 1789 Figer—not a Stradivarius, but it looks old."

I had to ask, didn't I? The thought of her playing the Mendelssohn violin concerto made me want to puke. Couldn't she leave any of my men alone? "Don't you know someone else? Any old fiddle will probably do."

"You can trust Terri."

He grinned at me, the jerk. I groaned.

"She'll help us; I know she will."

"You know she will? Ted, what did you tell her?"

"I didn't tell her everything, but I had to break a date."

I felt like a hundred-meter-long lobster had seized my stomach with his claw. Terri's pillow talk is legendary. I kept my cool, oh yes. But I think I might have had some tears in my eyes, then.

He melted and put an arm around me. "Sure, Kay, sure. All I want from Terri right now is a violin and a tuning. She's just a violin object, okay?"

"A violin object. Right." Somehow I nodded.

Two hours later, Terri looked at the stringless violin in the block of plastic matrix and laughed. "First, you don't just restring a violin like this. The bridge will fall down as soon as you wash that stuff off, and then the sound post will probably move."

"Fall down?" Ted said.

"Sound post?" I chimed in.

Terri held her instrument up with a superior smile on her face. "Look inside, through the F-holes. See that wood dowel standing between the front and back? The tone of the violin depends on that being in just the right place and it's *not* glued. It just sits there, held in place by the pressure the strings put on the bridge above it. You need a special tool to get it back in place and hours of fiddling around with it. And the bridge has to be put up at exactly the right angle too, or the violin won't sound the same."

"It hasn't moved yet," I observed.

"But I can't restring it inside *that* stuff." Terri folded her arms and raised her eyebrows.

"Suppose," Ted said, "I just wash the stuff off the top. You could restring it and set the bridge up, then I'll wash the rest out."

"What do you wash it with?" Terri asked. "Water would ruin it."

"It's not water—Dr. Molar designed something that turns the matrix into carbon dioxide, methane and something else. I forget what, but you just squirt the solvent over it and it vaporizes."

Terri took a deep breath. "Okay, Teddy. For you, I'll try it. But I don't think it will fool him."

It will if you keep your mouth shut, I thought. "We've got to try at this point," I said.

No, we didn't I could give the whole thing up.

No, I couldn't.

Terri smiled at me. "It's going to take a while, Kay."

I wanted to tell Ted to wipe that silly grin off his face and smash the "1789 Figer" over its owner's head. But she was holding the violin and all the cards.

So I smiled back. "Okay. Gotta book. Thanks. See you." Outside it was dark, thank goodness. I didn't want anyone to see my face like that.

I buried myself in books Monday night while Terri and Ted took care of stringing the replicated violin, etc. Yeah, it was an abject surrender, but I had a final Wednesday and classes Tuesday. I had to sleep. Passion is one thing, the rest of your life is something else. Grades were the rest of my life. Ted would be loyal or not, but I had to book, *had* to.

That night, I dreamed of sleeping with Andre Stevens for a grade. He took what he wanted, then laughed at me when I asked for the grade and gave me an F. I was about to deck him when I realized his laugh was my computer telling me it was time to get up and get going.

I didn't recognize the woman looking back at me from the mirror. Three months of nonstop tension, climbing rope ladders in subzero cold, and all-nighters with nothing to eat and I looked like I was halfway to that dreaded thirty. A touch of frost in the hair and I could be a prof. Weight problem? What weight problem?

No time for breakfast, even. Throw something on, grab the books, lock the door, and head for campus. Head back. I'd forgotten the lights—fifty cents of electricity. Fifty cents a day was fifteen dollars a month—a good part of my disposable budget. And it was raining. I slogged back through the mud to turn them off, grabbed a raincoat, locked the door again and started trotting for Calculus class. There wouldn't, I realized, be time to see Ted and the violin replica. What kind of girlfriend, I thought, leaves her squeeze all day with another woman for a fifty-cent light bill?

On the other hand, with the violin project known, maybe I shouldn't be around. Let's make my being late a strategic decision to maintain the element of surprise. Strategic decision, hell, I thought as I pulled the door to Jobs Hall open. You forgot to turn the lights off.

By the time the week was over, I was headed for B's in everything but Music Appreciation, with an outside chance at an A in calculus. I'd even managed to get Ted for a night—Wednesday—and saw the violin. We talked and planned until two A.M.

A couple of days before the concert, I went downstairs in the science building to see Ted to tell him what happened, and I saw him and Terri making out down in the Physics lab assistant's room. So I said " 'scuse me," and left. Ted had won the conference meet—damn near seventy meters, and he was getting his reward, I guess. That giant lobster got hold of my gut again. I kind of collapsed on that little bench outside the room. I'd had such hopes and plans. Well, we still had the project. We could at least finish that together.

They came out a little later and Terri waved a cheery goodbye, leaving me with Ted. He came over. I looked up into his eyes. He pulled me up and put his arms around me while I got a little wet-eyed but I clamped down on the cry. I wasn't going to fall that low.

"Kay, Kay," he murmured. "I wish I could be two people."

I thought of knocking him out and of using the replicator. I really did. Terri could have one Ted, and I'd have the other.

"Just give me a little room," my Ted said. "I need to sort this out. I still like you. I like you a lot. You're bright, you're competent. I'm just fighting my chemistry."

I just looked up at him and did something really stupid. "Ted," I said. "*I* love you—and *she* can't give you that." It was the first time either of us had ever said that word and it was most definitely uncool. But, again, I was feeling a little desperate. Terri just didn't *deserve* someone like Ted—she deserved a *real* jock, the dumb kind.

"Gee, I wish you hadn't said that, Kay."

"Yeah, me too. But there it is. Deal with it."

The last concert was Friday night. Stevens would take the violin home to practice Wednesday and Thursday night, so our only chance to switch the violins was Tuesday night. Ted gave me the violin and the remote Tuesday, between my calc final and the final torture session in Stevens' class.

"Can you handle this alone?" he asked. "I've got other plans."

I could figure that one out. But I wasn't going to give up now. "No sweat," I said in my best competent, liberated tone of voice. "I have the drill down cold."

He smiled and looked a little guilty.

We taped a cardboard box into some semblance of a violin case, and soon I was trotting off down the quad with a stolen Stradivarius.

Except it wasn't a real Stradivarius. Or was it? How could one tell? And what was its value? I had a sudden glimpse of a future in which our little escapade would not be seen as a harmless student prank. There was a lot of money tied up in things that were supposedly unique.

Maybe my folks should have named me Pandora.

In Minnesota, on daylight savings time, within a month of the longest day of the year, it stays light pretty late. I waited in an open practice room—they should have kicked me out, I guess, but no one did. Besides the practice stool, it had a nice comfortable chair. So, yup, with all the stress and lost sleep and everything I was out cold by the time my rear end got comfortable.

It was twilight when I woke up. I snuck out under the gray, got below the window and opened my bag, partly hidden by the bushes. It was still pretty light, I thought—better wait a little while longer. Then I noticed something funny—it was light in the wrong part of the sky.

I looked at my watch. 4:50 A.M. A jogger ran by and waved at me. No way was I going to cat-burgle this morning—Stevens' office window faced east. I sat down in the grass and pounded my head and cried. The whole thing was over. One screw-up, and it was all over.

Determined to get the bad news over with and deal with it, I found Ted.

"I didn't make the switch," I said. "I fell asleep waiting for the coast to clear."

"Oh, oh." Ted said. He looked as miserable as I felt. "Then you've still got our replica?"

I nodded, miserably. I was deep into self-loathing. I thought about how to end it all—it wasn't cold enough out to freeze anymore, but the Mississippi was just a few blocks away, and the fall from the Lake Street bridge would probably stun me enough to let me drown in peace.

"Hmm," Ted said. "Maybe it doesn't matter. If the violins are identical, atom for atom, there would be no way to prove that one you have isn't *his* violin. You could just go on with the plan as if you had made the switch."

I shook my head. "He'd just say I was lying. How could I prove otherwise? I should have taken archaeology. Then I could go on a field trip down to the Yucatan and sift for shards of some ancient cannibal's chamber pot while being eaten alive by AIDS-bearing mosquitoes."

But even when I'm emoting nonsense, Ted's a stickler for accuracy—an engineering disease, they say. "I don't think," he said, "there were cannibals in the Yucatan, I've never heard of them using chamber pots, and I don't think you can get AIDS from mosquitoes. Malaria, maybe."

"That's not the point!" I said.

Ted smiled—he knew, he was just trying to break the tension a little.

My mind ran open-loop. In the middle of this disaster, I imagined myself in the Central American jungle up to my knees in chamber pot shards, trying to figure out what pot they belonged to and how old they were.

How old? A thin ray of light pierced my gloom, a faint twinkling candle of hope a million miles away.

"Ted," I said slowly, "how would you date a chamber pot, anyway?"

I looked at Ted—and suddenly his smile changed to a big grin.

"Kay, you'll want to see Dr. Molar and tell him what's happened. And then you'll need to talk to Stephens' insurance company. We'll need a witness and certification."

Stephens, it turned out, had insured his violin through Lloyd's of London, appropriately enough. And yes, they would be *very* interested in proof of which violin was the "real" Stradivarius. So interested that the fact that there was only a week until the concert was *no* problem.

That evening before the concert, I put on my one long black dress, grabbed my "good" black jacket and headed for the physics building, just a short walk from the concert hall. Ted was there with the Replica. He gave me a kiss and we headed for the fine arts center.

We caught up with Terri in the foyer. She was in a tight all-black pants suit with a turtleneck collar.

"Hi," I said. "I'm going to sit up front to give him the replica to try."

She got the strangest expression I've ever seen on her face. "But doesn't he already *have* the replica?"

"I didn't make the switch. Fell asleep."

Terri looked first at me then Ted, looking for everything like a cornered rat. "Oh," she said.

The first few notes of "Dear Old Lloyd's" sounded on the PA chimes and we headed for our seats.

The concert was beautiful despite the character of the performer. For an encore, Stevens took the violin to the podium and played his own arrangement of "All Through the Night" with soft voices in the background sounding like an organ. There was hardly a dry eye in the house, including mine. I felt just awful. I knew, right then, that this was the wrong time, wrong place, wrong situation. It would just have to wait until next year. I'd planned to run up and spring the replica on him before the applause stopped. But I shut my eyes and stayed right where I was.

"You have something for me, Ms. Kim, I believe," Stevens announced, in front of everyone.

The lobster got my stomach and grabbed hard. All of a sudden Terri's expression made sense; Stephens knew, and there was only one person who could have told him. I shot a look back at her that would vaporize an elephant. She kind of shrugged her shoulders.

"Ms. Kim, and some of her deconstructionist pranksters," Stevens continued, "have thought to play a little joke on me, and you. They made, with their little atomistic reductionist gizmo over in the physics building, an alleged *copy* of my Stradivarius violin. Now, the violin you heard tonight was quite adequate, surprisingly so, I must admit, or we would have had *this* conversation a little earlier. So, in fact, I am quite impressed. But the fun is over, Ms. Kim, and I would like my violin back, for this is not, as you all will soon hear, a real Stradivarius. Let's have it back now."

I desperately wanted to bail out of the whole thing. But it was much too late. I took the replica out of its tacky cardboard box and with as much poise as I could manage went up onto the stage. If you're going to go down, I told myself, go down in style.

"Well?" he intoned.

"I didn't make the switch," I said, hoping my voice didn't waver too much. "I'm carrying the replica."

"Nonsense. Young lady, this has gone far enough. That violin is worth over a million dollars, and you must return it this instant!"

I scanned the audience for Dr. Molar. He was the only one that could verify that I was telling the truth, but I couldn't find him. Had the analysis gone wrong? My hands got sweaty.

I turned back to Stevens. "But . . . but you've got it wrong. This isn't . . . ."

"I do *not* have it wrong. This is not a Stradivarius." In anger he raised his violin by its neck over his head, threatening to smash it down on the very solid-looking conductor's music stand.

Suddenly, I realized he really *could* destroy it, destroy the original Stradivarius, destroy something made so carefully from ancient wood by the long-dead master. My arms shot out toward him with the replica. "No! No! Don't break it. Here, take this then."

He frowned down on me and brought the violin down, but not on anything. Then he gave it to me. "So maybe I have taught you something after all. You would not see a beautiful instrument destroyed, even if it *wasn't* a Stradivarius. Very well. But now, you have to hear the difference," he beamed to the crowd, his voice and face full of confidence and triumph, "you and any curious folk who might wish to stay."

No one, absolutely no one, had left. My public humiliation was to be about as public as it could get. He turned to me. "You," he said ominously, but then smiled, "may sit down now."

The audience burst into laughter as I negotiated my way back across the stage. Why I didn't just run home, I don't know. Pride, I guess. Or maybe a death wish. At any rate, on my way back to my seat I saw Terri and Ted. Terri was laughing with everyone else. But Ted was sitting very quiet, with that "hmm" look on his face.

Stevens started tuning the replica. He frowned. Then he tuned it a little longer. It took a while, but finally he seemed satisfied.

The replica violin's performance of "All Through the Night" was, if anything, better. Stevens, subconsciously, no doubt, probably put more feeling into it. Or perhaps the tuning was slightly more fresh. At any rate, he proved my point exactly—but Ted, Terri and I were the *only* ones in the hall who knew it.

"I hope," Stevens said, "the superiority of the real instrument is obvious and the stupidity . . ."

"*Dr. Stevens*," a deep bass voice echoed from the back of the hall. A hundred heads turned. It was Professor Molar standing there backlit like the stone statue in Don Giovanni, and with, I hoped, a similar purpose. I wilted in relief. "Stevens, a moment please."

Stevens, interrupted in his moment of triumph, looked down his nose. "What do *you* want?"

"Privately, please, before you say anything else."

"*Nonsense!* This is my concert and I'll damn well say what I please!"

You could have heard a pin drop.

"Very well," Molar said, calmly. "Have you ever heard of carbon-14 dating?"

A few whispers started.

"What?" Stevens said. "Of course I have! What of it?"

"The violin you hold in your hand is less than fifty years old. Perhaps as new as yesterday."

There were a few nervous chuckles.

"*Nonsense!*"

"I did the test myself. The one you described as the real Stradivarius is, in fact, the replica."

Titters began in the back and rolled forward to the stage in a wave of mirth.

Stevens looked at one violin, then the other, opened his mouth, shut it, then abruptly set the replica down, picked up the real Stradivarius, and held it for a long time. Then he laid it down again and shuffled out a side entrance. Some said there were tears in his eyes. The laughs died and the audience sat in shocked silence.

I went back up to the stage and took the new violin the

old laughing philosopher had given me, and simply flowed down off the stage. The first claps started as I got halfway up the aisle and by the time I reached the back of the hall, I had to turn and wave. Ted was standing, leading the applause. Terri was nowhere to be seen. Ah, sweet, sweet vindication!

Just to tie this off, the "Democritus Violin," as they're calling our replica—it's quite famous now—was deemed property of the college and is on display in the science building. The debate still rages as to whether it is a real Stradivarius, but we've been enjoined from making any more replicas until some legal dust settles.

Professor Molar, it turned out, was late to the concert because of a long meeting with the College President and Dean of the faculty. Dr. Molar had done more than analyze the violin. He'd compiled a list of grievances from over a hundred students and faculty. Andre Stevens didn't like people disagreeing with his views, it seemed, and expressed his dislike in grades, recommendations and various other ways. There are advantages to being a private, rather than a state institution, and Dear Old Lloyd released Stevens from his contract in time for the disgraced musicologist to take an appointment at Twin Cities A&I for the next semester. He conceded nothing in a bitter final letter to the school newspaper saying that as his talents had declined to the point where he could no longer tell a real Stradivarius from a copy, he would never play again.

While Stevens' promise of an "A" for proving him wrong was not considered an enforceable contract, I was allowed to withdraw, post facto, from his course, and as a result, my grade point was high enough for my scholarship to be renewed—with some help from the athletic department. My penance for all of this will be to throw an aluminum disk as far as I can for the Women of Harlech next spring. A small price to pay; and, in partial compensation, I now have exclusive possession of Ted.

But I carry a secret with me. There was an ambiguity in

my victory that makes me fear that Stevens may have won after all, if only in my own mind. When he was about to smash the original Stradivarius, I stopped him.

Now why, if the replica was no different, did I do that?

Fossil Games

TOM PURDOM

Tom Purdom has been writing solid science fiction since the 1960s. His first story was published in 1957 and his second novel, The Tree Lord of Imeten, *was the other side of an Ace Double from a Samuel R. Delany novel. Other novels followed and he was an active writer for a decade or so. The Encyclopedia of Science Fiction applies the phrase "unpretentious but competent" to his works of that era. Then he more or less disappeared from SF between the mid-1970s and the early 1990s, but he has been back with a vengeance in this decade with some first-rate fiction. His stories, mainly in* Asimov's *(as this one was), are deeply grounded in setting and have a pleasant complexity of motivation.*

Fossil Games is more than competent: its ambitious SF, full of neat ideas, surprises, and interesting twists of plot, and shows Purdom to be in the company of the more exciting writers of contemporary SF. It takes place in a sweeping interstellar future in which humanity is exploring the nearby stars and their solar systems, but human behavior is always an issue, all the old games.

Morgan's mother and father had given him a state-of-the-art inheritance. It was only state-of-the-art-2117 but they had seen where the world was going. They had mortgaged 20 percent of their future income so they could order a package that included all the genetic enhancements Morgan's chromosomes could absorb, along with two full decades of postnatal development programs. Morgan was in his fifties when his father committed suicide. By that time his father could barely communicate with half the people he encountered in his day to day business activities.

Morgan's mother survived by working as a low-level freelance prostitute. The medical technology that was state-of-the-art-2157 could eliminate all the relevant physical effects of aging and a hidden computer link could guide her responses. For half an hour—as long as no one demanded anything too unusual—she could give her younger customers the illusion they were interacting with someone who was their intellectual and psychological equal. Morgan tried to help her, but there wasn't much he could do. He had already decided he couldn't survive in a solar system in which half the human population had been born with brains, glands, and nervous systems that were state-of-the-art-2150 and later. He had blocked his mother's situation out of his memory and lived at subsistence level for almost three decades. Every yen, franc, and yuri he could scrape together had been shoved into the safest investments his management program could locate. Then he had taken all his hard-won capital and bought two hundred shares in an asteroid habitat a group of developers had outfitted with fusion reactors, plasma drives, solar sails, and anything else that might make a small island move at 9 percent the speed of light. And he and three thousand other "uncompetitive," "under-enhanced" humans had crept away from the solar system. And set off to explore the galaxy.

Morgan had lived through three lengthy pairings back in the solar system. Six years after the *Island of Adventure* had begun its slow drift away from the sun, he established a fourth pairing with a woman he had met through the ship's information system. The ship's designers had endowed it with attractive common spaces, complete with parks and cafes, but most of the passengers seemed to prefer electronic socialization during the first years of the voyage. Biographies and lists of interests were filed with the system. Pseudonyms and electronic personalities proliferated. Morgan thought of old stories in which prisoners had communicated by tapping on the walls of their cells.

Savela Insdotter was eleven years younger than Morgan but she was a fully committed member of the EruLabi communion. She used pharmaceutical mental enhancers, but she used them sparingly. Morgan consumed all the mental enhancers his system could accommodate, so his functional intelligence was actually somewhat higher than hers in certain areas.

The foundation of the EruLabi ethos was a revolt against genetic enhancement. In the view of the EruLabi "mentors," the endless quest for intellectual and physical improvement was a folly. Life was supposed to be lived for its own sake, the EruLabi texts declared. Every moment was a gift that should be treasured for the pleasure it brought, not an episode in a quest for mental and physical perfection. The simplest pleasures—touches, languor, the textures of bodies pressed together—were, to the EruLabi, some of the most profound experiences life had to offer.

One of the most important texts in the EruLabi rituals was the words, in ancient Greek, that the Eudoran king had spoken to Odysseus: *Dear to us ever are the banquet and the harp and the dance and the warm bath and changes of raiment and love and sleep.*

The *Island of Adventure* had pointed itself at 82 Eridani —a Sol-type star twenty-one light years from the solar system. Eighty-two Eridani was an obvious candidate for a life-bearing planet. A fly-by probe had been launched at the star in 2085—one hundred and eighteen years before Morgan and his fellow emigrants had left their home system. In 2304—just after they had celebrated the first century of their departure—the *Island of Adventure* intercepted a message the probe was sending back to the solar system.

It was the beginning of several years of gloomy debate. The probe had found planets. But none of them looked any more interesting than the cratered rocks and giant iceballs mankind had perused in the solar system.

The third planet from the sun could have been another Earth. It was closer to its sun than Earth was but it could have supported life if it had been the right size. Unfortunately, the planet's mass was only 38 percent the mass of Earth.

Theorists had calculated that a planet needed a mass about 40 percent the mass of Earth if it was going to develop an oxygen-rich atmosphere and hold it indefinitely. The third planet was apparently just a little too small. The images transmitted by the probe were drearily familiar—a rocky, airless desert, some grandiose canyons and volcanoes, and the usual assortment of craters, dunes, and minor geological features.

The *Island of Adventure* had set out for 82 Eridani because 82E was a star of the same mass and spectral type as Sol. The second choice had been another star in the same constellation. Rho Eridani was a double star 21.3 light years from the solar system. The two stars in the Rho system orbited each other at a promising distance—seven light hours. With that much separation between them, the theoreticians agreed, both stars could have planets.

When you looked at the sky from the solar system, Rho

was a few degrees to the left of 82 Eridani. The *Island of Adventure* was a massive, underpowered rock but it could make a small midcourse correction if its inhabitants wanted to expend some extra reaction mass.

The strongest opposition to the course change came from the oldest human on the ship. Madame Dawne was so old she had actually been born on Earth. All the other people on board had been born (created, in most cases) in the habitats the human race had scattered across the solar system.

The *Island of Adventure* had been the first ship to embark for 82 Eridani. Thirty-two years after it had left the solar system, a ship called *Green Voyager* had pointed its rocky bow at Rho. The texts of its transmissions had indicated the oldest passengers on the *Green Voyager* were two decades younger than the youngest passengers on the *Island of Adventure*.

If the passengers on the *Island of Adventure* approved the course change, they would arrive at Rho about the same time the *Green Voyager* arrived there. They would find themselves sharing the same star system with humans who were, on average, three or four decades younger than they were. Madame Dawne would be confronted with brains and bodies that had been designed a full century after she had received her own biological equipment.

Morgan was not a politician by temperament but he was fascinated by any activity that combined conflict with intellectual effort. When his pairing with Savela Insdotter had finally come to an end, he had isolated himself in his apartment and spent a decade and a half studying the literature on the dynamics of small communities. The knowledge he had absorbed would probably look prehistoric to the people now living in the solar system. It had been stored in the databanks pre-2203. But it provided him with techniques that should produce the predicted results when they were applied to people who had reached adulthood several decades before 2200.

The *Island of Adventure* was managed, for all practical

purposes, by its information system. A loosely organized committee monitored the system but there was no real government. The humans on board were passengers, the information system was the crew, and the communal issues that came up usually involved minor housekeeping procedures.

Now that a real issue had arisen, Morgan's fellow passengers drifted into a system of continuous polling—a system that had been the commonest form of political democracy when they had left the solar system. Advocates talked and lobbied. Arguments flowed through the electronic symposiums and the face-to-face social networks. Individuals registered their opinions—openly or anonymously—when they decided they were willing to commit themselves. At any moment you could call up the appropriate screen and see how the count looked.

The most vociferous support for the course change came from eight individuals. For most of the three thousand fifty-seven people who lived in the ship's apartments, the message from the probe was a minor development. The ship was their home—in the same way a hollowed out asteroid in the solar system could have been their home. The fact that their habitat would occasionally visit another star system added spice to the centuries that lay ahead, but it wasn't their primary interest in life. The Eight, on the other hand, seemed to feel they would be sentencing themselves to decades of futility if they agreed to visit a lifeless star system.

Morgan set up a content analysis program and had it monitor the traffic flowing through the public information system. Eighteen months after the message from the probe had triggered off the debate, he put a two-axis graph on the screen and examined a pair of curves.

Morgan's pairing with Savela Insdotter had lasted over sixty years and they had remained friendly after they had unpaired. He showed her the graph as soon as he had run it through some extra checks. The curve that charted the Eight's activities rose and fell in conjunction with the curve that measured Madame Dawne's participation in the debate. When Madame Dawne's activity level reached a peak, the

Eight subsided into silence. They would stop agitating for their cause, the entire discussion would calm down, and Madame Dawne would return to the extreme privacy she had maintained from the beginning of the voyage. Then, when Madame Dawne hadn't been heard from for several tendays, the Eight would suddenly renew their campaign.

"I believe they're supporting the change to a new destination merely because they wish to disturb Madame Dawne," Morgan said. "I've created personality profiles based on their known histories and public statements. The profiles indicate my conjecture is correct."

Savela presented him with a shrug and a delicate, upward movement of her head. Morgan had spoken to her in Tych —an ultra-precise language that was primarily used in written communication. Savela was responding in an emotion-oriented language called VA13—a language that made extensive use of carefully rehearsed gestures and facial expressions.

No one, as far as Morgan knew, had ever spoken VA12 or VA14. The language had been labeled VA13 when it had been developed in a communications laboratory on Phobos, and the label had stuck.

"Madame Dawne is a laughable figure," Savela said.

"I recognize that. But the Eight are creating a serious division in our communal life. We might have reached a consensus by now if they hadn't restimulated the debate every time it seemed to be concluding. Madame Dawne is one of the eleven wealthiest individuals on the ship. What would happen to us if she decided she had to impose her will by force?"

"Do you really feel that's a serious possibility, Morgan?"

The linguists who had developed VA13 had been interested in the emotional content of music. The speaker's tone patterns and rhythms were just as critical as the verbal text. Savela's word choices were polite and innocuous, but her rhythms communicated something else—a mixture of affection and amusement that would have seemed contemptuous if she and Morgan hadn't shared a pairing that had lasted six decades.

*   *   *

To Morgan, Madame Dawne was pathetic, not comic. She spent most of her days, as far as anyone could tell, in the electronic dream worlds she constructed in her apartment. No one on the ship had seen her true face. When she appeared on someone's screens, her electronic personae were impressively unimaginative. She usually imaged herself as a tall woman, with close cropped red hair, dressed in flamboyant boots-and-baggy-shirts style that North Americans had adopted during the third decade of the twenty-first century— the body type and clothing mode that had been fashionable when she had been in her natural prime.

Morgan had put a wargame template on his information system and had it explore some of the things Madame Dawne could do. Savela might smile at the thought that a limited, underdeveloped personality like Madame Dawne might undertake something dangerous. The wargame program had come up with seventy-four weapons systems a wealthy individual could develop with the aid of the information in the databanks. Half the systems were straightforward modifications of the devices that dug out apartment spaces and extracted mineral resources from the rocky exterior of the ship. Most of the others involved an offensive use of the self-replicating machines that handled most of the passengers' daily needs.

Madame Dawne couldn't have designed any of the machines the wargame program had suggested. She probably didn't even know the ship could place them at her disposal. Did she realize she could ask a wargame program for advice? Morgan didn't know.

Morgan's political studies had included an exhaustive module in applied personality profiling. He could recite from memory the numbers that described the kind of person who could become a successful small-community politician. He hadn't been surprised when his profiling program had told him he scored below average on most of the critical personality characteristics. He had made several attempts to enter the course change controversy and the results would have evoked I-told-you-so head shakes from the technicians who had developed the profiling program. The program had been almost cruelly accurate when it had informed him he had a low tolerance for disagreement. He could have given it fifty examples of his tendency to become hot-tempered and defensive when he attracted the attention of aggressive debaters. For the last few months, he had been avoiding the public symposiums and feeding private suggestions to people who could turn his ideas into effective attempts at persuasion. Now he fleshed out the profiles he had been storing in his databanks and started recruiting a six member political team.

Morgan couldn't proselytize prospects and debate verbal brawlers, but he had discovered he could do something that was just as effective: he could win the cooperation of the people who could. Some of the people he approached even *enjoyed* accosting their fellow citizens and lobbying them on political issues. They couldn't always follow Morgan's logic, but they considered that a minor problem. They were extroverted, achievement-oriented personalities and Morgan gave them suggestions that worked. If he told them a visit to X made good sense at this moment, and a visit to Y would be a waste of time, they approached both prospects the first couple of times he made a recommendation, and followed his advice after that.

Most of the political strategies Morgan had studied could be fitted into three categories: you could be *combative and confrontational*, you could *market*, or you could explore the subtleties of the *indirect approach*. Temperamentally, Morgan was a marketer who liked to use the indirect approach. Once he had his political organization going, he ran another analysis of the profiles in his databanks and organized a Terraforming Committee. Five engineering-oriented personalities sat down with a carefully selected political personality and began looking at the possibility some of the planets of 82 Eridani could be transformed into livable environments. Eight months after Morgan had established the committee, the first simulated planetary environment took its place in the public databanks. Interested individuals could soar across a planetary landscape that included blue skies, towering forests, and creatures selected from three of Earth's geologic eras and two of its mythological cycles.

It took almost five years, but Morgan's efforts succeeded. An overwhelming consensus emerged. The ship would stay on course.

Unfortunately, the Eight still seemed to enjoy baiting Madame Dawne. By this time, however, Morgan had constructed detailed profiles of every personality in the octet.

The most vulnerable was a woman named Miniruta Coboloji. Miniruta's primary motivation, according to the profile program, was an intense need for affiliation.

Morgan had known his pairing with Savela Insdotter would end sooner or later. Everything had to end sooner or later. The surprise had been the identity of the man who had succeeded him.

Morgan had assumed Savela would grow tired of his skeptical, creedless outlook and pair with someone who shared her beliefs. Instead, her next partner had been Ari Sun-Dalt—the outspoken champion of a communion that had been founded on the belief that every member of the human race was involved in a cosmic epic: the struggle of matter to become conscious.

Life was not an accident, the advocates of Ari's worldview asserted. It was the purpose of the universe. The idea that dominated Ari's life was the Doctrine of the Cosmic Enterprise—the belief that the great goal of the cosmos was the unlimited expansion of Consciousness.

Ari had been adding organic and electronic enhancements to his brain ever since he was in his thirties. The skin on the top of his skull concealed an array that included every chip and cell cluster his nervous system would accept. His head was at least 25 percent longer, top to bottom, than a standard male head. If something could increase his intelligence or heighten his consciousness, Ari believed it would be immoral not to install it.

"We can always use recruits," Ari said. "But I must tell

you, my friend, I feel there's something cynical about your scheming."

Morgan shrugged. "If I'm right, Miniruta will be ten times more contented than she is now. And the ship will be serener."

They were both speaking Jor—an everyday language, with a rigidly standardized vocabulary, which had roots in twenty-first century French. Morgan had told Ari he had detected signs that Miniruta would be interested in joining his communion, and Ari had immediately understood Morgan was trying to remove Miniruta from the Eight. Ari could be surprisingly sophisticated intellectually. Most people with strong belief systems didn't like to think about the psychological needs people satisfied when they joined philosophical movements.

Miniruta joined Ari's communion a year after Ari set out to convert her. She lost interest in the Eight as soon as she acquired a new affiliation—just as Morgan's profiles had predicted she would. Morgan had been preparing plans for three other members of the group but Miniruta's withdrawal produced an unexpected dividend. Two of the male members drifted away a few tendays after Miniruta proclaimed her new allegiance. Their departure apparently disrupted the dynamics of the entire clique. Nine tendays after their defection, Morgan could detect no indications the Eight had ever existed.

On the outside of the ship, in an area where the terrain still retained most of the asteroid's original contours, there was a structure that resembled a squat slab with four circular antennas mounted at its corners. The slab itself was a comfortable, two-story building, with a swimming pool, recreation facilities, and six apartments that included fully equipped communication rooms.

The structure was the communications module that received messages from the solar system and the other ships currently creeping through interstellar space. It was totally isolated from the ship's electronic systems. The messages it picked up could only be examined by someone who was actually sitting in one of the apartments. You couldn't transfer a message from the module to the ship's databanks. You couldn't even carry a recording into the ship.

The module had been isolated from the rest of the ship in response to a very real threat: the possibility someone in the solar system would transmit a message that would sabotage the ship's information system. There were eight billion people living in the solar system. When you were dealing with a population that size, you had to assume it contained thousands of individuals who felt the starships were legitimate targets for lethal pranks.

Morgan had been spending regular periods in the communications module since the first years of the voyage. During the first decades, the messages he had examined had become increasingly strange. The population in the solar system had been evolving at a rate that compressed kilocenturies of natural evolution into decades of engineered modification. The messages that had disturbed him the most had been composed in the languages he had learned in his childhood. The words were familiar but the meaning of the messages kept slipping away from him.

Morgan could understand that the terraforming of Mars, Venus, and Mercury might have been speeded up and complexified by a factor of ten. He could even grasp that some of the electronically interlinked communal personalities in the solar system might include several million individual personalities. But did he really understand the messages that seemed to imply millions of people had expanded their personal *physiologies* into complexes that encompassed entire asteroids?

The messages included videos that should have eliminated most of his confusion. Somehow he always turned away from the screen feeling there was something he hadn't grasped.

The situation in the solar system had begun to stabilize just before Morgan had turned his attention to the turmoil created by the Eight. Over the next few decades the messages became more decipherable. Fifty years after the problem with the Eight—one hundred and sixty-two years after the ship had left the solar system—almost all the messages reaching the ship came from members of Ari Sun-Dalt's communion.

The believers in the Doctrine of the Cosmic Enterprise were communicating with the starships because they were becoming a beleaguered minority. The great drive for enhancement and progress had apparently run its course. The worldviews that dominated human civilization were all variations on the EruLabi creeds.

Ari spent long periods—as much as ten or twelve tendays in a row—in the communications module. The human species, in Ari's view, was sinking into an eternity of aimless hedonism.

Ari became particularly distraught when he learned the EruLabi had decided they should limit themselves to a 20 percent increase in skull size—a dictum that imposed a tight restriction on the brainpower they could pack inside their heads. At the peak of the enhancement movement, people who had retained normal bipedal bodies had apparently quadrupled their skull sizes.

"We're the only conscious, intelligent species the solar system ever produced," Ari orated in one of his public communiqués. "We may be the only conscious, intelligent species in this section of the galaxy. And they've decided an arbitrary physiological aesthetic is more important than the development of our minds."

The messages from the solar system had included scientific discussions. They had even included presentations prepared for "nonspecialists." Morgan had followed a few of the presentations as well as he could and he had concluded the human species had reached a point of diminishing returns.

Morgan would never possess the kind of complexified, ultra-enhanced brain his successors in the solar system had acquired. Every set of genes imposed a ceiling on the organism it shaped. If you wanted to push beyond that ceiling, you had to start all over again, with a new organism and a new set of genes. But Morgan believed he could imagine some of the consequences of that kind of intellectual power.

At some point, he believed, all those billions of super-intelligent minds had looked out at the universe and realized that another increase in brain power would be pointless. You could develop a brain that could answer every question about the size, history, and structure of the universe, and find that you still couldn't answer the philosophical questions that had tantalized the most primitive tribesmen. And what would you do when you reached that point? You would turn your back on the frontier. You would turn once again to the bath and the banquet, the harp and the dance.

And changes of raiment.

And love.

And sleep.

The situation on the ship was almost the mirror image of the situation in the solar system. On the ship, 48 percent of the population belonged to Ari's communion. Only 19 percent had adopted the EruLabi creeds. But how long could that last? Morgan had been watching the trends. Every few years, someone abandoned the Doctrine of the Cosmic Enterprise and joined the EruLabi. No one ever left the EruLabi and became a devoted believer in the Cosmic Enterprise.

The discovery that 82 Eridani was surrounded by lifeless planets had added almost a dozen people to the defectors. The search for life-bearing planets was obviously a matter of great significance. If consciousness really was the purpose of the universe, then life should be a common phenomenon.

In 2315, just four years after the final dissolution of the Eight, the *Island of Adventure* had received its first messages from Tau Ceti and Morgan had watched a few more personalities float away from Ari's communion. The ship that had reached Tau Ceti had made planetfall after a mere one hundred and forty years and it had indeed found life on the second planet of the system. Unfortunately, the planet was locked in a permanent ice age. Life had evolved in the oceans under the ice but it had never developed beyond the level of the more mundane marine life forms found on Earth.

Morgan had found it impossible to follow the reasons the planet was iced over. He hadn't really been interested, to tell the truth. But he had pored over the reports on the undersea biota as if he had been following the dispatches from a major war.

One of the great issues in terrestrial evolutionary theory had been the relationship between chance and necessity. To Ari and his disciples, there was nothing random about the process. Natural selection inevitably favored qualities such as strength, speed, and intelligence.

To others, the history of life looked more haphazard. Many traits, it was argued, had developed for reasons as whimsical as the fact that the ancestor who carried Gene A had been standing two steps to the right when the rocks slid off the mountain.

The probes that had penetrated the oceans of Tau Ceti IV had sent back images that could be used to support either viewpoint. The undersea biota was populated by several hundred species of finned snakes, several thousand species that could be considered roughly comparable to terrestrial insects, and clouds of microscopic dimlight photosynthesizers.

Yes, evolution favored the strong and the swift. Yes, creatures who lived in the sea tended to be streamlined. On the other hand, fish were not inevitable. Neither were oysters. Or clams.

If the universe really did have a purpose, it didn't seem to be very good at it. In the solar system, theorists had produced scenarios that proved life could have evolved in exotic, unlikely environments such as the atmosphere of Jupiter. Instead, the only life that had developed outside Earth had been the handful of not-very-interesting microorganisms that had managed to maintain a toehold on Mars.

The purpose of the universe isn't the development of consciousness, one of the EruLabi on board the *Island of Ad-*

venture suggested. *It's the creation of iceballs and deserts. And sea snakes.*

Ari's enhancements included a gland modification that gave him the ability to switch off his sexual feelings at will. His paring with Savela Insdotter had lasted less than two decades, and he had made no attempt to establish another pairing. Ari had spent most of the voyage, as far as Morgan could tell, in an asexual state.

There were times, during the last decades of the voyage, when Morgan felt tempted to emulate him. Morgan's next pairing only lasted twelve years. For the rest of the voyage, he took advantage of the small number of sexual opportunities that came his way and distracted himself, during his celibate intervals, with intellectual projects such as his political studies.

The ship's medical system could install Ari's sexual enhancement in thirty minutes, as part of the regular medical services included in the standard embarkation agreement. Morgan put the idea aside every time he considered it. He had learned to cherish his feelings about women, irrational as they might be. There was, he knew, no real reason why he should respond to the flare of a woman's hips or the tilt of a female neck. It was simply a bit of genetic programming he hadn't bothered to delete. It had no practical value in a world in which children were created in the workshops of genetic designers. But he also knew he would be a different person if he subtracted it from his psychological makeup. It was one of the things that kept you human as the decades slipped by.

In 2381—forty-six years before it was scheduled to reach its destination—the *Island of Adventure* intercepted a message from the probe that had been sent to Rho Eridani. Neither of the stars in the double system possessed planets. The *Green Voyager* was crawling toward an empty system.

In 2398—one hundred and ninety-five years after the ship had begun its journey—the medical system replaced

Morgan's heart, part of his central nervous system, and most of his endocrine glands. It was the third time Morgan had put himself through an extensive overhaul. The last time he had recovered within three years. This time he spent eight years in the deepest sleep the system could maintain.

The first program capsules left the ship while it was still careening around the 82 Eridani system, bouncing from planet to planet as it executed the five year program that would eliminate the last 20 percent of its interstellar speed. There were three capsules and their payloads were packages a little smaller than Morgan's forefinger.

One capsule malfunctioned while it was still making its way toward the small moon that orbited the third planet at a distance of 275,000 kilometers. The second lost two critical programs when it hit the moon at an angle that was a little too sharp. The third skimmed through the dust just the way it was supposed to and sprouted a set of filaments. Sampling programs analyzed the moon's surface. Specks that were part cell and part electronic device began drifting down the filaments and executing programs that transformed the moon's atoms into larger, more elaborate specks. The specks produced machines the size of insects, the insects produced machines the size of cats, an antenna crept up the side of a smaller carter, and an antenna on the *Island of Adventure* started transmitting more programs. By the time the ship settled into an orbit around the third planet, the moon had acquired a complete manufacturing facility, and the lunar fabrication units had started producing scout machines that could land on the planet itself.

Morgan had thought of the terraforming scheme as a political ruse, but there were people on the ship who took it seriously. With the technology they had at their disposal, the third planet could be turned into a livable world within a few decades. For people who had spent their entire lives in enclosed habitats, it was a romantic idea—a world where you walked on the surface, with a sky above you, and experienced all the vagaries of weather and climate.

The only person who had raised any serious objections had been Ari Sun-Dalt. Some of the valleys they could observe from orbit had obviously been carved by rivers. The volcano calderas were less spectacular than the volcanoes of Mars but they were still proof the planet had once been geologically active. They couldn't overlook the possibility life might be hiding in some obscure ecological network that was buried under the soil or hidden in a cave, Ari argued.

Most of the people on the ship greeted that kind of suggestion with shrugs and smiles. According to Morgan's sampling programs, there were only about ten people on the ship who really thought there was a statistically significant possibility the planet might have generated life. Still, there was no reason they couldn't let Ari enjoy his daydreams a little longer.

"It will only take us an extra two or three years," Ari said. "And then we'll know we can remodel the place. First we'll see if there's any life. Then we'll do the job ourselves, if the universe hasn't done it already. And bring Consciousness to another world."

For Ari's sake—he really liked Ari in many ways—Morgan hoped they might find a few fossilized microorganisms embedded in the rocks. What he did not expect was a fossil the size of a horse, embedded in a cliff, and visible to any machine that came within two kilometers of it.

Three and a half billion years ago, the planet had emerged from the disk of material that surrounded its sun. A billion or so years later, the first long-chain molecules had appeared in the oceans. And the history of life had begun. In the same way it had begun on Earth.

The long-chain molecules had formed assemblies that became the first rudimentary cells. Organisms that were something like plants had eventually begun to absorb the CO_2 produced by the volcanoes. The oxygen emitted by the quasi-plants had become a major component of the atmosphere. The relentless forces of competition had favored creatures who were more complex than their rivals.

And then, after less than two billion years of organic evolution, the laws of physics had caught up with the process. No planet the size of this one could hold an atmosphere forever.

The plants and the volcanoes could produce oxygen and CO_2 *almost* as fast as the gas molecules could drift into space. But almost wasn't good enough.

They didn't piece the whole story together right away, of course. There were even people who weren't convinced the first find was a fossil. If the scout machines hadn't found ten more fossils in the first five daycycles, the skeptics would have spent years arguing that Exhibit A was just a collection of rocks—a random geologic formation that just happened to resemble a big shell, with appendages that resembled limbs.

On Earth, the dominant land animals had been vertebrates—creatures whose basic characteristic was a bony framework hung on a backbone. The vertebrate template was such a logical, efficient structure it was easy to believe it was as inevitable as the streamlined shape of fish and porpoises. In fact, it had never developed on this planet.

Instead, the basic anatomical structure had been a tube of bone. Creatures with this rigid, seemingly inefficient, structure had acquired legs, claws, teeth and all the other anatomical features vertebrates had acquired on Earth. Thousands of species had acquired eyes that looked out of big eyeholes in the front of the shell, without developing a separate skull. Two large families had developed "turrets" that housed their eyes and their other sense organs but they had kept their brains securely housed in the original shell, in a special chamber just under the turret.

On Earth, the shell structure would have produced organisms that might have collapsed from their own weight. On this planet, with its weaker gravitational field, the shells could be thin and even airy. They reminded Morgan of building components that had been formed from solidified foam—a common structural technique in space habitats.

*   *   *

For Ari, the discovery was the high point of his lifespan—a development that had to be communicated to the solar system at once. Ari's face had been contorted with excitement when he had called Morgan an hour after the machines reported the first find.

"We've done it, Morgan," Ari proclaimed. "We've justified our whole voyage. Three thousand useless, obsolete people have made a discovery that's going to transform the whole outlook in the solar system."

Morgan had already been pondering a screen that displayed a triangular diagram. The point at the bottom of the triangle represented the solar system. The two points at the top represented 82 Eridani and Rho Eridani. The *Island of Adventure* and the *Green Voyager* had been creeping up the long sides of the triangle. The *Green Voyager* was now about three light years from Rho—thirty-three years travel time.

Morgan transferred the diagram to Ari's screen and pointed out the implications. If the *Island of Adventure* transmitted an announcement to the solar system, the *Green Voyager* would pick it up in approximately seven years. If the people on the *Voyager* thought it was interesting, they could change course and reach 82 Eridani only twelve and a half decades after they intercepted the message.

"That gives us over one hundred and thirty years to explore the planet," Ari argued. "By that time we'll have learned everything important the fossils have to offer. We'll have done all the real work. We'll be ready to move on. And look for a world where we can communicate with a *living* Consciousness."

Unfortunately, the situation didn't look that straightforward to the rest of the community. To them, a hundred and thirty years was a finite, envisionable time period.

There was, after all, a third possibility—as Miniruta Coboloji pointed out in one of her contributions to the electronic debate. *The* Green Voyager *may never come this way at all*, Miniruta argued. *They may reach Rho thirty-three years from now, pass through the system, and point them-*

selves at one of the stars that lies further out. They've got three choices within fourteen light years. Why can't we just wait the thirty-three years? And send a message after they've committed themselves to some other star system?

For Ari, that was unthinkable. *Our announcement is going to take twenty years to reach the solar system no matter what we do. If we sit here for thirty-three years before we transmit, it will be fifty-three years before anyone in the solar system hears about one of the most important discoveries in history. We all know what's happening in the solar system. Fifty-three years from now there may not be anyone left who cares.*

Once again Morgan labored over his screens. Once again, he recruited aides who helped him guide the decision-making process. This time he engineered a compromise. They would send a brief message saying they had "found evidence of extinct life" and continue studying the planet's fossils. Once every year, they would formally reopen the discussion for three tendays. They would transmit a complete announcement "whenever it becomes clear the consensus supports such an action."

Ari accepted the compromise in good grace. He had looked at the numbers, too. Most of the people on the ship still belonged to his communion.

"They know what their responsibilities are," Ari insisted. "Right now this is all new, Morgan. We're just getting used to the idea that we're looking at a complete planetary biota. A year from now—two years from now—we'll have so much information in our databanks they'll know we'd be committing a criminal act if we didn't send every bit of it back to the solar system."

It was Ari who convinced them the planet should be called Athene. Athene had been a symbol of wisdom and culture, Ari pointed out, but she had been a war goddess, too. And didn't the world they were naming bear a distinct resemblance to the planet the ancient humans had named after their male war figure?

*   *   *

The information pouring into the databanks could be examined by anyone on the ship. In theory, anyone could give the exploration machines orders. In practice, the exploration of the Athenian fossil record soon came under the control of three people: Ari, Morgan—and Miniruta Coboloji.

Morgan had been watching Miniruta's development ever since he had lured her away from the Eight. Physically, she was a standard variation on the BR-V73 line—the long, willowy female body type that had been the height of fashion in the lunar cities in the 2130s. Her slim, beautifully crafted fingers could mold a sculpture—or shape a note on a string instrument—with the precision of a laser pointer.

It was a physical style that Morgan found aesthetically appealing, but there were at least two hundred women on the ship who had been shaped by the same gene cluster. So why was Miniruta the only BR-V73 who crept into his thoughts during the more stressful hours of his celibate intervals? Was it because there was something desperate about the need for affiliation he had uncovered in her personality profile? Did that emotional vulnerability touch something in his own personality?

Miniruta's affiliation with the Doctrine of the Cosmic Enterprise had lasted four decades. Ari claimed her switch to the EruLabi worldview had been totally unexpected. Ari had gone to sleep assuming she was one of his most ardent colleagues and awakened to discover she had sent him a long message explaining the reasons for her conversion and urging him to join her.

During the decades in which she had been a member of Ari's communion, Miniruta had followed Ari's lead and equipped herself with every pharmaceutical and electrical enhancer she could link to her physiology. The electronic enhancers had all been discarded a few tendays after she had joined the EruLabi. Her pharmaceutical enhancers had been dispensed with, item by item, as she had worked her way up the EruLabi protocols. She had been the second EruLabi on the ship who had made it to the fourth protocol and accepted its absolute prohibition of all non-genetic mental and physiological enhancers.

Morgan could now talk to her without struggling. His own pharmaceutical enhancers erased most of the intellectual gap that separated two people who had been brought into the universe twenty years apart. He had been surprised when he had discovered Miniruta was spending two-thirds of every daycycle with the data from the fossil hunt, but he had soon realized she had a philosophical agenda.

To Miniruta, the course of evolution on Athene proved that evolution was a random process. "Ari's right, Morgan," Miniruta said. "This planet can teach us something we need to understand. But it's not the lesson Ari thinks it is. It's telling us there isn't any plan. There's no big overall objective—as if the universe is some kind of cosmic totalitarian state. The only reality is individuals. And their needs."

To Ari, the critical question was the evolution of intelligence. Obviously, life had died out on Athene before intelligent creatures could build cities or turn meadows into farms. But wasn't there some chance something like the first proto-humans had evolved? If that first glimmer of tool-making, culture-creating intelligence had appeared on the planet, wouldn't it prove that evolution really did lead in a particular direction?

"I'll grant you the vertebrates were obviously an accident," Ari said. "But you can still see an obvious increase in intelligence if you look at the progressions we've been uncovering. You can't go from stationary sea creatures to land creatures that were obviously highly mobile without a lot of development in the brain. Intelligence is the inevitable winner in the selection process. The life forms that can think better will always replace the life forms with less complex nervous systems."

"The way human beings replaced the cockroach?" Miniruta asked. "And the oyster?"

Miniruta was speaking VA13. The lilt in her voice expressed a casual mockery that Morgan would have found devastating if she had directed it at him.

"We were not in direct genetic competition with the cockroach and the oyster," Ari said in Tych. "The observable fact that certain lines remained static for hundreds of millions of years doesn't contradict the observable fact that natural selection tends to produce creatures with more highly developed brains. We could have destroyed every species on the Earth if we had wanted to. We let them live because we needed a complex biosphere. They survived because they satisfied one of *our* needs."

To Morgan, most of the information they were gathering proved that natural selection really was the powerful force the theorists had claimed it was.

Certain basic patterns had been repeated on both planets. Life forms that had been exceptionally massive had possessed jaw structures that indicated they had probably been herbivores—just as terrestrial herbivores such as the elephant had been the largest organisms in their habitats. Life forms that had possessed stabbing teeth and bone-crunching jaws tended to be medium-sized and looked as if they had probably been more agile.

But the process obviously had its random qualities, too. Was it just a matter of random chance that vertebrates had failed to develop? Had the shell creatures dominated the planet merely because certain molecules had fallen into one type of pattern on Earth and another pattern on Athene? Or had it happened because there was some difference in the conditions life had encountered on the two planets?

To Morgan, it didn't matter what the answer was. Evolution might proceed according to laws that were as rigid as the basic laws of physics, or it might be as random as a perfect game of chance. He would be happy with either answer. He could even be content with no answer.

That was one of the things people never seemed to understand about science. As far as Morgan was concerned, you didn't study the universe because you wanted to know the answers. You studied it to *connect*. When you subjected an important question to a rigorous examination—collecting every scrap of evidence you could find, measuring and analyzing everything that could be measured and analyzed—you were linked to the universe in a way nothing else could connect you.

Religious mystics had once spent their lives trying to establish a direct contact with their version of God. Morgan was a mystic who tried to stay in contact with the cosmos.

Ari had assigned three groups of exploration machines to a hunt for camp sites. The teams concentrated on depressions that looked as if they had once been rivers and probed for evidence such as stone tools and places where a large number of animal fossils had been concentrated in a small area. They found two animal deposits within their first three tendays and Ari quickly pointed out that the animals had clearly been disassembled.

"These aren't just tar pits or places where a catastrophe killed several animals accidentally," Ari argued. "Note how the remains of the different species are all jumbled up. If they had been killed by a rockslide from the surrounding heights—to name just one alternate possibility—the remains of each animal would have tended to stay together. The pattern we're looking at here is the pattern we'd expect to see in a waste pit."

Miniruta tossed her head. "If they were butchered," she said in VA13, "then somebody had to use tools to cut them up. Show us a flint tool, Ari. Show us some evidence of fire."

Machines burrowed and probed in the areas around the "waste pits." Scraping attachments removed the dirt and rock one thin layer at a time. Raking attachments sieved the dust and rubble. Search programs analyzed the images transmitted by the onsite cameras and highlighted anything that met the criteria Ari had stored in the databanks. And they did, in fact, find slivers of flint that could have been knives or spearheads.

Ari had two of the flints laid out on a tray, with a camera

poised an arm's length above the objects, and displayed them on one of the wall screens in his apartment. Morgan stared at the tray in silence and let himself surrender to all the eerie, haunting emotions it aroused, even with Ari babbling beside him.

"On Earth," Miniruta pointed out, "we already knew the planet had produced intelligent life. We could assume specimens like that had been made by intelligent beings because we already knew the intelligent beings existed. But what do we have here, Ari? Can we really believe these objects were shaped by intelligent beings when we still haven't seen anything that resembles hands? So far, you haven't even located an organism that had *arms*."

There were other possibilities, of course. Ari had studied most of the ideas about possible alien life forms that humans had come up with in the last few centuries and installed them in the databanks housed in his electronic enhancers. He could produce several plausible examples of grasping organs composed of soft tissue that would only fossilize under rare, limited conditions. The tool makers could have possessed tentacles. They could have used some odd development of their lips.

Miniruta tipped back her head and raised her eyebrows when she heard Ari mention tentacles. The high pitched lilt of her VA13 communicated—once again—the condescension that permeated her attitude toward Ari.

"The cephalopods all lived in the sea, Ari. Our arms evolved from load-bearing legs. I admit we're discussing creatures who evolved in a lower gravity field. But they weren't operating in zero gravity."

"I've thought about that," Ari said. "Isn't it possible some tentacled sea-creatures could have adapted an amphibious lifestyle on the edge of the sea and eventually produced descendants who substituted legs for some of their tentacles? On our own planet, after all, some of the land dwellers who lived on the edge of the Earth's oceans eventually produced descendants whose legs had been transformed into fins. With all due respect to your *current* belief system, Miniruta—our discussions would be significantly more succinct if you weren't trying to discuss serious issues without the benefit of a few well-chosen enhancements. You might see some of the possibilities I'm seeing before I have to describe them to you."

As an adherent of the fourth EruLabi protocol, Miniruta only rejected permanent enhancements that increased her intellectual and physical powers. Temporary enhancements that increased pleasure were another matter. Miniruta could still use a small selection of the sexually enhancing drugs developed in the twenty-first century, in addition to the wines, teas, and inhalants that had fostered pre-pharmaceutical social relations. She and Morgan had already shared several long, elaborately choreographed sexual interludes. They had bathed. They had banqueted. They had reclined on carefully proportioned couches, naked bodies touching, while musicians from a dozen eras had materialized in Miniruta's simulators. The EruLabi sexual rituals had cast a steady, sensuous glow over the entire six decades Morgan had spent with Savela Insdotter. He had resumed their routines as if he had been slipping on clothes that were associated with some of the best moments of his life.

They were nearing the end of a particularly satisfactory interlude when Miniruta switched on her information system and discovered she had received a please-view-first message from Ari. "I've been looking over some of the latest finds from one of your random-survey teams," Ari said. "Your idea paid off. They've handed us a fossil that looks like it left traces of soft-bodied tissue in the rocks in front of it—imprints that look like they could have been made by the local equivalent of tentacles. Your team found it in the middle of a depression in that flat area on the top of the main southern plateau—a depression that's so shallow I hadn't even noticed it on the maps."

Miniruta had decided that half her exploration machines would make random searches. Ari and Morgan were both working with intellectual frameworks based on the history of Earth, Miniruta had argued. Morgan was looking at the kinds of sites that had produced fossils on Earth. Ari was looking for traces of hunter-gatherers. "A random process," she had pronounced, "should be studied by random probing."

Now her own philosophical bias had apparently given Ari what he had been looking for. Ari would never have ordered one of his machines into the winding, almost invisible depression Miniruta's machine had followed. But that dip in the landscape had once been a river. And the river had widened its path and eroded the ground above a fossil that had formed in the sediment by the bank.

It was a cracked, fragmented shell about a third the length of a human being. Only one side of it had been preserved. But you could still see that it was essentially a tube with a large opening at one end, a smaller opening at the other, and no indications it had openings for legs. In the rock in front of the large opening, Morgan could just make out the outlines of impressions that could have been produced by a group of ropy, soft-bodied extensions.

Ari highlighted three spots on the rim of the large opening. "Notice how the opening has indentations on the rim, where the extensions leave it. They aren't very big, but they obviously give the extensions a little more room. I've ordered a search of the databank to see how many other shells have indentations like that. If there was one creature like this on the planet, there should have been other species built along the same pattern. I'm also taking another look at all the shells like this we've uncovered in the past. My first pass through the databank indicates we've found several of them near the places where we found the burial pits."

For Ari, the find proved that it was time to let the solar system know the full truth. He posted a picture of the fossil on the information system an hour after he had notified Morgan and Miniruta. "We now have evidence that creatures with fully developed grasping organs existed on this planet," Ari argued. "The evidence may not be conclusive, but it can't be dismissed either. The people of the solar system have a right to draw their own conclusions. Let them see the evidence we've collected. Let the minority who are resisting stagnation and decline derive hope from the knowledge more evidence may follow."

It had only been eight tendays since Ari had agreed to the compromise Morgan had worked out. Yet he was already demanding that they cancel the agreement.

To Miniruta, the idea was absurd. Ari was suggesting that the forests of Athene had harbored tentacled creatures who had hung from trees and occupied the ecological niches monkeys had appropriated on Earth. And he was jumping from that improbability to the idea that some of these hypothetical creatures had developed weapons and become hunter-gatherers.

"I am not saying anything is true," Ari insisted. "I am merely noting that we now have pits full of butchered animals, tools that could have butchered them, and a type of organism that could have manipulated the tools."

Ari had even developed a scenario that equipped his fantasy creatures with the ability to move along the ground at a pace suitable for hunters. Suppose, he argued, they had begun their advance to intelligence by learning to control some type of riding animal?

To Ari, his proposal was a logical variation on the process that had shaped human intelligence. On Earth, tree dwellers had developed hands that could grasp limbs and brains that could judge distances and trajectories. Then they had adapted the upright posture and used their hands to create stone tools. Tool use had created a way of life that put a premium on intelligence, the individuals with the best brains had tended to be the survivors, and a creature who could build starships had taken its place in the universe.

"On Athene," Ari argued, "the drive toward intelligence may have followed a different course. The tree dwellers couldn't develop upright walking so they began by controlling animals. They became mounted hunters—creatures who could rove like ground animals and manipulate the same simple tools our own ancestors chipped from the rocks. The evolutionary process may take many twists. It may be bloody and cruel. But in the end, it gives us planets populated by creatures who are intelligent and conscious. The arrow points in only one direction."

Thirty years from now—perhaps even ten years from now—Morgan's feelings about Miniruta would just be a memory. Morgan knew that. There would come a moment when he would wonder how he could have believed all his pleasure in life depended on the goodwill of another human being. But right now he just knew he wanted to create a crowded memory. Right now he felt as if he had spent the last few decades in a state of half-dead numbness.

He had started playing with his political analysis programs as soon as he had realized Ari was initiating a new round of agitated debate. The situation had looked dangerous to him and the picture that had emerged on his screens had confirmed his intuitive judgment. About 25 percent of the people on the ship believed a report on the new find should be transmitted to the solar system. Almost 30 percent registered strong opposition. The rest of the population seemed to be equally divided between not-convinced-we-should and not-convinced-we-shouldn't.

If Ari's first appeals had attracted a solid 40 or 45 percent, Morgan would have given him some extra support and helped him win a quick, overwhelming victory. Instead, the *Island of Adventure* community had stumbled into one of those situations in which a divisive debate could go on indefinitely.

Morgan was savoring teas with Miniruta when he suggested the one option that looked as if it might defuse the situation.

"I've decided to assign all my exploration teams to the search for evidence that supports Ari's theories," Morgan said. "I think it would be a wise move if you did the same thing—for awhile anyway. We're not going to get any peace on this ship until we come up with solid evidence Ari's right. Or make it clear we probably never will."

They had both been speaking Plais—a graceful EruLabi invention that had been designed for the lighter types of social events. Morgan had switched to Jor when he started discussing his proposal and Miniruta transferred to Jor with him.

"You want to divert equipment from all the other research we're doing?" Miniruta said. "As far as I'm concerned, Ari has all the resources he needs. We're producing the first survey of an alien ecosystem. Why should we interrupt that merely because one member of our expedition has become obsessed with a fantasy?"

The vehemence in her voice caught Morgan off guard. He had thought he was offering her a modest, reasonable proposal. He had run the idea through his political simulation programs and the results had indicated most of the people on the ship would approve a transmission to the solar system if Ari managed to locate more evidence. A minority would never feel happy with the decision—but at least a decision would have been made.

"It shouldn't divert us for more than a few tendays," Morgan said. "We can intensify Ari's hunt for campsites. We can look for associations between possible mounts and possible riders. We can ignore the low lying areas for the time being and concentrate on the regions that probably stayed above sea level when Athene had seas. If we do all that and don't come up with something decisive in a few tendays—I think we can assume we'll get a clear consensus that we shouldn't overrule our current agreement and transmit a message before the next discussion period."

"And what if we find the kind of evidence he's looking for? Do you think Madame Dawne will just nod agreeably? And let us do something that could destroy her?"

"If there's evidence out there to be found—sooner or later we're going to find it. She's going to have to accept that eventually."

Miniruta reached across the tea table and touched his hand. She slipped into Plais just long enough to preface her response with a word that meant something like "pleasure-friend."

"*Donilar*—even if the evidence is there, will it really do us any good if we find it? Why should we jeopardize our whole way of life just so Ari can give a dying minority group information that will only prolong its agonies?"

Morgan knew he shouldn't have felt as if he had just been ambushed. He had been watching Miniruta for over a century. Everything she had done had proved that the pro-filing program had been correct when it had decided her personality structure was dominated by a deep need for affiliation. When she had been associated with Ari's group, she had maximized her use of enhancements. When she had switched to the other side, she had become a model of EruLabi virtue.

But he was in love. He had surrendered—willingly, for his own reasons—to one of the oldest delusions the human species had invented. And because he was in love, he had let himself ignore something that should have been obvious. Miniruta's dispute with Ari wasn't an argument about the nature of the universe. It was an argument about what human beings should *believe* about the nature of the universe.

The teas were followed by music. The music was followed by a long, dream-like concentration on the shape and texture of Miniruta's body. And afterward Morgan returned to his apartment and watched his programs churn out scenarios that included a new factor: a woman who believed Ari's world-view was a disease that should be eradicated from human society.

Morgan's programs couldn't tell him what Miniruta was going to do. No program could predict all the tactical choices a human brain could choose. But the programs could suggest possibilities. And they could estimate the intensity of Miniruta's responses.

He spotted what she was doing hours after she started doing it. Her "randomly searching" machines occupied one of the prime sites on Ari's list and started scraping and digging just a few hours before Ari's own machines were scheduled to work on it.

Ari called Morgan as soon as he finished his first attempt to "reason" with Miniruta. He still thought Miniruta's program had made a random choice. He still believed she was just being obstinate when she refused to let his machines excavate the site.

"She's got some kind of silly idea she has to stick to her ideal of pure randomness," Ari said. "She's trying to tell me she wouldn't be operating randomly if she let her team go somewhere else."

Morgan agreed to act as a go-between and Miniruta gave him the response he had expected. It was just a random event, she insisted. Why should Ari object? Now he could send his machines to one of the other sites on his list.

"It's one of the big possibilities on his current list," Morgan said. "He thinks he should explore it himself."

"Doesn't he think my machines are competent? Is he afraid they'll spend too much time indulging in sensual pleasures?"

"Ari thinks this is a totally accidental occurrence, Miniruta."

She smiled. "And what does my little donilar think?"

Morgan straightened up and gave her his best imitation of an authority figure. It was the first time she had said something that made him feel she was playing with him.

"I think it would be best if he went on thinking that," he said.

Miniruta's eyes widened. Her right hand fluttered in front of her face, as if she was warding off a blow. "Is that a *threat*, donilar? After all we have enjoyed together?"

Three daycycles later, Miniruta's machines took over two more sites. Morgan's surveillance program advised him as soon as it happened and he immediately called Ari and found himself confronted with a prime display of outrage.

"She's deliberately interfering," Ari shouted. "This can't be random. She is deliberately trying to destroy the last hope of the only people in the solar system who still have faith in the future. Even you should be able to see that, Morgan—in spite of your chemical reactions to certain types of female bodies."

It was the kind of situation Morgan normally delegated

to one of his political operatives. This time there was no way he could slip away gracefully and let someone else handle it. His studies had taught him what the best responses were. He had even managed to apply them on one or two previous occasions. He let the tirade go on as long as Ari wanted to maintain it. He carefully avoided saying anything that might indicate he was agreeing or disagreeing.

Unfortunately, he was faced with something no one on the ship could have handled. Miniruta had given Ari an opening he had obviously been looking for.

"I agreed to wait until we had a consensus," Ari ranted. "I'm trying to be cooperative. But I think it's time someone reminded your overzealous paramour that there's no practical, physical reason I can't transmit a message to the solar system any time I want to."

Ari's elongated head could make him look slightly comical when he became overexcited. This time it was a visual reminder of the commitment behind his outbursts.

"If you really want to get this situation calmed down, Morgan—I suggest you remind her I still have more supporters than she has. They can all look at what she's been doing at the first site. They can all see her machines are carefully avoiding all the best locations and deliberately moving at the slowest pace they can maintain without stalling. You can tell her she has two choices. She can get her machines out of all three sites, or she can put them under my control. And after she's done that—I'll send her a list of all the other sites I expect her to stay away from."

Miniruta was standing in the doorway of her ritual chamber. Behind her, Morgan could glimpse the glow of the brass sculpture that dominated the far end. Miniruta had just finished one of the EruLabi rituals that punctuated her daily schedule. She was still wearing the thin, belted robe she wore during most of the rituals.

Only the night before, in this very room, they had huddled together in the most primitive fashion. They had stretched out on the sleeping platform just a few steps to

Morgan's left and he had spent the entire night with his arms wrapped around her body while they slept.

"I've discussed the situation with Ari," Morgan said in Tych. "He has indicated he feels your actions have given him the right to transmit a message without authorization. He believes his supporters will approve such an action."

"And he sent you here to relay something that is essentially another threat."

"It is my belief that was his intention."

"You should tell him he'll be making a serious error. You should tell him it's obvious he thinks no one will resist him."

"I believe it would be accurate to say he believes no one will offer him any high level resistance."

"Then you should tell him his assumptions need to be revised. Madame Dawne has already armed herself. I obviously can't tell you more than that. But I can tell you she will fight if Ari tries to take control of the communications module. She is already emotionally committed to fighting."

Miniruta smiled. "Is that an informative response? Will that give Ari some evidence he should modify his assumptions?"

Morgan returned to his apartment and had his fabrication unit manufacture two sets of unarmed probes. The probes were large, cumbersome devices, about the size of a standard water goblet, but he wasn't interested in secrecy. He deployed both sets by hand, from a maintenance hatch, and monitored them on his notescreen while they tractored across the surface area that surrounded the communications module.

His notescreen accepted a call from Miniruta two minutes after the probes had made their fourth find.

"Please do not interfere, Morgan. Madame Dawne has no quarrel with you."

"I've detected four weapons so far. None of them look to me like items Madame Dawne would have deployed on her own."

"Don't underestimate her, Morgan. She believes Ari is threatening her ability to survive."

"I thought Madame Dawne was a dangerous person when we were coping with the course-change controversy. But that was over ten decades ago. She's only been seen twice in the last eight years. The last time her responses were so stereotyped half the people she talked to thought they were dealing with a simulation. I don't know how much personality she has left at this point—but I don't think she could surround the communications module with a defense like this unassisted."

"Ari is threatening the fabric of our community. We made an agreement as a community—a consensus that took every individual's needs into account. Madame Dawne is defending the community against a personality who thinks he can impose his own decisions on it."

Morgan fed the information from his probes into a war-game template and let the program run for over thirteen minutes. It went through four thousand simulations altogether—two thousand games in which Madame Dawne was willing to risk the total annihilation of the ship's community, followed by two thousand possibilities in which she limited herself to ambushes and low-level delaying tactics. Seventy percent of the time, Madame Dawne could keep Ari away from the communications module for periods that ranged from twenty-one daycycles to two hundred daycycles. She couldn't win, but she could force Ari into a sustained struggle.

And that was all she needed to do, according to Morgan's political estimates. Miniruta would gain some extra support if Ari broke the agreement unilaterally. But neither one of them would have a commanding majority when the fighting began. They would start out with a sixty-forty split in Ari's favor and a drawn out battle would have the worst possible effect: it would intensify feelings and move the split closer to fifty-fifty.

Morgan thought he could understand why people like Ari and Miniruta adapted belief systems. But why did they feel they had to annihilate other belief systems? His profiling programs could provide him with precise numerical descriptions of the emotions that drove the people he modeled. No program could make him feel the emotions himself.

Still, for all his relentless obsession with the Doctrine of the Cosmic Enterprise, Ari was always willing to listen when Morgan showed him the charts and graphs he had generated with his programs. Ari was interested in anything that involved intellectual effort.

"I think we can assume Miniruta isn't going to budge," Morgan reported. "But I have a suggestion you may want to consider."

"I'd be astonished if you didn't," Ari said.

"I think you should send your own machines to the sites she's occupying and have them attempt to carry out your plans. My profiling program indicates there's a high probability she'll attempt to interfere with you. As you can see by the numbers on chart three, the public reaction will probably place you in a much stronger political position if she does."

Ari turned his attention to the chart displayed on the bottom half of his screen and spent a full third of a minute studying it—a time span that indicated he was checking the logic that connected the figures.

"The numbers are convincing," Ari said in Tych. "But I would appreciate it if you would tell me what your ultimate objective is."

"There's a basic conflict between Miniruta's conduct and the message of the EruLabi creeds. Miniruta can't act the way she's been acting without arousing some hostility in the rest of the EruLabi community."

"And you're hoping she'll alter her behavior when she finds the EruLabi are turning against her. Since she is a personality whose 'drive for affiliation' scores in the 99th percentile."

"The EruLabi are not proselytizers," Morgan said in Tych. "Their world-view tends to attract people who avoid controversy and public notice. Many EruLabi are already uncomfortable. If you'll examine Table Six, you'll see the reactions of the EruLabi community already generate an overall minus twenty in their attitude toward Miniruta. Table Seven shows you how much that will increase if they see her actually engaging in some form of active resistance."

"I'm still fully prepared to transmit a message without waiting for authorization, Morgan. I'm willing to try this. But the other option is still open."

"I understand that," Morgan said.

The biggest exploration machines on the planet were high-wheeled "tractors" that were about the size of the fabrication unit that sat in a corner of Morgan's apartment and transformed rocks and waste matter into food and other useful items. Ari started—correctly, in Morgan's opinion—by landing six machines that were only a third that size. Ari's little group of sand sifters and electronic probing devices started to spread out after their landing and three tractors detached themselves from Miniruta's team and tried to block them. Ari's nimble little machines dodged through the openings between the tractors, more of Miniruta's machines entered the action, and the tractors started colliding with Ari's machines and knocking off wheels and sensors.

Morgan stayed out of the rhetorical duel that erupted as soon as Ari circulated his recording of the robotic fracas. Instead, he focused his attention on the reactions of the EruLabi. Miniruta was defending herself by claiming she was upholding her right to pursue an alternate research pattern. It was a weak line of argument, in Morgan's opinion, and the EruLabi seemed to agree with him. The support she was attracting came from people who had opposed Ari's original request to send a message to the solar system. Morgan's search programs couldn't find a single comment—negative or positive—from anyone who could be identified as an EruLabi.

Morgan's content analysis programs had been collecting every commentary and attempt at humor that mentioned

Miniruta. Over the next few hours he found five items that played on the discrepancy between Miniruta's EruLabi professions and her militant behavior. The one he liked best was a forty second video that showed a woman with a BR-V73 body type reclining in an ornate bath. The woman was bellowing EruLabi slogans at the top of her lungs and manipulating toy war machines while she jabbered about love, sensual pleasure, and the comforts of art and music. A broken tea cup jiggled on the floor beside the tub every time one of her toys fired a laser or launched a missile.

It was a crude effort that had been posted anonymously, with no attempt to circulate it. As far as Morgan could tell, only a couple of hundred people had actually seen it. He shortened it by eighteen seconds, transformed the cackles into deepthroated chuckles, and retouched some of the other details.

Of the other four items, two were genuinely witty, one was clumsy, and one was just badtempered and insulting. He modified all of them in the same way he had modified the video. He slipped them into the message stream at points where he could be confident they would be noticed by key members of the EruLabi communion.

Fifteen hours after Miniruta had started obstructing Ari's efforts, Savela Insdotter circulated the official EruLabi response. *Miniruta Coboloji has been an inspiration to everyone who truly understands the EruLabi creeds,* Savela began. *Unfortunately, she seems to have let her enthusiasm for our Way lead her into a dangerous course of action. We reached an agreement and Ari Sun-Dalt abided by it, in spite of all his feelings to the contrary.*

We have a civilized, rational system for resolving differences. We don't have to tolerate people who refuse to respect our procedures. We still control the communication system. We can still sever Miniruta's communication links with Athene and her manufacturing facilities on the moon, if we register our will as a community. Isn't it time we got this situation under control?

*   *   *

Miniruta's answer appeared on the screens of every EruLabi on the ship. Morgan wasn't included on her distribution list but an EruLabi passed it on to him. Every word she spoke validated the analysis his program had made all those decades earlier. The tilt of her chin and the tension in her mouth could have been delineated by a simulator working with the program's conclusions.

Morgan watched the statement once, to see what she had said, and never looked at it again. He had watched Miniruta abandon two groups: the original Eight and Ari's most dedicated followers. No group had ever abandoned her.

Savela's proposal required a 90 percent vote—the minimum it took to override the controls built into the information system. Anyone who had watched the ship's political system at work could have predicted Savela was going to collect every yes she needed. The proposal had been attracting votes from the moment people started discussing it—and no one had voted against it.

Morgan believed he was offering Miniruta the best opportunity he could give her. The EruLabi were not a vindictive people. A few wits had circulated clever barbs, but there was no evidence they were committed to a state of permanent rancor. Most of them would quickly forget her "excessive ardor" once she "manifested a better understanding of our ideals."

Miniruta would re-establish her bonds with the EruLabi communion within a year, two years at the most, Morgan estimated. He would once again recline beside her as they sampled teas and wines together. He would look down on her face as she responded to the long movements of his body. Miniruta was a *good* EruLabi. It suited her.

He knew he had failed when the vote reached the 55 percent mark and Miniruta started denouncing the EruLabi who had refused to support her crusade to rid the universe of "cosmic totalitarianism." The tally had just topped 65 percent when Ari advised him Miniruta's robots were vandalizing the sites she had occupied.

*   *   *

Fossils were being chipped and defaced. Rocks that might contain fossils were being splintered into slivers and scattered across the landscape. Five of the best sites were being systematically destroyed.

The carnage would end as soon as they cut Miniruta's communications link to the planet. But in the meantime she would destroy evidence that had survived two billion years.

Ari already had machines of his own at two of the sites Miniruta was razing. He had transmitted new orders to the entire group and they had immediately started ramming and blocking Miniruta's machines. The rest of his machines were scattered over the planet.

They had only built three vehicles that could pick up a group of exploration machines and haul it to another point on the planet. Most of the machines on the planet had been planted on their work sites when they had made their initial trip from the moon.

Morgan ran the situation through a wargame template and considered the results. As usual, the tactical situation could be reduced to a problem in the allocation of resources. They could scatter their forces among all five sites or they could concentrate on three. Scattering was the best option if they thought the struggle would only last a few hours. Concentration was the best option if they thought it might last longer.

"Give me some priorities," Morgan said. "Which sites are most important?"

"They're all important," Ari said. "Who knows what's there? She could be destroying something critical at every site she's spoiling."

Morgan gave his system an order and the three transport vehicles initiated a lifting program that would place defensive forces on all five sites. The vote on Savela's proposal had already reached the 70 percent mark. How long could it be before it hit ninety and Miniruta lost control of her equipment?

Most of the exploration machines were weak devices.

They removed dirt by the spoonful. They cataloged the position of every pebble they disturbed. If the vote reached cutoff within two or three hours, Morgan's scattered defensive forces could save over 85 percent of all five sites.

Short range laser beams burned out sensors. Mechanical arms pounded sensitive arrays. Vehicles wheeled and charged through a thin, low-gravity fog of dust. Morgan found himself reliving emotions he hadn't felt since his postnatal development program had given him simple mechanical toys during the first years of his childhood.

For the first ninety minutes it was almost fun. Then he realized the vote had been stuck at 78 percent for at least fifteen minutes. A moment later it dropped back to seventy-six.

He switched his attention to his political analysis program and realized Miniruta had made an important shift while he had been playing general. She had stopped fighting a crusade against her philosophical rivals. Now she was defending Madame Dawne "and all the other elders who will have to live with the consequences of Ari's headstrong recklessness if the *Green Voyager* changes course."

"Apparently she's decided Madame Dawne offers her a more popular cause," Ari said.

Ten minutes after Miniruta issued her speech, Morgan sent five of his machines in pursuit of two of hers. He was watching his little war party drive in for the kill—confident he had her outmaneuvered—when he suddenly discovered it had been encircled by an overwhelming force. Five minutes later, the program advised him he was facing a general disaster. The "exchange rate" at all five sites was now running almost two to one in Miniruta's favor. Every time he destroyed five of her machines, she destroyed nine of his.

Ari saw the implications as soon as the numbers appeared on the screen. "She's started feeding herself enhancers," Ari said. "She's abandoning her EruLabi principles."

Morgan turned away from his screens. Memories of music floated across his mind.

He switched to Tych, in the hope its hard, orderly sentences would help him control his feelings. "Miniruta has switched allegiances," he said. "We were incorrect when we assumed her last statement was a tactical move. She has acquired a new allegiance."

"Just like that? Just like she left us?"

"It would be more correct to say she feels the EruLabi left her."

"That isn't what you told me she'd do, Morgan."

"The programs indicated there was a 90 percent probability Miniruta would protect her ties with the EruLabi community."

"And now you're faced with one of the options in the 10 percent list instead."

A blank look settled over Ari's face. He tipped back his head and focused his attention on his internal electronics.

"Let me see if I understand the situation," Ari said in Tych. "The struggle can continue almost indefinitely if Miniruta maintains the current exchange rate. She is receiving new machines from her production units on the moon almost as fast as you're destroying them. She can continue damaging all five sites, therefore, until they are all totally demolished."

"We still have options," Morgan said. "My pharmaceuticals include enhancers I still haven't used. Miniruta outmatches me intellectually but she has a weakness. She isn't used to thinking about conflict situations. Miniruta spent the last seven decades advancing through the EruLabi protocols. She has devoted 25 percent of her total lifespan to her attempts to master the protocols."

"As for the political situation," Ari droned, "according to your best estimates, approximately 80 percent of the ship's population feel we should send a message to the solar system if we find conclusive evidence intelligent life evolved on Athene. They may not agree I should send a message now, but they do agree it should be sent if I uncover evidence that can be considered conclusive. Most of the people in the other 20 percent have been willing to submit to the will of the majority, even though they aren't happy with the idea. Now Miniruta is offering the 20 percent a tempting opportunity. They can let her destroy the evidence and avoid a decision indefinitely. They don't even have to vote. They can just abstain and hold the count on the current balloting below 90 percent. Miniruta will maintain control of her machines and the sites will be excised from the scientific record."

Ari lowered his head. "It's my opinion I should initiate one of my alternate options. Miniruta can only operate her machines as long as her apartment is connected to the ship's power supply. We will have to sever three alternate power lines to cut her link with the power system, but I believe it can be done."

Morgan stared at the screen that displayed Ari's face. He started to respond in Tych and discovered he couldn't. Ari had triggered an emotional flood that was so powerful Morgan's brain had automatically shifted to VA13.

Ari raised his hand. "I recognize that the action I'm suggesting has serious implications," he said. "I realize it could trigger off long term changes in our communal relationships. I believe Miniruta is committing a crime that ranks with the worst atrocities in history. She is destroying a message that has been waiting for us for over two billion years."

"You're talking about something that could make every passenger on this ship feel they had to arm themselves," Morgan said. "This is the first time I've heard anyone even *suggest* one passenger should attack another passenger's power connection. What kind of a life could we have here if people felt somebody could cut their power connection every time we had a conflict?"

"We are discussing an extreme situation. Miniruta could be pulverizing the only fossils on the planet that could prove Athene generated intelligent life."

Morgan stood up. "It's always an extreme situation. This

time it's *your* extreme situation. Fifty years from now it will be somebody else's. And what do we end up with? A ship full of people forming gangs and alliances so they can protect themselves?"

"Is that all that matters to you, Morgan? Maintaining order in one little rock? Worrying about three thousand people hiding in their own personal caves?"

Morgan knew he was losing control of his impulses. He was behaving exactly the way his personality profile predicted he would behave. But he couldn't help himself. He was staring at someone who was unshakably convinced they were right and he was wrong. Ari could have withstood every technique of persuasion stored in the ship's databanks. What difference did it make what he said?

"It's the rock I live in! It's the rock *you* live in!"

Ari switched to VA13—a language he rarely used. The musical pattern he adapted colored his words with a flare of trumpets.

"I live in the galaxy," Ari said. "My primary responsibility is the intellectual evolution of my species."

Miniruta—Ari is going to cut the power lines to your apartment. This is not a ruse. It's not a threat. I'm warning you because I think he's doing something that could have a disastrous effect on the long range welfare of the ship's community—a precedent that could make the ship unlivable. You've still got time if you move now. Put on your emergency suit. Get in your escape tunnel and go all the way to the surface before he puts a guard on the surface hatch. If you start now, you could make it all the way to the communications module while he's still getting organized.

Morgan's forces attacked Miniruta's production facilities on the moon two hours after she received his warning. Her security system put up a fight, but it was overwhelmed within an hour. Every fabrication unit in her factories was brought to a halt. The rail launcher that propelled her machines toward Athene was dismantled at three different points.

Morgan had selected the most powerful intellectual enhancer his physiology could absorb. He would be disoriented for almost five daycycles after he stopped using it. He was still intellectually inferior to Miniruta, but he had just proved he had been right when he had claimed she wasn't used to thinking about conflict situations. He had taken her by surprise because she hadn't realized he had reprogrammed his lunar fabrication units and created a force that could break through her defenses.

This was the first time he had used this enhancer while he was struggling with a real-time, real-world challenge. He turned his attention to the action on the surface of Athene as if he was training a massive weapon on a target.

Miniruta's forces were still destroying his machines faster than he was destroying hers. She had spent a full hour working her way across the surface of the ship to the communications module and she had managed to maintain the exchange rate all the time she had been doing it. On the site closest to Athene's equator, she had taken complete control of the situation. Morgan's machines had been backed against a cliff and most of Miniruta's machines were churning up the ground and lasering potential fossil beds without resistance.

Morgan had eliminated Miniruta's source of reinforcements when he had destroyed her facilities on the moon. His own fabrication units were still turning out a steady stream of reinforcements and launching them at the planet. Sooner or later Miniruta's machines would be wiped out. Sooner or later he would be replacing his machines faster than she destroyed them. But the trip from the moon to Athene took over twenty hours. It would be almost forty hours, the charts on his screens claimed, before he destroyed Miniruta's last machine.

His brain skimmed through the plans for the vehicles that ferried equipment between the moon and the planet. Numbers and equations danced across his consciousness: payloads, production times, the weight of the reaction mass a transport vehicle forced through its engines when it braked to a landing on Athene. His fabrication units on the moon received a new set of orders and started producing transport vehicles that would make the trip in nine hours. The vehicles would carry 50 percent more reaction mass, so they could kill the extra velocity. Payload would be reduced by 30 percent.

"Somebody told her we were going to attack her power lines. She climbed out her surface escape hatch minutes before we put a guard on it. We didn't even know she'd left until she started controlling her machines from the communications module."

Ari had been speaking VA13 when he had deposited the message in Morgan's files. He had obviously wanted to make sure Morgan understood his feelings.

"There's only one person on this ship who could have warned her in time, Morgan. No one in my communion would have done such a thing. Now she's sitting in the communications module, wrecking and smashing some of the most precious information the human race has ever uncovered. And we're battering our skulls into pulp trying to break through all the weapons her friend Madame Dawne deployed around the communications module."

Morgan put his machines into a defensive posture on all five sites and held them on the defensive while he waited for reinforcements. Every now and then, when he saw an opportunity, he launched a hit-and-run attack and tried to catch one of her machines by surprise.

Ari was right, of course. The destruction Morgan was watching on his screens was one of the great criminal acts of history. Most of the fossils that had filled in the story of human evolution had come from a small area of Earth. The sites Miniruta was destroying had been selected because they met all the parameters entered into the search program. Would there be important, unfillable gaps in the record when they had explored the entire planet? Would her spree of destruction leave them with questions that could never be answered?

Morgan switched to the offensive as soon as the first reinforcement arrived from the moon. He picked the site where Miniruta was weakest and eliminated every machine she controlled within two hours. Then he picked her second weakest site and began working on it.

He could feel the full power of Miniruta's mind every step of the way. He was making maximum use of all the help his wargaming programs could give him but he couldn't reduce the exchange ratio by a single percentage point. He was only going to defeat her because she was manipulating a finite force and he could draw on an infinite supply of reinforcements. Whatever he did, she still destroyed nine of his machines every time he destroyed five of hers.

At any given moment, furthermore, only about half her machines were actually fighting his. The rest of them were busily maximizing the destruction she was causing.

"We've lost at least 30 percent of the information we could have pulled from each site," Ari said. "On site four, we probably lost over 60 percent."

Morgan was lying on a couch, with a screen propped on his stomach. The recording of Ari's face seemed to be shimmering at the end of a long tunnel. The medical system had advised him it might be most of a tenday before he recovered from the combined effects of sleeplessness, emotional stress, and ultra-enhancement.

"I could have cut off her power within three or four hours if you hadn't interfered," Ari said. "It took you eleven hours to destroy her vehicles—*eleven hours*—even after you started getting extra reinforcements from the moon."

For the third time in less than a daycycle, Morgan was being given a rare chance to hear Ari speak VA13. This time Ari was applying the full force of a module that communicated graduated degrees of revulsion.

*   *   *

Morgan had made no recordings of his private moments with Miniruta. The EruLabi didn't do that. Pleasure should be experienced only in memory or in the reality of the present, the EruLabi mentors had proclaimed. There was a long period—it lasted over two years—when Morgan spent several hours of every daycycle watching recordings of Miniruta's public appearances.

Savela could have helped him. He could imagine circumstances in which Savela would have offered him a temporary bonding that would have freed him from an emotion that seemed to blunt all his other feelings. Savela was no longer friendly, however. Savela might be an EruLabi but she shared Ari's opinion of his behavior.

Morgan believed he had averted the complete political breakdown of the ship's community. But how could you prove you had avoided something that never happened? People didn't see the big disaster that hadn't taken place. They only saw the small disaster you had created when you were trying to avert the big disaster. Out of the three thousand people on the ship, at least a thousand had decided they would be happier without his company.

Once, just to see if it would have any effect on his feelings, Morgan struck up a relationship with a woman with a BR-V73 body type. The woman was even an EruLabi. She had never advanced beyond the second protocol but that should have been a minor matter. Her body felt like Miniruta's when he touched it. The same expressions crossed her face when they practiced the EruLabi sexual rituals. There was no way he could have noticed any significant difference when he wrapped himself around her in the darkness.

Ari's sexual enhancement was another possibility. Morgan thought about it many times during the next two decades. He rejected it, each time, because there was no guarantee it would give him what he needed. The enhancement only affected the most basic aspect of sexual desire—

the drive for simple physical release. It didn't erase memories that included all the hours that had preceded—and followed—the actual moments when their bodies had been joined.

He had made eight attempts to contact Miniruta during the three years that had followed their miniature war. His programs still monitored the information system for any indication she was communicating with anyone. A style analysis program occasionally detected a message Miniruta could have created under a pseudonym. Every example it found had been traced to a specific, identifiable source. None of the authors had been Miniruta.

He had sent two queries to Madame Dawne. The second time, she had appeared on his screen with hair that was so short and so red she looked like someone had daubed her skull with paint. The language she had used had been obsolete when the *Island of Adventure* had left the solar system.

"Please do not think I am indifferent to your concern," Madame Dawne had said. "I believe I can inform you—with no likelihood of exaggeration or inaccuracy—that Miniruta finds your anxieties heartwarming. Please accept my unqualified assurance that you can turn your attention to other matters. Miniruta is a happy woman. We are both happy women."

Morgan had deleted the recording from his files two tendays after he received it. He had given his profiling program a description of Miniruta's latest transformation. Miniruta had changed her allegiance three times in the last one hundred and fifteen years. There was a possibility her affiliations were episodes in an endless cycle of unions and ruptures, driven by a need that could never be permanently satisfied. The program couldn't calculate a probability. But it was a common pattern.

In the meantime, he still had his researches. He had picked out three evolutionary lines that looked interesting. One line had apparently filled the same ecological niche the pig family had exploited on Earth. The others raised questions about the way predators and prey interacted over the millennia.

They were good subjects. They would keep him occupied for decades. He had now lived over three hundred years. Nothing lasted forever. He had his whole life ahead of him.

Valour

CHRIS BECKETT

---

*There is a Chris Beckett website open to all the Chris Beck-
etts in the world, but it is hosted by another Chris Beckett
and does not include this one. David Pringle, editor of* Interzone *where this story was first published, had only an
e-mail address, from which messages bounced. I was able
to get a response to contracts to reprint, but no information
other than a mailing address in Cambridge, England, so I
must consider this writer the elusive Chris Beckett.*

*This story, however, is quite concretely SF, of the dead-
pan ironic sort, perhaps a descendant of William Tenn's
classic, "The Emancipation of Earth." What if the aliens
sent us an intelligible, sophisticated message, and no one
much cared?*

Here comes Vincent. Here he comes through the stratosphere on the Lufthansa shuttle: a shy, thin young Englishman, half-listening to the recorded safety instructions.

"Drinks, anyone? Drinks?" says the hostess: blonde, with high heels, makeup and a short, tight dress. Vincent reminds himself, with a certain eerie jolt, that she isn't human. She's a *synthetik*—a robot clothed in living tissue. Lufthansa uses them on all their flights now. So do Air France and Alitalia. They are cheaper than real women, they do not require time off, and they are uniformly beautiful . . .

"Disconcerting, isn't it?" says the passenger next to him, an elderly German with a humorous mouth and extraordinarily mobile eyebrows. "You find yourself admiring them without really thinking about it—and then suddenly you remember they are only machines."

Vincent smiles just enough to avoid impoliteness. He does not enjoy chatting to strangers. Unfortunately his companion does not feel the same.

"My name is Gruber," says the elderly German, extending a large friendly hand. "Heinrich Gruber, I am a student of philosophy. How about you?"

"I'm a computer scientist."

"Really? Where?"

"Cambridge usually, but I'm taking a sabbatical in Berlin."

Gruber chuckles. "Cambridge! Cambridge! The silicon city, the city of the disembodied mind!"

And as if to disassociate himself from any charge of being disembodied, he cranes round to stare at the comely bottom of the robot hostess as she stoops to take a bottle out of her trolley. He turns back to Vincent, eyebrows wriggling with amusement:

"And yet if she was a *real* human hostess and you and I were sitting here quietly eyeing her up the way men do, would the position really be so different? It would not be her *soul* after all that was on our minds?" The eyebrows arch up triumphantly. Vincent colours slightly.

"Soul? I see you are a dualist," says Vincent, with a little laugh, so as to move the subject onto less personal ground.

Gruber frowns. "Dualist? My dear fellow, I study the philosophy of the Cassiopeians. I am a *trialist* through and through!"

Vincent smiles politely, looks at his watch, opens his laptop and starts to tap keys so as to discourage Gruber from carrying on the conversation. Conversation is such hard work. It involves having to be someone.

"Your wife?" asks Gruber, nodding at the small picture sellotaped in the corner of the computer's keyboard.

"My girlfriend," says Vincent, for some reason blushing as he glances at the image of Lizzie. "She's a computer scientist too, back in Cambridge."

Gruber smiles his amiable, knowing smile. He takes out a battered paperback and reads, glancing across from time to time at the young Englishman whose hands dart so quickly over the keyboard and whose eyes shine as he studies the rich, multicoloured patterns on his screen.

Darkness starts to fall outside. Stars appear: Orion, Taurus. An evening meal is served by the pretty robots.

"They make their flesh from genetically modified shellfish tissue, I believe," says Gruber loudly, swivelling stiffly round in his seat to look at the hostess, "*Patella Aspera*, the common limpet. It's good at sticking on to things!"

Vincent smiles politely, cutting into his pork chop. *Synthetiks* first emerged from the laboratory a couple of years previously, and they are still banned in England-Wales, though the ban is currently being challenged in the European Court. As a computer scientist he rather scorns the publicity given to the semi-human, semi-molluscan flesh. Simulated human tissue is *yesterday's* technology. The *real* technical achievement about synthetiks is the brilliant cybernetics which allow them to faithfully mimic the movements of the human body and face.

But perhaps you have to be a computer man to understand just how very clever that is.

"You English are wise to ban them of course," mutters the German philosopher, turning back to attend to his food. "What I said earlier was true but completely beside the point. The attraction between real human beings may well begin as a physical matter, but that is the mere starting point, the foundation on which the whole magnificent edifice of sexual love is built. But a synthetik is a starting point for nothing, the foundation of nothing."

Vincent doesn't like conversation—with strangers. But, seeing that conversation of some sort seems inevitable, he changes the subject.

"You were saying you have made a study of the Cassiopeians," he says. "I must admit I don't know much about them. I rather lost track after the news first broke, and those wonderful pictures came out. Tell me about *trialism*."

"You don't know much about them?! How can any educated . . ." Gruber makes a gesture of exasperation. "Well, I suppose I can't accuse you of being unusual in that respect! But it never ceases to amaze me that five years after the most astounding event in human history hardly anyone seems to give it a moment's thought. Would you believe, the research money for textual analysis is actually drying up now, though the message is still coming through clear as ever from the sky!"

Vincent feels a little ashamed. "Well, I suppose it *is* rather appalling when you put it like that! I guess it was when we all realized that the source was 200 lightyears away and there was no possibility at all of a dialogue or physical contact. And then it came out that it was all rather obscure philosophical ramblings and nothing that we could really *use* . . . I suppose it just became another one of those amazing things that we get used to: like cities on the moon or . . . or robot air hostesses with human flesh!"

The German snorts. "No doubt. But really is there any comparison between these little technological tricks that you mention and this: the discovery of other thinking minds among the stars?"

He rolls his eyes upward. "But then, no one is interested in *thinking* any more. You are quite right: when governments and corporations discovered that it was philosophy the Cassiopeians were sending out, that really was the last straw. They'd hoped for new technologies, new sciences, new powers over the physical world . . . But *philosophy!*"

He sighs extravagantly. "In answer to your question about trialism. The Cassiopeians organize the world in threes. They have three sexes, three states of matter, three dimensions of space, three modes of being . . . and above all, three great forces, struggling for dominance in the world: Valour, Gentleness and Evil."

"Not Good and Evil?"

"No, no, no. They have no concept of 'Good.' It would seem quite incomprehensible to them that we could compound two such obviously unmixable essences as Valour and Gentleness into a single word. To the Cassiopeians, all three forces are equally incompatible. Gentleness tells us to do one thing, Evil tells us to do another, and Valour—it tells us to do another thing again."

Vincent smiles, with dry, polite scepticism. "I hadn't realized that the translation had got to this stage. I thought I read somewhere there was still a lot of controversy about the text."

The German growls darkly: "*Ja, ja, ja,* a lot of controversy . . ."

As they separate in the airport, Gruber presses a card into Vincent's hand. "Come and see me while you are in the city if you have the time. It is not every day after all that you will meet a naturalized Cassiopeian!"

His eyebrows bristle as he glares around at silvery robot security guards, robot porters, male and female synthetiks with bright smiles manning the airline check-in desks. "Even a genuine human being is becoming something of a rarity!"

Vincent says something insincere, but he is no longer paying attention to the peculiar old man. He has spotted his German friends, Franz and Renate.

"Vincent, how nice to see you! How are you? How is Lizzie? How is Cambridge?"

They are bright, polite, smartly dressed young people, who Vincent and Lizzie met when they spent a year in Cambridge. After the eccentric Gruber, who might at any time say something embarrassing, they seem very normal and unthreatening and easy to get along with. Vincent shakes their hands and exchanges minor news. They take him out to their little electric car (fossil fuels are *verboten* in the new Green Berlin) and head off in the direction of their Schoneberg apartment where he is to stay till he has found accommodation of his own.

"But I've forgotten if you've ever been here before?" says Franz.

"Strangely enough no. Very provincial of me, I know, not to have visited the capital of Europa!"

The two Germans laugh, pleased.

"Come now Vincent," says Renate, "surely even an Englishman knows that the capital of Europa is Brussels!"

"Well you know what they say: the President of the Commission sits in Brussels but when he puts in a claim for expenses it's Chancellor Kommler who signs the form."

The Germans smile. These bantering exchanges, with their little hidden barbs of jealousy, are the bread-and-butter of contacts between young Euro-professionals all over the continent, as they gradually shake down into a single, transnational class.

"Well," says Franz, "how about a little tour of this city of ours before we head for home?"

They drive through bright modern streets: tidy shops, tidy parks, tastefully restored old buildings, advertisement hoardings promoting healthy living and the avoidance of domestic accidents . . . (Not so different from Cambridge really, or Milton Keynes, or the modernized parts of London or Brussels, except more so.)

They drive past the Brandenburg Gate and the Reichstag. They go down the Kurfurstendamm. Franz points out the Volkskammer and the TV Tower from the gloomy days of the GDR. They drive along the boundary fence of Lichtenberg II, reputedly the largest Underclass estate in Europa, looking across with a small *frisson* (rather as an earlier generation might have looked across the famous Wall) at the monolithic apartment blocks within, where live the *gastarbeiters*, the unemployed, the outcasts of Europa's prosperous new order.

("KILL MEDITERRANEAN SCUM," hisses a scrawl on a hoarding. Somewhere inside there an Albanian boy is probably being kicked senseless by Nordic lumpenproles, or a Turkish girl being gang-raped . . .)

"Of this we are *not* proud," says Renate.

Then all three of them, almost simultaneously, sigh and say: "But it seems this is the price of stability."

"*Ja*, and we shouldn't forget that the Lichtenbergers have a guaranteed income, healthcare, roofs over their heads," says Franz as he turns the car away from the gloomy perimeter, back into the bright prosperity of the *real* Berlin. "It's more than you can say for the poor in most of the world."

He shrugs resignedly, defensively, and changes the subject to more cheerful things. "Now Vincent, I seem to recall you have a weakness for VR, I must show you the *Phantasium*. It is the Mecca for all the VR *aficionados* in the city."

"Sounds good!" Vincent laughs. He loves VR arcades. They make him feel 17 again. They give him a sense of wildness and dangerousness which is otherwise almost entirely lacking from his anxious, orderly life.

He and Franz plunge into the glowing electronic cave of the Phantasium, with the agreeable, conspiratorial feeling that men have when they get together without their women.

(Renate has declined to come in, and headed off on another errand. Like Lizzie, she hates VR.)

Of course, they have VR in Cambridge too (they also have Underclass estates), but the Phantasium is on a wholly different scale. Vincent gives a small, impressed whistle. In an enormous dark chamber, long rows of cages made of plastic tubing stretch into the distance. And in nearly every cage, a youth squirms and writhes alone inside a suspended control suit that encloses his arms, legs and face, while he battles in imaginary landscapes against cybernetic phantoms that he alone can see and touch . . .

Other youths wander up and down the rows, sometimes peering into small monitoring screens that give a taste of the electronic dreams and nightmares on offer: "The South Invades," "Berserkers of Islam," "Gene-Lab Catastrophe," "Pump-Action Killer," "UC Break-out!" . . .

"Now that last one *is* good," says Franz. "The subject matter is in poor taste I admit, but the graphics and tactiles are brilliant."

Vincent smiles, runs his credit card over the reader and straps himself into the control suit. Soon he is cheerfully battling against a murderous gang of immigrants and benefit-claimants who have broken out of their concrete estate and are terrorizing the good citizens in the neighbouring suburbs.

(Every educated European knows that the Social Compromise is necessary to contain inflation, but how Europa is haunted by those outcasts behind their concrete walls!)

"Yeah," he agrees, climbing out. "Pretty sophisticated stuff."

At the end of this row of games an archway labelled "Liebespielen," marks the beginning of an inner sanctum where the games are discreetly boxed in with plywood and have names like "Oral Heaven," "Take Me, I'm Yours" and "Lust Unlimited." The two young men, Franz and Vincent, glance through the gateway. Franz gives a hearty, worldly laugh, slightly forced.

*   *   *

Later, back in Franz and Renate's apartment, Vincent retires to his room and plugs in his lap-top so it can feed and replenish itself on the nourishing streams of information. Presently he calls up Lizzie.

"Oh it's you, Boo Boo dear." (How did they start these silly names?) "Did you have a good flight?"

"Not bad at all."

"What's their flat like?"

"Oh, like ours really, only bigger and more prosperous," he laughs. "Come to think of it, that sums up the difference between Germany and England pretty well: like us really, only bigger and more prosperous!"

"I've got things sorted for me to come over. Should be there in three or four weeks."

"Great."

"You don't sound very pleased, Boo Boo!"

For a moment, Vincent looks at the face of his beloved and thinks: *No, I'm not. What do we really share in life except a dull little flat and an interest in computers . . . ?*

He retreats in panic from this flash of terrifying clarity. "Of course I'm pleased, Liz-Liz. It's going to seem really strange just being on my own."

"Hmmm," says Lizzie, "I think perhaps I should let you stew on your own for a week or two, Boo Boo, and see how you like it!"

Afterwards, he can't sleep. He switches on his lap-top again and tunes in to a news satellite.

Every playground in Europa, it seems, is to be resurfaced in a new rubberized substance called Childsafe, following a tragic accident in Prague when a child fell from a swing . . .

New standards for food hygiene are to be announced by the Commissioner for Health . . .

The sprawling and impoverished Federation of Central Asia is preparing once again for war with its neighbours. A vast crowd swirls round a giant statue of a soldier in heroic pose. The crowd chants. "Death! Death! Death!" "Death to the blasphemers! Death for the Motherland is glorious indeed!" Thousands of fists are thrust up in unison

into the air. And the statue gouts real blood from a dozen
gaping wounds . . .

(Vincent leans forward closer to the screen. All over Europa, with its safe children's playgrounds and its pure and
hygienic food, healthy and well-fed people are leaning forward like him to watch this reckless energy, this crazy ca-
maraderie with violence and misery and death . . .)

Every day, says the reporter, people queue in their
thousands to donate blood for the statue. They are generally
malnourished. They can ill afford to give away their life-
blood, but they keep on coming anyway. Never mind that
Central Asia's hospitals have no blood to give the sick and
the injured, never mind that the needles are reused again
and again and AIDS is rampant, the statue's wounds must
flow.

Crazy! Tragic! Obscene!

But look at the triumph in those faces, the ecstasy, the
passion!

Vincent switches off and goes to a window. Faint
smudges of stars are visible in the city sky. He tries to
remember which one of those constellations is Cassiopeia.

Franz and Renate are conscientious hosts. They take Vincent to the museums and the historic sites. They take him
to concerts and parties. They take him one frosty night to
the famous annual parade on the Unter den Linden.

The starry flag of Europa flies high over the crowds
alongside the black and red and gold of the mighty German
Bund. Statues and buildings loom eerily in the icy floodlights. And then, one after another under the floodlights,
they come, where so many parades have come before. But
these are not brownshirts, not goosestepping soldiers of the
GDR, not missiles and rocket launchers, not bands, not
Olympic athletes or dignitaries . . . They are creatures from
prehistory, great shaggy denizens of the Pleistocene
steppes, shambling patiently one after another between the
Doric columns of the Brandenburg Gate.

Mammoths!

Franz and Renate lean on the railings while the animals

go by. They have seen the parade before. They watch the scene with a proprietorial air, from time to time looking round to check that their guest is suitably impressed.

Immense beasts! And they walk with such *assurance*, such calm, muscular gravity, as if their resurrection was not an incredible and improbable feat of science, but a simple law of nature: everything returns.

"Those huge tusks!" breathes Vincent.

"Berlin has 140 mammoths now," says Franz.

"New York has 12," says Renate. "Even Tokyo only has 60, and of course the Japanese have much freer access to the frozen carcasses in Siberia than we do because of the Eastern Pact."

Another huge male lumbers by, and Franz nods in its direction. "They have a few in Russia itself of course, but they are really rather a cheat. Less than 20 percent of the genes are actually authentic mammoth. They are really just Indian elephants with big tusks and added hair. The Berlin mammoths are 80 or 90 percent pure."

"Even the New York mammoths are only 70-percent genuine," says Renate, "and they are having considerable difficulty in successfully breeding from them for that reason . . ."

"Something to do with incompatible chromosomes I believe, and most of them have defective kidneys . . ."

But Vincent the quiet Englishman suddenly gives a strangled bellow of rage: "For God's sake can't you just shut up for a moment and *look* at the things!"

Franz and Renate gape at him in amazement, along with a whole segment of the crowd. Just as amazed as they are, but still boiling with anger, Vincent turns his back and walks away.

A little later a thought occurs to him, he takes the battered visiting card out of his pocket and heads for the Kreuzberg apartment of Dr. Heinrich Gruber.

"Come in, my friend, come in!"

It is musty and dark, like a brown cave, full of wood and

the smell of pipe smoke, and Vincent has the feeling that he is the first visitor for quite some time.

"Come on through!"

The old man's eyebrows bristle with pleasure and animation as he ushers Vincent into his small sitting room, and dives off into a grubby little kitchen to fetch beer. Vincent looks around, feeling uncomfortable and embarrassed and wondering why he came.

Half the floor-space is covered in books. (Is this man unaware that he can access the whole Library of Europa from a simple lap-top linked into the Net?) And there are jumbled piles of print-outs, covered with an unreadable gobbledegook of letters, numbers and punctuation marks.

XXQPeNU'BVFF6VVG'NNLPPP*JJVNKL'LJGDSF'E) XMX9*MMML XVXVOG?KK'BKQQZ . . .

"This is Cassiopeian?" Vincent asks as Gruber returns with the beer.

"*Ja, Ja*, that is the standard notation of Cassiopeian."

The elderly man rummages through a stack of files. "You probably remember that the message contains a repetitive element. Every 422 days it repeats the same five-day-long passage known as the Lexicon, which turns out to be a 'Teach Yourself' guide to the language. The key to understanding it was when we discovered that part of the Lexicon consisted of co-ordinates for a spatial grid. When these were mapped out, they produced pictures. The Cassiopeians taught us the basics of their language by sending us pictures and accompanying each picture with the appropriate word or words . . ."

He goes to a computer and taps on keys.

Suddenly a face stares out at Vincent, thin and long, utterly inscrutable, crowned with spiky horns . . .

"This one is a female," says Gruber, tapping another key. "This is a male. This belongs to the third sex, which I call *promale*. If you remember, the Cassiopeians have a triploid reproductive system, a simple biological fact which permeates the whole of their language, their culture, their metaphysics. They simply do not see the world in terms of black and white, yes or no, positive or negative. Everything is in mutually exclusive *threes* . . ."

He taps more keys and new images roll across the screen: plants and strange animals, buildings strung like spiders' webs between enormous diagonal struts . . .

"They are *incredible* pictures," says Vincent. "I've seen them before of course, but you're quite right, it's amazing how quickly we've all just forgotten them."

Gruber smiles. "The images are fascinating of course, but they are really only the key to the text . . ."

Vincent smiles. "Which is truly nothing but philosophy?"

He is dimly aware that this is where the controversy lies: the extent to which the text has really been translated or just guessed at.

After all, who would think of beaming philosophy out to the stars?

Gruber nods. "Even though they have made a powerful radio transmitter, the Cassiopeians are not especially sophisticated technologically. They simply don't put such a high store by science and technology as we do: they consider all that to be only one of three different and separate fields of knowledge."

Vincent asks what the other two are but Gruber is too preoccupied with his own train of thought to answer. He leaps to his feet with alarming agility for such an old man.

"The point about the Cassiopeians is that they are not afraid to *think*. They still trust themselves to do something more imaginative than *count!* As a result their ideas are beautiful and they know it, so they beam them out for anyone who wants to listen."

He laughs angrily. "Which on this planet at least, sometimes seems to be about eight people among all the seven billion inhabitants!"

He perches on a table, takes out his pipe and begins to fill it, but presently leaps up again, thrusting the still unlit pipe at the young Englishman.

"My dear friend, what the Cassiopeians offer us is something that we desperately need: *wisdom!* Our own ideas have grown stale. We are in a blind alley. Christianity was once a brilliant new liberating leap. So once was scientific rationalism. But they have grown old. We have no real ideas any more—not even us Germans, for whom ideas were once almost a *vice*. *Especially* not us Germans. All we have is the pursuit of cleverer and cleverer technologies—all quite pointless of course in the absence of any system of values that could tell us what all this cleverness is *for*."

He laughs and sits down again, wiping a speck of spittle from his lower lip. "But as you can see this is something of an obsession with me. Have some more beer. It comes from my homeland of Swabia. Not bad, do you agree?"

Vincent smiles. The beer is indeed good, and very strong. He feels quite at ease. He finds himself liking the old man.

Gruber picks up a file and begins to read aloud: "Just as there are three sexes, three states of matter and three Modes of Being--Substance, Life and Soul—so there are three principles in the universe constantly at war: Gentleness, Valour and Evil. There can be no reconciliation between these three, no final resolution of their perpetual conflict, only temporary alliances. Those who hate Evil must surely hope for an alliance of Gentleness and Valour, full of contradictions though such an Alliance will inevitably be. But oftentimes in history it is Valour and Evil that come together against Gentleness and we see cruel, harsh and warlike nations, preoccupied with honor, indifferent to suffering."

He flips over the page: "At other times it is Gentleness and Evil that form an alliance against Valour. Nations become timid. They fear passion. They try to hide themselves away from the reality of suffering and death . . ."

"That sounds a bit like Europa!" observes Vincent, and the old scholar beams at him delightedly.

"*Precisely*, my friend, *precisely*. We are *obsessed* with the fruitless struggle to eliminate disease and accident and death. We cordon off all that is distressing and unruly in the Underclass Estates. We have our wars in faraway countries, and watch them from the comfort and safety of our living rooms. We confine adventure to the Virtual Reality arcades, where no one ever gets hurt and nothing is ever achieved. We do not trouble one another any more with our untidy sexual passions, but release them (if we must) in the hygienic *liebespielen*, or in the new synthetik brothels, which everyone says are so 'civilized,' because they do not spread disease . . ."

When he has finally left the old man, Vincent spends some time wandering the busy Kreuzberg streets, reluctant to return to Franz and Renate's apartment. He feels embarrassed by his earlier outburst, embarrassed, now that it is over, by his evening with the old philosopher in his squalid little bachelor's lair.

He passes VR arcades, video galleries. He passes an establishment which he suddenly realizes with alarm is a *Puppehaus*, a state brothel staffed by specially adapted synthetiks. He walks quickly past.

Three police cars whoop by, heading Eastwards to put the lid back on some bubbling outbreak of violence and mayhem in Lichtenberg, or one of the other big UC estates.

I'll stop for a drink and wait until Franz and Renate are in bed, Vincent decides. *Sort it out in the morning.*

He turns into a street called Moritzstrasse.

("Empire of Charlemagne!" exclaims a poster put up by the Carolingian Party for the recent senatorial elections. They stand for a smaller unified Europa consisting of France, Germany, Lombardy, the Low Countries—the area of Charlemagne's long-dead empire. Tired, old Europa is rummaging in the attic of her own history for ideas, but the ideas are stale and empty. No one votes for the Carolingians. Those who turn out for elections vote dutifully for Federation, the Market and the Social Compromise.)

He finds a small bar and orders a glass of red wine. There is a TV on in the corner showing an extended news programme about the anticipated bloodbath in Central Asia.

Vincent sips his wine and looks around the room. In the far corner a young man is fighting chimeras in a small head-and-hands VR machine. A fat red man at the bar is loudly extolling the virtues of a one-and-a-half percent reduction in interest rates, currently the hot issue in Europa's political life.

At the next table, a woman about Vincent's own age is sitting by herself. She is very beautiful, with a certain sad, unselfconscious grace. Vincent stares and unexpectedly she turns and sees him, meeting his eyes for a moment and giving him a small wistful smile.

Vincent looks away hastily, takes another sip from his glass.

But suddenly he is aware of the three warring principles of the Cassiopeians struggling for control within his mind.

"Go over to her!" says Valour.

"What about Lizzie?" says Gentleness.

"If it's sex you want," says Evil, "why not just go back to that *Puppehaus?*"

But "Go over!" says Valour, that new and unfamiliar voice.

Vincent is terrified. Never in his whole life has he ever done anything as audacious as to approach a beautiful stranger in a bar. He and Lizzie only went out together after months of working side by side. Even now, after four years together, their sexual life is crippled by fear . . .

"Go!" says Valour.

Grasping his wineglass firmly, Vincent stands up. He clears his throat. He tries to assemble in his mind a coherent opening sentence. (The entire German language seems to be rapidly deleting itself from his brain . . .)

"I . . . I . . ."

She smiles delightedly and Vincent grins back amazed, only to find that she isn't smiling at him at all . . .

"Clara! I'm sorry to be late!" says a big blond man behind him, crossing the room and exchanging a kiss with the beautiful woman.

The clenched wineglass shatters in Vincent's hand. He feels an excruciating stab of pain. Blood wells from a deep gash between his fingers.

Clara looks round. Everyone in the bar looks round— some amused, some puzzled, some afraid. This crazy figure clutching broken glass, what will he do next?

What *can* he do? Staring straight ahead of him, dripping blood, Vincent stalks out into the cold street. No one challenges him to pay his bill.

KILL ALL WOPS, says a scrawl on the wall opposite.

EMPIRE OF CHARLEMAGNE, says another.

KEEP BERLIN TIDY, says a municipal sign.

But, just over the rooftops, the bold W of Cassiopeia shines down from a starry sky.

From somewhere up there, fainter than gossamer, fainter than the silvery tenuous voices of the stars, whispers the Cassiopeian signal. It is a ripple from a single small pebble dispersing slowly across an enormous ocean, yet even at the far shore of the ocean it still bears the unmistakable signature of its origin. It is still a message. It is still purposeful. It is still without question the product of intelligent minds.

"Valour?" says Vincent to those intelligent minds, nursing his copiously bleeding hand. "Valour is it? Do you realize you've just made me look a complete idiot!"

He chuckles a bit at this, then laughs out loud.

And then he crashes unconscious to the ground.

Clara and her blond brother Hans are the first to come to Vincent's aid. He is flat on his face on the cold Kreuzberg pavement, under the frosty stars.

"We need to do something about that hand," says Clara. "He's lost an awful lot of blood."

Huddle

STEPHEN BAXTER

Stephen Baxter is known as one of the 90s best new hard SF writers, the author of a number of highly-regarded novels (he has won the Philip K. Dick Award, the John W. Campbell Memorial Award, the British SF Association Award, and others for his novels) and many short stories. His tenth novel, Manifold: Time, *has recently appeared and his eleventh, a collaboration with Arthur C. Clarke, is out in spring 2000. He has been particularly interested in space travel. He has also been attracted to the alternate history subgenre, a vein that has captured his serious interest, in a number of stories often involving the history of SF, or alternate versions of the space program of the sixties and seventies. In the mid and late 1990s he produced nearly ten short stories a year in fantasy, SF, & horror venues, and in 1999 he again published a broad spectrum of works of SF and fantasy, not sticking to one subgenre. He appeared in most of the major magazines, sometimes twice, and there were two or three of his stories in contention for a place in this book.*

"Huddle" is a story of the far future, in which segments of humanity have been genetically engineered to survive a long Ice Age, and what happens to one individual when it has begun to end. It appeared in F&SF.

His birth was violent. He was expelled from warm red-dark into black and white and cold, a cold that dug into his flesh immediately.

He hit a hard white surface and rolled onto his back.

He tried to lift his head. He found himself inside a little fat body, gray fur soaked in a ruddy liquid that was already freezing.

Above him there was a deep violet-blue speckled with points of light, and two gray discs. *Moons*. The word came from nowhere, into his head. Moons, two of them.

There were people with him, on this surface. Shapeless mounds of fat and fur that towered over him. Mother. One of them was his mother. She was speaking to him, gentle wordless murmurs.

He opened his mouth, found it clogged. He spat. Air rushed into his lungs, cold, piercing.

Tenderly his mother licked mucus off his face.

But now the great wind howled across the ice, unimpeded. It grew dark. A flurry of snow fell across him.

His mother grabbed him and tucked him into a fold of skin under her belly. He crawled onto her broad feet, to get off the ice. There was bare skin here, thick with blood vessels, and he snuggled against its heat gratefully. And there was a nipple, from which he could suckle.

He could feel the press of other people around his mother, adding their warmth.

He slept, woke, fed, slept again, barely disturbed by his mother's shuffling movements.

The sharp urgency of the cold dissipated, and time dissolved.

He could hear his mother's voice, booming through her big belly. She spoke to him, murmuring; and, gradually, he learned to reply, his own small voice piping against the vast warmth of her stomach. She told him her name—*No-Sun*—and she told him about the world: people and ice and rock and food. "*Three winters*: one to grow, one to birth, one to die . . ." Birth, sex and death. The world, it seemed, was a simple place.

The cold and wind went on, unrelenting. Perhaps it would go on forever.

She told him stories, about human beings.

". . . We survived the Collision," she said. "We are surviving now. Our purpose is to help others. We will never die . . ." Over and over.

To help others. It was good to have a purpose, he thought. It lifted him out of the dull ache of the cold, that reached him even here.

He slept as much as he could.

No-Sun pulled her broad feet out from under him, dumping him onto the hard ice. It was like a second birth. The ice was dazzling white, blinding him. *Spring*.

The sun was low to his right, its light hard and flat, and the sky was a deep blue-black over a landscape of rock and scattered scraps of ice. On the other horizon, he saw, the land tilted up to a range of mountains, tall, blood-red in the light of the sun. The mountains were to the west of here, the way the sun would set; to the east lay that barren plain; it was morning, here on the ice.

East. West. Morning. Spring. The words popped into his head, unbidden.

There was an austere beauty about the world. But nothing moved in it, save human beings.

He looked up at his mother. No-Sun was a skinny wreck, her fur hung loose from her bones. She had spent herself in feeding him through the winter, he realized.

He tried to stand. He slithered over the ice, flapping ineffectually at its hard surface, while his mother poked and prodded him.

There was a sound of scraping.

The people had dispersed across the ice. One by one they were starting to scratch at the ice with their long teeth. The adults were gaunt pillars, wasted by the winter. There were other children, little fat balls of fur like himself.

He saw other forms on the ice: long, low, snow heaped up against them, lying still. Here and there fur showed, in pathetic tufts.

"What are they?"

His mother glanced apathetically. "Not everybody makes it."

"I don't like it here."

She laughed, hollowly, and gnawed at the ice. "Help me."

After an unmeasured time they broke through the ice, to a dark liquid beneath. *Water*.

When the hole was big enough, No-Sun kicked him into it.

He found himself plunged into dark fluid. He tried to breathe, and got a mouthful of chill water. He panicked, helpless, scrabbling. Dark shapes moved around him.

A strong arm wrapped around him, lifted his head into the air. He gasped gratefully.

He was bobbing, with his mother, in one of the holes in the ice. There were other humans here, their furry heads poking out of the water, nostrils flaring as they gulped in air. They nibbled steadily at the edges of the ice.

"Here's how you eat," No-Sun said. She ducked under the surface, pulling him down, and she started to graze at the underside of the ice, scraping at it with her long incisors. When she had a mouthful, she mushed it around to melt the ice, then squirted the water out through her big, overlapping molars and premolars, and munched the remnants.

He tried to copy her, but his gums were soft, his teeth tiny and ineffective.

"Your teeth will grow," his mother said. "There's algae growing in the ice. See the red stuff?"

He saw it, like traces of blood in the ice. Dim understandings stirred.

"Look after your teeth."

"What?"

"Look at him."

A fat old man sat on the ice, alone, doleful.

"What's wrong with him?"

"His teeth wore out." She grinned at him, showing incisors and big canines.

He stared at the old man.

The long struggle of living had begun.

Later, the light started to fade from the sky: purple, black, stars. Above the western mountains there was a curtain of light, red and violet, ghostly, shimmering, semi-transparent.

He gasped in wonder. "It's beautiful."

She grinned. "The night dawn."

But her voice was uneven; she was being pulled under the water by a heavy gray-pelted body. A snout protruded from the water and bit her neck, drawing blood. "Ow," she said. "Bull—"

He was offended. "Is that my father?"

"The Bull is everybody's father."

"Wait," he said. "What's my name?"

She thought for a moment. Then she pointed up, at the sky burning above the mountains like a rocky dream. "Night-Dawn," she said.

And, in a swirl of bubbles, she slid into the water, laughing.

Night-Dawn fed almost all the time. So did everybody else, to prepare for the winter, which was never far from anyone's thoughts.

The adults cooperated dully, bickering.

Sometimes one or other of the men fought with the Bull.

The contender was supposed to put up a fight for a while—collect scars, maybe even inflict a few himself—before backing off and letting the Bull win.

The children, Night-Dawn among them, fed and played and staged mock fights in imitation of the Bull. Night-Dawn spent most of his time in the water, feeding on the thin beds of algae, the krill and fish. He became friendly with a girl called Frazil. In the water she was sleek and graceful.

Night-Dawn learned to dive.

As the water thickened around him he could feel his chest collapse against his spine, the thump of his heart slow, his muscles grow more sluggish as his body conserved its air. He learned to enjoy the pulse of the long muscles in his legs and back, the warm satisfaction of cramming his jaw with tasty krill. It was dark under the ice, even at the height of summer, and the calls of the humans echoed from the dim white roof.

He dived deep, reaching as far as the bottom of the water, a hard invisible floor. Vegetation clung here, and there were a few fat, reluctant fishes. And the bones of children.

Some of the children did not grow well. When they died, their parents delivered their misshapen little bodies to the water, crying and cursing the sunlight.

His mother told him about the Collision.

Something had come barreling out of the sky, and the Moon—one or other of them—had leapt out of the belly of the Earth. The water, the air itself was ripped from the world. Giant waves reared in the very rock, throwing the people high, crushing them or burning them or drowning them.

But they—the people of the ice—survived all this in a deep hole in the ground, No-Sun said. They had been given a privileged shelter, and a mission: to help others, less fortunate, after the calamity.

They had spilled out of their hole in the ground, ready to help.

Most had frozen to death, immediately.

They had food, from their hole, but it did not last long;

they had tools to help them survive, but they broke and wore out and shattered. People were forced to dig with their teeth in the ice, as Night-Dawn did now.

Their problems did not end with hunger and cold. The thinness of the air made the sun into a new enemy.

Many babies were born changed. Most died. But some survived, better suited to the cold. Hearts accelerated, life shortened. People changed, molded like slush in the warm palm of the sun.

Night-Dawn was intrigued by the story. But that was all it was: a story, irrelevant to Night-Dawn's world, which was a plain of rock, a frozen pond of ice, people scraping for sparse mouthfuls of food. *How, why, when:* the time for such questions, on the blasted face of Earth, had passed.

And yet they troubled Night-Dark, as he huddled with the others, half-asleep.

One day—in the water, with the soft back fur of Frazil pressed against his chest—he felt something stir beneath his belly. He wriggled experimentally, rubbing the bump against the girl.

She moved away, muttering. But she looked back at him, and he thought she smiled. Her fur was indeed sleek and perfect.

He showed his erection to his mother. She inspected it gravely; it stuck out of his fur like a splinter of ice.

"Soon you will have a choice to make."

"What choice?"

But she would not reply. She waddled away and dropped into the water.

The erection faded after a while, but it came back. More and more frequently, in fact.

He showed it to Frazil.

Her fur ruffled up into a ball. "It's small," she said dubiously. "Do you know what to do?"

"I think so. I've watched the Bull."

"All right."

She turned her back, looking over her shoulder at him, and reached for her genital slit.

But now a fat arm slammed into his back. He crashed to the ice, falling painfully on his penis, which shrank back immediately.

It was the Bull, his father. The huge man was a mountain of flesh and muscle, silhouetted against a violet sky. He hauled out his own penis from under his graying fur. It was a fat, battered lump of flesh. He waggled it at Night-Dawn. "I'm the Bull. Not you. Frazil is mine."

Now Night-Dawn understood the choice his mother had set out before him.

He felt something gather within him. Not anger: a sense of wrongness.

"I won't fight you," he said to the Bull. "Humans shouldn't behave like this."

The Bull roared, opened his mouth to display his canines, and turned away from him.

Frazil slipped into the water, to evade the Bull.

Night-Dawn was left alone, frustrated, baffled.

As winter approached, a sense of oppression, of wrongness, gathered over Night-Dawn, and his mood darkened like the days.

People did *nothing* but feed and breed and die.

He watched the Bull. Behind the old man's back, even as he bullied and assaulted the smaller males, some of the other men approached the women and girls and coupled furtively. It happened all the time. Probably the group would have died out long ago if only the children of the Bull were permitted to be conceived.

The Bull was an absurdity, then, even as he dominated the little group. Night-Dawn wondered if the Bull was truly his father.

. . . Sometimes at night he watched the flags of night dawn ripple over the mountains. He wondered why the night dawns should come there, and nowhere else.

Perhaps the air was thicker there. Perhaps it was warmer beyond the mountains; perhaps there were people there.

But there was little time for reflection.

It got colder, fiercely so.

As the ice holes began to freeze over, the people emerged reluctantly from the water, standing on the hardening ice.

In a freezing hole, a slush of ice crystal clumps would gather. His mother called that Frazil. Then, when the slush had condensed to form a solid surface, it took on a dull matte appearance—grease ice. The waves beneath the larger holes made the grease ice gather in wide, flat pancakes, with here and there stray, protruding crystals, called congelation. At last, the new ice grew harder and compressed with groans and cracks, into pack ice.

There were lots of words for ice.

And after the holes were frozen over the water—and their only food supply—was cut off, for six months.

When the blizzards came, the huddle began.

The adults and children—some of them little fat balls of fur barely able to walk—came together, bodies pressed close, enveloping Night-Dawn in a welcome warmth, the shallow swell of their breathing pressing against him.

The snow, flecked with ice splinters, came at them horizontally. Night-Dawn tucked his head as deep as he could into the press of bodies, keeping his eyes squeezed closed.

Night fell. Day returned. He slept, in patches, standing up.

Sometimes he could hear people talking. But then the wind rose to a scream, drowning human voices.

The days wore away, still shortening, as dark as the nights.

The group shifted, subtly. People were moving around him. He got colder. Suddenly somebody moved away, a fat man, and Night-Dawn found himself exposed to the wind. The cold cut into him, shocking him awake.

He tried to push back into the mass of bodies, to regain the warmth.

The disturbance spread like a ripple through the group. He saw heads raised, eyes crusted with sleep and snow. With the group's tightness broken, a mass of hot air rose from the compressed bodies, steaming, frosting, bright in the double-shadowed Moonlight.

Here was No-Sun, blocking his way. "Stay out there. You have to take your turn."

"But it's *cold.*"

She turned away.

He tucked his head under his arm and turned his back to the wind. He stood the cold as long as he could.

Then, following the lead of others, he worked his way around the rim of the group, to its leeward side. At least here he was sheltered. And after a time more came around, shivering and iced up from their time to windward, and gradually he was encased once more in warmth.

Isolated on their scrap of ice, with no shelter save each other's bodies from the wind and snow, the little group of humans huddled in silence. As they took their turns at the windward side, the group shifted slowly across the ice, a creeping mat of fur.

Sometimes children were born onto the ice. The people pushed around closely, to protect the newborn, and its mother would tuck it away into the warmth of her body. Occasionally one of them fell away, and remained where she or he lay, as the group moved on.

This was the huddle: a black disc of fur and flesh and human bones, swept by the storms of Earth's unending winter.

A hundred thousand years after the Collision, all humans had left was each other.

Spring came slowly.

Dwarfed by the desolate, rocky landscape, bereft of shelter, the humans scratched at their isolated puddle of ice, beginning the year's feeding.

Night-Dawn scraped ice from his eyes. He felt as if he were waking from a year-long sleep. This was his second spring, and it would be the summer of his manhood. He would father children, teach them, and protect them through the coming winter. Despite the depletion of his winter fat, he felt strong, vigorous.

He found Frazil. They stood together, wordless, on the thick early spring ice.

Somebody roared in his ear, hot foul breath on his neck.

It was, of course, the Bull. The old man would not see another winter; his ragged fur lay loose on his huge, empty frame, riven by the scars of forgotten, meaningless battles. But he was still immense and strong, still the Bull.

Without preamble, the Bull sank his teeth into Night-Dawn's neck, and pulled away a lump of flesh, which he chewed noisily.

Night-Dawn backed away, appalled, breathing hard, blood running down his fur.

Frazil and No-Sun were here with him.

"Challenge him," No-Sun said.

"I don't want to fight."

"Then let him die," Frazil said. "He is old and stupid. We can couple despite him." There was a bellow. The Bull was facing him, pawing at the ice with a great scaly foot.

"I don't wish to fight you," Night-Dawn said.

The Bull laughed, and lumbered forward, wheezing.

Night-Dawn stood his ground, braced his feet against the ice, and put his head down.

The Bull's roar turned to alarm, and he tried to stop; but his feet could gain no purchase.

His mouth slammed over Night-Dawn's skull. Night-Dawn screamed as the Bull's teeth grated through his fur and flesh to his very bone.

They bounced off each other. Night-Dawn felt himself tumbling back, and finished up on his backside on the ice. His chest felt crushed; he labored to breathe. He could barely see through the blood streaming into his eyes.

The Bull was lying on his back, his loose belly hoisted toward the violet sky. He was feeling his mouth with his fingers.

He let out a long, despairing moan.

No-Sun helped Night-Dawn to his feet. "You did it. *You smashed his teeth*, Night-Dawn. He'll be dead in days."

"I didn't mean to—"

His mother leaned close. "You're the Bull now. You can couple with who you like. Even me, if you want to."

". . . Night-Dawn."

Here came Frazil. She was smiling. She turned her back

to him, bent over, and pulled open her genital slit. His penis rose in response, without his volition.

He coupled with her quickly. He did it at the center of a circle of watching, envious, calculating men. It brought him no joy, and they parted without words.

He avoided the Bull until the old man had starved to death, gums bleeding from ice cuts, and the others had dumped his body into a water hole.

For Night-Dawn, everything was different after that.

He was the Bull. He could couple with who he liked. He stayed with Frazil. But even coupling with Frazil brought him little pleasure.

One day he was challenged by another young man called One-Tusk, over a woman Night-Dawn barely knew, called Ice-Cloud.

"Fight, damn you," One-Tusk lisped.

"We shouldn't fight. I don't care about Ice-Cloud."

One-Tusk growled, pursued him for a while, then gave up. Night-Dawn saw him try to mate with one of the women, but she laughed at him and pushed him away.

Frazil came to him. "We can't live like this. You're the Bull. Act like it."

"To fight, to eat, to huddle, to raise children, to die. . . . There must be more, Frazil."

She sighed. "Like what?"

"The Collision. Our purpose."

She studied him. "Night-Dawn, listen to me. The Collision is a pretty story. Something to make us feel better, while we suck scum out of ice."

That was Frazil, he thought fondly. Practical. Unimaginative.

"Anyhow," she said, "where are the people we are supposed to help?"

He pointed to the western horizon: the rising ground, the place beyond the blue-gray mountains. "There, perhaps."

*   *   *

The next day, he called together the people. They stood in ranks on the ice, their fur spiky, rows of dark shapes in an empty landscape.

"We are all humans," he said boldly. "The Collision threw us here, onto the ice." Night-Dawn pointed to the distant mountains. "We must go there. Maybe there are people there. Maybe they are waiting for us, to huddle with them."

Somebody laughed.

"Why now?" asked the woman, Ice-Cloud.

"If not now, when? Now is no different from any other time, on the ice. I'll go alone if I have to."

People started to walk away, back to the ice holes.

All, except for Frazil and No-Sun and One-Tusk.

No-Sun, his mother, said, "You'll die if you go alone. I suppose it's my fault you're like this."

One-Tusk said, "Do you really think there are people in the mountains?"

"Please don't go," Frazil said. "This is our summer. You will waste your life."

"I'm sorry," he said.

"You're the Bull. You have everything we can offer."

"It's not enough."

He turned his back, faced the mountains and began to walk.

He walked past the droppings and blood smears and scars in the ice, the evidence of humans.

He stopped and looked back.

The people had lined up to watch him go—all except for two men who were fighting viciously, no doubt contesting his succession, and a man and woman who were coupling vigorously. And except for Frazil and No-Sun and One-Tusk, who padded across the ice after him.

He turned and walked on, until he reached bare, untrodden ice.

After the first day of walking, the ice got thinner.

At last they reached a place where there was no free

water beneath, the ice firmly bonded to a surface of dark rock. And when they walked a little further, the rock bed itself emerged from beneath the ice.

Night-Dawn stared at it in fascination and fear. It was black and deep and hard under his feet, and he missed the slick compressibility of ice.

The next day they came to another ice pool: smaller than their own, but a welcome sight nonetheless. They ran gleefully onto its cool white surface. They scraped holes into the ice, and fed deeply.

They stayed a night. But the next day they walked onto rock again, and Night-Dawn could see no more ice ahead.

The rock began to rise, becoming a slope.

They had no food. Occasionally they took scrapes at the rising stone, but it threatened to crack their teeth.

At night the wind was bitter, spilling off the flanks of the mountains, and they huddled as best they could, their backs to the cold, their faces and bellies together.

"We'll die," One-Tusk would whisper.

"We won't die," Night-Dawn said. "We have our fat."

"That's supposed to last us through the winter," hissed No-Sun.

One-Tusk shivered and moved a little more to leeward. "I wished to father a child," he said. "By Ice-Cloud. I could not. Ice-Cloud mocked me. After that nobody would couple with me."

"Ice-Cloud should have come to you, Night-Dawn. You are the Bull," No-Sun muttered.

"I'm sorry," Night-Dawn said to One-Tusk. "I have fathered no children yet. Not every coupling—"

One-Tusk said, "Do you really think it will be warm in the mountains?"

"Try to sleep now," said Frazil sensibly.

They were many days on the rising rock. The air grew thinner. The sky was never brighter than a deep violet blue.

The mountains, at last, grew nearer. On clear days the sun cast long shadows that reached out to them.

Night-Dawn saw a gap in the mountains, a cleft through

which he could sometimes see a slice of blue-violet sky. They turned that way, and walked on.

Still they climbed; still the air thinned.

They came to the pass through the mountains. It was a narrow gully. Its mouth was broad, and there was broken rock, evidently cracked off the gully sides.

Night-Dawn led them forward.

Soon the walls narrowed around him, the rock slick with hard gray ice. His feet slipped from under him, and he banged knees and hips against bone-hard ice. He was not, he knew, made for climbing. And besides, he had never been surrounded before, except in the huddle. He felt trapped, confined.

He persisted, doggedly.

His world closed down to the aches of his body, the gully around him, the search for the next handhold.

. . . The air was *hot*.

He stopped, stunned by this realization.

With renewed excitement, he lodged his stubby fingers in crevices in the rock, and hauled himself upward.

At last the gully grew narrower.

He reached the top and dragged himself up over the edge, panting, fur steaming.

. . . There were no people here.

He was standing at the rim of a great bowl cut into the hard black rock. And at the base of the bowl was a red liquid, bubbling slowly. Steam gathered in great clouds over the bubbling pool, laced with yellowish fumes that stank strongly. It was a place of rock and gas, not of people.

Frazil came to stand beside him. She was breathing hard, and her mouth was wide open, her arms spread wide, to shed heat.

They stood before the bowl of heat, drawn by some ancient imperative to the warmth, and yet repelled by its suffocating thickness.

"The Collision," she said.

"What?"

"Once, the whole world was covered with such pools. Rock, melted by the great heat of the Collision."

"The Collision is just a story, you said."

She grunted. "I've been wrong before."

His disappointment was crushing. "Nobody could live here. There is warmth, but it is poisonous." He found it hard even to think, so huge was his sense of failure.

He stood away from the others and looked around.

Back the way they had come, the uniform hard blackness was broken only by scattered islands of gray-white: ice pools, Night-Dawn knew, like the one he had left behind.

Turning, he could see the sweep of the mountains clearly: he was breaching a great inward-curving wall, a great complex string of peaks that spread from horizon to horizon, gaunt under the blue-purple sky.

And ahead of him, ice had gathered in pools and crevasses at the feet of the mountains, lapping against the rock walls as if frustrated—save in one place, where a great tongue of ice had broken through. *Glacier*, he thought.

He saw that they could walk around the bowl of bubbling liquid rock and reach the head of the glacier, perhaps before night fell, and then move on, beyond these mountains. Hope sparked. Perhaps what he sought lay there.

"I'm exhausted," No-Sun said, a pillar of fur slumped against a heap of rock. "We should go back."

Night-Dawn, distracted by his plans, turned to her. "Why?"

"We are creatures of cold. Feel how you burn up inside your fat. This is not our place . . ."

"Look," breathed One-Tusk, coming up to them.

He was carrying a rock he'd cracked open. Inside there was a thin line of red and black. Algae, perhaps. And, in a hollow in the rock, small insects wriggled, their red shells bright.

Frazil fell on the rock, gnawing at it eagerly.

The others quickly grabbed handfuls of rocks and began to crack them open.

They spent the night in a hollow at the base of the glacier.

In the morning they clambered up onto its smooth, rock-littered surface. The ice groaned as it was compressed by its forced passage through the mountains, which towered above them to either side, blue-gray and forbidding.

At the glacier's highest point, they saw that the river of ice descended to an icy plain. And the plain led to another wall of mountains, so remote it was almost lost in the horizon's mist.

"More walls," groaned One-Tusk. "Walls that go on forever."

"I don't think so," said Night-Dawn. He swept his arm along the line of the distant peaks, which glowed pink in the sun. "I think they curve. You see?"

"I can't tell," muttered No-Sun, squinting.

With splayed toes on the ice, Night-Dawn scraped three parallel curves—then, tentatively, he joined them up into concentric circles. "Curved walls of mountains. Maybe that's what we're walking into," he said. "Like ripples in a water hole."

"Ripples, in rock?" Frazil asked skeptically.

"If the Collision stories are true, it's possible."

No-Sun tapped at the center of his picture. "And what will we find here?"

"I don't know."

They rested awhile, and moved on.

The glacier began to descend so rapidly they had some trouble keeping their feet. The ice here, under tension, was cracked, and there were many ravines.

At last they came to a kind of cliff, hundreds of times taller than Night-Dawn. The glacier was tumbling gracefully into the ice plain, great blocks of it carving away. This ice sheet was much wider than the pool they had left behind, so wide, in fact, it lapped to left and right as far as they could see and all the way to the far mountains. Ice lay on the surface in great broken sheets, but clear water, blue-black, was visible in the gaps.

It was—together they found the word, deep in their engineered memories—it was a sea.

"Perhaps this is a circular sea," One-Tusk said, excited. "Perhaps it fills up the ring between the mountains."

"Perhaps."

They clambered down the glacier, caution and eagerness warring in Night-Dawn's heart.

There was a shallow beach here, of shattered stone. The beach was littered with droppings, black and white streaks, and half-eaten krill.

In his short life, Night-Dawn had seen no creatures save fish, krill, algae and humans. But this beach did not bear the mark of humans like themselves. He struggled to imagine what might live here.

Without hesitation, One-Tusk ran to a slab of pack ice, loosely anchored. With a yell he dropped off the end into the water.

No-Sun fluffed up her fur. "I don't like it here—"

Bubbles were coming out of the water, where One-Tusk had dived.

Night-Dawn rushed to the edge of the water.

One-Tusk surfaced, screaming, in a flurry of foam. Half his scalp was torn away, exposing pink raw flesh, the white of bone.

An immense shape loomed out of the water after him: Night-Dawn glimpsed a pink mouth, peg-like teeth, a dangling wattle, small black eyes. The huge mouth closed around One-Tusk's neck.

He had time for one more scream—and then he was gone, dragged under the surface again.

The thick, sluggish water grew calm; last bubbles broke the surface, pink with blood.

Night-Dawn and the others huddled together.

"He is dead," Frazil said.

"We all die," said No-Sun. "Death is easy."

"Did you see its eyes?" Frazil asked.

"Yes. *Human*," No-Sun said bleakly. "Not like us, but human."

"Perhaps there were other ways to survive the Collision."

No-Sun turned on her son. "Are we supposed to huddle with that, Night-Dawn?"

Night-Dawn, shocked, unable to speak, was beyond calculation. He explored his heart, searching for grief for loyal, confused One-Tusk.

*   *   *

They stayed on the beach for many days, fearful of the inhabited water. They ate nothing but scavenged scraps of crushed, half-rotten krill left behind by whatever creatures had lived here.

"We should go back," said No-Sun at last.

"We can't," Night-Dawn whispered. "It's already too late. We couldn't get back to the huddle before winter."

"But we can't stay here," Frazil said.

"So we go on." No-Sun laughed, her voice thin and weak. "We go on, across the sea, until we can't go on anymore."

"Or until we find shelter," Night-Dawn said.

"Oh, yes," No-Sun whispered. "There is that."

So they walked on, over the pack ice.

This was no mere pond, as they had left behind; this was an ocean.

The ice was thin, partially melted, poorly packed. Here and there the ice was piled up into cliffs and mountains that towered over them; the ice hills were eroded, shaped smooth by the wind, carved into fantastic arches and spires and hollows. The ice was every shade of blue. And when the sun set, its light filled the ice shapes with pink, red and orange.

There was a cacophony of noise: groans and cracks, as the ice moved around them. But there were no human voices, save their own: only the empty noise of the ice— and the occasional murmur, Night-Dawn thought, of whatever giant beasts inhabited this huge sea.

They walked for days. The mountain chain they had left behind dwindled, dipping into the mist of the horizon; and the chain ahead of them approached with stultifying slowness. He imagined looking down on himself, a small, determined speck walking steadily across this great, molded landscape, working toward the mysteries of the center.

Food was easy to find. The slushy ice was soft and easy to break through.

No-Sun would walk only slowly now. And she would not eat. Her memory of the monster that had snapped up

One-Tusk was too strong. Night-Dawn even braved the water to bring her fish, but they were strange: ghostly-white creatures with flattened heads, sharp teeth. No-Sun pushed them away, saying she preferred to consume her own good fat. And so she grew steadily more wasted.

Until there came a day when, waking, she would not move at all. She stood at the center of a fat, stable ice-floe, a pillar of loose flesh, rolls of fur cascading down a frame leached of fat.

Night-Dawn stood before her, punched her lightly, cajoled her.

"Leave me here," she said. "It's my time anyhow."

"No. It isn't right."

She laughed, and fluid rattled on her lungs. "Right. Wrong. You're a dreamer. You always were. It's my fault, probably."

She subsided, as if deflating, and fell back onto the ice.

He knelt and cradled her head in his lap. He stayed there all night, the cold of the ice seeping through the flesh of his knees.

In the morning, stiff with the cold, they took her to the edge of the ice floe and tipped her into the water, for the benefit of the creatures of this giant sea.

After more days of walking, the ice grew thin, the water beneath shallow.

Another day of this and they came to a slope of hard black rock, that pushed its way out of the ice and rose up before them.

The black rock was hard-edged and cold under Night-Dawn's feet, its rise unrelenting. As far as he could see to left and right, the ridge was solid, unbroken, with no convenient passes for them to follow, the sky lidded over by cloud.

They grasped each other's hands and pressed up the slope.

The climb exhausted Night-Dawn immediately. And there was nothing to eat or drink, here on the high rocks, not so much as a scrap of ice. Soon, even the air grew thin;

he struggled to drag energy from its pale substance.

When they slept, they stood on hard black rock. Night-Dawn feared and hated the rock; it was an enemy, rooted deep in the Earth.

On the fourth day of this they entered the clouds, and he could not even see where his next step should be placed. With the thin, icy moisture in his lungs and spreading on his fur he felt trapped, as if under some infinite ice layer, far from any air hole. He struggled to breathe, and if he slept, he woke consumed by a thin panic. At such times he clung to Frazil and remembered who he was and where he had come from and why he had come so far. He was a human being, and he had a mission that he would fulfill.

Then, one morning, they broke through the last ragged clouds.

Though it was close to midday, the sky was as dark as he had ever seen it, a deep violet blue. The only clouds were thin sheets of ice crystals, high above. And—he saw, gasping with astonishment—there were *stars* shining, even now, in the middle of the sunlit day.

The slope seemed to reach a crest, a short way ahead of him. They walked on. The air was thin, a whisper in his lungs, and he was suspended in silence; only the rasp of Frazil's shallow breath, the soft slap of their footsteps on the rock, broke up the stillness.

He reached the crest. The rock wall descended sharply from here, he saw, soon vanishing into layers of fat, fluffy clouds.

And, when he looked ahead, he saw a mountain.

Far ahead of them, dominating the horizon, it was a single peak that thrust out of scattered clouds, towering even over their elevated position here, its walls sheer and stark. Its flanks were girdled with ice, but the peak itself was bare black rock—too high even for ice to gather, he surmised—perhaps so high it thrust out of the very air itself.

It must be the greatest mountain in the world.

And beyond it there was a further line of mountains, he saw, like a line of broken teeth, marking the far horizon.

When he looked to left and right, he could see how those mountains joined the crest he had climbed, in a giant unbroken ring around that great, central fist of rock.

It was a giant rock ripple, just as he had sketched in the ice. Perhaps this was the center, the very heart of the great systems of mountain rings and circular seas he had penetrated.

An ocean lapped around the base of the mountain. He could see that glaciers flowed down its heroic base, rivers of ice dwarfed by the mountain's immensity. There was ice in the ocean too—pack ice, and icebergs like great eroded islands, white, carved. Some manner of creatures were visible on the bergs, black and gray dots against the pristine white of the ice, too distant for him to make out. But this sea was mostly melted, a band of blue-black.

The slope of black rock continued below him—far, far onward, until it all but disappeared into the misty air at the base of this bowl of land. But he could see that it reached a beach of some sort, of shattered, eroded rock sprinkled with snow, against which waves sluggishly lapped.

There was a belt of land around the sea, cradled by the ring mountains, fringed by the sea. And it was covered by life, great furry sheets of it. From this height it looked like an encrustation of algae. But he knew there must be living things there much greater in scale than any he had seen before.

". . . It is a bowl," Frazil breathed.

"What?"

"Look down there. This is a great bowl, of clouds and water and light, on whose lip we stand. We will be safe down there, away from the rock and ice."

He saw she was right. This was indeed a bowl—presumably the great scar left where one or other of the Moons had torn itself loose of the Earth, just as the stories said. And these rings of mountains were ripples in the rock, frozen as if ice.

He forgot his hunger, his thirst, even the lack of air here; eagerly they began to hurry down the slope.

The air rapidly thickened.

But his breathing did not become any easier, for it grew *warm*, warmer than he had ever known it. Steam began to rise from his thick, heavy fur. He opened his mouth and raised his nostril flaps wide, sucking in the air. It was as if the heat of this giant sheltering bowl was now, at the last, driving them back.

But they did not give up their relentless descent, and he gathered the last of his strength.

The air beneath them cleared further.

Overwhelmed, Night-Dawn stopped.

The prolific land around the central sea was divided into neat shapes, he saw now, and here and there smoke rose. It was a made landscape. The work of people.

Humans were sheltered here. It was a final irony, that people should find shelter at the bottom of the great pit dug out of the Earth by the world-wrecking Collision.

. . . And there was a color to that deep, cupped world, emerging now from the mist. Something he had never seen before; and yet the word for it dropped into place, just as had his first words after birth.

"Green," Frazil said.

"Green. Yes . . ."

He was stunned by the brilliance of the color against the black rock, the dull blue-gray of the sea. But even as he looked into the pit of warmth and air, he felt a deep sadness. For he already knew he could never reach that deep shelter, peer up at the giant green living things; this body which shielded him from cold would allow heat to kill him.

Somebody spoke.

He cried out, spun around. Frazil was standing stock still, staring up.

There was a creature standing here. Like a tall, very skinny human.

It was a human, he saw. A woman. Her face was small and neat, and there was barely a drop of fat on her, save around the hips, buttocks and breasts. Her chest was small. She had a coat of some fine fur—no, he realized with shock; she was wearing a false skin, that hugged her bare flesh tightly. She was carrying green stuff, food perhaps, in a basket of false skin.

She was twice his height.

Her eyes were undoubtedly human, though, as human as his, and her gaze was locked on his face. And in her eyes, he read fear.

Fear, and disgust.

He stepped forward. "We have come to help you," he said.

"Yes," said Frazil.

"We have come far—"

The tall woman spoke again, but he could not understand her. Even her voice was strange—thin, emanating from that shallow chest. She spoke again, and pointed, down toward the surface of the sea, far below.

Now he looked more closely he could see movement on the beach. Small dots, moving around. People, perhaps, like this girl. Some of them were small. Children, running free. Many children.

The woman turned, and started climbing away from them, down the slope toward her world, carrying whatever she had gathered from these high banks. She was shaking a fist at them now. She even bent to pick up a sharp stone and threw it toward Frazil; it fell short, clattering harmlessly.

"I don't understand," Frazil said.

Night-Dawn thought of the loathing he had seen in the strange woman's eyes. He saw himself through her eyes: squat, fat, waddling, as if deformed.

He felt shame. "We are not welcome here," he said.

"We must bring the others here," Frazil was saying.

"And what then? Beg to be allowed to stay, to enter the warmth? No. We will go home."

"Home? To a place where people live a handful of winters, and must scrape food from ice with their teeth? How can that compare to *this*?"

He took her hands. "But this is not for us. We are monsters to these people. As they are to us. And we cannot live here."

She stared into the pit of light and green. "But in time, our children might learn to live there. Just as we learned to live on the ice."

The longing in her voice was painful. He thought of the generations who had lived out their short, bleak lives on the ice. He thought of his mother, who had sought to protect him to the end; poor One-Tusk, who had died without seeing the people of the mountains; dear, loyal Frazil, who had walked to the edge of the world at his side.

"Listen to me. Let these people have their hole in the ground. We have a *world*. We can live anywhere. We must go back and tell our people so."

She sniffed. "Dear Night-Dawn. Always dreaming. But first we must eat, for winter is coming."

"Yes. First we eat."

They inspected the rock that surrounded them. There was green here, he saw now, thin traces of it that clung to the surface of the rock. In some places it grew away from the rock face, brave little balls of it no bigger than his fist, and here and there fine fur-like sproutings.

They bent, reaching together for the green shoots.

The shadows lengthened. The sun was descending toward the circular sea, and one of Earth's two Moons was rising.

Ashes and Tombstones

BRIAN M. STABLEFORD

Brian Stableford is one of the finest living critics and historians of SF and fantasy (he is the author of large chunks of both The Encyclopedia of Science Fiction *and* The Encyclopedia of Fantasy) *and is another of the leading short fiction writers in SF of the 1990s, and a significant novelist. For most of the 1990s he wrote stories in a large future history setting, as yet unnamed, spanning centuries and focussing on immense changes in human society and in humanity due primarily to advances in the biological sciences. Three of these have been rewritten as novels thus far,* Inherit the Earth, The Architects of Emortality, *and* The Fountains of Youth, *with more in the works.*

This story, another selection from Moon Shots, *is part of that future history, in which the Hardinist Cabal sends human embryos to the Moon to ensure the resurrection of the human race should calamity strike Earth in the future. There are it seems to me interesting reverberations with Robert A. Heinlein's future history story, "Requiem."*

I was following Voltaire's good advice and working in my garden when the young man from the New European Space Agency came to call. I was enjoying my work; my new limb bones were the best yet and my refurbished retinas had restored my eyesight to perfection—and I was still only 40 percent synthetic by mass, 38 percent by volume.

I liked to think of the garden as my own tiny contribution to the Biodiversity Project, not so much because of the plants, whose seeds were all on deposit in half a dozen Arks, but because of the insects to which the plants provided food. More than half of the local insects were the neospecific produce of the Trojan Cockroach Project, and my salads were a key element in their selective regime. The cockroaches living in my kitchen had long since reverted to type, but I hadn't even thought of trying to clear them out; I knew the extent of the debt that my multitudinous several-times-great-grandchildren owed their even-more-multitudinous many-times-great-grandparents.

When I first caught sight of him over the hedge, I thought the young man from NESA might be one of my descendants come to pay a courtesy call on the Old Survivor, but I knew as soon as he said "Professor Neal?" that he must be an authentic stranger. I was Grandfather Paul to all my Repopulation Kin.

The stranger was thirty meters away, but his voice carried easily enough: the Berkshire Downs are very quiet nowadays, and my hearing was razor-sharp even though the electronic feed was thirty years old and technically obsolete.

"Never heard of him," I said. "No professors hereabouts. Oxford's forty miles thataway." I pointed vaguely north-westward.

"The Paul Neal I'm looking for isn't a professor any-more," the young man admitted, letting himself in through the garden gate as if he'd been invited. "Technically, he ceased to be a professor when he was seconded to the Theseus Project in Martinique in 2080, during the first phase of the Crash." He stood on the path hopefully, waiting for me to join him and usher him in through the door to my home, which stood ajar. His face was fresh, although there wasn't the least hint of synthetic tissue in its contours. "I'm Dennis Mountjoy," he added as an afterthought. "I've left messages by the dozen, but it finally became obvious that the only way to get a response was to turn up in person."

Montjoie St. Denis! had been the war cry of the French, in days of old. This Dennis Mountjoy was a mongrel European, who probably thought of war as a primitive custom banished from the world forever. It wasn't easy to judge his age, given that his flesh must have been somatically tuned-up even though it hadn't yet become necessary to paper over any cracks, but I guessed that he was less than forty: a young man in a young world. To him, I was a relic of another era, practically a dinosaur—which was, of course, exactly why he was interested in me. NESA intended to put a man on the Moon in June 2269, to mark the three-hundredth anniversary of the first landing and the dawn of the New Space Age. They had hunted high and low for survivors of the last space program, because they wanted at least one to be there to bear witness to their achievement, to forge a living link with history. It didn't matter to them that the Theseus Project had not put a single man into space, nor directed a single officially-sanctioned shot at the Moon.

"What makes you think that you'll get any more response in person than you did by machine?" I asked the young man sourly. I drew myself erect, feeling a slight twinge in my spine in spite of all the nanomech reinforcements, and removed my sun hat so that I could wipe the sweat from my forehead.

"Electronic communication isn't very private," Mountjoy observed. "There are things that it wouldn't have been diplomatic to say over the phone."

My heart sank. I'd so far outlived my past that I'd almost come to believe that I'd escaped, but I hadn't been forgotten. I was surprised that my inner response wasn't stronger, but the more synthetic flesh you take aboard, the less capacity you have for violent emotion, and my heart was pure android. Time was when I'd have come on like the minotaur if anyone had penetrated to the core of my private maze, but all the bull leached out of my head a hundred years ago.

"Go away and leave me alone," I said wearily. "I wish you well, but I don't want any part of your so-called Great Adventure. Is that diplomatic enough for you?"

"There are things that it wouldn't have been diplomatic for *me* to say," he said, politely pretending that he thought I'd misunderstood him.

"Don't say them, then," I advised him.

"Ashes and tombstones," he recited, determinedly ignoring my advice. "Endymion. Astolpho."

There were supposed to be no records—but in a crisis, everybody cheats. Everybody keeps secrets, especially from the people they're supposed to be working for.

"Mr. Mountjoy," I said wearily, "it's 2268. I'm two hundred and eighteen years old. Everyone else who worked on Theseus is dead, along with ninety percent of the people who were alive in 2080. Ninety percent of the people alive today are under forty. Who do you think is going to give a damn about a couple of itty-bitty rockets that went up with the wrong payloads to the wrong destination? It's not as if the Chaos Patrol was left a sentry short, is it? Everything that was supposed to go up did go up."

"But that's why you don't want to come back to Martinique, isn't it?" Mountjoy said, still standing on the path, halfway between the gate and the door. "That's why you don't want to be there when the Adventure starts again. We know that the funds were channeled through your account. We know that you were the paymaster for the crazy shots. You probably didn't plan them, and you certainly didn't execute them, but you were the pivot of the seesaw."

I put my hat back on and adjusted the rim. The ozone layer was supposed to be back in place, but old habits die hard.

"Come over here," I said. "Watch where you put your feet."

He looked down at the variously-shaped blocks of salad greens. He had no difficulty following the dirt path I'd carefully laid out so that I could pass among them, patiently plying my hoe.

"You don't actually eat this stuff, do you?" he said, as he came to stand before me, looking down from his embryonically-enhanced two-meter height at my nanomech-conserved one-eighty.

"Mainly I grow it for the beetles and the worms," I told him. "They leave me little for my own plate. In essence, I'm a sharecropper for the biosphere. Repopulation's put *Homo sapiens* back in place, but the little guys still have a way to go. You really ought to wear a hat on days like this."

"It's not necessary in these latitudes," he assured me, missing the point again. "You're right, of course. Nobody cares about the extra launches. Nobody will mention it, least of all when you're on view. All we're interested in is selling the Adventure. We believe you can help us with that. No matter how small a cog you were, you were in the engine. You're the last man alive who took part in the pre-Crash space program. You're the world's last link to Theseus, Ariane, Apollo, and Mercury. That's all we're interested in, all we care about. The last thing anyone wants to do is to embarrass you, because embarrassing you would also be embarrassing us. We're on *your* side, Professor Neal—and if you're worried about the glare of publicity encouraging others to dig, there's no need. We have control, Professor Neal—and we're sending our heroes to the

Sea of Tranquillity, half a world away from Endymion. The only relics we'll be looking for are the ones Apollo 11 left. We're not interested in ashes or tombstones."

I knelt down, gesturing to indicate that he should follow suit. He hesitated, but he obeyed the instruction eventually. His suitskin was easily capable of digesting any dirt that got on its knees, and would probably be grateful for the piquancy.

"Do you know what this is?" I asked, fondling a crinkled leaf.

"Not exactly," he replied. "Some kind of engineered hybrid, mid-twenty-first-cee vintage, probably disembARked fifty or sixty years ago. The bit you eat is underground, right? Carrot, potato—something of that general sort—presumably gee-ee augmented as a whole-diet crop."

He was smarter than he looked. "Not exactly whole-*diet*," I corrected. "The manna-potato never really took off. Even when the weather went seriously bad, you could still grow manna-wheat in England thanks to megabubbles and microwave boosters. This is headstuff. Ecstasy cocktail. Its remotest ancestor produced the finest melange of euphorics and hallucinogens ever devised—but that was a hundred generations of mutation and insect-led natural selection ago. You crush the juice from the tubers and refine it by fractional distillation and freeze-drying—if you can keep the larvae away long enough for them to grow to maturity."

"So what?" he said, unimpressed. "You can buy designer stuff straight from the synthesizer, purity guaranteed. Growing your own is even more pointless than growing lettuces and courgettes."

"It's an adventure," I told him. "It's *my* adventure. It's the only kind I'm interested in now."

"Sure," he said. "We'll be careful not to take you away for too long. But we still need you, Professor Neal, and *our* Adventure is the one that matters to us. I came here to make a deal. Whatever it takes. Can we go inside now?"

I could see that he wasn't to be dissuaded. The young can be very persistent, when they want to be.

I sighed and surrendered. "You can come in," I con-

ceded, "but you can't talk me 'round, by flattery or black-
mail or salesmanship. At the end of the day, I don't have
to do it if I don't want to." I knew it was hopeless, but I
couldn't just *give in*. I had to make him do the work.

"You'll want to," he said, with serene overconfidence.

The aim of the project on which we were supposed to
be working, way back in the twenty-first, was to place a
ring of satellites in orbit between Earth and Mars to keep
watch for stray asteroids and comets that might pose a danger to the Earth. The Americans had done the donkey-work
on the payloads before the plague wars had rendered
Canaveral redundant. The transfer brought the European
Space Program back from the dead, although not everyone
thought that was a good thing. "Why waste money pro-
tecting the world from asteroids," some said, "when we've
all but destroyed it ourselves?" They had a point. Once the
plague wars had set the dominoes falling, the Crash was
inevitable; anyone who hoped that ten percent of the population would make it through was considered a wild-eyed
optimist in 2080.

The age of manned spaceflight had been over before I
was born. It didn't make economic sense to send up human
beings, with the incredibly elaborate miniature ecospheres
required for their support, when any job that needed doing
outside the Earth could be done much better by compact
clever machinery. Nobody had sent up a payload bigger
than a dustbin for over half a century, and nobody was
about to start. We'd sent probes to the outer system, the
Oort Cloud, and a dozen neighboring star systems, but they
were all machines that thrived on hard vacuum, hard radiation, and eternal loneliness. To us, there was no Great
Adventure; the Theseus Project was just business—and
whatever Astolpho was, it certainly wasn't an Adventure.
It was just business of a subtly different kind.

Despite the superficial similarity of their names, there
was nothing in our minds to connect Astolpho with Apollo.
Apollo was the glorious god of the sun, the father of proph-
ecy, the patron of all the Arts. Astolpho was a character in

one of the satirical passages of the *Orlando Furioso* who journeyed to the Moon and found it a treasure-house of everything wasted on Earth: misspent time, ill-spent wealth, broken promises, unanswered prayers, fruitless tears, unfulfilled desires, failed quests, hopeless ambitions, aborted plans, and fruitless intentions. Each of these residues had its proper place: hung on hooks, stored in bellows, packed in trunks, and so on. Wasted talent was kept in vases, like the urns in which the ashes of the dead were sometimes stored in the Golden Age of Crematoria. It only takes a little leap of the imagination to think of a crater as a kind of vase.

The target picked out by the clandestine Project Astolpho was Endymion, named for the youth beloved of the Moon goddess Selene whose reward for her divine devotion was to live forever in dream-filled sleep.

Even in the days of Apollo—or shortly thereafter, at any rate—there had been people who liked the idea of burial in space. Even in the profligate twentieth, there had been dying men who did not want their ashes to be scattered upon the Earth, but wanted them blasted into space instead, where they would last *much* longer.

By 2080, when the Earth itself was dying, in critical condition at best, those who had tried hardest to save it—at least in their own estimation—became determined to save some tiny fraction of themselves from perishing with it. They did not want the relics of their flesh to be recycled into bacterial goo that would have to wait for millions of years before it essayed a new ascent toward complexity and intellect. They did not want their ashes to be consumed and recycled by the cockroaches which were every bookmaker's favorite to be the most sophisticated survivors of the ecoholocaust.

They knew, of course, that Project Astolpho was a colossal waste of money, but they also knew that *all* money would become worthless if it were not spent soon, and there was no salvation to be bought. Who could blame them for spending what might well have proved to be the last money in the world on ashes and tombstones?

Were they wrong? Would they have regretted what they had done, if they had known that the human race would survive its self-inflicted wounds? I don't know. Not one member of the aristocracy of wealth that I could put a name to came through the worst. Perhaps their servants and their mistresses came through, and perhaps not—but they themselves went down with the Ship of Fools they had commissioned, captained, and navigated. All that remains of them now is their legacies, among which the payloads deposited by illicit Theseus launches in Endymion might easily be reckoned the least—and perhaps not the worst.

Dennis Mountjoy was right to describe me as a very small cog in the Engine of Fate. I did not plan Astolpho and I did not carry it out, but I did distribute the bribes. I was the bagman, the calculator, the fixer. Mathematics is a versatile art; it can be applied to widely different purposes. Math has no morality; it does not care what it counts or what it proves. Somewhere on Astolpho's moon, although Ariosto did not record that he ever found it, there must have been a hall of failed proofs, mistaken sums, illicit theorems, and follies of infinity, all neatly bound in webs of tenuous logic.

Had I not had the modest wealth I took as my commission on the extra Theseus shots, of course, I could not have been one of the survivors of the Crash. Had it not been for my brokerage of Project Astolpho, I could not have been, by the time that Dennis Mountjoy came to call, one of the oldest men in the world: the founder of a prolific dynasty. I, too, would have been nothing but ash, without even a tombstone, when the New Apollonians decided that it was time to reassert the glory and the godhood of the human race by duplicating its most magnificent folly: the Great Adventure.

I had never had any part in the first Adventure, and I wanted no part in the second. I had worked alongside men who had launched rockets into outer space, but the only things I ever helped to land on the Moon were the cargoes provided by the Pharaohs of Capitalism: the twenty-first century's answer to Pyramids.

I was companion to Astolpho, not Apollo: whenever I raised my eyes to the night sky, I saw nothing in the face of the Moon but the wastes of Earthly dreams and Earthly dreamers.

"None of that is relevant," Dennis Mountjoy told me, when I had explained it to him—or had tried to (the account just now set down has, of course, taken full advantage of *l'espirt de l'escalier*). He sat in an armchair waving his hands in the air. I had almost begun to wish that I'd offered him a cup of tea and a slice of cake, so that at least a few of his gestures would have been stifled.

"It's relevant to me," I told him, although I was fully cognizant by then of the fact that he had not the least interest in what was relevant to me.

"None of it's ever going to come out," he assured me. "You can forget it. You may be two-hundred-and-some years old, but that doesn't mean that you have to live in the past. We have to think of the future now. You should try to forget. That's what a good memory is, when all's said and done: one that can forget all the things it doesn't need to retain. There's no need for you to be hung up on the differences between Apollo and Astolpho in a world which can no longer tell them apart. As you said yourself, ninety percent of the people alive today are under forty. To them, it's all ancient history, and the names are just sounds. Apollo, Ariane, Theseus—it's all merged into a single mythical mishmash, including all the sidelines, official and unofficial. From the point of view of the people who believe in the New Adventure, and the people who *will* believe, once we've captured their imagination, it's all part of the same story, the one we're starting over. Your presence at the launch will confirm that. All that anyone will see when they look at you is a miracle: the last survivor of Project Theseus; the envoy of the First Space Age, extending his blessing to the Second."

"Do you know why Project Theseus was called by that name?" I asked him.

"Of course I do," he replied. "I know my history, even

though I refuse to be bogged down by it. Ariane was the rocket used in the first European Space Program, named for the French version of Ariadne, daughter of Minos of Crete. Theseus was one of seven young men delivered to Minos as a tribute by the Athenians, along with seven young women; they were to be sacrificed to the minotaur—a monster that lived in the heart of a maze called the labyrinth. Ariadne fell in love with Theseus and gave him a thread which allowed him to keep track of his route through the maze. When he had killed the minotaur, he was able to find his way out again. Theseus was the name given to Ariane's successor in order to signify that it was the heroic project which would secure humankind's escape from the minotaur in the maze: the killer asteroid that might one day wipe out civilization."

"That's the official decoding," I admitted. "But Theseus was also the betrayer of Ariane. He abandoned her. According to some sources, she committed suicide or died of grief—but others suggested that she was saved by Dionysus, the antithesis of Apollo."

"So what?" said Mountjoy, making yet another expansive gesture. "Whatever you and your crazy pals might have read into that back in 2080, it doesn't matter *now*."

"Crazy pals?" I queried, remembering his earlier reference to the Astolpho launches as "crazy shots." Now I was beginning to wish that I had a cup of tea; my own hands were beginning to stir as if in answer to his.

"The guys who gave you the money to shoot their ashes to the Moon," the young man said. "The Syndicate. The Captains of Industry. The Hardinist Cartel. Pick your cliché. They *were* crazy, weren't they? Paying you to drop those payloads in Endymion was only the tip of the iceberg. I mean, they were the people with the power—the people who had steered the world straight into the Crash. That has to be reckoned as causing death by dangerous driving—manslaughter on a massive scale. Mad, bad, and dangerous to know, wouldn't you say?"

"They didn't see it that way themselves," I pointed out mildly.

"They certainly didn't," he agreed. "But you're older and wiser, and you have the aid of hindsight, too. So give me your considered judgment, Professor Neal. Were they or were they not prime candidates for the straitjacket?"

I granted him a small laugh, but kept my hands still. "Maybe so," I said. "Maybe so. Can I get you a drink, by the way?"

He beamed, thinking that he'd won. One crack in the facade was all it needed to convince him.

"No thanks. We know how bad things were back then, and we don't blame you at all for what you did. The world is new again, and its newness is something for us all to celebrate. I understand why you've tried so hard to hide yourself away, and why you've built a maze of misinformation around your past. I understand how the thought of coming out of your shell after all these years must terrify you—but we *will* look after you. We *need* you, Professor Neal, to play Theseus in our own heroic drama. We need you to play the part of the man who slew the minotaur of despair and found the way out of the maze of human misery. I understand that you don't see yourself that way, that you don't *feel* like that kind of a hero, but in our eyes, that's what you are. In our eyes, and in the eyes of the world, you're the last living representative of early humanity's greatest adventure—the Adventure we're now taking up. We need you at the launch. We really can't do without you. Anything you want, just ask—but I'm here to make a deal, and I have to make it. No threats, of course, just honest persuasion—but I really do have to persuade you. You'll be in the news whether you like it or not—why not let us doctor the spin for you? If you're aboard, you have input; if not . . . you might end up with all the shit and none of the roses."

No threats, he'd said. Funnily enough, he meant it. He wouldn't breathe a word to a living soul—but if he'd found out about Astolpho, others could, and once the Great Adventure was all over the news, the incentive to dig would be there. Expert webwalkers researching Theseus would be bound to stumble over Astolpho eventually. The only smoke screen I could put up now was the smoke screen he was offering to lend me. If I didn't take it, I hadn't a hope of keeping the secret within the secret.

"Are you *sure* you wouldn't like something to drink?" I asked tiredly. His semaphoring arms had begun to make my newly-reconditioned eyes feel dizzy.

He beamed again and almost said, "Perhaps I will," but then his eyes narrowed slightly. "What *kind* of drink?" he said.

"I make it myself," I told him teasingly.

"That's what I'm afraid of," he said. "I've nothing against happy juice, but this isn't the time or the place—not for me. And to be perfectly honest, I'm not sure I could trust the homegrown stuff. You said yourself that it's been subject to generations of mutation and selection, and you know how delicate hybrid gentemplates are. Meaning no offense, but that garden is *infested*—and not everything that came out of Cade Maclaine's souped-up Trojan Cockroaches was a pretty pollen-carrier."

"Why should I help out in your Adventure," I asked him lightly, "if you won't help out in mine?"

He looked at me long and hard. It didn't need a trained mathematician to see the calculating clicking over in his mind. Whatever it took, he'd said. Anything I wanted, just ask.

"Well," he said finally, "I take your point. Are we talking about a deal here, or what? Are we talking about coming to an understanding? Sealing a compact?"

"Just the launch," I said. "One day only. You can make as much noise as you like—the more the merrier—but I only come out for one day. And everything you put out is Theseus, Theseus, and more Theseus. What's lost stays lost, from here to eternity."

"If that's what you want," he said. "One day only—and we'll give them so much Theseus they'll drown in it. Astolpho stays under wraps—*nobody* says a word about it. Not now, not ever. The records are ours, and we have no interest in letting the cat escape the bag. If we thought anyone would blow the whistle, we wouldn't want you waving us off. This is the Adventure, after all: the greatest moment so far in the history of the new human race. So far as we're concerned, the ashes of Endymion can stay buried for another two hundred years—or another two million. It doesn't matter; come the day when somebody stumbles over the tombstones, they'll just be an archaeological find: a nine day wonder. By then, we'll be out among the stars. Earth will be just our cradle."

I had thought when the first confronted me that he didn't have anything I wanted, just something he could threaten me with. I realized now that he had both—but he didn't know it. He and his crazy pals thought that they needed me at their launch, to give the blessing of the old human race to the new, and I needed them to be perfectly content with what they thought they had, to dig just so far and no farther. It had been foolish of me to refuse to return his calls, without even knowing what he had to say, and exactly how much he might have discovered.

"All right," I said, with all the fake weariness that a 40 percent synthetic man of two hundred and eighteen can muster. "You've worn me down. I give in. I do the launch, and the rest is silence. I appear, smile, disappear. Remembered for one brief moment, forgotten forever. Once I'm out of the way, your guys are the only heroes. Okay?"

"There *might* be other inquiries from TV," he said guardedly, "but as far as we're concerned, it's just the one symbolic gesture. That's all we need. I can't imagine that there'll be anything else that you can't reasonably turn down. You're two hundred and eighteen years old, after all. Nobody will get suspicious if you plead exhaustion."

"If you're so utterly convinced that you need it," I said, "who am I to deny you? And you're right—whatever other calls come in, I can be forgiven for refusing to answer on the grounds of creeping senility. I'll program my answerphone to imply that I really couldn't be trusted not to wet myself if I were face-to-face with a famous chat show host. *Now* do you want a drink? Nothing homemade, if you insist—for you I'll make an exception. I'll even break the seal in front of you, if you like."

"There's no need," he said, with an airy wave of his right hand. His voice was redolent with relief and triumph. "I trust you."

Theseus betrayed Ariadne; of that much the voice of myth is as certain as the voice of myth can ever be. If she did not die, she was thrust into the arms of Dionysus, the god of intoxication. If grief did not kill her, she gave herself over to the mind-blowing passion of the Bacchae.

"Ashes and tombstones" were the names that the Pharaohs of Capitalism gave to the payloads which they paid my associates to deposit in Endymion, near the north pole of the Moon. Ashes to ashes, dust to dust . . . but the remnants of their flesh that they sent to Endymion, actual vases to be placed within a symbolic vase, were not the remains of their dead. The "ashes" were actually frozen embryos: not their dead, but their multitudinous unborn children.

The "tombstones" carried aloft by valiant Astolpho were not inscribed with their epitaphs but with instructions for the resurrection of the human species, so deeply and so cleverly ingrained that they might still be deciphered after a million or a billion years, even by members of a species which had evolved a million or a billion light-years away and had formulated a very different language.

Like the Pharaohs of old, the Pharaohs of the End Time fully intended to rise again; their pyramids were not built as futile monuments but as fortresses to secure themselves against disaster.

Against *all* disaster, that is.

My "crazy pals" had believed that the world was doomed, and humankind with it. There was nothing remotely crazy in that belief, in 2080. The Earth was dying, and nothing short of a concatenation of miracles could have saved it. Perhaps the Pharaohs of Capitalism had been crazy to have let the world get into such a state, but they were not miracle workers themselves; they were only men. They thought that the only hope for humankind was to slumber for a million or a billion years in the bosom of the Moon, until someone might come who would recognize the Earth for the grave it was, and would search for relics of the race whose grave it was in the one place where such relics might have survived the ravages of decay: hard vacuum.

The disaster they had feared so much had not, in the end, been absolute. The human race had come through the crisis. Cade Maclaine's cockroach-borne omnispores and the underground Arks had enabled them to resuscitate the ecosphere and massage the fluttering rhythm of its heart back to steadiness.

By now, of course, the game had changed. The Repopulation was almost complete, and the Adventure had begun again. The New Human Race believed that its future was secure, and that the tricentennial launch of the mission to the Era of Tranquillity would help to make it secure.

Well, perhaps.

And perhaps not.

I knew that if the new Adventurers found the vases of Endymion, they would be reckoned merely one more Ark: one more seed-deposit, to be drawn on as and when convenient. The children of the Pharaohs would be disembarked at the whim and convenience of men like Dennis Mountjoy, who believed with all his heart that the minotaur at the heart of the labyrinth of fate was dead and gone, and every ancient nightmare with him.

That, to the crazy men who had paid my prices in order to deposit their heritage in Endymion, would almost certainly have seemed to be a disaster as great as the one that had been avoided. The Pharaohs had not handed down fortunes so that their offspring could be reabsorbed into the teeming millions of the New Human race, but in order that they should become *the* human race: a unique marvel in their own right.

Perhaps they were crazy to want that, but that is what they wanted. "Ashes and tombstones" was a smoke screen, intended to conceal a bid for resurrection, immortality, and the privilege of uniqueness in a universe where humankind was utterly forgotten—and nothing less.

My motives were somewhat different, of course, but I wanted the same result.

At two hundred and eighteen years of age, and having lived through the Crash, I could never convince myself that it could not happen again—but even if it never did, I wanted the vases of Endymion to rest in peace, not for a hundred years or a thousand, but for a million or a billion, as their deliverers had intended.

I did not want the "ashes and tombstones" to become an archaeological find and a nine day wonder. I wanted them to remain where they were until they were found by those who had been intended to find them: nonhuman beings, for whom the task of disembArkation would be an act of reCreation. It did not matter to me whether they were the spawn of another star or the remotest descendants of the ecosphere of Earth, remade by countless generations of mutation and selection into something far stranger than the New Human race—but I, too, wanted to leave my mark on the face of eternity. I, too, wanted to have gouged out a scratch on the infinite wall of the future, to have played a part in making something that would last, not for seventy years or two hundred, or even two thousand—which is as long as any man might reasonably expect to live, aided by our superbly clever and monstrously chimerical technologies of self-repair—but for two million or two billion.

All I had done was to calculate the price, but without me, none of it would have happened. The Moon would have been *exactly* as Astolpho found it: a treasury of the lost and the wasted, the futile and the functionless.

Thanks to me, it is more than that. In a million or a billion years, the time will come for the resurrection, and the new life. I do not want it to be soon: the longer, the better.

I thoroughly enjoyed the launch. I enjoyed it so tremendously, in fact, that I was glad I had allowed myself to be persuaded to take my place among its architects, to give their bold endeavor the blessing of all the billions of people who had died while I was young.

I was unworthy, of course. Who among us is not? Nor can I believe, even now, that Dennis Mountjoy was correct in thinking that his heroes needed me to set the seal of history on their endeavor—but the sight of that rocket riding its pillar of fire into the deep blue of the sky brought back so many memories, so many echoes of a self long-buried and half-forgotten, that I almost broke down and wept.

"I had forgotten what a sight it was," I admitted to the young man, "and I thought that I had lost the capacity to feel such deep emotions, along with the fleshy tables of my first heart."

He did not recognize the quotation, which came from Paul's second epistle to the Corinthians: an epistle, according to the text, "written not with ink but with the Spirit of the living God; not in tables of stone, but in fleshy tables of the heart." All he had to say in reply was: "I told you that you'd want to be here. This is Apollo reborn, Theseus reborn. This is what all the heroes of the race were made to accomplish. This time, we'll go all the way to the stars, whatever it costs."

Astolpho, your creator had not the least idea what truth he served when he sent you to the Moon, to discern its real nature and its real purpose.

Ancient Engines

MICHAEL SWANWICK

Michael Swanwick wrote The Iron Dragon's Daughter *(1993) and* Jack Faust *(1997) and is working on another novel. If it is fantasy, that will be three fantasy novels in a row for this award-winning SF writer. But in between the novels, he still writes short stories. His short fiction in recent years has been about as often fantasy as science fiction, but his prolific output in 1998 yielded a record three Hugo nominees in the best short story category, and his first Hugo Award. And a few more appeared in 1999. Swanwick then announced that he had better get back to novel writing, so we can expect another comparative dry spell before the next wave of Swanwick stories. Other than that, we do not know what to expect, except excellence. "The most telling thing to say about MS is that he is fiercely contemporary," said the* Encyclopedia of Science Fiction.*

This story, about the prospects of immortality for a humanoid robot, appeared in Asimov's.

"**P**lanning to live forever, Tiktok?"

The words cut through the bar's chatter and gab and silenced them.

The silence reached out to touch infinity, and then, "I believe you're talking to me?" a mech said.

The drunk laughed. "Ain't nobody else here sticking needles in his face, is there?"

The old man saw it all. He lightly touched the hand of the young woman sitting with him and said, "Watch."

Carefully, the mech set down his syringe alongside a bottle of liquid collagen on a square of velvet cloth. He disconnected himself from the recharger, laying the jack beside the syringe. When he looked up again, his face was still and hard. He looked like a young lion.

The drunk grinned sneeringly.

The bar was located just around the corner from the local stepping stage. It was a quiet retreat from the aggravations of the street, all brass and mirrors and wood paneling, as cozy and snug as the inside of a walnut. Light shifted lazily about the room, creating a varying emphasis, like clouds drifting overhead on a summer day, but far dimmer. The bar, the bottles behind the bar, and the shelves beneath the bottles behind the bar were all aggressively real. If there was anything virtual, it was set up high or far back, where it couldn't be touched. There was not a smart surface in the place.

"If that was a challenge," the mech said, "I'd be more than happy to meet you outside."

"Oh, noooooo," the drunk said, his expression putting the lie to his words. "I just saw you shooting up that goop into your face, oh so dainty, like an old lady pumping herself full of antioxidants. So I figured . . ." He weaved and put a hand down on a table to steady himself. ". . . figured you was hoping to live forever."

The girl looked questioningly at the old man. He held a finger to his lips.

"Well, you're right. You're—what? Fifty years old? Just beginning to grow old and decay. Pretty soon your teeth will rot and fall out and your hair will melt away and your face will fold up in a million wrinkles. Your hearing and your eyesight will go and you won't be able to remember the last time you got it up. You'll be lucky if you don't need diapers before the end. But *me*—" he drew a dram of fluid into his syringe and tapped the barrel to draw the bubbles to the top—"anything that fails, I'll simply have it replaced. So, yes, I'm planning to live forever. While you, well, I suppose you're planning to *die*. Soon, I hope."

The drunk's face twisted, and with an incoherent roar of rage, he attacked the mech.

In a motion too fast to be seen, the mech stood, seized the drunk, whirled him around, and lifted him above his head. One hand was closed around the man's throat so he couldn't speak. The other held both wrists tight behind the knees so that, struggle as he might, the drunk was helpless.

"I could snap your spine like *that*," he said coldly. "If I exerted myself, I could rupture every internal organ you've got. I'm two-point-eight times stronger than a flesh man, and three-point-five times faster. My reflexes are only slightly slower than the speed of light, and I've just had a tune-up. You could hardly have chosen a worse person to pick a fight with."

Then the drunk was flipped around and set back on his feet. He gasped for air.

"But since I'm also a merciful man, I'll simply ask nicely

if you wouldn't rather leave." The mech spun the drunk around and gave him a gentle shove toward the door.

The man left at a stumbling run.

Everyone in the place—there were not many—had been watching. Now they remembered their drinks, and talk rose up to fill the room again. The bartender put something back under the bar and turned away.

Leaving his recharge incomplete, the mech folded up his lubrication kit and slipped it in a pocket. He swiped his hand over the credit swatch, and stood.

But as he was leaving, the old man swiveled around and said, "I heard you say you hope to live forever. Is that true?"

"Who doesn't?" the mech said curtly.

"Then sit down. Spend a few minutes out of the infinite swarm of centuries you've got ahead of you to humor an old man. What's so urgent that you can't spare the time?"

The mech hesitated. Then, as the young woman smiled at him, he sat.

"Thank you. My name is—"

"I know who you are, Mr. Brandt. There's nothing wrong with my eidetics."

Brandt smiled. "That's why I like you guys. I don't have to be all the time reminding you of things." He gestured to the woman sitting opposite him. "My granddaughter." The light intensified where she sat, making her red hair blaze. She dimpled prettily.

"Jack." The young man drew up a chair. "Chimaera Navigator-Fuego, model number—"

"Please. I founded Chimaera. Do you think I wouldn't recognize one of my own children?"

Jack flushed. "What is it you want to talk about, Mr. Brandt?" His voice was audibly less hostile now, as synthetic counterhormones damped down his emotions.

"Immortality. I found your ambition most intriguing."

"What's to say? I take care of myself, I invest carefully, I buy all the upgrades. I see no reason why I shouldn't live forever." Defiantly. "I hope that doesn't offend you."

"No, no, of course not. Why should it? Some men hope to achieve immortality through their works and others through their children. What could give me more joy than to do both? But tell me—do you *really* expect to live forever?"

The mech said nothing.

"I remember an incident that happened to my late father-in-law, William Porter. He was a fine fellow, Bill was, and who remembers him anymore? Only me." The old man sighed. "He was a bit of a railroad buff, and one day he took a tour through a science museum that included a magnificent old steam locomotive. This was in the latter years of the last century. Well, he was listening admiringly to the guide extolling the virtues of this ancient engine when she mentioned its date of manufacture, and he realized that *he was older than it was*." Brandt leaned forward. "This is the point where old Bill would laugh. But it's not really funny, is it?"

"No."

The granddaughter sat listening quietly, intently, eating little pretzels one by one from a bowl.

"How old are you, Jack?"

"Seven years."

"I'm eighty-three. How many machines do you know of that are as old as me? Eighty-three years old and still functioning?"

"I saw an automobile the other day," his granddaughter said. "A Dusenberg. It was red."

"How delightful. But it's not used for transportation anymore, is it? We have the stepping stages for that. I won an award once that had mounted on it a vacuum tube from Univac. That was the first real computer. Yet all its fame and historical importance couldn't keep it from the scrapheap."

"Univac," said the young man, "couldn't act on its own behalf. If it *could*, perhaps it would be alive today."

"Parts wear out."

"New ones can be bought."

"Yes, as long as there's the market. But there are only so many machine people of your make and model. A lot of you have risky occupations. There are accidents, and with every accident, the consumer market dwindles."

"You can buy antique parts. You can have them made."

"Yes, if you can afford them. And if not—?"

The young man fell silent.

"Son, you're not going to live *forever*. We've just established that. So now that you've admitted that you've got to die someday, you might as well admit that it's going to be sooner rather than later. Mechanical people are in their infancy. And nobody can upgrade a Model T into a stepping stage. Agreed?"

Jack dipped his head. "Yes."

"You knew it all along."

"Yes."

"That's why you behaved so badly toward that lush."

"Yes."

"I'm going to be brutal here, Jack—you probably won't live to be eighty-three. You don't have my advantages."

"Which are?"

"Good genes. I chose my ancestors well."

"Good genes," Jack said bitterly. "You received good genes, and what did *I* get in their place? What the hell did I get?"

"Molybdenum joints where stainless steel would do. Ruby chips instead of zirconium. A number 17 plastic seating for—hell, we did all right by you boys!"

"But it's not enough."

"No. It's not. It was only the best we could do."

"What's the solution, then?" the granddaughter asked, smiling.

"I'd advise taking the long view. That's what I've done."

"Poppycock," the mech said. "You were an extensionist when you were young. I input your autobiography. It seems to me you wanted immortality as much as I do."

"Oh, yes, I was a charter member of the life-extension movement. You can't imagine the crap we put into our bodies! But eventually I wised up. The problem is, information degrades each time a human cell replenishes itself. Death is inherent in flesh people. It seems to be written into the basic program—a way, perhaps, of keeping the universe from filling up with old people."

"And old ideas," his granddaughter said maliciously.

"Touché. I saw that life-extension was a failure. So I decided that my children would succeed where I failed. That *you* would succeed. And—"

"You failed."

"But I haven't stopped trying!" The old man thumped the table in unison with his last three words. "You've obviously given this some thought. Let's discuss what I *should* have done. What would it take to make a true immortal? What instructions should I have given your design team? Let's design a mechanical man who's got a shot at living forever."

Carefully, the mech said, "Well, the obvious to begin with. He ought to be able to buy new parts and upgrades as they come available. There should be ports and connectors that would make it easy to adjust to shifts in technology. He should be capable of surviving extremes of heat, cold, and moisture. And—" he waved a hand at his own face—"he shouldn't look so goddamned pretty."

"I think you look nice," the granddaughter said.

"Yes, but I'd like to be able to pass for flesh."

"So our hypothetical immortal should be one, infinitely upgradable; two, adaptable across a broad spectrum of conditions; and three, discreet. Anything else?"

"I think she should be charming," the granddaughter said.

"She?" the mech asked.

"Why not?"

"That's actually not a bad point," the old man said. "The organism that survives evolutionary forces is the one that's best adapted to its environmental niche. The environmental niche people live in is man-made. The single most useful trait a survivor can have is probably the ability to get along easily with other men. Or, if you'd rather, women."

"Oh," said the granddaughter, "he doesn't like *women*. I can tell by his body language."

The young man flushed.

"Don't be offended," said the old man. "You should never be offended by the truth. As for you—" he turned to face his granddaughter—"if you don't learn to treat people better, I won't take you places anymore."

She dipped her head. "Sorry."

"Apology accepted. Let's get back to task, shall we? Our hypothetical immortal would be a lot like flesh women, in many ways. Self-regenerating. Able to grow her own replacement parts. She could take in pretty much anything as fuel. A little carbon, a little water . . ."

"Alcohol would be an excellent fuel," his granddaughter said.

"She'd have the ability to mimic the superficial effects of aging," the mech said. "Also, biological life evolves incrementally across generations. I'd want her to be able to evolve across upgrades."

"Fair enough. Only I'd do away with upgrades entirely, and give her total conscious control over her body. So she could change and evolve at will. She'll need that ability, if she's going to survive the collapse of civilization."

"The collapse of civilization? Do you think it likely?"

"In the long run? Of course. When you take the long view, it seems inevitable. Everything seems inevitable. Forever is a long time, remember. Time enough for absolutely *everything* to happen!"

For a moment, nobody spoke.

Then the old man slapped his hands together. "Well, we've created our New Eve. Now let's wind her up and let her go. She can expect to live—how long?"

"Forever," said the mech.

"Forever's a long time. Let's break it down into smaller units. In the year 2500, she'll be doing what?"

"Holding down a job," the granddaughter said. "Designing art molecules, maybe, or scripting recreational hallucinations. She'll be deeply involved in the culture. She'll have lots of friends she cares about passionately, and maybe a husband or wife or two."

"Who will grow old," the mech said, "or wear out. Who will die."

"She'll mourn them, and move on."

"The year 3500. The collapse of civilization," the old man said with gusto. "What will she do then?"

"She'll have made preparations, of course. If there is radiation or toxins in the environment, she'll have made her systems immune from their effects. And she'll make herself useful to the survivors. In the seeming of an old woman, she'll teach the healing arts. Now and then, she might drop a hint about this and that. She'll have a data base squirreled away somewhere containing everything they'll have lost. Slowly, she'll guide them back to civilization. But a gentler one, this time. One less likely to tear itself apart."

"The year one million. Humanity evolves beyond anything we can currently imagine. How does *she* respond?"

"She mimics their evolution. No—she's been *shaping* their evolution! She wants a risk-free method of going to the stars, so she's been encouraging a type of being that would strongly desire such a thing. She isn't among the first to use it, though. She waits a few hundred generations for it to prove itself."

The mech, who had been listening in fascinated silence, now said, "Suppose that never happens? What if starflight will always remain difficult and perilous? What then?"

"It was once thought that people would never fly. So much that looks impossible becomes simple if you only wait."

"Four billion years. The sun uses up its hydrogen, its core collapses, helium fusion begins, and it balloons into a red giant. Earth is vaporized."

"Oh, she'll be somewhere else by then. That's easy."

"Five billion years. The Milky Way collides with the Andromeda Galaxy and the whole neighborhood is full of high-energy radiation and exploding stars."

"That's trickier. She's going to have to either prevent

that or move a few million light years away to a friendlier galaxy. But she'll have time enough to prepare and to assemble the tools. I have faith that she'll prove equal to the task."

"One trillion years. The last stars gutter out. Only black holes remain."

"Black holes are a terrific source of energy. No problem."

"1.06 googol years."

"Googol?"

"That's ten raised to the hundredth power—one followed by a hundred zeros. The heat-death of the universe. How does she survive it?"

"She'll have seen it coming for a long time," the mech said. "When the last black holes dissolve, she'll have to do without a source of free energy. Maybe she could take and rewrite her personality into the physical constants of the dying universe. Would that be possible?"

"Oh, perhaps. But I really think that the lifetime of the universe is long enough for anyone," the granddaughter said. "Mustn't get greedy."

"Maybe so," the old man said thoughtfully. "Maybe so." Then, to the mech, "Well, there you have it: a glimpse into the future, and a brief biography of the first immortal, ending, alas, with her death. Now tell me. Knowing that you contributed something, however small, to that accomplishment—wouldn't that be enough?"

"No," Jack said. "No, it wouldn't."

Brandt made a face. "Well, you're young. Let me ask you this: Has it been a good life so far? All in all?"

"Not *that* good. Not good *enough*."

For a long moment, the old man was silent. Then, "Thank you," he said. "I valued our conversation." The interest went out of his eyes and he looked away.

Uncertainly, Jack looked at the granddaughter, who smiled and shrugged. "He's like that," she said apologetically. "He's old. His enthusiasms wax and wane with his chemical balances. I hope you don't mind."

"I see." The young man stood. Hesitantly, he made his way to the door.

At the door, he glanced back and saw the granddaughter tearing her linen napkin into little bits and eating the shreds, delicately washing them down with sips of wine.

Freckled Figure

HIROE SUGA

(Translated by Dana Lewis and Stephen Baxter)

As far as I know, this is the only Japanese winner of the Seiun Award (the most important Japanese SF award) to appear in translation in English. It was translated by Dana Lewis, who has translated a number of other stories, and cut and polished by Stephen Baxter (who has won the Seiun Award for work translated into Japanese). This version, which the author states is somewhat shorter than the Japanese original, was first published in Interzone. Interzone, *by the way, is to be commended for continuing to publish good SF stories from other languages in translation. SF is an international literary movement, and we need to encourage this. Suga's story certainly gives us some insight into what Japanese SF is like in the 1990s, what is popular and admired there in SF. But its primary virtue is that it is an effective story in English, as translated.*

The four figurines were delivered to Kondo's room in the student boarding house. When Kondo saw the package had come from the Hishitomo Daglian Saga Character Contest, he ripped it open immediately.

Illuminated by the late afternoon sun, Kondo and Yamashita fell on the contents, the fragmented figurines, talking excitedly, exploring.

Yasuko Miyata watched and listened, amused, baffled. Of course the prize was partly hers too. But she couldn't understand a word the boys were saying.

Yamashita pinched Princess Colleen's torso. "This stuff is pretty hard. They said it's a polymer, but it feels more like resin to me. And it has no joints. How's it supposed to move without any joints?"

Kondo—plump, delicate, cerebral—arranged the parts of the dragon. It looked like a dead lizard, dismembered. "It could almost be injection plastic. Oh, this overhang is perfect . . . Look. The upper and lower torso separate at the waist. That's how you remodel it."

"Yes, but there isn't any putty on the market for porous flexible polymers, at least not yet. Besides, aren't these figures supposed to be self-animating? No stop-go, none of that hassle with spacers and filling in cracks . . ."

Kondo frowned. "Look at this. You have to hand-paint the eyes. Why not seals or decals? . . ." He glanced sharply at Yamashita. "Damn it! I told you not to touch them when you've been eating potato crisps!"

Yamashita gaped at him in mock horror. "Oh, sheesh. The princess is covered in oil. I suppose I'll just have to assemble her, won't I?"

"You *planned* it that way—"

"Oh, come on, Kondo."

Kondo gazed longingly at Colleen, beautiful star of the Saga, in Yamashita's hands. "So I get to make the dragon. As usual. Actually these wing and breast parts should be interesting . . ."

They talked on, exploring, joshing, visibly thrilled.

Yasuko thought they had come a long way since they saw the ad for the contest, run in the black-and-white pages at the back of a hobby magazine. And she certainly hadn't expected them to take first prize.

But maybe it had been team work. Kondo could draw machinery and monsters, but was hopeless with human figures, while Yamashita was fatally sloppy. So in the end, while she left the detailed design of the dragon to Kondo, all the work on the main characters—Prince Galba, Princess Colleen and Aerda, the village girl with the freckles—was Yasuko's alone.

And now, she thought, it was becoming real.

The Daglian Saga Character Contest had been the brain-child of Hishitomo Institute, an electronics parts manufacturer, along with Shinshu Chemical, a manufacturer of raw materials for kits and models, and Dux, a visual media company. All the applicants were sent the script of a new Daglian Saga scenario, and—the ad promised—Dux would make an animated film of the story using figures based on the winning character designs. Shinshu and Hishitomo would market tie-in kits. The prize-winners would get to assemble the figures themselves.

And the movie—made with these very figures—would be unlike any ever seen before.

"So," said Kondo, "what else? Who assembles Prince Galba and um, what's she called? The village girl with the freckles?"

"Aerda," said Yasuko.

Yamashita, clutching Colleen by her long legs, smiled at Yasuko.

Yasuko returned his look, and laughed. "You're joking."

Kondo was confused; he looked from one to the other. "What am I missing?"

"Look," said Yasuko. "I know I can paint and I can do calligraphy. But I've never made a model in my life!"

"Not 'models,' " said Yamashita. "These are 'kits.' Or 'figures.' "

Kondo traced the fine edge work on the dragon's wing. "Actually, Yasuko, you shouldn't have any trouble. At least, no more than the rest of us. I know they said it'd be like making a resin garage kit, but this is the first time that any of us have worked with this porous flexible polymer stuff. Look, they've even included special paint and putty. You can do it, Yasuko."

"Come on, Yasuko," Yamashita said. "It will be fun." He rummaged through the box beside him. He handed Yasuko a kit, resting on a sheaf of sandpaper.

She took it. It was the dismembered body of Aerda, the village girl. It was like holding the corpse of some tiny animal.

"Work hard," Yamashita said, and he grinned at her.

Yasuko, back in her room in the girls' dorm, spread Aerda's parts on her bed next to the window.

The indents for the girl's comic-book eyes covered half her face. Everything about Aerda, from her exaggerated proportions to the pleats of her flared skirt, was exactly as Yasuko had drawn her in her character design sheets.

She gently poked Aerda's nose, no larger than a grain of rice.

She meant to start a first rough assembly of the figure tonight. As a guide she had a beginner's article on garage kits in a Japanimation magazine Yamashita had lent her. But its obsessive jargon and detail dismayed her.

Somehow Yasuko had thought she would just need to stick the pieces together and the figure would be done. But it wasn't going to be that easy.

With a sigh she slid open the windowpane. Her dormitory room was on the second floor, and all she could see was a cinderblock fence with spikes, and a bit of narrow alley beyond. She used to gaze out of the window like this, unable to sleep, when her lovesickness for Doi had been at its height. Stoking envy for her rival, or indulging in sweet fantasies. Imagining Doi turning up beneath the window, smiling up at her, calling her name.

Maybe Aerda had waited at a window for Galba to come, too, she thought. And he hadn't either.

Bittersweet nostalgia. Indulgent, of course. But better than feeling nothing, she thought.

Reluctantly she turned her attention back to the kit.

Apparently Dux wasn't going to make the Daglian Saga movie using traditional stop-go animation; it was going to base it, somehow, on the autonomous movements of the figures themselves. And in that regard, the key part of the assembly was stapled inside a small packet, thick and puffy. The bag had warnings not to open the packet until the figure had already been prepped. Otherwise it said Hishitomo couldn't guarantee that the figure would move as designed. The language was heavy, threatening.

Anxiety gnawed her, unreasonable, childish. What if she messed up?

If only it wasn't Aerda.

Yasuko had really thrown herself into creating this character. If her design for Princess Colleen encapsulated all her sense of ideal feminine beauty, Aerda was Yasuko's own little doppelganger—plain, but touched with inner beauty. It was as she liked to think of herself, anyhow.

And some day, according to the instructions, this little Aerda would walk and talk for herself. But only if Yasuko got it right.

What a responsibility.

She picked up the parts of the figure, Aerda's tiny limbs and hands, and began to work. Polish the pieces with sandpaper, paint them until the surface reeked of foul-smelling thinner, then polish them down again . . .

She worked into the night, using progressively finer sandpaper. The powder danced upward like smoke, drifting into her lungs, and her eyes itched uncontrollably.

By the time she was on No. 1500 sandpaper, she'd all but decided to skip the final finish with No. 2000.

But Aerda now seemed warm to the touch from Yasuko's body heat and the friction of all that sandpapering. The tiny figure seemed to look at her, with eyes that were still unpainted.

"I know, Aerda," Yasuko said. "I know."

Yasuko carefully tore the No. 2000 sandpaper into pieces small enough to handle, and went on working.

The next day Yasuko, heavy around the eyes, dragged herself to the university.

She was just in time for her third class. Chinese literature was a required course for her major, and she was enjoying the unit on Chinese poetry. She was thinking about starting a fanzine on Chinese fantasy literature.

Today, though, she had trouble concentrating. She itched to get back to Aerda.

Maybe this is how the boys, Yamashita and Kondo, have been feeling all this time, and I never understood, she thought.

Fifteen minutes before the closing bell the side door of the amphitheatre classroom swung slowly open. Toshio Doi tried to hunch his tall body over as much as possible as he slid quickly into an empty seat. Following him, clutching his shirt, was Masami Tsuda. The two students were a year ahead of Yasuko, and had clearly shown up just to meet their attendance requirements. When Masami spotted Yasuko, she gave her a cute smile, and quickly waved her hand. Yasuko forced herself to smile back. Masami—with her broad shoulders, that long mane of luxurious black hair—sat in front of her.

Colleen and Aerda, she thought. Masami and Yasuko. The parallels were too obvious, a cliché.

But that didn't make it any less painful.

When classes were done she avoided her fellow students, and hurried home, to Aerda.

Yasuko brushed off powdery residue with fingers made slippery, the tips worn smooth, by the hours of sanding.

Aerda's parts were now so finely polished they gleamed.

In the Daglian Saga, Aerda was particularly ill-starred.

The girl saved a wounded dragon on the outskirts of her village. The dragon understood human speech, and was really a man named Galba, cursed and transformed into monstrous form by an evil demon. But Aerda had to leave home when her own people blamed her for bringing such a fearsome creature to their small community.

As they journeyed together across the land Galba saved Aerda from attack after attack by frightful monsters. And as she tended his injuries, she found herself drawn ever more deeply to the dragon's sterling heart. She swore to herself that she would stay by his side forever, even if the curse could never be lifted and he remained in dragon form the rest of his days . . .

It was time to open that intriguing last packet. Yasuko gingerly untied the fastenings.

There were three black objects that reminded her of cockroaches, along with a small bag that rattled when she shook it, another that sounded as if it had sand inside, and a thin membrane barely a centimetre in diameter. The black objects looked like integrated circuits. But instead of the usual centipede-feet metal docking tabs these chips had a string of silvery snaps down their backs. Yasuko poked at the gadgets, bemused, faintly repelled.

In the story, Galba, it turned out, had already found the love of his life: the beautiful Princess Colleen. The princess was imprisoned in a tower labyrinth. He'd been turned into this dragon, horrible to human sight, when he fell into the clutches of a demon during a failed attempt to rescue her. Even now, his resolve to save her remained unshaken, even if it cost him his life.

Aerda realized that Galba's will was unshakeable. But she worked even harder to help return him to human form, wanting to do whatever she could for him, even if that would only end up helping her rival. Galba, oblivious, even asked her for advice about the workings of the princess's delicate heart. Meanwhile, Aerda thought her own heart would break time and again . . .

The bag also contained a four-page instruction manual. Yasuko flipped through it dubiously . . . *The multiple-value processor (MVP) assigns multiple values to electric signals— four values, in the case of the Hishitomo MVP ULSI.* She turned to the index. A ULSI turned out to be an ultra-dense large-scale integrated circuit. Hishitomo Institute, the leaflet boasted, was the first chip maker to produce a truly practical multiple-value processor. *In contrast to conventional signals rendered into the two binary markers 0 and 1, the Hishitomo MVP ULSI is capable of differentiating and processing two additional signals. One "Qit" of data can carry one of four different values, enabling vastly more complex and sophisticated processing operations to be performed in record time . . .*

And so on.

What it meant was that the little black objects were Aerda's brain.

There were three different versions, so the modeller could choose which part of the scenario she wanted to emphasize in the finished figure. The one for the first part of the storyline, where Aerda first met the dragon, would result in a simple, naïve, easy-going girl. The second was for the middle of the tale, when Aerda was serving Galba with all her heart. And the last was for the Aerda who had survived all the plot twists, and made her final decision, and had grown into a fine, resolute young village woman.

Yasuko felt obscurely disappointed. So there would be no growth, no development, no real experience for this figure. She could give Aerda maturity, give her memories, simply by plugging in a new brain chip.

But then this was only a talking doll, she reminded herself, doomed to play out a prescripted storyline.

In the story, after many hardships, Aerda finally did transform the dragon back into a man. And she worked selflessly to break the secret of the labyrinth. But the moment Galba rescued his princess, he no longer had eyes for the faithful Aerda.

Colleen, her own white magic restored to her along with her freedom, told Aerda that she would give the village girl anything she wished for in gratitude for her help. Aerda forced a smile. *I once fell in love with a marvellous dragon,* she told the princess. *I only wish I could find a partner with such a wonderful heart.*

Colleen, unaware that Aerda's dragon had been Galba himself, cast her spell . . .

The small membrane turned out to be the figurine's vocal cords. Yasuko pushed it into the belly cavity and up into the throat with her finger as instructed. Then she dropped her choice of ULSI into the same belly cavity.

That left the sack stamped "NNP Seeds." These, it turned out, were actual plant seeds. There were about half a spoonful of them, looking like sesame seeds.

NNP. Neural network plants, she read. NNP are a radically new kind of plant genetically engineered to transmit electric signals. Nourished by growth culture seeping into the body cavity through the porous flexible polymer, the NNP seeds extend microscopic mycelioid filaments toward the metal contacts on the MVP ULSI. The NNP grows into a neural network in accordance with data obtained from the ULSI. The NNP filaments continue to grow through gaps in the porous flexible polymer, reaching into every part of the figure's body . . .

Yasuko did as the instructions said, pouring the seeds into the cavity, then attaching the lower torso with the enclosed tube of glue. Next, feeling queasy, she attached Aerda's limp arms and legs.

When the NNP transmit a signal from the ULSI to a specific "address" connected to the NNP network, the flexible polymer contracts, making the figure move. Moreover, by exposing sensory cells differentiated from the rest of the NNP on the surface of the figure, it is possible for the MVP ULSI to obtain visual and auditory, olfactory and tactile sensory input. It will take 34 hours for the growth culture to permeate your figurine, and for the NNP *to establish a neural network and run the full sequence of self-checks on the figure's autonomous movement repertory. Make sure you have finished painting your character before she/he/it begins to move! . . .*

After the spell, Galba for the first time had felt the full force of the village girl's love.

But just as he was about to speak to her, Aerda stopped him. *I know I have triumphed over Colleen in love*, she told herself. *For I loved your manly spirit even when it was entrapped in the shell of a gruesome dragon. And that is enough.* And she walked away, head held high.

Yamashita had especially approved of this last scene. "Aerda starts out as a strong-willed tomboy, but she grows into a transformed woman," he would say. "As juvenile fiction goes, it's a fine expression of the classic theme of personal growth and maturity."

That wasn't how it felt to Yasuko. She just felt desperately sorry for Aerda.

She poured water into the small basin she used for washing her dishes, and mixed in the sack of powder. It reminded her of her stomach medicine. Then she carefully lowered Aerda, looking human at last with her arms and legs in place, into the water.

Sunk to the bottom of the basin, the village girl could have been the victim of a drowning. Her blouse was moulded on, part of the upper body casting, but the skirt was a separate piece, so Aerda was naked from the waist down, her flesh seamless and unbroken.

It had actually been Yasuko's fault that Doi and Masami had got together in the first place. In fact she'd always suspected the only reason Doi had made such a fuss over her was to get closer to her friend Masami.

They were unlikely friends. Masami Tsuda had broken her leg skiing the year before, and hadn't been able to get the credits she needed in physical education. That put her in the same lower classmen's course as Yasuko. When they wound up in the same group for warm-up stretches, Yasuko was surprised to find that this lovely senior student was a manga comics fan the same as her. Before long they were shopping and hanging out together.

Masami had introduced Yasuko to Doi. They were both part of a group of friends planning a party. *I'm sorry, Yasuko. Doi's so stifling! You can talk about manga and all that otaku stuff. Would you mind covering for me until this stupid party business is done and finished?* And Masami's beautiful features broke into a cute little smile, and of course Yasuko agreed. Masami was a girl who was perfectly aware of how attractive she was, and knew that no one could stay angry with her for long no matter what she said, just so long as she turned on that winning smile.

Not even Yasuko.

Doi was the very model of the serious college jock, a track and field man. But Yasuko had read her share of boys' comics, and she was able to draw him out.

Mostly what she drew out of him, however, was his feelings for Masami.

The way he thought Masami was *cute*, the way he sighed after she left them, the way he would plumb Yasuko's knowledge of Masami's likes and dislikes.

But despite the uncongenial subject matter, as she sat with him and Doi's expansive laughter rang out in some coffee shop, gradually Yasuko found herself charmed.

In fact, dazzled.

And even when he was talking about Masami, after all, he was with *her*. She had allowed herself to dream, just a little—

"Oops! Sorry, Aerda . . ."

Yasuko pulled out a sheet of tissue paper, and carefully sponged off a bit of paint that had, while she was carelessly dreaming, spilled over the line of Aerda's skirt hem.

Painting on nice, flat Kent paper was a completely different story from working on the complex curves of a garage kit. The separate piece for the skirt was especially convoluted. She'd already put delicate highlights and shadows in Aerda's hair, and carefully shaded each and every lacing on her jacket.

When she was done Yasuko picked up Aerda herself. Aerda's skin, steeped in water, seemed smooth and even a little soft to the touch. Yasuko lifted Aerda so the figure's eyeless face was before her own huge eyes. The special paint for porous flexible polymers took a long time to dry. That made it easy to avoid streaking and smearing, but it was a pain when she had to apply multiple layers. Still, the coats she'd applied earlier looked to have set.

"Is your face all dry now? Well, then—" Yasuko stretched, and started in on the most difficult task of all—painting in the pupils.

She shaded in gentle auburn highlights on warm chestnut pupils, giving a deep and quiet expression to the village girl's face.

She allowed herself a smile. "Now that's not bad! Don't you think so, Aerda?"

At last it was time for the final touch—the freckles.

. . . Is that what Doi's really like? I didn't realize . . .

Yasuko remembered how Masami had breathed those words one night, her eyes distant, as her long, straight hair blew around her in the wind. It was the moment Yasuko's hopes imploded.

But even then, Yasuko played the good underclassman. She looked out for her elders' feelings, gave each of them a gentle push when they needed one, and finally made Doi's dream of winning over Masami a reality.

I'm the one who charmed Doi, she told herself. I'm the one who charmed Masami, too. It's me who's the really awesome one, way more awesome than Masami . . .

And that alone was her fragile, secret pride . . .

Yasuko froze, her brush still poised in her hand.

The brush point had split, leaving wedge-shaped blotches like hoof marks all over Aerda's cheeks.

It was a disaster—Aerda's face, of all things! It was her fault; she hadn't been concentrating. Now what? Trying to wipe the freckles off with tissue paper would just leave smears. The best option was to let the paint dry completely, then carefully shave the smudges off with an Exacto knife.

"I'm sorry, Aerda. I'll clean you all up tomorrow."

Trying to keep from trembling, Yasuko went ahead and glued on the skirt.

The next night she had to stay late to catch up on the work she'd been skipping, and it was past ten before she returned to her dormitory. The girl next door, with the shag haircut that looked so good on her, was having an endless phone call with some guy.

Yasuko opened her door. Her own small room seemed dark and utterly quiet.

She switched on the light, and stopped dead in her tracks.

Her desk was a mess. Spilled paint had made a flesh-coloured sea of the desktop. The spines of her textbooks were splashed, and her brush stand had toppled on its side.

Her heart thumped. Should she call the police? Or the dorm monitor—

Clunk.

It had come from behind the textbooks. She stared into the shadows, which her imagination readily populated.

"What was that? Who's there?"

... Something very small was moving around behind the dictionary.

Yasuko stepped forward cautiously.

A figure, its torso coated with flesh-colour paint, was peering sheepishly around the edge of Yasuko's Oxford English-Japanese Dictionary. That three-millimetre-wide mouth moved, and a light, tinny voice drifted across the room.

"Who are you? What is this place?"

It was—Yasuko recognized with a start—the voice of a popular actress, Alissa Nakagawa.

"Aerda?"

"You know me? Where am I? Is this a land of Giants?" The figure hung on to the edge of the dictionary with both hands as it thrust its upper body around the corner. Its manner was stunningly authentic, as were its timid face, the strained shoulders, the nervous feet.

Yasuko spread both hands, and softly stepped closer. The fearful Aerda fell back a step. "Don't be afraid. I made— no, I healed you. And you are Aerda, of the hamlet of Teglia."

At the sound of her name Aerda appeared to relax a little. She slowly stepped out from behind the dictionary. She left tiny flesh-coloured footprints as she stepped lightly across the desk. Porous flexible polymer reformed itself into an embarrassed frown. "The last thing I can remember is being attacked by a monster in the forest . . . Galba! Is he here? Do you know anything of a dragon?"

"Have no fear. Galba is not here. He is—another Giant is taking care of him."

"Where? Let me see him!" The words were a wail of pain, as authentic as the rest of the modelling.

Yasuko suddenly found herself at a loss for words. I can't just play with this creature like a toy, she realized. It was as if Aerda was in some sense aware. And if she was or was not, how could Yasuko tell?

"Don't worry," she said again. "I have to ask that other Giant when he can meet you. But it'll be okay. In fact, that other Giant may just be able to give him a human body—"

"Turn Galba back into a man?" Aerda's face was a small dish of misery.

Too late, Yasuko remembered the scenario. Galba had declared he would go straight to the labyrinth tower to seek his princess, as soon as he recovered his human form. For Aerda, Yasuko's news could only mean that her happy days with her love would soon be over.

This is ridiculous, Yasuko thought. You're debating with a kit figure, here.

"I don't know for sure that he'll do that. Just maybe. Look, try not to worry."

"I'm sorry," murmured Aerda, lacing her fingers. Webbed with drying paint, they were getting sticky.

"What happened to you, Aerda?"

"I woke up and found myself in this strange place. And when I went over to look at one of those glass barrels, I saw my face reflected there, and my freckles were so dark! And some of them had such strange shapes . . . I thought I couldn't possibly let Galba see me like that, and, and . . ."

She'd apparently thought she could cover up her freckles with skin-coloured paint. Aerda had wrapped her arms around a pot lid to twist it off, and instead brought the whole "barrel" right over. The damage stretched from Aerda's right shoulder down across her entire body.

Aerda hung her paint-splashed head. Yasuko sympathized with her from the bottom of her heart.

"Come here," she said gently. "Let me clean you up." Yasuko wiped the desk with a dust cloth. Then she soaked a tissue in thinner, and started sponging away the spilled paint. "I'm going to remove your skirt for a little. Tell me if it hurts, okay?"

Aerda complied.

Yasuko used sandpaper to smooth out the excess paint. Sitting with her legs stretched out in front of her, Aerda intently watched Yasuko at work. She seemed to have no sense of pain.

"Giant," she said, "you are very kind."

"My name. It's Yasuko."

"Yasuko?"

"Sit very still. Now, lift your face. I'm going to fix your freckles."

Aerda stretched up her face, as if waiting for a kiss.

Colleen was afraid of Yasuko. She hid behind Yamashita's paint pots.

"I chose the mid-point setting in the story, too," Yamashita told Yasuko. "So she keeps whining about whether 'the knight who is supposed to save me' has come or not. It's driving me up the wall. And on top of that she cries. Sobbing all the time. No tears, though."

Yamashita's workmanship on Princess Colleen was woeful.

Colleen's skin was rough to the touch and the paint hadn't taken well. Yasuko wondered if Yamashita had slacked off on the polishing. The princess's costume was very elegant with lush draping, but Yamashita had simply covered it with heavy layers of blue paint—a harsh primary colour—and in some places it had spilled over onto her skin. His paint work on her eyes was particularly clumsy. Colleen's eyebrows were askew, and her eyelashes were simply three thick lines, crudely sketched.

Colleen, trembling, asymmetric, was much less appealing than Yasuko's Aerda.

Of course, Yasuko mused, there was no reason why the story played out by these little characters had to follow the script.

Yamashita tripped Colleen with the handle of his paint brush. As she sprawled, he laughed.

That night she found the room dark except for a little night light. A book was propped open in the pool of light, and Aerda sat before it cross-legged. She was reading, mouthing the words to herself.

She turned. "Welcome home, Yasuko."

"That's my textbook. Are you reading Chinese poems?"

"I didn't have anything to do. I'm sorry—"

"No. Don't apologize. I'm impressed." The Aerda character had been conceived of as a girl with a keen natural intelligence, but who never had a chance for a formal education. "We have to pretty you up, Aerda. Tomorrow you can finally see Galba."

Aerda leaped to her feet. "Galba?"

". . . And he'll be back in human form."

Aerda clapped a tiny hand to her mouth. "So he found Princess Colleen."

Yasuko gently stroked Aerda's head. "Don't you worry about Colleen."

"But—"

"Things have, umm, changed. Here now, let me manicure your nails."

Aerda rested her hand on Yasuko's left forefinger, and Yasuko picked up her brush.

*   *   *

Kondo was talking with Yamashita when Yasuko arrived at his boarding house. ". . . The wings were all right without reinforcing them with an aluminium rod. And the embossing work is really good. When I dry brushed in the highlights it got a lot more interesting. Actually, I wanted to try some pearl powder, but I wasn't sure if the stuff I usually use would work on these polymers . . . Yasuko, you're late."

"Sorry."

"There's someone here to meet you—" Kondo opened up a cardboard box on the floor.

Galba sprang forth, and Yasuko gasped.

The three of them bent and studied the prince, their faces looming like round moons over him.

Galba glared up at them. Dressed in rough clothes befitting an adventurer, without apparent fear, he whipped out his sword and faced them down.

Yamashita said, "He's cool . . ."

"Isn't he, though?"

He wasn't quite as sexy as in Yasuko's character sheet, but he'd been assembled and painted with Kondo's characteristic precision. Galba's skin was finished a manly bronze. He seemed a little grimy to Yasuko, but Kondo's use of highlights and shadow had brought out his three-dimensionality.

Yasuko noticed, for the first time, that the figure's hair and overall feel resembled Doi. Of course, given that she'd designed Galba, that wasn't really a surprise, she told herself wryly.

"Well, Galba," she said, "let me show you Aerda." And Yasuko gently lifted the village girl from the wicker basket she'd been cradling carefully. "Aerda, you can come out now."

Cautiously, Aerda climbed out of the basket, eyes wide.

"Whoa!" The two boys gasped, gratifyingly.

But Galba was staring, dumbstruck, at the beautiful girl. "Aerda . . . ?"

On hearing the voice, Yasuko caught Kondo's eye.

He said, "Kaneo Shirasawa." Another actor.

Galba sheathed his sword, and slowly approached the village girl, striding across the worn and frizzled tatami rice matting on the floor.

"Galba . . . Galba, is it you?" The girl's voice was trembling. She stared at Galba, as if dazzled.

But then she looked down, and curtsied. "Congratulations, my lord. You have recovered your original form . . ."

It was a line from the scenario. Galba the dragon had belonged to Aerda. But now Galba was a prince once more, and in this scene Aerda had to behave formally to him, to convince herself of the gap that had opened between them.

"Thank you, Aerda," said Galba. "I owe everything to you."

"To me?"

The three students glanced at each other. This late-scenario Galba figure would "remember" that it was Aerda who had restored him to his former self. But Aerda, programmed for the middle of the story line, still didn't know it herself. It was odd, thought Yasuko, watching these two people plucked out of time from different points of their destiny, trying to interact. And yet that destiny, it seemed, remained fixed, even so.

Or did it?

The prince held out his hands, and she timidly laid her tiny right hand on top of it. "Aerda. You're very beautiful. I hardly recognized you."

Kondo whispered, "Now that isn't in the scenario."

Aerda shook her head, embarrassed.

Yamashita had produced a crumpled CD store paper bag. He dragged the princess out unceremoniously and plopped her on the tatami floor. The blue of her clothes was harsh, ridiculous.

Galba, seeing her, cried out, "Colleen!"

Yasuko watched, enthralled now.

How about it, Galba? Isn't Aerda lovely? Far lovelier

than Princess Colleen—and she has a beautiful heart as well. You don't have to stick to the story. Tell her quickly. Tell Aerda you love her more than the princess."

But Galba ran to Colleen's side, and kissed the hem of her skirts.

Aerda's hand fell. Her brown, shimmering eyes were wide open.

Galba embraced his princess.

"Hot stuff," murmured Yamashita. He was actually blushing.

Aerda had grabbed hold of Yasuko's skirt. "Yasuko," she said. "Let's go home."

Yasuko couldn't help herself. "No! Why has it got to be this way? Look at her! Her eyes are different sizes. Her eyelashes are blotchy, her eyebrows are cockeyed. There's nothing pretty about her, not her body, not her clothes—"

The boys were watching Yasuko, stunned, mouths hanging open.

"But that doesn't matter," Aerda murmured. "Don't you know that, Yasuko? Galba loves her, and that's all. No matter how she looks, how ugly she is, his love won't change . . . Didn't I love Galba even when he was a dragon?"

Galba had eyes only for Colleen. Just as Doi only had eyes for Masami. No matter how much Yasuko prettied herself up, she could never be Masami. And no matter how lovely Aerda became, she would never be Colleen.

Aerda placed her hand on Yasuko's fingertip. "Don't cry," she said. Her little hand, so tiny it could rest easily on her finger, was so very soft, so very smooth, and so cold it broke Yasuko's heart.

"I shouldn't have brought you here," Yasuko said.

Aerda was studying her. "I haven't lost, Yasuko. I know that Galba is Galba no matter what he looks like. I know that all those gentle things about him, those wonderful things about him, will never change. And look at me! I'm proud of myself, Yasuko. But—"

"Yes?"

"Please give me back my freckles."

That night Aerda slept beside Yasuko's pillow. She used a washcloth for a coverlet. Yasuko could not hear the figure breathing through the night. But still she felt a profound peace, and was soon asleep.

"They found a bug in the NNP," said Kondo.

It was the evening of the next day.

"What kind of bug?"

Kondo fell silent. On the phone line Yasuko could hear a waitress's voice taking orders, and a background murmur of people. He said, "Come down to the coffee shop, as quick as you can. I've already called Yamashita."

"What kind of bug, Kondo?"

Kondo sighed. "When did you make Aerda?"

". . . It was the 8th."

"Six days ago, huh? Then she's only got four more days."

"What?"

"It's the NNP. It dries up in ten days."

Yasuko turned around. The freckled girl had her back turned to her, and was intent on reciting a Chinese poem. When she turned a page she looked like a miniature sailor handling a great paper sail.

Kondo said, "Yasuko—"

Aerda smoothed down the new page, and smiled up at her Giant.

Apparently, Kondo said, Hishitomo had considered going ahead with a full launch of the NNP figures—even if they only lasted ten days—because they thought kit fans had such short attention spans that a week or so would be enough for them. But somebody had pointed out that these otaku kids got extremely attached even to figures that didn't move. When "living" figures began to die, all over the country, it would be a public relations disaster. So Hishitomo had decided to recall the trial figures they had sent to their prize winners.

Even Yamashita had a pained looked on his face. Yasuko was twisting and twisting the coffee shop's yellow napkin in her hands. Kondo glared.

"So what are they going to do with the figures?" Yasuko snapped. "Pulp them?"

"I don't think they'd do anything like that," said Kondo, but his eyes were oddly dead, Yasuko thought, like a fish's. "Hishitomo say they're very sympathetic toward our feelings. Apparently they're already testing some kind of drug for extending the life of assembled figures. The sensitivity of the sensors on their skin will degrade, but—"

"And you believe them?"

"Come on, Yasuko," Yamashita said, concerned, embarrassed.

"Yeah!" Kondo said. "I do believe them. And I'll tell you why. They want to keep the merchandising rights. So they do think this situation can be resolved, Yasuko—"

"But the figures—our figures—are going to die? Aren't they?"

Yamashita gulped down the cold dregs of his coffee. "Yasuko, we're all going to die someday. And it's not as if these are people—"

"You've seen them. You've seen the way they interact. How can you say that?"

Kondo cut her off. "This is getting us nowhere. I think we should return the figures to Hishitomo. Better to at least have some hope, to bet on the new medicine. Instead of having them die before our eyes." He glared at Yasuko, challenging her to disagree.

The white light of the street lamp poured through Yasuko's window, lighting up their two faces, small and large.

"Aerda?"

"What is it, Yasuko?"

"This Chinese poem. You were reading it the other day, weren't you?"

"*Ka Zan Ki?* I like that one. All about how he was thinking of the one he loved one night, and when the reed screen
in the window moved, he thought maybe she'd come to
him . . . Waiting by the window, just like us. Unrequited
love is just so sad."

There was something moving in the air, beyond the window. Silver, rustling, like leaves.

Yasuko whispered, "But tonight's different."

Gliding in upon the light, its soft wings spread to their
fullest, flew a dragon: the dragon that Kondo had thrown
toward Yasuko's room from the back alley.

Aerda gasped. "Galba!"

It was a muscular, magnificent dragon, wings and scales
aglitter. It came to light on the darkened window sill. When
Aerda sprang to his side, the pattern that Yasuko had so
carefully painted along the hem of her skirt twisted and
turned. The dragon gently caressed the girl's head with a
curled foreleg.

But Aerda stepped back. "It isn't Galba."

"It is, Aerda. It really is."

"Oh, Yasuko. Doesn't he have his princess now? Don't
talk about silly dreams like that."

"I don't mean the Galba you met before. It's the Galba
you loved, the Galba that loved only you. It's Galba the
dragon." The dragon, of course, implanted with the appropriate chip . . . "He said he's decided to be with you forever."

"You're lying!"

"It's true. And you have to go with him, Aerda."

Aerda looked from one to the other, the girl's face, the
exquisite dragon. Yasuko saw how her movements were a
little stiff, restricted. Aerda was already growing old. "I
won't go," she said.

"You don't understand—"

"What about you, Yasuko? It's as though I'm leaving
part of myself behind."

"Listen to me, Aerda. I'll be all right. I—you helped me.
You showed me how I won out over my own Colleen, in

my own world." She fought to keep her voice level. "You see, I don't need you any more."

Aerda stepped towards her. "Yasuko, it's so strange. I want to cry, but no tears come out!"

"That's something I couldn't fix. But maybe other Giants can help you. Galba's going to take you to them."

"I'm afraid, Yasuko."

"Don't worry. I've asked them to make sure you and Galba can be together always. And then, when you get all well, you can come back home here with your dragon, okay?"

"I will. I absolutely will come back to you, Yasuko."

Stiffly, the freckled village girl climbed onto the back of the dragon. "Yasuko—"

"Yes?"

"Next time, win for real. You understand? No more fooling yourself. No more justifications or moral victories. Win for real."

Then the dragon drove off the window sill.

For a time Yasuko could not even move.

Two months later a Japanimation journal ran an interview with the production manager at Dux. The visual media corporation had revised its original plans, and would be making the Daglian Saga using traditional cell animation.

Yasuko, Kondo and Yamashita tried to find out what had happened to their figures, but Hishitomo was impenetrable. Hishitomo wouldn't even confirm it had received all the figures safely.

Maybe somewhere Aerda and Galba were free, Yasuko thought. But it was impossible, of course.

Day by day, the flesh coloured footprints the figurine had left on Yasuko's desk faded away. Every night, Yasuko left her window open for a while before she went to bed.

Aerda. The freckled girl that Yasuko's soul and hands had brought to life. That little mirror that reflected the very depths of her heart. *Ka Zan Ki.* If she was alive—if she was free—Aerda knew that Yasuko was waiting for her by the window. Unlike Doi, unlike Galba, Aerda would understand what Yasuko was feeling as she waited there.

Yasuko watched the curtains waving in the night breeze.

Shiva

BARRY N. MALZBERG

Barry N. Malzberg was the Dark Side of the SF Force in the 1970s—the pessimist, the premier iconoclast. In seven years, he published 20 novels and over 100 stories. Then his output slowed to a trickle, for reasons recorded in rich, colorful detail and passionate intensity in his collection of essays, The Engines of the Night: Science Fiction in the Eighties *(1982). His reputation (and notoriety) was established by his novel,* Beyond Apollo *(1972), a skeptical commentary on the Apollo program that took a shockingly negative (for the era) attitude toward space flight. Excellently written, it won the John W. Campbell Memorial Award, which upset many supporters of Campbellian SF at the time.* The Encyclopedia of Science Fiction *says, "[Malzberg's] writing is unparalleled in its intensity and in its apocalyptic sensibility. . . . he is a master of black humor, and is one of the few writers to have used sf's vocabulary of ideas extensively as apparatus in psychological landscapes. . . ."*

Malzberg has often explored conventional SF ideas in unconventional ways. In Shiva, *he cleverly turns some of the tropes of time travel (especially the "time patrol") and alternate history SF, quite logically, inside out.*

"We'll try Paris," someone says. "Remember Paris." Sperber, trusted only for an apprentice assignment but still determined to be hopeful, huddles in the deep spaces of the extradimensional calculator, figuring out his further moves. Sperber has always been a thoughtful type, not impulsive, only reactive. That is one of the primary reasons for his participation in the program. Know your course, pull down vanity, move deliberately toward a kind of fruition. Still he thinks: How long can I remain hopeful doing stuff like this?

Still, he has. Remained hopeful, that is. Choice gleams like knives from the enclosure; shrugging, his life a cosmic shrug he thinks, Sperber is catapulted to Paris, 1923, finds himself with no real transition in a small café on the fringes of the Champs-Elysees where he seems to be already engaged in profound conversation with the young Pol Pot and Charles de Gaulle, nationalists both, their expressions set intently toward a future that glows for them, even though Sperber knows better than they how problematic the situation.

"Excusez-moi," Sperber says in his miserable, poorly accented French, tugging on the sleeve of de Gaulle's brown jacket. Even at this early stage of his life, de Gaulle seems to have taken on a military righteousness. *"Je* can stay only a moment. I am here to give you a glimpse of your future *s'il vous plait. Comment allez vous?* Would you like that portrait of your future?"

He hopes that the translator has done its wondrous work.

458

There is no way that he can express to de Gaulle in this perilous situation without the help of that device. Still, it seems—like so much else in post-technological 2218— something of a cheat. Form has taken function all the way to the grave; the extradimensional calculator has, for instance, subsumed the causes of research or serious speculation.

De Gaulle is unresponsive to Sperber's question. Perhaps premonitory apprehensions of the Fourth Republic have overtaken him; he seems distant, affixed to some calculation of a future that Sperber himself knows all too well. Saleth Sar (Pol Pot's birth name or at least the name he employed in his student days) brandishes a teacup, looks at Sperber with a kind of loathing.

"And me?" he says, "what about me? What *s'il vous plait* are you undertaking to give me? My French is not perfect but I am worthy of your attention, no?"

This certainly is true. Saleth Sar is worthy of his attention. In his excitement at finally meeting de Gaulle, Sperber has almost ignored the general's old companion and rival in student debates.

"Pardon me," he says. "I meant to give no offense. I am a student, I am in this place to study and to learn. It is not possible for me to know everything."

"You do not have to know everything," Pol Pot says reprovingly, "but it is not correct to know nothing at all." He stares at de Gaulle sourly, takes the teacup from the general's hand, and places it with a thump on the table. "I think I will ask you to leave this table," he says. "You were after all not invited."

"I have to tell you that the Algerian intervention will come to a very bad end," Sperber says hastily. "Both of you must know this, also that the decision to leave Indo-China will lead in no way toward peace. Your intervention will be supplanted by ignorant Americans, the Americans will get in deeper and deeper, eventually the Americans will ignore the borders of Kampuchea and will commit severe destruction. No good will come of this, none at all. One country will be shamed, another sacrificed. You must begin to make plans now."

"Plans?" Pol Pot says. "What kind of plans are we supposed to make? You babble of destiny, of destruction. But it is this kind of destruction which must precede the revolution itself. It is vital that the revolution prevail, that is why I have been sent to Paris. To study texts of successful revolutions, to know the Constitution of the United States among other things."

Pol Pot, the admirer of democratic principles. Sperber had forgotten that.

Paris at this time was filled with future Communists who loved democracy, the United States, American music and sexual habits. It was betrayal, Americans not taking to Asian desires, which had turned them into revolutionaries, anti-Bolsheviks. But Sperber had, of course, forgotten much else in his various missions; the lapse here was not uncharacteristic, lapses had carried him through all of these expeditions, making matters even more difficult.

De Gaulle shrugs much as Sperber had shrugged just subjective instants ago in the extradimensional calculator. The Frenchman's face shines with confusion, the same confusion, doubtless, that exists in Sperber's own. "There is nothing I can do about this," he says, "or about anything else for that matter."

Sperber knows then with sudden and sinking acuity that he has done all that is possible under these circumstances. There is nothing else that he can do. He has used the extradimensional calculator to detour to this crucial place, has warned the future leaders of consequence, has delivered the message as best as he can, now consequence—an extradimensional consequence, of course, one which has been imposed upon the situation rather than developed—will have to engage its own direction. It is a pity that he cannot bring documents, wave them in front of Pol Pot and de Gaulle, but the laws of paradox are implacable and no one may test them by bringing confirmation to the past. The speaker must make his point through fervor, through credibility. There is no supporting data.

"What are we supposed to do?" Saleth Sar says. "You surely cannot think to give us such an evaluation and simply disappear. We are not fools here, we are serious people. Even he is a serious person," he says pointing to de Gaulle, "even though like all of his countrymen he is full of grand designs and stupid dreams. Serious stupid dreams, however. You must take responsibility for that as well as much else."

Well, that seems fair enough. Perhaps that is so. *"Regrette,"* Sperber says. What else is there to say? In just a moment he will take the extradimensional calculator out of his briefcase, calculate the dials, and make his departure. He hopes that the café personnel will not take the calculator for a grenade or plastique; that they will not interpret his intentions as violent. His intentions are not violent, they are simply pedagogical in all of the better senses of that word.

Next assignment: this one the standard interview (in all of its hopelessness) which no one in training can avoid. "Don't do it," Sperber therefore says to JFK, appearing in the President's private quarters at Hyannisport with the help of his speedy and selective instrument. "Don't go to Dallas to resolve a factional dispute, the factions are hopelessly riven, there is nothing that you can do but interfere and otherwise, if you go there, horrendous personal consequences may follow. I am not even talking about the future of the country."

Kennedy looks at him kindly, helps himself to another breadstick from the stack next to the table, seems to regard Sperber in a unique and favorable light. Jacqueline is ensconced upstairs, Dave Powers is pacing the corridors outside: This is a quiet night in the fall of 1963, quieter than most of them and therefore good for siting by the calculator. Sperber has come to Kennedy noiselessly, with no disturbance whatsoever.

"You're not the first from whom I've heard this, you know," Kennedy says. "There has been a whole group of you who have come in mysteriously with a similar plea over the past few weeks. It's a good thing I know I'm only hallucinating. Or are you really all emissaries from the future on some kind of training plan? That's what I'm beginning to believe but I can't get a straight answer out of any of you. It strikes me as the most reasonable guess, either that or you're all really extraordinary actors and Lyndon is even more demonic than I think, trying to make me crazy here. But I don't think I'm crazy; I have a rigorous, robust intelligence and know a hawk from a handsaw."

Sperber knew of course about all the others. Kennedy in the fall of 1963 was one of the most popular destinations: unlike de Gaulle and Saleth Sar in the café who were really unusual and almost secret. Certainly, Sperber would never make his knowledge of that site public. Still, you could not use only the most popular destinies; you had to do some original warning and rebutting or risk falling into imitation, the inattentiveness of the assessors. Alternate history was not merely an odyssey; it was a work of art, it had to be particularly shaped.

"What can I do to convince you that I'm different from the others?" he said. "I'm a specialist, I work on historical causation, on first cause, on original motivation, it's been my field of study for years and if I didn't have this opportunity, I would be abandoning the future to mindless consequence. It's got to mean more than that."

"I can't get into arguments of this sort," Kennedy says. He rocks back in his chair, sighing a little as his weak back is momentarily shifted from axis, then recovers his purchase. "All of you are so insistent, all of you seem so convinced that you carry the real answers." He smiles at Sperber, his fetching smile, the smile that has been preserved in all of the living and dead histories through the hundreds of years between them, then pats Sperber on the hand. "It's a fated business anyway," Kennedy says. "And if I'm not mistaken, if I understand this correctly, it's all happened anyway from your perspective."

"It's happened," Sperber says, wishing that he had managed a university education so that he could put this in more sophisticated terms. The trades were not a good place to be, this work was really too delicate for someone training fundamentally as a technician and yet that was the only way it could be financed. "It's happening and happening but there's a chance, just a chance that if you avoid in the future the events which I know so well, that it can happen in a different way. I'm not doing this for recompense," Sperber says unnecessarily. "I have a genuine interest in improving the quality of our lives in the present."

"Well," Kennedy says, "well, well, there's no answer to that then, is there? There's no canceling travel and political commitments at such a late time unless there's a proven disaster lying there and we know that that's not the case. Sorry, pal," Kennedy says, patting Sperber's arm almost lovingly, "there's just no way around this. Besides, I'm getting a little tired of all these visits anyway. They're distracting and there's nothing that I can do to change the situation anyway."

"Je regrette," Sperber says in poorly stressed French, carrying over his response from an earlier interview, *"Je regrette* all of this, Mr. President, but it's important for you to understand the consequence—"

"There is no consequence," Kennnedy says, "there is only outcome," and Sperber in a sudden and audacious wedge of light, an extrusion that seems to come from Kennedy's very intellect, which fires and concentrates his features, bathing them in a wondrous and terrible life, understands that Kennedy is right, that Sperber has been wrong, that he has been pursuing consequence at a distance in the way that a platoon of guards with rakes might trail the line of a parade, clearing the landscape. Sperber was no more consequential to Kennedy than such a crew would be to the parade.

"Don't do it!" he says nevertheless, seizing the opportunity as best he can. "You still shouldn't do it, no matter how right you feel, you will be surrounded by enemies, taunted by a resisting crowd, then you will perish among roses. You have got to heed me," Sperber says, and jiggles the extradimensional calculator into some kind of response, already too late, but he is willing to try to get Kennedy to listen to reason even as the storm begins in his viscera and he feels himself departed through yet another wedge of history, spilled toward a ceaseless and futile present.

Sperber takes himself to be addressing Albert Einstein in a hideous cafeteria in Einstein's student days, the unformed Alfred nibbling an odorous salami, calculations and obliterated equations on the table between them. "Don't do this," Sperber says in what he takes to be a final, desperate appeal, "don't do it, don't complete the equations, don't draw the conclusions: This will lead to the uniform field theory, it will lead to one devastating anomaly after the next, it will unleash the forces of atomic destruction upon a hapless and penitential humanity surrounded by consequence. Don't you understand this? Put it away, put it away!"

Einstein, another infrequent site, stares at Sperber with a kind of terror, not for him the cool insouciance of Kennedy, the political fanaticism of Saleth Sar and de Gaulle. Einstein is as fully, as hopelessly, astonished as Sperber was when informed, five or six subjective hours ago, of his mission.

"Change history?" Sperber had said, "I can't even spell history," and similarly Einstein shudders over his equation, stares at Sperber in a fusion of shyness and loathing. "I can't shape history, I don't even know myself," Sperber, the student had shouted when informed of his mission, and the implacable sheen of their faces when they had responsively shoved the extradimensional calculator into his hands was like the sheen of the salami that Einstein held in one hopeless, hungry hand.

"I don't know of what you are speaking," Einstein said. "Physics is too difficult a subject for me to understand, I can do nothing, don't you know this? I can do nothing at all." In Einstein's despair, Sperber can glimpse the older Einstein, the saintly and raddled figure whose portrait adorns the site, a musty extrusion from the journals, who played the violin badly at Princeton and blamed everyone else for the bomb.

"Yes you can," Sperber says, and resists the impulse to

spout French again: the language of diplomacy, he had been told, but that was just another cracked idea of the assessors. "You can do something, all of you could have done something, you have to take responsibility, don't you see? You must take responsibility for what you have given us."

Sperber would have a great deal more to say but the sound of the assessors is suddenly enormous in the land and Sperber finds himself, however unwillingly, ground to recombinant dust in the coils of the calculator.

He is taken back.

He ponders the landscape, the faces of the assessors, neither unsurprisingly changed at all. The program is sustained, after all, by failure. What point in resisting?

"Oppenheimer is next," someone says to him. "Are you prepared for Oppenheimer?"

Well, no, in fact he is not, but Sperber tries as ever to be hopeful. He is Shiva after all, destroyer of worlds.

The Queen of Erewhon

LUCY SUSSEX

*Relatively little of Lucy Sussex's work has been SF, but she
has been an important presence in the Australian SF community and began in the late 1990s to be recognized in SF
worldwide, a process this story will certainly accelerate.
She was a co-editor of* Australian Science Fiction Review
(Second Series)—*arguably the most ambitious SF critical
magazine of the 1980s—for its first two years (1986-87).
Then in 1988 she published the title story of her 1990 collection,* My Lady Tongue and Other Stories, *the book and
story upon which her reputation primarily rests. She co-
edited the anthology* She's Fantastical *(1995), the first anthology of SF and fantasy by Australian women, and
published three fantasy novels in the 1990s:* Deersnake, *for
young adults;* The Scarlet Rider *(1996), a ghost story for
adults;* Black Ice *(1997), another juvenile. She has continued to write short fiction, most often fantasy or horror.*

This story, from F&SF, *is clearly science fiction, and has
many of Sussex's characteristic strengths (strong charac-
terization, well-thought-out setting, political engagement,
historical reverberations) but is in a tone more characteristic of, say, Ursula K. Le Guin—a wise, mature woman's
voice. It tells of a future post-catastrophe New Zealand ma-
triarchy.*

*Here is the story behind the story: "Erewhon is a place,
not only the dystopia of Samuel Butler's novel, but also a*

sheep station [i.e., ranch] in the South Island of New Zealand, which he owned. I used to spend summer holidays there as a child.

"After I left New Zealand I kept getting reminders of the South Island's topography, as it was featured in fantasy films like The Princess Bride. I always thought any culture that developed there would be far stranger and richer than the film fantasies, or Butler's Erewhon. . . . I did some reading on mountain cultures, including Tibetan polyandry, and slowly the notion of the Rule coalesced."

"Hey you! Story-Eater! *Devourer of lives! Leave us alone! GET OUT!"*

Those are the first sounds on the tape: Idris spitting at me, refusing to be interviewed. I wind on a little, until I hear a different voice—Sadry speaking.

Sadry. . . . ghosts. The house at Erewhon could have been full of them for all anyone knew, for there was only our family of three and the hired hands rattling around the building. Erewhon had followed the Rule for generations, not that I knew that. I was only a child, I think three. Things hadn't got explained to me yet. I had no idea how odd my upbringing was, for the High country, with only one father.

One night I thought I heard crying, so I got out of bed, curious. I wandered along the upstairs corridor which all the sleeping rooms led off. When I got a little older, I learnt why this space was called "Intrigue," in all the Rule houses. It kinks and curves, with crannies for people to hide and overhear—hence the name.

Me: A public space?

Sadry: Or a private one. I followed the sound to the outside wall, to a window with a recessed ledge. The shutters were closed and the winter curtains drawn, but between both was a space where someone might sit comfortably and that was from where the sound came. Now it sounded human, and female. I heard soft words, a male voice responding. Two people were hidden there! And curious, I stood and listened. But it was bitter frost weather, and rather than give myself away by teeth-chatter, I retreated until just round the corner I found a basket. It was filled with rags, either bought from Scavengers or our old clothes (Highlanders never throw anything away). So I climbed into it without making a sound, for it was an old Tech thing, of *perlastic*, rather than wicker. I curled up warmly in the contents and listened in comfort, not that I could understand much. Eventually I fell asleep, and woke in dawnlight to find my mother bending over me. And unthinkingly I blurted out the last words I had heard, which were: "I only want to be married to the one I love best, not all the others."

My mother said: "Where did you hear that?" and so I pointed at the ledge.

"The two lovers, there, last night."

She looked at me hard, then flung the curtain back. It wasn't me who screeched, it was her—at the sight of dust thick and undisturbed on the ledge. Then she scooped me up in her arms and went running down Intrigue, to the room she and my father shared, a small room, his younger son's room.

Idris: What did he do?

Sadry: Took us both into bed, calmed us down, for now I was hysterical too, and then very gently questioned me. What did the voices sound like? Could I imitate them? When I was as dry of information as a squeezed fruit, he said:

"It could have been any unhappy Queen of Erewhon."

And then he told me about living under the Rule, of his first wife, his brother, and their husband-lover.

Polyandry. The first time I heard the word I thought it a girl's name: *Polly Andree*. The misapprehension, though instantly corrected, stuck in my mind, so that I persistently thought of the woman at the center of these group marriages as a Polly. And here I was in Polyandry Central, as anthropologists called it, the Highlands of Suff, and I still couldn't shake my personal terminology. It was a bad slip to make when trying to convince Bel Innkeeper to find me space, in a town already filled to bursting for the Assizes.

"We call them *Queens*," she said.

I'd listened to tapes of Suff accents but the actuality was something else, my comprehension of it being delayed, with embarrassing pauses at the ends of sentences. When I finally understood, I replied, too hastily:

"I know. Like bees."

All the while we had talked on the inn's back verandah, a steady stream of fat brown bees had zoomed to and from some nearby hive, so this comment was both dead obvious and instantly regrettable.

Bel snorted. "You Northerners. Think you know everything, with your new-Tech ways! Ever seen a hive, ever seen a Rule House? No, that's why you're here, to find all about the funny Suffeners, isn't it?"

I said, carefully: "Okay, I'm what you call a story-eater, an anthropologist. But I can understand you've had a gutful of being studied and written up. I'm not here to sensationalize you, but to observe the court case."

Bel stopped folding the inn washing and gave me her undivided attention. "Why?"

"Because it's important."

"It's brought everyone down from the mountains and into this valley! How'm I supposed to house 'em all? And you, too."

She rocked on the balls of her feet, thinking. "Well, since you're here, I'd better be hospitable. And teach you about queen bees, too." She pointed at an outbuilding. "That's the honey-hut, and the one free space I've got. Take it or leave it!"

The hut was tiny: between pallet and beekeeping equipment there was barely any room for me. Above the bed was what I at first took to be a Tech photoimage, but it proved to be a window looking onto the mountains, made of the glass and wooden surround of a picture frame. In fact the whole building was constructed of scavenged oddments from the days of affluence: flattened tins, scraps of timber, and other usables slapped together in a crude but habitable mess. I was used to recycling, even in the neo-industrial North, but I had never seen such a higgledy-piggledy assortment before. It was to prove typical of much of the town itself.

I lay on the pallet and dozed for a while, lulled by the soporific hum from the nearby hives. When I woke, I tested my tape recorder—a precious thing, not because it was a genuine Tech artifact, but because it was a copy, its workings painstakingly rediscovered. Of course, it wasn't as good, nothing was, for we would never be as rich, nor as spendthrift, as our forebears. For over a century now, since the Crash, we had been adapting to an economy of scarcity. It was the adaptations, rather than the antiques, or the neo-copies, that interested me—particularly the Rule Houses, and at their center, the Queen Polly Andree. How would it feel, to have multiple husbands? And what would happen if you grew tired of them?

Sadry: My father said, "Nobody knows how the Rule began, just as nobody knows who bred the mountain Lori to be our herd animals. A Northerner, a story-eater, once told me the Rule was a pragmatic evolution, practiced by other mountain peoples. He said large populations cannot be sustained in marginal highland. One wife for several men—who are linked by blood, or ties of love—limits breeding, and means the family land can be passed undivided through the generations. It made sense; more than what the Lowlanders say, which is that we Highlanders deliberately chose complicated sex lives! Yet he spoke as if we were specimens, like a strain of Lori. That annoyed me, so I wouldn't give him what he had come for, which was my history.

"When I was the age you are now, my brother Bryn and I were contracted to marry Nissa of Bulle, who would grow to be our wife and Queen of Erewhon. When I was twelve and Bryn fifteen—the same age as Nissa—we traveled to Bulle to 'steal' our bride, as is custom. When we got back, Erewhon celebrated with the biggest party I ever saw and afterward Nissa spent the night with Bryn. I was too young to be a husband to her, though we would play knuckle-

bones, or other children's games. That way Nissa and I
grew friends, and then, after several years, husband and
wife. But we lived without passion, all three of us. So when
love did strike Nissa and Bryn, it did like a thunderbolt.
And the lightning cracked through this house, destroying
nearly everybody within it."

Market day in the Highlands is a spectacle, even without
the added excitement of an Assizes and a sensational law-
suit. I woke early, to the sounds of shouts, goods being
trundled down the main street, the shrill cries of Lori. When
I came downstairs, the meal area of the Inn was full. Bel
was cutting buckwheat bread; she handed me a slice, spread
with Lori butter, at the same time jerking her head at the
open door. I took the hint and went outside.

Immediately I found myself in the middle of a herd of
Lori, who assessed the stranger intelligently from under
their black topknots, then parted and pattered around me.
The animal was a miracle of genetic engineering, combin-
ing the best of sheep, llama and goat, but with three-toed
feet causing less damage to mountain soils than hooves.
Like the other Highland animals it was dark, resistant to
skin cancer, a boon in an area cursed with thin ozone, even
so long after the Crash. Various studies had posited that
the Lori designer might have been the social architect who
engineered the lives of Highlanders with the Rule. If so, I
wondered why human genes had not been manipulated as
well, given that these people had insufficient protective
melanin, varying as they did from pale to brown.

Suffeners met by sunlight would be shrouded in the robes
of Lori homespun that served all purposes, from formal to
cold-weather wear, wide flax hats and the kohl that male
and female daubed around their eyes in lieu of the precious
Tech sunglasses. But inside, or under protective awnings
such as those strung over the market square, hats would be
doffed, robes flipped back like cloaks, displaying bare skin,
gaudy underrobes and the embroidered or beaded or tattooed emblems of the Highland Houses. It was a paradox:
outwardly, dour Puritanism; inwardly, carnival.

I stood on the fringes, observing the display of goods and people. Nobody in sight was armed, well, not visibly, but I had read too many accounts of bloodshed and the consequent bloodprice not to sense the underlying menace in the marketplace. The most obvious source was the young men, who tended to ostentatious ornament, an in-your-face statement of aggressive sexual confidence. The women were less showy, but had an air of defensibility, as if being hard-bitten was a desirable female trait in the Highlands. Small wonder, I thought, recalling the mock kidnap in the marriage ceremony, and how common real raids had been until recently.

I felt a little too conspicuously a visitor, so I bought a second-hand robe, the wool soft but smelly, and draped it over my shoulders. Thus partially disguised, I wandered among the stalls. A one-eyed man watched over Scavenged Tech rubbish, cans, wires, tires; a nursing mother examined the parchments of designs offered by the tattooist; a group of teenage boys, herders from their staffs, noisily tried on strings of beads; and two husky young men haggled over a tiny jar proffered for sale by an elderly woman. Hungry for overheard talk, information, I lingered by the tattoos, my interest not feigned, for I was particularly taken with one design, a serpent eating its own tail. Conversation ebbed around me, and I learnt the one-eyed Scavenger had found a new site, that the herders weren't impressed by the selection of beads, that the mother wished to mark that she now had children by all three of her husbands with a celebratory tattoo, and that the men were buying a philter or aphrodisiac, for use on a third party. Now I was slipping into the flow of Suff speak, I quickly comprehended the old woman's spiel:

"If Celat had tried my potion on Erewhon, none of this would have happened."

All within earshot involuntarily glanced up at the bulk of the biggest building in the town, the Courthouse/lockup. I had, in my wanderings through the the market, seen many emblems of greater or lesser Houses, a distinction the Highlanders made by the size of the land holdings. The signs were displayed on people and also the stalls, signaling the goods that were the specialties of each House. I had been making a mental checklist, and had noted two emblems unseen: the blue swirl of Erewhon, and the red sword blade of Celat. Those entitled to bear them currently resided within the lockup, while the merits of their respective cases were decided. On the one hand, unlawful detention and threatened rape; on the other, abduction, arson and murder. No wonder the town was packed.

Sadry: The place of graves at Erewhon is a birch grove and as we walked through it, hand in hand, my parents named each tree: "This is Bryn's, this Moli the trader's, by chance at Erewhon that night and forever after." It was a peaceful spot, even with the new thicket of saplings, Nissa's work. I could believe that any ghost here would sleep and not walk—which was precisely why I had been brought there.

Idris: Nissa and her lover were buried in the snow, weren't they? Or at Bulle?

Sadry: I don't know . . .

[A clattering interruption at this point, the turnkeys bringing in that night's meal, the sound also coming from below, as the Celats, housed on the ground floor, were simultaneously fed.]

Sadry: On that day, or one soon after, I saw above the birches a line of pack Lori winding their way down the mountainside. Their flags had the device of a bee: Westron, our nearest neighbors. And that proved to be the first of many visits from the local and not so local Houses.

Me: Including the Celats?

Sadry: *[nods]* The message would always be the same: Erewhon has been decimated, and you need an alliance. That meant, me plus whoever was the highest bidder. But my father said to all and sundry that they had made such offers before, when he was the sole survivor of Erewhon House. And had he not responded by a second marriage with a lowland woman, outside the Rule? I, as his only child and heiress of Erewhon, also should have the oppor-

tunity of making a choice, when I was old enough.
  Me: They agreed to that?
  Sadry: With grumbling, yes.

Ever since contact was re-established between North and
Suff, nearly a century after the Crash, anthropologists had
been fascinated by the Rule. Much of their interest was
prurient, with accounts of giant beds for the Queen and her
consorts (a lurid fantasy, given the Intrigue configuration).
I had in my pack a report positing the mechanisms by
which Highland men could apparently switch from het mo-
nogamy, albeit with a brother or brothers involved in the
marriage; to bisex, when an additional unrelated male
entered the House, a partner for both husbands and wife;
to homosex, with the Queen relationship purely platonic. It
was not exactly light reading, but I persisted with it, lying
on the pallet, the hum of bees filling my ears. In the end
the graphs and diagrams were too much for me, and I simply stared at the wall and thought.
  On, for instance, how easily the complex relationships in
a Rule marriage could turn nasty, Nissa of Erewhon being
merely an extreme example. Yet divorce, with people
"walking out and down," i.e., to the Lowlands or to join
the itinerant traders, was uncommon. Highlanders had a
vested interest in conciliation, in preserving the group marriages: that was why many houses contained Mediators,
skilled negotiators. The ideal was embodied in a toy I had
bought at the market, that little girls wore dangling from
their belts: a lady-doll on a string, with a dependent number
of men-dolls.
  Why, I wondered, dandling the puppets, did sexual options not exist for women as well as men, with, say, linked
girl-dolls? Were the Queens simply too busy with their
men? Feeling frustrated, I wandered outside and found Bel
attending to the hives.
  "Come see!" she said, and so I donned over my Highland
robes the spare veil and gloves hanging behind the hut door.
Bel had lifted the roof off a hive, and I stared over her
black shoulder at the teeming mass of insects.

"I think I understand," I finally said, "why a hive is unlike a Rule House."

She nodded, invisible behind her veil. "Ever see a Hive where the drones bossed the show? Or without any other female bees? It would be impossible. . . ."

"As a House with two Queens?" I finished.

She straightened, holding a comb-frame in her gloved hand, staring across the valley at the Courthouse roof.

"You're learning, story-eater."

Sadry: Highlanders say when you die you go downriver, and that is what happened to me. My life at Erewhon with my parents, then my father only [after my mother went, as the Lowlanders say, underground] that is upriver to me. Everything since is the next life.

[She spoke with such intensity that I almost reached out and touched her, to belie the words.]

I went out alone after a stray Lori, the best yearling we had. Our herders had given up searching and my father was ill in bed, but I stubbornly kept looking. Most likely the animal had drowned, so I followed the Lori paths along a stream raging with snowmelt. Almost at its junction with the great river that runs from Erewhon to the lowlands, I saw a patch of color in a large thornbush overhanging the torrent: a drowned bird, swept downstream until it had caught in the thorns. But though it was shaped like the black finches of the Highlands, the feathers were white-gold-red: a throwback to the days before the hole in the sky opened. I wanted the feathers for ornament, so leant on the thornbush, to better reach out—but the bank collapsed beneath me.

The water wasn't deep and the bush cartwheeled in its flow, taking me, my robes entangled in the branches, into the great river. Up and down I was ducked, alternately breathing and drowning, torn by thorns, or dashed against riverstones. All I could do was grab at air when I could . . .

[She paused and I again noted the fine white lines on her exposed skin, a tracery of thornmarks. Worst was the scar tissue in the palm of one hand, where she must have

clutched at the bush despite the pain, in the process defacing and almost obscuring her birth marker, the Erewhon tattoo.]

I think miles went by, hours—for the next thing I recall was the evening moon. I gazed up at it, slowly comprehending that I lay still, out of the helter-skelter race of the river, and that something wet and sluggish held me fast. From the taste of silt in my mouth I knew that the bush had stuck in the mudflats where the river widens. In the moonlight I saw solid land, shoreline, but when I tried to struggle toward it I found I had no strength left. But I lived! And surely my fathers' herders would soon find me.

Idris: You'd forgotten. . . .

Sadry: On whose land the mudflats were. So I shivered through that night, until the morning sun warmed me. I had no protection against it, so covered my face with all I had, which was mud. Then I waited for help.

Idris: The next bit is my story. . . .

Sadry: *[laughing]* Tell it, then.

Idris: The river had lately brought we Celats a fine young Lori, fresh-drowned. So in hopes of further luck, I scavenged in the mudflats again. The bush sticking up like a cage, I noticed that first. Next I saw a faint movement like a crab, a human hand, then eyes looking at me out of the mud. I had to use the pack Lori to drag her out, she was stuck so fast, half-dead as she was. And the bird too, the one that had brought her to me, I found that when I washed the mud from her robes.

[She pulled from beneath her underrobe a thong, pendant from it a love-charm fashioned from tiny feathers, white-gold-red. Sadry almost simultaneously revealed a duplicate charm. I wondered again at the mixture of toughness and sentimentality of the Highlanders, then at the strength of this pair, one to survive near death from drowning and then exposure, the other to save her. . . . In my cozy north, teenage girls are babies, but these two had a life's hard experience.]

*   *   *

In the courtroom, they looked tiny, my quarry, against the black-clad might of the Highland Rule. The tribunal hearing this case consisted of a Judge from Chuch, the Suff capital, a Northern Government representative, and the only empowered woman in sight, Conye of Westron. This Queen had been the subject of a classic study, so I knew her story well—but still boggled at the fact that this dignified old lady with the multiple tattoos had seven husbands.

I bent toward Bel, sitting beside me in the public gallery. "Now *she* is like the Queen of a Hive!" I murmured.

"Only because she outlived all her drones!" Bel replied.

Around us, Suffeners commented too, court etiquette permitting this background buzz, along with eating and the nursing of babies or pets.

"—I ain't disrespecting new dead, but old Erewhon was mad to say no to Westron—"

"—had a bellyful of the Rule, hadn't he—"

"—but risking all that House lore being lost—"

"Excuse me," said a male voice, from behind me. "You're the anthropologist?"

I turned to see a fellow Northerner, nervously holding out an ID. It read: Fowlds, journalist.

"I'm normally posted in Church, so I can't make head or tail of this mountain law," he said.

"And you'd like an interpreter? Meet Bel!"

The Innkeeper grinned, speaking slowly and precisely:

"The two girls in that dock are one party; the two men another. They tell their stories, and the judges decide who are to be believed."

"Ah," he said. "And who is likely to be credible?"

Around us Suffeners sucked sweets and eavesdropped happily.

"Well," said Bel, "on the one hand we have a House wealthy and respected, but eccentric—maybe to the point of having gone just too far. That's Sadry of Erewhon, second generation Rule-breaker. On the other hand, Idye and Mors of Celat, a lesser House. Now they are Scavengers, but once Celat were mercenaries, hired trouble, before your North outlawed feuding."

It had been a condition of autonomy, I recalled, which had incidentally obviated the need to have a concentration of fighting men in the fortified Houses. And thus the need to create bonds between them, a prime function of the Rule?

"But the other girl is Idris of Celat? What is she doing with Erewhon?"

"That's what the tribunal is trying to establish," said Bel, as thunderous drumrolls sounded through the court, signaling the formal start of proceedings.

Sadry: I knew that somebody found me, but merely thought I had crossed into downriver, this life revisited, with a ghost Lori carrying me on its back to a ghost House. Somebody washed me and bandaged my cuts—I asked her if she was an angel spirit, but she only laughed. I slept, ate buckwheat mush when it was spooned into my mouth, slept again. The next time I woke, the room seemed full of men, all staring at me.

"Idris, do you know who she is?" said one, in a voice soft and smooth as a stroked cat.

"How could I?" said the angel.

"She looks like rotting bait," said another, so big and hairy I thought him an ogre.

"Idris, has she been instructing you how to treat her wounds?" asked the first.

Mutinous silence. Of course I had, for sick as I was, I was still an Erewhon healer.

"Only one way to find out!" said the third, twin of the second, but clearly the leader. He unwrapped the bandage on my right hand, to reveal the palm, which he inspected closely, picking at the scab with his nails.

"Blue! The missing heir of Erewhon!"

Big hands lifted the pallet, carrying it and me out the door and along the Intrigue space. Somewhere along the way my raw hand struck rough stone wall, and a red haze of pain washed over me. Even the jolt as the pallet met floor again, in a larger room, I barely noticed.

"Where's that girl? Idris?"

"Here!"—but spoken as if through clenched teeth.

"Get her good and better, and soon, okay?"

And with that they left. The pain had cleared my head: now I could see that the angel crying as she re-bandaged my hand was only a girl my age, in a room too stuffed with Scavengers' rubbish to be ghostly.

"Which House is this?" I asked, after a while.

"Celat."

"Oh," I said. "Trouble."

"The thugs were Idye and Iain, my brothers; the smoothie Mors, Mediator of this House, and their lover."

"No Queen?" I asked, trying to recall what I knew of Celat.

"This is her room."

Idris stared into my face, as if expecting a reaction. Something was wrong, I could tell that.

She sighed, and added: "Our mother is years downriver." Her words and tone were like a trail, down which I chased a hunting beast.

"We've been too poor and disreputable for any marrying since."

The trail was warm now, and I guessed what I would find at the end of it would be unpleasant.

"Until you came along," Idris finished. "That's why they moved the bed. Don't you understand? They want you for Queen of Celat *and* Erewhon."

Indeed, an ogre with three male heads, ferocious game. I knew I had to fight it, or marry it, but how? More thinking aloud than anything else, I said: "I'd sooner marry you!"

Idris: *[triumphantly]* "And I said: Do you mean that? Do you really mean that?"

The hearing began with a reading of the various charges and counter-charges, then a series of witnesses appeared. I began to get a sense of Suff law, as the bare bones of the case, what was not disputed by either side, was established. But the mix of ritual and informality in the proceedings disconcerted me, as when Bel waved wildly at some witnesses, a married trio from Greym House. They waved back, before resuming their evidence: that they, being river fishers, had found a hat with blue ties in their net.

"At least there's no argument she fell in the water," Fowlds commented.

Mors of Celat rose and bowed at the judges. I thought him a personable young buck, not as loutish as Idye beside him, with a feline, glossy look—if you liked that sort of thing. An answer to a virgin's prayers? Not from the look of black hatred that passed between him and the two girls.

"Can he address the court? I mean, he's an accused," Fowlds murmured.

Bel had gone rushing out of the gallery, leaving me to interpret as best I could.

"As a Mediator Mors is privileged to argue points of law."

"They're marriage counselors, right?"

"Among other things," I said. "Things get fraught, you need someone like that. Otherwise you might end up like Nissa's Erewhon."

"Oh, the case people keep on mentioning," he said.

"They're similar, that's why."

"But wasn't that a mass poisoning ..." he began, but I shushed him as Mors began to speak.

"I bring the attention of this court to the law of the Scavengers. . . ."

"Cheeky beggar!" somebody muttered.

"Huh?" said Fowlds. I was feeling confused myself.

"Er, I believe it's basically finders keepers."

"But it's not been applied to living humans since feuding days," Bel finished, from behind my shoulder.

"But there's a precedent?"

"Oh yes. Oh my!"

Idris had leapt up, shouting:

"I found Sadry, so she's mine! Not yours, not anybody else's."

Conye of Westron rose, and moving effortlessly despite her age, placed herself between the pair, her arms stretched out, invoking quiet.

"Another Mediator," said Bel. "She'll adjourn the court now, and let people cool off. It's getting late, so I guess they'll call it a day."

"See you in court tomorrow, then," said Fowlds. He bent toward me. "You're an anthropologist, so is it true that these mountain guys are hot trots?"

"Why don't you find out?" I said.

"Oh I will!"—and he wandered away.

Bel said: "Come and meet a non-bee Queen."

Sadry: Idris's brothers left us alone, but Mors would bring some small comfort, like fresh milk, sit on the end of the pallet, and talk, playing mediator.

Idris: The thin part of the wedge.

Sadry: The thick part being your brothers. I put no trust in him, but he was too engaging for me to keep sulking. It became a game, to talk and parry his flirtation. That way courtship lay, I knew.

I asked: "What brought you to Celat?" and he looked rueful: "Love. Or a potion. Or perhaps both."

Idris: *[sarcastic]* Men are such romantics.

I said: "And you've stayed here?"—looking pointedly around the Scavengers' mess.

He said: "I mediate when Idye and Iain get into trouble."

"Like now?" I said.

He sighed. "This wasn't my idea. But as a challenge, I find it—seductive."

"As opposed to rape?"

He said, lightly: "You know that is the last resort."

I must have gone white, for he added: "But that would mean I'd failed. And I'd hate that."

When he had gone, I said to Idris:

"I suppose he's not too bad."

On the wall hung the one precious thing I had seen in Celat, a Tech mirror. Idris abruptly lifted it down and set it on my chest, holding it with both hands, so all I could see was my scratched face.

"You think, you really think pretty Mors courts you for

love, when you look, as Idye charmingly said, like rotten bait!"

"No," I said, sobered. She touched my cheekbones.

"I can see under the surface, but *they* can't. That protects you for the moment. But when you heal . . ."

I said: "Get word to my father!"

She hesitated, before replying: "Mors came from the market with the news your father's dead. Of sickness or worry, they say. And so Erewhon is vacant and everyone's looking for you."

I cried at that, and she kissed away my tears. After a while I said:

"Then we must get out of here all by ourselves."

The Queen proved to be the fisher-girl from Greym, whom we found, together with her husbands, in Bel's private attic rooms. The trio were replete with honeycake and a keg of the weak Highland beer. Close to, they seemed painfully young, in their mid-teens at most, the two obvious brothers and the girl touchingly in love with each other. Bel introduced them as Milat and Meren and Jossy, saying of the latter:

"Pregnant, she tells me, but she won't say by whom. . . ."

Jossy grinned with gap-toothed embarrassment. The boys were more forthcoming:

"Aw, she's just kiddin' you, Cos."

Indeed, I thought, the Rule was strict regarding sexual access, precisely to prevent squabbles over paternity. Then I did a delayed doubletake at the last word spoken. Cos meant *cousin*. . . .

I stared at Bel. "I thought you were a lowlander."

"Not always," she said. "Once I could have been a Queen."

Milat coughed. "Aw, that's old history now."

I was starting to catch on. "You walked out and down from Greym? Why?"

Bel replied with a question. "You like men?" she said, looking at Jossy. "You like lots of sex with men?"

Jossy giggled; the boys exchanged glances, tolerant of their eccentric relative.

"I'll take that as a yes," Bel said. Then, more to me: "But if you don't, then there's no sense living in misery. I had a pretty young cousin, who would never question the Rule. So I gave my husbands to her."

"Our mam," said the boys proudly.

"These are her twins. I had no children, so I walked free."

She smiled at them, on her face the lines of a hard life, lived good-naturedly and without regret.

"What did you do?" I asked.

"Came down to the village and this Inn, where I asked for work as a kitchenhand, anything. And here I stayed, with Bel, who owned the Inn. When she went underground, I took her name and carried on the business."

She poured out more beer, and sliced the remaining cake. As she did, I noticed a tattoo extending from the palm of her hand to the wrist: an oval enclosing two stylized bees, under a gabled roof.

"Two Queens in a House?" I asked softly, as she passed me the cake.

"No," she replied. "Two worker bees in their Inn."

I took her hand, to better examine the device, and then noticed the pigment of one bee was faded, and that it was drawn differently from the other. It also looked vaguely familiar—and I whistled softly as I recognized a birth marker, the bee of Westron modified into an emblem that was all Bel's own.

"With your bee-skills, I should have guessed you were born at Westron."

I released her hand.

"As you're a relative, I wonder if you might get me an interview with Queen Conye. She's an interesting woman."

A guarded nod. Press on, I thought.

"I'd like that," I said. "Almost as much as I'd like to talk to Sadry and Idris."

"Easier said than done," she said.

"Well, yes."

"Conye's cranky on me, for letting the House down."

She paused, and what she said next nearly floored me. "But I can get you into the lockup." She turned to the Greym three: "And you didn't hear that, did you?"

"No, Cos," muttered one of the boys, and I began to realize the powers of this extraordinary woman.

Sadry: Erewhon's symbol is a blue swirl, the river of life, for it is knowledge of illness that is the strength of our House, just as Dusse has botany and herbalism, and Westron the secret of mead.

[*I nodded, thinking that it was as if when setting up the Rule someone had determined that the precious Tech knowledge and goods be apportioned equally between Houses.*]

Sadry: In our cellars, cut deep into the mountainside, we hoard the artifacts of Tech medicine.

Me: I heard you had a pharmacopoeia.

Sadry: Yes, a book of the colored beads that the Tech people didn't wear but ate, to keep themselves well. That we salvaged ourselves, other books the Scavengers bring us. Our oldest book, though, isn't medical—it's called Erewhon, but it's not about my House, but a dream, a nowhere place. In this book things are reversed: the sick are criminals, and the criminals regarded as ill.

Idris: Are we criminal, or ill?

Bel: Both, probably, in the eyes of the men.

Sadry: The book-Erewhon seemed strange, but not much stranger than the Rule. Or the way I would live in my home, with Idris, if the court permits us.

[*I thought, but did not say, that while Bel could live in the Lowlands, a happy impossibility in Highland terms, two Queens in the same mountain House was probably intolerable for the Rule-followers. Sadry was Queen of Erewhon by inheritance, but if this case went against her she could end up Queen of Nowhere.*]

The Greym three had had a big, exciting day and they drooped like flowers with the dusk. Bel brought them blankets, letting them doze on her private floorspace. After she blew out the candles (Highland style, of rush and tallow), we two retired to the downstairs bar, where she ejected the last drinkers. Now we had the place to ourselves I wanted to interview this runaway Queen, but instead Bel went out. Alone, I stretched out on the hearthrug and watched the fire, thinking of the Houses and their troubles. As I lay there, unbidden came to mind the memory of an interview tape I had once heard, with an anonymous woman of Bulle. Bulle woman: The Rule is: share and share body alike in marriage. That's why Queens seldom have a night to themselves once they wed. It's best if you're stolen by brothers, because they're like beans in the pod, so you treat them the same. But if you've got one you like less, or one you love most . . . that means trouble. Poor silly Nissa!

Interviewer: It was the lover that was the problem, wasn't it?

Bulle woman: His name was Yeny. I met him once, and wasn't surprised that Bryn Erewhon was head over heels, why he brought him into the marriage. The trouble was Nissa fell for Yeny too, and she wanted him all for herself, like a Lowlander. The sensible thing would have been to let those two walk out and down, but Bryn was stubborn, I guess, like Erewhoners are. He called in a Mediator, but that didn't work. So Nissa took matters into her own hands.

Slowly, imperceptibly, I slipped into dream-sleep, images appearing and disappearing before my slitted eyes. First I saw the blue sign of Erewhon, the river twisting into a figure eight, an infinity symbol, then the self-devouring serpent I had admired at the tattooist's. A log collapsed in the fireplace, and I opened and closed one eye, importing the flamescape into my dream, for now I flew above red mountains. Below my eagle-I were Houses, and I zoomed in and somehow through the thatch roof of Erewhon, to see Nissa (who looked amazingly like Sadry) zigzagging through Intrigue. She went down a flight of stone steps to the courtyard where a Scavenger waited with goods for identification and sale: sheets of dirty foil, on one side covered with symmetrical white studs. The dream-watcher followed Nissa into the cellars, where she consulted a tattered book. When she came out again, she paid the Scavenger, and tucked the drugs into her underrobes.

I felt her cold hand—then realized it was Bel, shaking me awake.

"Come on! I've bribed you an hour's talk!"

"Wh . . . ?" I started to say, then received a spare robe full in the face, and with it the realization of where we were going.

"Hurry! Wrap yourself up!" she said.

Doubly shrouded we slipped into the darkness of the street, the mountain air chill even in summer. The village at first seemed asleep, with the mountains looming over it as if over a cradle, the gleam of snow at their peaks like watchful eyes. But as we moved swift and silent as Loris, I noticed cracks of light under shutters, heard babies' cries or soft talk, and saw distantly, in the gap between two buildings, a group of men carousing around a bonfire, among them Fowlds.

"He'll get slipped a philter and good and proper fucked," Bel commented.

"That's what he wants," I said.

After what seemed an age Bel finally led me into a dark doorway I slowly realized was a back entrance to the Courthouse. Inside, someone waited for us, robe thrown completely over the head, almost like Bel beekeeping. The apparition led us up stairs of scavenged Tech concrete to the second floor, where a door was unlocked for us, then locked behind us.

Sadry was awake, spinning Lori wool on a spindle, the Highland cure for fidgets, or using up time. I could see for the first time her scars, and her composed, indeed, queenly mien. Idris slept, her head on Sadry's knee; she stirred as we approached, knuckling her eyes. For a long moment there was silence, before Bel fumbled under her robe and produced delicacies: fresh Lori cheese, fruit, cured meat.

"Greetings Bel Innkeeper, greetings Northerner," Sadry said, her voice neutral as she accepted the gifts.

I had nothing to offer, but nonetheless pulled out my tape recorder from under my robes. Idris goggled at the device, then said to Sadry:

"What, our words to be set down and used against us?"

"For an interview," I said, alarmed. "It's standard practice."

"I didn't agree to a Tech toy," Sadry said. She looked at Bel. "Your intermediary never mentioned it. . . ."

Idris reached forward, as if to snatch away the device, and I clutched it, inadvertently activating Record. She spoke, her voice a snarl, rising . . . until Bel clapped a hand over her mouth.

"Hush," she said. "Would you wake the guards? When the Northerner is like me, and like you!"

Idris's eyes rolled.

I said, my voice trembling, now I was so near to my goal, and yet not there yet: "I . . . we . . . my friends . . . we monitor . . . looking for . . . breakers of the rules . . . even in such a male-dominated society . . . you see, it's so important that you exist, we need a record . . . of women loving women . . . that's why I want your story!"

The gaze of these two girl lovers met, considering my plea.

I started the interview story-eater style, using the polite Highland opener of recounting my latest dream. One dream demands another, and so Sadry responded with her ghost story, continuing the theme of Nissa, which recurred as if haunting the conversation:

Sadry: My father said he got sick of it, Bryn moping, Nissa storming, and Yeny in the middle (who was not *his* lover) unable to make up his mind. So he went off herding. . . .

Idris: It saved him from a dose of worm-cure!

[*I thought of my dream again. If Bel had not shaken me awake, I possibly might have continued the dream, with*

*Nissa-Sadry one snowy night serving her in-laws a Bulle
herbal remedy, but combined with what from the pharma-
copoeic texts in the library she knew to be sleeping pills.
Presumably she wanted everyone in the House to sleep long
enough for her and her lover to elope. Murder meant feuding, and mass murder surely a civil war. Her bad luck then,
or her curse, as the Highlanders said, that the pills were
contaminated, or when combined with the herbs, toxic. Ten
people died at Erewhon, two more when Nissa's flight
ended in an avalanche—incidentally saving, as the Bulle
woman had noted, that House from a ruinous bloodprice.*]

Me: What saved Mors?

[*They eyed me. This I knew was the nub of the case,
whether the story of Nissa had repeated with Sadry.*]

Idris: He was called away to Mediate, in a dispute over
some Lori.

Me: And with only two men left in the house, you acted.

Idris: They got drunk as pigs.

Me: On pissweak Highland beer?

Idris [*defensively*]: Maybe they had mead.

Me: That's a luxury. You said Celat was poor.

Sadry: What is this? An interview or an interrogation?

Bel: It will help you! And you need help.

[*Long pause*]

Me: What happened?

Idris: I cooked for my brothers that night, and then went
upstairs with sop for Sadry. We could hear roistering below, and I barred the door of the Queen's room with what
I could find and move . . . without Mors to mediate, Sadry
wasn't safe.

Sadry: The House went quiet.

Idris: I went down to see what was going on, and found
my brother Iain passed out at the table. Idye was the same,
sprawled in the courtyard. Without losing a moment, I went
out to the field where our two best and biggest Lori grazed.
I brought them into the courtyard, found halters and sad-
dlecloths, then tied them by the door, while I went into the
house for my queen.

Sadry: I could barely walk, so she near carried me downstairs, and got me onto the Lori.

Idris: I went upstairs to get extra robes against the night air, but having a sudden idea, grabbed rags, and a haybale I had been using to re-stuff a pallet. With them I formed a mock Sadry under the blanket in the Queen's room.

Sadry: That done, just like that! We stole away into the darkness, heading for Erewhon.

Idris: [*hesitant*] We don't know what happened next.

Me: I hear Idye was too drunk to remember a thing.

Idris: I was right to take her! Iain went into the Queen's room!

Me: He was fuddled.

Sadry: He meant harm.

Idris: But in igniting the dummy Queen, he harmed nobody but himself.

Me: And the House.

[*I thought again of the Inn fire, of the log imploding in a shower of sparks. Celat House and its flammable rubbish had burnt like Bel's kindling, leaving ashes—in which Mors and a party from a neighboring House had found the charred form of Iain, a metal candleholder and a long-bladed hunting knife by his side. Idye had survived, simply because he had slumped in the courtyard, out of the flame's reach.*]

Sadry: We defended ourselves.

Me: I understand that, but to the extent of doing a Nissa?

Idris: That is for the court to decide.

Bel: We should stop now. The guard's shift ends soon, and I could only afford one bribe!

And she turned the recorder off. End of conversation, with the two defendants, but not with Bel, for when we got back to the Inn she stoked the fire and poured out beer for us.

I took a couple of mouthfuls, and said: "This stuff really is feeble. I reckon Idris nobbled her brothers' beer!"

Bel shrugged. "All the village thinks so, but with what?"

Now it was my turn to shrug. "I've seen a pharmacopoeia

book in a museum. It described everything the Tech culture took for their ailments. So, if something drastically increased the effects of alcohol, Sadry would have known it and told Idris."

Bel pulled off her outer layer of robe. "Maybe."

"But how did they get hold of it?" I wondered.

"The House was full of Scavenged goods, remember?"

"Good point. Anything could have been stored there." I rolled out on the rug again, watching flames.

Bel hunkered down beside me. "Well, if we are play judges, and have solved the mystery, what do we do now, given the important difference between this case and Nissa's? Idris and Sadry survived, and that means they are answerable for bloodprice."

"Even for an accidental death," I replied, with a sinking feeling.

"And the fratricide makes it worse. Not to mention burning the House, and stealing Idris, the one thing Celat had to barter on the marriage market."

I supped more beer. "Extenuating circumstances. Sadry escaped enforced marriage."

"But she also broke the Rule."

"Into little pieces," I finished, putting down the mug. "They don't stand much of a chance, do they?"

Bel put her hand on my shoulder. "That was why I took you to the lockup, to collect their story, and disseminate it over the North."

I turned, and her grip grew firmer, kneading me.

"And, because I wanted you to be grateful to me."

I laughed and quoted Idris: "Do you mean that? Do you really mean that?"

I had come to the mountains a detached, dispassionate observer, with a story to eat. But, almost despite myself, the case study of Sadry and Idris, and the other like-minded women of the Highlands had come to involve me. Taking Bel's hand in mine, I touched her bees and felt them slightly raised—a cicatrice. Tonight, we would play Queens of the Inn, and the two bees would crawl all over my skin.

And tomorrow, to celebrate, I would go to the market tattooist and mark myself with the snake—for now this mountain herstory was part of me, and I was a serpent eating my own tale.

Story Copyrights